ICEFALL

Guy Hallowes

Published by OMNE Publishing in 2018
Guy Hallowes © 2014

A catalogue record for this book is available from the National Library of Australia

Internal layout by OMNE Author Services www.omneauthorservices.com.au
Cover by Designerbility https://www.designerbility.com.au/
Printed by OMNE Publishing www.omnepublishing.com.au

This book is available in print and ebook formats.

For Diana

Contents

I acknowledge I am indebted to the following publication
for alerting us to the danger we face:
Published on Friday December 1st 2006 by the New Zealand Herald

Massive Ice Shelf 'May Collapse without Warning'

The Ross Ice Shelf, a massive piece of ice the size of France, could break off without warning causing a dramatic rise in sea levels, warn New Zealand scientists working in Antarctica.

A New Zealand-led ice drilling team has recovered three million years of climate history from samples which gives clues as to what may happen in the future.

The team's co-chief scientist, Tim Naish, told The Press newspaper the sediment record was important because it provided crucial evidence about how the Ross Ice Shelf would react to climate change, with potential to dramatically increase sea levels.

"If the past is any indication of the future, then the ice shelf will collapse," he said.

In January, British Antarctic Survey researchers predicted that its collapse would make sea levels rise by at least 5m, with other estimates predicting a rise of up to 17m.

Book One

CHAPTER ONE
Upbringing

Tanya was brought up in the mean streets of the lowly Sydney suburb of Cabramatta. With her blonde tresses, she was slim, tall and, even as a teenager, growing up into a stunningly beautiful woman. Her honest, solid parents always tried to do the right thing by their very smart, but wilful, only child. Both had two, low-paying menial jobs to keep food on the table and a roof over their heads. On most days they were away for as much as sixteen hours, so by the time Tanya was in her early teens, her parents had, to all intents and purposes, lost control of their daughter.

At fifteen, looking for excitement, she was persuaded to join a local gang led by Demetriou Smith, three years her senior. At first it was just great fun. They stole sweets and various items of small value from the shops in the vicinity, and shared the spoils out among gang members. To start with, Demetriou took little notice of her. So she pushed herself forward, her skimpy clothes and competent thievery soon attracting his attention. When the gang moved on to stealing cars for joyriding, she persuaded Demetriou to teach her to drive so she could participate.

Tanya had always done reasonably well at school without doing any work at all. As far as she was concerned, belonging to the gang was just fun and soon became her focus. They learnt all sorts of minor criminal skills like how to pick a lock and how to hide items on one's person without it being detected. Most of all she learnt how people behaved when under stress; many were unable to cope, giving up at the first sign of trouble. Only a few others, and she found that she was one of the latter, managed to bluff their way through virtually any difficulty and almost always escaped detection or punishment.

It all changed when Demetriou asked her to help him with a very special job. He had recently taught her how to hot-wire a car and she was already a reasonably competent driver, although still unlicensed due to her age.

'All you have to do is steal a car and drive it to this address.' He handed her a piece of paper. 'I'll be there. We'll make a few deliveries; afterwards you dump the car. Should be easy.'

Tanya did exactly as she had been told. At dusk, she rapidly surveyed a local unattended car park, selected a car and within minutes had carefully driven the vehicle to the appointed address. Demetriou was waiting outside holding a small bag. They stopped at six addresses. Tanya saw him handing over some of the contents to individuals standing in the shadows in exchange for what she determined was cash. Eventually, Demetriou asked her to drop him off.

He handed her two ten dollar notes and said, 'Thanks, you did very well. Dump the car and go home.'

Tanya was worldly enough to understand they had been delivering drugs and that she had been massively underpaid. Not that she minded, finding it all very exciting. Demetriou, well-built, six foot tall and darkly handsome had a devil-may-care attitude to life which the immature Tanya found very attractive. Being mildly interested in sex, and having only had one or two unsatisfactory encounters with boys in the gang, she suspected it might be different with Demetriou.

The fourth or fifth time Tanya had driven the delivery car, the last address was close to home. Knowing that her parents would still be out, she stopped the car in front of her home saying boldly to Demetriou, 'Come and have a cup of tea or coffee, or a beer if you like. Dad has some beer in the fridge. I'll drop the car off later.'

Demetriou needed no second invitation. 'Forget the beer, come here.'

They were kissing as the front door closed. Within minutes, all vestiges of clothing had been discarded and they were making passionate love on her bed. Half an hour later, they made love again.

Looking at her watch, Tanya said, 'Mum and Dad will be back soon, I've got to drop the car.' They scrambled into their clothes.

Demetriou scooted off on foot, leaving Tanya to deal with the car. She arrived back home a few minutes before her parents.

Tanya was thrilled with the lovemaking; it was everything she had imagined and she relived the experience time and again; she loved Demetriou's rough and tumble approach. She couldn't wait until their next encounter.

Tanya drove for Demetriou's drug deliveries for another four months. She stole the car, they made the deliveries, and either returned home or went to

Demetriou's place and made love. Tanya, early on in the piece, had made an appointment at the local family planning clinic and was now on the pill. Her new life was thrilling and exciting. She was meticulous about how and where she stole cars, never from the same place twice, and she was always exactly where Demetriou told her to be at the right time. She had no fear and it almost never occurred to her that she might be in danger either from the police or drug suppliers. She wasn't sure whether she was in love with Demetriou or not, but she loved the rough, fearless sex. No thought was given to the future or how long her new life, as she saw it, would last.

Then, Tanya noticed something had changed. Demetriou seemed nervous. He appeared more than once with a black eye and bruises on his body. On one occasion, there were flecks of what appeared to be blood on his shirt. He refused to discuss it when asked. He was also taking a bit too much notice, from Tanya's perspective, of another slightly older girl in the group. Tanya became increasingly watchful, wondering how long her relationship with Demetriou would last. But then all those negative thoughts would be swept away when they made love, always persuading herself afterwards that all was well.

The last time she saw him, they had completed the usual deliveries and had returned to his home and made love. Going to the toilet, she was shocked to see a shirt in the tattered laundry basket covered in dried blood. Gingerly picking up the shirt, Tanya was about to return to the bedroom to confront Demetriou when she heard an unusual sound outside. Standing on the toilet bowl and peering out into the street, she saw to her horror two police cars parked and another arriving. A dozen or more policemen, uniformed and plain clothes, were standing around waiting for something.

Suddenly Tanya understood she was in real trouble. Her personal survival instinct made her focus solely on her own situation. Without thinking, still clutching the bloody shirt and leaving Demetriou asleep in bed, she grabbed all her belongings, making sure she had left nothing behind. Running naked into the garage, she looked around briefly before clambering onto the roof of the parked car and up into the ceiling space. She carefully replaced the manhole cover then dressed silently, hiding behind some stored boxes. Shivering with fright, she sat uncomfortably on a roof beam in the dark, wondering what would happen next.

Within minutes all hell broke loose. She could hear police everywhere, thoroughly searching the premises; some came over the back fence, so if she had tried to escape that way she would certainly have been apprehended. They clumsily crashed about in the garage for a few minutes, but missed the manhole.

The raid lasted an hour. She didn't move, apart from her terrified shivering.

She heard an unfamiliar female voice say, 'Just him, I've looked everywhere. There's no sign of anyone else.'

'There's a young girl, we need to find her.'

'Not here mate. We've looked everywhere.'

Once Tanya was certain the raid was over and all was quiet, she noticed, with horror, the bloodied shirt lying where she had discarded it on top of a box. Half emptying it, she carefully folded the shirt, placed it inside, and covered it with the papers and other jumbled clothing. At about noon the following day, Tanya emerged from her hideout. She crept around the side of the house to find the stolen car still parked in front; obviously the police had not identified the vehicle. Making sure there was nobody about, she jumped into the driver's seat. She drove it carefully to the nearest shopping centre, parked it, and walked home.

Her frantic mother was, unusually, still at home. 'Where have you been? Why aren't you at school?'

Tanya, helping herself to breakfast cereal, said, 'It's all okay now. I can't go to school today. I need to sleep, but when you and Dad are here I will explain everything.'

'I called the police.'

Tanya almost panicked, 'Call them back. Tell them not to worry, I'm back now.'

Noticing Tanya's clothes all covered in dust, her mother started fussing again, 'Look at you. Where have you been?' She tried to dust Tanya off.

Tanya escaped her mother's anxious clutches. While she was in the bath, she heard her mother talking to someone, probably a policeman, at the door.

'Sorry I called you. She stayed with a friend last night and forgot to tell us. She is back home now, unharmed.'

Over the evening meal, she quietly told her horrified parents everything; the teenage gang, the carjacking and finally the drug deliveries. Thinking it was irrelevant, she spared them the sex. No mention was made of the bloodied shirt or the fact that she had parked the stolen car where she thought it would eventually be found.

'Demetriou is certainly under arrest and will go to jail for drug dealing. The police might look for me since I drove a car for him on at least two dozen occasions while he was doing his deliveries. I really have learnt my lesson, but now I need to go somewhere else. I don't think the police will look very hard if they don't find me soon.' Tanya, although badly frightened, was quite calm and coherent.

'Did you take any drugs?' asked her father anxiously.

'No. I saw one or two in the gang who did and decided it wasn't for me.'

'Maybe you can go to my sister Cara, since she is now on her own. I will ask. Her flat is small, but Bronte is a long way from here.'

Both Tanya's parents had hopes for Tanya and were determined to help her achieve her potential.

'I couldn't care less about the drug deliveries,' her father said to her mother later. 'We must get her as far away from here as possible. If Cara will have her that will be a good solution.' They were mortified by Tanya's behaviour and blamed themselves for not being able to supervise her more closely. However, they understood how people, in their position, at the bottom of the heap could fall into such a trap.

'Tanya,' her father said to her kindly, 'If Cara will have you; it will give you another chance. But make the most of it. Don't foul up again.'

He had Tanya's full attention. Badly frightened, she could see that her life could have been ruined by her foolishness and she had no wish to wind up in juvenile detention. So she cooperated fully with her parent's suggestion.

Within days, Tanya had moved in with her aunt. Cara was sensitive and asked few questions. But gradually, as trust developed, Tanya unburdened herself and told Cara nearly everything, even the sex; she made no mention of the bloodied shirt.

'I think you've had several lucky escapes. At worst you could be pregnant and in jail,' Cara said, unemotionally a few weeks into her niece's stay. 'I hope you've learnt your lesson. But you can make a significant change now. Your teachers say you're very clever and will easily get into university, if that is what you want. Since you were enrolled under my name, the police shouldn't track you here. Another piece of advice—don't go anywhere near Cabramatta and stay away from your old friends, if you want to stay out of jail.'

Tanya took her aunt's advice for now, although she thought she might contact a few of her old friends when the fuss had blown over.

After several months of Cara's non-judgmental tutelage, Tanya gradually formed a view of what life might be like outside her previous grubby world. She was concentrating hard on her studies and steering clear of trouble.

'Don't come back home, at all,' her father advised. 'Maybe the police are still looking for you.'

Tanya's parents, on one of their regular visits to see their daughter, showed her a short piece cut from a local paper.

"Demetriou Smith, aged nineteen, was convicted in the local district court of two counts of drug dealing and was sentenced to three years jail. A further charge of manslaughter was dismissed due to lack of evidence."

Tanya shivered with fright, then, and whenever she thought of Demetriou. *That's what might have happened to me*, she reflected. She occasionally revisited their lovemaking, and not always successfully tried put the memories of it out of her head. She took full responsibility for her own actions and placed no blame on Demetriou: *You knew what you were doing*, she said to herself. *If you had given the situation a moment's thought, you silly bitch, you could see where it was heading. Same for Demetriou. He knew the risks and got what was coming to him.* She went quite cold when she thought of the bloodied shirt. *He must have killed someone.* She wondered why she had touched the shirt at all and who he had killed.

CHAPTER TWO

Transformation

Tanya, carefully guided by Aunt Cara, transformed her life and worked hard at school, finishing top of her class in the remaining three years in academic and sporting subjects.

'I will be here when you get home from school, every day, so come straight back. Leave the boys alone, they are just trouble,' Cara told her. Her aunt had a part-time job at a local supermarket and was always on hand if she needed anything.

Tanya met Mark Bower at university. Mark, in his final year, was intrigued by the clever, slim, and beautiful first year student even though he could see she had come from a poor background.

'Going slumming?' and, 'Fancy a bit of rough, do you?' were typical comments from his more well-to-do friends.

Tanya had no shortage of dates, including Mark, once she had established herself at university. Cara, realising she would not be able to keep Tanya away from the opposite sex forever, gave her a lecture on birth control.

'I have bought you a dozen condoms. I don't want to encourage you, but you need to be prepared.'

A surprised Tanya took the condoms; she was well aware of the need for birth control, but did not want to upset her aunt.

Mark tried to ignore Tanya's background and the competition for her attention, and they had several dates. Tanya could see she did not fit in with the middle class norms at the university, but she was flattered by Mark's attention. With his easy charm and tall, good looks, he could have had the pick of the girls. He had been head boy at school and captain of the rugby team.

She was smart enough to keep her eyes open and learn from her new world, free from the strains of the poverty she had been raised in and away from any temptations of the drug dealing world she had been a part of until three years or so earlier. She started to dress more conventionally, copying what some of her classmates wore. She even had the courage to ask one of the more friendly girls to help her. 'I would like to fit in a bit better. I don't want to put Mark off by looking like a dag.'

She liked and admired Mark, but was not yet sure of her relationship with him. He was shy around her and, to her surprise, had not made any attempt to sleep with her, even after three months dating. He eventually had the courage to take her home to dinner with his parents David and Chloe Bower, where she was able to charm them with her looks and modest demeanour.

'She only makes conversation when she has something sensible to say,' said David afterwards. 'I like that.'

Tanya was amazed by the opulence of the Bower household. It gave her hope that with her brains and a lot of hard work she would be able to have a similar life. She became a regular and welcome visitor and was soon familiar with the house Mark had grown up in. But when invited to stay over, she was always in a room far away from Mark.

One Friday night, with the elder Bowers travelling overseas, she found she and Mark had the place to themselves.

'Maybe we could stay in?' Mark said. 'I'll help you cook if that's okay; my cooking skills are rudimentary.'

'No problem.' She looked at him speculatively, a little amused, with a frisson of desire unfurling in her stomach. *He seems a bit inexperienced*, she thought.

Tanya was familiar with the well-appointed kitchen, having sometimes helped Chloe, and soon produced a delicious seafood pasta from the ingredients in the fridge and cupboards. Mark, sitting on a nearby kitchen stool, poured some wine. 'Should we stay here or do you want to sit at the dining room table like we always do with your parents?'

'This is fine,' answered Mark. 'Mmm, what a great smell.'

After they had cleaned up, Mark held her around the waist and kissed her on the cheek.

It's time I took control, Tanya thought.

Putting her arms around his neck, they kissed more deeply. She led him to the large settee in the living room. Mark continued to kiss her, while he clumsily tried to undo her bra strap. She quickly undid the clasp, releasing her breasts, her nipples standing erect. Mark continued to kiss her and shyly fondle her breasts, making no further moves.

Tanya said gently, 'Here, help me off with these.'

Putting his hand between her legs and onto her now damp panties, Mark became more animated and, with Tanya's help, removed them. She quietly started to undress him and then said, 'Bed—it will be more comfortable there.'

Now both naked, Tanya ran to Mark's bedroom holding him by the hand. They leapt into bed, with Mark rushing back to fish a condom from his trouser pocket.

'Here, let me help you with that,' said Tanya, expertly unwrapping it and rolling it down his impressive erection. 'Gently, gently,' coaxed Tanya. 'Here, hold me for a minute.' She placed his hand on her sex.

Mark then rose up and clumsily entered her. A few quick thrusts and it was all over. He rolled off, knowing he had somehow disappointed her.

She stroked his face, saying, 'Don't worry, it will be fine again in a few minutes. I'll help you. It'll be better for both of us then. Just relax.'

Mark went to sleep. Tanya woke him an hour later. 'Come on lover boy, let's try again.' She had crawled out of bed, while he was asleep and found another condom in his trouser pocket. She held his hand, knowing she would have to take the lead. 'Hold me, please. Put your finger inside me. Yes, that's better, keep going. I'm going to get on top of you and take you inside me. Just take it easy, try to let me come first.' Tanya focussed on her own pleasure and with a few sharp cries was engulfed in ecstasy. 'That was wonderful,' she said. 'Now your turn.'

Afterwards, he looked at her admiringly, saying nothing.

They woke together in the early hours of the morning. This time Tanya encouraged Mark to take the lead. 'I don't have any more condoms,' he said sheepishly. Tanya leant over and found one in her handbag, kept there since her discussion with Cara.

'Always better to be safe than sorry,' she said, handing it to him.

From then on the sex was more satisfactory, with Tanya trying to leave it to Mark to take the lead. They spent most of the weekend in bed, with the occasional break for meals.

Tanya decided to go home to her Aunt Cara's before the Bowers returned. The weekend had helped her feel more secure in her relationship with Mark and she began to see a long-term future for them. She sought Cara out in her tiny kitchen, kissing her fondly on the cheek before helping with dinner. Cara glanced at her, but as always did not question where or what she had been doing. If Tanya wanted to tell her anything she would do that in her own time.

Over dinner, Tanya told her about the weekend with Mark, leaving nothing out. Mark had been to dinner at Cara's place, so she knew something of him.

'Are you in love with him?' asked Cara.

'I think so,' Tanya shrugged.

'You need to be certain of a man like him. He'll expect to be in charge, but you are the stronger person, so it might lead to difficulties. If he was struggling to lead during sex, where else would he fall short? I think he is a good man, and probably clever, but if this relationship goes any further you'll have to take care.'

Tanya nodded. She thought her aunt, as always, had hit the nail on the head.

~

Two weeks later, after the senior Bowers had returned home, Tanya was again invited for the weekend. She wondered what the sleeping arrangements would be. Had Mark told his mother she would be sharing his bed? On arrival she could see that nothing had changed and Chloe assumed she would still be using the spare room.

Helping Chloe prepare the dinner, Tanya said, 'I've put my bag in Mark's room, I hope you don't mind.'

Chloe hesitated for a split second, then gave Tanya a big hug, saying, 'Bless you, you are a brave girl.' They continued their task in companionable silence, until Chloe added, 'I appreciate the honesty. I'm glad you didn't feel it necessary to creep about in the night pretending nothing had happened.'

From then on, a relationship of trust continued to develop with the Bowers, firstly with David and Chloe and then with Mark's siblings. She even persuaded him to share her bed in Aunt Cara's little flat.

~

After graduating with high results, Tanya was much sought after by a number of Sydney's leading law practices. She settled on one firm after a number of interviews.

Before she was made a formal offer she said to the junior partner dealing with the matter, 'I would like to speak to the senior partner please. It has to be one-on-one.'

'This is very irregular. I can deal with any queries you may have.'

'You have answered all my questions,' said Tanya, 'most impressively. There is something I have to tell your senior partner in confidence; I am not prepared to speak to anyone else about it.'

The man looked at her across the table and, after some thought, left the room. He returned twenty minutes later.

'He'll see you now, please come this way.'

Tanya was ushered into a well-furnished but workmanlike office. A man in his fifties was sitting at a round conference table looking at Tanya's personal file. He stood up and introduced himself as John Chambers, senior partner.

'You wanted to tell me something,' he said, once they were alone.

'Yes,' said Tanya, with her heart in her mouth, 'It's about my background …

'

'We know all that, it's one of the reasons we would like you to join us. Most of our new recruits have grown up with a silver spoon in their mouths. You have had to fight for what you have and I think that will be valuable to us.'

'There's more to it than that … ' said Tanya, looking directly at Chambers as she interrupted him.

'You mean the inconsistency between the name on your birth certificate and the surname on your degree?'

'Yes, if I could just explain …'

'You don't need to. We run background checks, and I have good contacts with the police. An old friend of yours, with permission from his seniors, George, now with the police … ' Tanya's eyes widened, 'has told me the full story.'

'Could you tell me what he told you please? I'm not here to justify anything; I just need you to know the truth.'

Tanya listened while Chambers gave her chapter and verse about her relationship with Demetriou, his drug dealing, and her move to live with her aunt. He also mentioned the references the school and university had provided. He even knew of her relationship with Mark.

'Well yes, that covers it. I don't have anything further to add,' said Tanya. 'I didn't want to come here under false pretences.' Rising to leave, she said, 'I'm sorry if I wasted your time.'

'Sit down for a minute. You most certainly have not wasted my time. I wondered how you would deal with the issue.' Chambers looked at her admiringly. 'Frankly, you could not have dealt with it in a more honest way; it must have been difficult for you.'

Tanya looked at him gratefully.

'The police have also informed me they no longer have any interest in you. None at all,' he emphasised.

'Thank you. I'm happy to know that,' she responded. George had already told her what the situation was with the police, but she felt no need to mention her ongoing contact with him. She was certain George would be a very useful asset in her new position.

'Enjoy working here,' said Chambers as he escorted her out of his office. 'We are looking forward to having you. By the way, everything I have told you remains between us.'

~

Tanya thought about telling Mark of her conversation with Chambers, but decided not to. She had explained some of her background to the Bowers but she did not want them to know anything about Demetriou and the drug dealing.

~

The relationship continued and, as most who knew the couple had expected, they were married in a tasteful but low-key ceremony at the Bowers' North Shore home. Mark had thought that Tanya would want a large fancy wedding.

'No,' she said. 'Could we make it as simple as possible? My parents will come, of course, and Aunt Cara, and a few old friends from Cabramatta, but I want them to feel comfortable.'

Finally about one hundred people attended, mostly friends and colleagues of the Bowers, but including some of Tanya's university friends. Tanya persuaded George to come. He was an old friend, now hidden away in a secret police department, as well as two from her ex-Cabramatta gang with whom she had kept in touch.

Tanya's father insisted on making a speech after the ceremony, along with David, and the best man. Despite his poor command of English, Tanya's dad succeeded in amusing the gathering with his wit and sincerity.

~

Prior to the wedding, Mark had produced some very elaborate looking brochures with a view to an extensive six week honeymoon trip. After looking at them unenthusiastically, Tanya sat next to him on the sofa in the Bower home. She kissed him gently on the mouth and hugged him. 'Do you know what would give me more pleasure than anything you can think of?' she whispered.

He looked at her curiously.

'It's my parents, they've given me everything, but they are still poor. I would love to pay off their mortgage. It would cost only a little more than this honeymoon. I would be happy with a weekend away, somewhere local.'

She handed him a mortgage statement, knowing the amount reflected was considerably more than the cost of anything Mark had planned. Mark looked at her wonderingly, but after talking and making love, he agreed.

As Tanya's parents left the wedding ceremony, Tanya's mother whispered to her, 'They fired him today, because he said he wanted to attend his daughter's wedding and couldn't do his shift. Don't tell him I told you.'

As she and Mark disappeared for a weekend in a resort in Pokolbin, Tanya's father's employers received a very forceful letter from a well-known Sydney law firm threatening massive legal action unless Tanya's father was reinstated, which he was a few days later.

'Bastards,' said Tanya as she heatedly told Mark the story on the one hour drive to Pokolbin and the Hunter Valley vineyards. 'It's just a fucking cleaning job. If I ever come across them again, I will cut their bloody bollocks off.' Mark smiled at the language; she might have meant every word.

CHAPTER THREE
Bombshell

A FEW YEARS LATER, 2010

Tanya bounced energetically into the room. She had, unusually for her in the middle of the week, arrived home early to the mansion she and Mark had recently purchased in the smart Sydney suburb of Mosman. She dumped her laptop and a sheaf of files untidily on a nearby coffee table. Normally, she would have been engrossed in one of many complicated legal cases. This time she had set aside the afternoon to try to summarise some research she had completed on global warming and the potential devastating conclusions. Her initiative was based on a conversation from a dinner party she and Mark had attended some three months earlier.

Soon after they were married, Tanya had become accustomed to being invited to what she thought of as "posh" dinner parties, mainly hosted by clients of the merchant bank where Mark was employed. Tanya believed the invitations aided their mutual ambition to rise to the very top of Sydney society.

Tanya, by now, had gathered a tasteful wardrobe, suited to occasions such as the anticipated dinner party. She asked, like an excited school kid, as she and Mark were dressing, 'Who's the host this time? I just love these parties. A chance to dress up and show off. And, if we are lucky, a conversation worth listening to.'

Mark looked at her admiringly, knowing she would turn many male heads at the party. 'You always look beautiful,' he said, 'but tonight there is a touch of elegance.' Tanya ignored the last pointed barb.

'It's a major client of the bank. The boss will be there and one of my senior colleagues. Don't be too disappointed though, we are well down the totem on this one.'

Tanya exclaimed, 'I'm rapt to be there at all; I don't care how far down. Anyway, many of the more interesting people are in the same boat as we are. Senior people seem too conscious of their positions. The most interesting question I heard asked at the last party was, "Where do your children go to school?" For God's sake!'

They drove east over the Sydney Harbour Bridge towards Vaucluse, one of the long-established suburbs developed in the early days of European settlement before the bridge was built.

'Try not to swear, if you can help it,' Mark said, as he gingerly found his way into the driveway of a large waterfront mansion with well-manicured lawns and, from what Tanya could see in the half-light, well-established flower beds and shrubs. There were several fancy limousines parked, one with a uniformed chauffeur.

Tanya's shoulders slumped a little at this second slight, reflecting, she supposed, Mark's anxiety about her upbringing. She wasn't going to take this one lying down though. 'You know as well as I do, Mark,' hiding her anger, 'that I come accross as well as anyone, including you, in the kind of company we are about to enjoy. I've never let you down in the past.'

They were introduced to the other dozen or so diners already present, standing around in a large, beautifully-appointed reception area. Two more couples arrived after the Bowers. Their host made a point of welcoming the stunning looking Tanya, introducing her to all those present. The men were especially effusive in their greetings, the host knowing Mark, who had wandered off to talk to colleagues, from his dealings with the bank.

'Congratulations are in order, I understand,' said the host in a quiet moment.

Tanya looked surprised, 'Oh yes, the partnership,' she muttered, looking embarrassed. 'Thank you. I am, of course, delighted and overwhelmed. I didn't know many people knew.'

'The youngest ever, I hear, and a woman at that.'

Tanya nodded, not wishing to continue the conversation or to draw any further attention to herself.

As Mark had predicted, they were placed towards the bottom of a long table seating sixteen people. The dinner, with a fish entrée, a main course of lamb, and an elaborate sweet, was beautifully served by two liveried servants. Tanya sipped sparingly at the several wines placed in front of her. She had become used to the confusing array of cutlery displayed at these affairs, but still watched carefully to ensure she used the right cutlery in the correct order. She briefly compared it to the sort of dinner she knew her parents would be enjoying at home in Cabramatta, probably parked uncomfortably on the old couch watching television.

That is, she thought, unless they are slaving away at one of their jobs.

Although she had learnt not to judge people by their appearance, she found herself sitting next to a thin, rather nerdy young man, much the same age as she was. He introduced himself as Theo, the only son of the host. Expecting a very dull conversation from a spoilt child, she soon realised that although the son had not inherited his father's evident charm and looks, he certainly had brains and intelligence and an independent viewpoint, probably in conflict with those of his parents. He regaled her with the science of climate change and the consequences of the probable collapse of the Ross Ice Shelf in the Antarctic.

Tanya started to enjoy the conversation and the intellectual challenge it presented. 'Where is this Ice Shelf? Nobody has ever heard of the bloody place.'

Theo drew a rough map of Antarctica and the Ross Ice Shelf, using a ballpoint pen, on his pristine, starched, linen table napkin. Tanya was a little shocked at the desecration.

'Don't worry,' said Theo, grinning. 'Keep it if you like.' He handed the napkin to Tanya and she, unnoticed, tucked the offending item into her handbag. 'He can afford another one.' He waved dismissively at his father sitting at the other end of the table, talking uninterestedly to an elderly woman seated next to him. The servant replaced the napkin without a word. His mother frowned at her son.

They had a very animated conversation, lasting most of the meal, with Tanya questioning and challenging his every assertion. 'You mean this,' she waved her hand around, indicating the opulent room and the surrounding suburbs, 'this whole f … place will be swamped and disappear? What does your father think?'

Theo laughed, appreciating the fact that Tanya was able to be herself, despite the rather formal setting. 'This and many other places around the world. If you don't believe me, I can give you a few pointers.' She fished a post-it note from her handbag and he wrote a half dozen references on it. After a moment's hesitation he added his phone number and e-mail address.

As the dinner finished, Theo's mother announced, 'The ladies will withdraw to the drawing room.'

Tanya looked surprised, wondering what was expected of her.

'We, the men, get to smoke a fancy cigar and have a glass or two of port,' explained a smiling Theo. 'The ladies are expected to enjoy a cup of tea.' He hesitated, 'I've enjoyed our conversation. Dad told me you were the brightest spark on the block tonight. It seems he was right.' He leant over and kissed her on the cheek, much to the amusement of all those present.

An hour or so later, Mark and Tanya took their leave from their smiling hosts. 'I hope Theo didn't bore you with all his climate change nonsense,' said their host as he also plucked up the courage to kiss Tanya on the cheek.

Tanya laughed, 'Not at all, it was a fascinating conversation. I have enjoyed the evening immensely, thank you.' Looking at Mark, as they walked the short distance to the car, Tanya said, 'I think it might be better if I drive. It would be dumb to be stopped for being over the limit.'

Mark handed over the keys without question. 'What was so fascinating about that funny little man you spent the whole night talking to?' asked Mark as they drove home.

'Our hosts' son Theo. We talked about global warming. It was really interesting. Much food for thought.'

'Do you fancy him?'

'Fancy him?' she laughed. 'Don't be daft.' She glanced at him, putting a hand on his leg, squeezing it as they sped along the now almost deserted streets. 'Not for a bloody nanosecond. I enjoyed the conversation though.'

Mark grunted, saying, 'There are more and more investment opportunities coming our way relating to green energy projects. I have not been able to get my head around any of them yet. Are the threats surrounding global warming real, or is it just a load of bull?'

'Don't know yet, but as sure as I am sitting here I'm going to find out. He was quite convincing.'

They lapsed into silence. Mark knew she would do her research and when she knew what she was talking about would discuss it with him.

Tanya retrieved her laptop from the coffee table. Before she moved it to her own study she glanced at the magnificent view of Sydney Harbour through the large picture window in the lounge. A view she was becoming used to. The beautiful-ly-furnished room flowed unobtrusively into a modern, open-plan kitchen with a marble-topped breakfast bar and top of the range appliances. The passage led to two studies and four bedrooms, an en-suite bathroom off the main bedroom, and two other bathrooms. In the few months since they had owned the house she had started to collect little knick-knacks as decoration. She had hidden at least half of them away in a cupboard, wondering why she had bought them in the first place.

She hadn't been able to get used to the cost of the new furnishings they had bought and glanced uneasily at some of the pictures on the walls, 'What did that set you back?' she had asked Mark, when he had proudly unwrapped one of the larger pieces.

'About ten.'

'Ten grand …?'

'It'll be worth twice that in a year, the artist is all the rage … ' He had looked at the expression on her face and said no more.

Before she started work on her summary from her readings about global warming and the consequences of the collapse of the Ross Ice Shelf, Tanya briefly reflected on how her life had transformed itself over the past ten years. And now the potentially devastating threat to all that, if the research she was about to complete turned out to be correct. She noticed with mild irritation the gaggle of yachts racing fruitlessly up and down the harbour in the sunlight.

Mark made his usual noisy entrance as she finished. Tanya returned to the lounge. 'How long have you been home?' he asked as he kissed her. As always, as the unwritten law in the merchant bank demanded, he was dressed in a regulation, but expensive, suit and tie.

'I was home early. You remember we talked about global warming after that dinner two or three months ago?'

'Global warming! I had some more immediate things I thought we could warm up,' he said as he started to undo the buttons on her blouse. Within minutes they were both lying naked on the plush lounge carpet, their clothes scattered. Mark's confident approach to their sex life was in complete contrast to their first sexual encounter.

Tanya loved it when he came home in such a mood. Inevitably they ended up making love, sometimes in the bedroom, but more often in various parts of the house—the lounge floor, bathroom, even the kitchen. They lay supine for a few minutes.

'What's for dinner?' asked Mark.

She giggled. 'Whatever you decide to rustle up. I will open a bottle while you do that and I want you to listen while I tell you about global warming.'

Tanya carefully collected all the clothes lying about, conscious of what they had cost, hanging up Mark's suit, tidying some items away, and putting others in the laundry basket. Afterwards, she tossed Mark his dressing gown and put on her own.

'Spag bol okay?' he asked as she handed him a glass of wine.

She nodded, fetching her laptop and placing it on the kitchen bench, as Mark was busily preparing the meal. 'Here, let me take over. Maybe you should read it for yourself.'

Mark moved to the other side of the bench. 'I read somewhere that the earth was something like point seven of a degree warmer now than it was at the start of the nineteenth century. That doesn't seem significant to me.'

Tanya remained silent as she fried up the mince and tossed into the mix, the selection of vegetables Mark had prepared. She popped the spaghetti into the now boiling water.

Mark started to expostulate, 'This is surely crap.' He jabbed at the computer as if, somehow, it was to blame. 'The sea levels will rise somewhere between seven and seventeen metres, when some piece of ice in the Antarctic, that nobody has ever heard of, collapses into the sea.'

'Yes, the Ross Ice Shelf. It's about the size of France.'

Mark continued to read, muttering under his breath.

Tanya pushed the loaded frying pan towards Mark, once she had placed a small amount of pasta on one plate and a much larger amount on the other. She explained, according to her research, almost all the hottest years in recorded history had been in the last ten or fifteen years. She pointed at the laptop, 'We had the typhoon in Queensland a year or two back and the Black Saturday bushfires in Victoria. More recently, there appear to be far more extreme weather events and they seem to be coming closer together. Also, there have been similar incidents in America, Hurricane Katrina for example, and always bushfires every summer.'

'There have been extreme weather events in the past,' argued Mark as he started to dish up the bolognese sauce onto both plates.

'Not too much please, I had lunch with a client today,' Tanya said. 'Certainly,' she continued, 'but not all together, which is what's happening now.'

Mark was looking at her as he started to slurp large mouthfuls of spaghetti into his mouth. 'And all this is caused by global warming?'

'Didn't you have any lunch today?' Tanya laughed.

'No, the boss was on about some pet theory of his and went on waffling for hours and then I had two back-to-back meetings.' He went on reading. 'Anyway, you say here,' Mark jabbed at the laptop again, 'that temperatures are forecast to rise by at least five degrees by the end of the century. Is that serious? I have no idea. It doesn't sound too dramatic. After all, the daily maximum temperature in Sydney often varies by more than that. Surely over that length of time we will be able to cope.'

'Yes, if it's correct, it's very serious. Someone somewhere needs to take drastic action.'

'How significant is the rise in sea levels?'

Tanya pulled the laptop towards her on the bench-top and spent a minute tapping a few keys, while Mark continued with his meal. 'I have just logged in to Google Earth where you can see heights above current sea levels in various places. Have a look at Sydney, George Street for example.'

'Here, let me,' Mark grabbed the mouse and started playing with it. 'Shit, at seventeen metres this place, our precious fucking house, will be prime waterfront. The city would be completely flooded. Holy shemoly, what do you think it all means?'

'Just take a look at the Kurnell Oil Refinery in Botany Bay.'

Mark moved the cursor. 'Gone, completely flooded!'

'Let's look at a few other cities.'

'London, buggered despite the flood barriers. New York, buggered. Melbourne, most of the city flooded.' Mark looking amazed and horrified, read on. 'Beijing, Moscow, Delhi, and Tehran will be okay. Still all this is dependent on the Ice Shelf collapsing. Many of the low-lying Pacific Islands will disappear altogether. Bangladesh with its enormous population will be inundated. Fuuuck,' he exclaimed.

'If what has been forecast actually happens the inland cities will not be flooded. But most of the ports and oil refineries will be, so unless they have a nearby food source it won't help them. There will be critical food shortages within days of the floods,' said Tanya. 'It does seem a helluva jump from what we have now,' Tanya waved vaguely in the direction of the harbour with its twinkling lights and busy streets, 'to almost total destruction.'

They sat in silence for a few minutes finishing their wine. Tanya packed the few dishes into the dishwasher.

'How much did that little turd, Theo, help with all this?' asked Mark, while she was busy.

'He gave me some references at the dinner party, and I talked with him on the phone a couple of times since.' She looked at Mark, wondering why he felt so insecure as far as she was concerned. Most people would have expected her to be the insecure one. She had not looked at another man since she had become involved with him. 'He's asked me to lunch more than once, an invitation I won't be taking up.' She walked around the bench and hugged him.

The next morning they were woken as usual by the five am alarm. They both leapt out of bed and dressed for their normal nine kilometre run. Mark was big and strong and tried to push the pace. Tanya was very fit and easily kept up with him through the still-deserted streets of their suburb, as the sky was lightening up in the East. They had a shower together, after a hasty breakfast of fruit and muesli. Tanya spent time dressing carefully, making sure, as always, that she looked her very best. She brushed her shining blonde hair.

'What's the occasion?' asked Mark playfully as he tried to kiss her.

'Sorry, I am in a bit of a hurry this morning,' she said as she quietly evaded his embrace. 'I have this shithead of a client. He's about to get himself into very big trouble and I need to steer him clear. I must have all the facts at my fingertips before our nine am appointment.'

'Well, your appearance will certainly distract him,' said Mark.

'I think he likes me to be well dressed. But he is gay, so hopefully he will be listening to what I have to say rather than gawping at my boobs.'

'Don't forget to send me your summary of the global warming thing when you get in. I will try to get opinions from other people in the office,' he said as Tanya marched out of the door, clutching her laptop and files.

They both arrived home at about seven pm. They kissed warmly, hugging each other for a minute. Tanya started to fix dinner. 'Did you show anyone the paper?'

'Yes. Rooney and Curtin.'

'Rooney!' Tanya glanced up with an exasperated look on her face. 'His idea of the long term is who he is going to sleep with the weekend after next. He will have dismissed it out of hand, right?'

'Right, he said it was a load of bull.'

'You might get a more thoughtful response from Curtin in a few months. He'll have to do all his own research.'

Mark was always amazed at Tanya's perceptiveness. She seemed to be able to assess people and their reactions after a very short acquaintance. 'Right, he said he would get back to me.'

'What do you think?'

'It is compelling, but I can't believe that all this … ' he held her by the arm as they walked over to the window overlooking the beautiful, peaceful harbour, 'will just disappear. If what you say is right, most of the people in the city will probably die, either by drowning or starvation, and much of the city will gradually crumble into the water. This wonderful thriving city and many others like it around the world. I find it very difficult to take in. My immediate instinct is to treat it all as bullshit. What do you think we should do about it?'

'I really don't know,' said Tanya. 'I would like to know what Curtin thinks and I will put more thought into it myself.'

CHAPTER FOUR
A Few Days Later

David Bower was nervous. Over many months now he had been researching some of the wider aspects of the effects of climate change and what, if anything, could be done about it. His conclusions were radical and drastic. David, though graying, was a slim, fit man. Not tall at five foot nine, but giving the impression of intense energy. On this occasion, he had dressed in a neat pair of grey flannel trousers and a jacket. Chloe had persuaded him to dispense with the tie, knowing their children would be wearing jeans and tee shirts when they arrived for dinner. He kept himself fit with regular runs, the occasional session in the gym, and golf. He was well liked by business associates for his forthrightness and honesty and, above all, his calmness under even intense pressure.

David sat for half an hour on the deck of his large house enjoying the warmth. He stared unseeingly into the bushland opposite. A large gathering of lorikeets were squawking and squabbling over the birdseed David had spread over a small table in the garden. A pair of king parrots looked nervously on from the safety of a nearby melaleuca tree, waiting their turn.

Not long after their engagement, Chloe had excitedly driven him to this very place, then an empty piece of land. David had tried not to show his enthusiasm by commenting on the steepness of the site. However, he agreed to talk to one of the builders he dealt with regularly once Chloe told him she had already asked an architect to have a look at what could be built there.

David had been concerned. 'I'll have to work through our finances. I've only had a year with the business, albeit a successful one.' With partners, he had started his own business about the time he had met Chloe.

'I'll go on working,' Chloe had offered, 'but this place is perfect. It's close to the city. If we do it right, we'll never have to move again.'

David thought back to that conversation, more than thirty years later. *We may indeed have to move if what I have concluded comes to pass.* 'I'm sure I'm right, but I wish to hell I wasn't,' he said aloud. He shuddered when thinking of his son Mark and his beautiful wife, obviously intending to take themselves to the very top. *They will dismiss the very idea of climate change.*

He emerged from his reverie when Chloe called him from the kitchen, asking him to help set the table. His daughter Patricia and her husband Joe, now in their early thirties, had arrived. Their eight year old daughter Kim was already headstrong unlike their son Jason, who was gentle and thoughtful at five.

Patricia bustled in. She liked to have them fed and in bed early, giving David an opportunity, if there was time, to read to them and tuck them up. Patricia had steadfastly resisted any thought of returning to work. 'It's more important to bring the children up properly. And I do help with mum's charities,' she added, when challenged by some of her more ambitious friends.

Joe and Patricia were committed environmentalists. Joe had a well-paid position as an accountant with a large retail operation in Sydney. 'I'm not sure I can see myself bean-counting for this lot for the next thirty or so years,' he had confided in David on a previous occasion. 'I really need something more fulfilling. We do provide a service, but it's not exactly saving humanity.'

Jonathan, their youngest at eighteen, was still living at home. He bustled in announcing that he was due to go out later to listen to some obscure band in Kings Cross. While he tried to give the appearance of non-conformity, when asked what he was going to do with his life, his stock answer was, 'Maths and Physics at Sydney Uni, the Royal Military College at Duntroon, and a commission in the Australian Army.'

Gentle Evan, aged twenty-five, was pursuing a career in music. 'Aussie is a bit of a backwater as far as music goes. I have an offer in England which I'll take up as soon as I've got my shit together,' he had told his mother a few days earlier.

Just as Chloe was wondering whether her dinner would be spoiled, Mark and Tanya made their high-profile entrance in a fancy sports car David couldn't identify. He had never been fooled by Tanya. He knew she was clever, ambitious, and ruthless. She had always downplayed her role in the law firm, but David was aware she had now been elevated to the partnership, something she hadn't mentioned. She appeared to be casually dressed, but her long blonde hair, beautifully patterned shirt, and the shortest skirt she could get away with, showing off her long legs, made her the standout among those present.

There were lots of ribald greetings between the siblings, and the children were made a fuss of by all the adults before they were put to bed. Everyone automatically helped serve and clear-up the sumptuous dinner making Chloe's role very easy.

From Chloe's perspective, she had the perfect life. They lived in a large, five bedroom house, in Sydney's leafy North Shore, which she helped design and had built. It was quiet, overlooking bushland, and was close to the city. She played golf once or twice a week and usually indulged in one bridge afternoon. With her children now grown up, she spent a good deal of time on her charities. David ran a very successful operation and, although she had noticed him being rather secretive of late, she thought that probably had something to do with the business. He shared some of his business issues with her, but to her relief had never bored her with the details. She foresaw this situation continuing for some time to come. The word "retirement" had not passed David's lips, although she was confident they would have sufficient funds to retire on when the time came. Both of them were in good health.

Some of the family had noticed a screen with a computer and projector on a small table in the lounge. When David asked Joe to help him set it up on the now cleared dining room table, most thought he was going to show them a few slides from a recent trip to India. With coffee or port in hand, the family were relaxing, having indulged in too much good wine over dinner. David noticed that Tanya, although she laughed and talked as much as the others, had barely touched any alcohol. He wondered whether she was pregnant, but then decided that she, alone, had sensed something different in the atmosphere and was on full alert. He glanced at her, but she gave nothing away.

David said, 'I have ten slides here that try to explain something I've been researching over past months.'

'So, it's not you and Mum riding camels in India,' joked Evan.

'Not this time,' David smiled. 'There is a discussion going on suggesting human activity has caused the world to heat up.'

There were some uneasy glances around the room. David was not given to lecturing and he normally did not force his opinions on the family.

Mark glanced at Tanya who imperceptibly shook her head as if to say, 'Let's hear what he has to say first.'

'The first slide shows that average world temperatures have increased by just less than one degree centigrade since the early 1800s … '

The sigh of relief at this insignificant amount came too soon. David continued with the rest of his slides, briefly showing the results of his research on climate change and his conclusion that the world was facing a catastrophe not seen since the advent of Noah's flood.

Tanya listened intently, Holy fucking shit, she thought, we have drawn the same conclusions.

David was finishing, 'Under this scenario, virtually every port in the world would be inundated and many of the oil refineries. The consequences would be that food distribution, among other things, would come to an immediate halt and I don't see how it could be restored to anything like its present state for years.'

There was a stunned silence. Most of the family could not believe what their sensible, down-to-earth father had said.

'I can't believe this,' said Mark, deliberately aggressive, 'especially from a sane person like you. Are you now about to tell us that you're going to join the ranks of the great unwashed and lie about in Martin Place smoking dope and chanting ridiculous slogans? Anyway, what can we possibly do about any of that? You are just winding us up.' Although he had listened to Tanya saying almost the same things a few days earlier, he still needed convincing of the veracity of the science. He sometimes used this particular technique in his business dealings to try and tease out the issues.

'No, I'm not winding you up.' David glanced at Tanya, her half-smile appearing to signify approval. 'I thought that with all the brain power around this table we could at least discuss the evidence. What we do about it is another question.'

'Isn't the jury out on this? Are we certain your conclusions are correct?' asked Mark.

Tanya looked at him, frowned, and again shook her head.

'The evidence is overwhelming,' said Joe quietly. 'If anything, what David has presented is understated.'

'If food distribution is disrupted, people will starve,' said Evan uncertainly.

'Yes,' said David. 'Just think of the situation here in Australia. The ports will be unusable, for years probably. There will be no fuel for our trucks, so while there may be some food in the fields, it won't be going anywhere. People will certainly try to get out of the main cities. Can you imagine what it will be like? There will be absolute gridlock and people will quickly run out of fuel and food. I can see people dying on the M4. The supermarkets will be looted within days. The communications systems will be more or less destroyed. The police will be caught up in this thing like everyone else.'

'Okay,' Tanya had said nothing up to that point. 'Let us assume you are right and the Ross Ice Shelf will collapse into the sea. As Mark asked, what do you think we can or should do about it?'

'Well we could all go on living like kings for another ten or twenty years and when it happens, if we are still doing what we are doing now, the most sensible solution would be for us all to commit suicide. I expect many people would take this option,' answered an unsmiling David.

They all looked at him as if he was mad.

Tanya continued, looking at David directly, 'You most certainly have not brought us all to this wonderful dinner to tell us that though, have you?' She looked at him shrewdly. 'You really do have another solution.'

'Maybe,' said David, 'but if anyone has any other ideas I would be happy to hear them first.'

There was silence.

'I suppose there is no chance you are wrong, and all this is a lot of mumbo-jumbo. I have read that the world has cooled down and warmed up over thousands of years and this is happening again.' said Mark quietly, avoiding Tanya's glances.

'During the past seventy or so years the human population has grown from just more than two billion to just under seven billion people. It is forecast to be about nine billion within another fifty years. I believe that to be an underestimate, bearing in mind the trends over recent years … '

Joe interrupted, 'Without doubt, the increase in the world population has already had a major effect on global warming. The third world is determined to achieve first world living standards in as short a time as possible, so unless something drastic is done the trend to a warmer climate is likely to accelerate.'

David looked thankfully at Joe for his support. He then dropped his bombshell, as he said quietly, 'The collapse of the Ross Ice Shelf will wipe out anything from half to three quarters of whatever world population exists at the time. There is no doubt it will be an apocalypse like nothing the earth has seen in recent times and it certainly appears that human activity will have caused the catastrophe.'

There was a brief silence while the people around the table tried to gather their thoughts.

'What about governments around the world, surely they should be addressing this issue?' asked Patricia.

'The only government that is remotely capable of doing anything significant is the Chinese government. The democracies will not be able to generate the will to do enough. People have been brought up to expect continuing improvement in their living standards; they will not accept a situation that requires major sacrifices on their part, particularly when there is some dispute about the science behind climate change. If we rely on governments then we are headed for the suicide option,' David responded calmly.

'You've obviously thought about this,' said Tanya. 'Please tell us what you think the solution might be.'

'There is no solution as such,' said David. 'However, I have no intention of sitting on my hands and watching while the human race destroys itself. In thinking about it I have decided there is one basic objective. Would anyone like to tell me what they think that might be?'

There was silence again and then Tanya said, glancing quickly around the table, 'Under this unlikely scenario, there is only one possible objective and that is survival, firstly of self, and then family, and after that one can start thinking of the wider community.'

David looked at her admiringly, 'Precisely. My thoughts exactly. Does anyone have any ideas as to what we might do?'

Another stunned silence. David was aware that Chloe was looking daggers at him as if he was personally responsible for trying to destroy her "perfect" life.

David waited a few moments. Everyone was fully engaged, but they were waiting for him to speak. 'If we stay in Sydney, or any other major centre, we will be caught up in the disaster. We could go to one of the outback towns like Orange—' Chloe pulled a face. 'But those who escape Sydney will make for those towns, especially if they have not planned anything. I foresee considerable social disruption, even anarchy. Maybe all rural towns, like Orange, will have to limit the number of people they allow in. But food and fuel will be a problem for them as well.'

No one spoke.

'Okay,' said David, 'I really need help on this. One solution I think could work would be to develop a place somewhere, perhaps in the Blue Mountains that we could make totally self-sufficient. It would have to be defensible, almost inaccessible or could be made inaccessible once the Ross Ice Shelf collapses.' He had been speaking matter-of-factly, ticking the points off on his fingers. His calm demeanour belied his anxiety; he really needed to be able to convince this, his precious family, of the seriousness of the situation if they were collectively going to be able to do anything. He could see that he had everyone's full attention. Most were leaning forward waiting, now quite anxiously, for what he would say next. Tanya alone was leaning back, giving nothing away.

He ran through his mental list, 'We would have to produce all our own food, clothing, and electricity. We would have to be self-sufficient in water.'

'What about phones and Internet?' asked Evan. He thought it was all complete nonsense, but he wanted to be a part of the conversation.

'Phones and Internet would be as they are today, until of course the Ice Shelf collapses, after which, who knows, they would probably cease to function altogether.'

'All the major businesses, such as banks and supermarkets, would disappear ... for a time anyway,' added Joe, warming to the theme.

David continued, 'Mining would cease, as would postal services and so on.' He hesitated, then continued, 'The rule of law would certainly collapse.' He looked at Jonathan, 'The military may survive and could therefore be the one cohesive force in the country.'

'Help me out now. I have probably forgotten a few things. It would be helpful if everyone put their minds to this,' David continued on determinedly.

'What I hear you saying is that we would find and develop a place deep in, say the Blue Mountains, which would have something like five hundred hectares of arable land, but would be protected by its location and would have limited access by road. The access would have to be able to be blocked once the Ice Shelf had collapsed, which would isolate the community established there, but it would also deny outsiders any access at all,' said Jonathan, carefully analysing the situation. He wasn't sure of the science yet, but was intrigued by the intellectual challenge.

'Something like that,' responded David.

'How many people do you envisage being part of this commune?' asked Evan. He wanted to dismiss the whole thing as rubbish, but he was very fond of both his parents so he was trying to humour his father.

'I suppose two or three hundred eventually, but it would have to start off very small, maybe a dozen people. Sooner or later we would need our own medical facilities, teachers, and so on as, for a period after the disaster first strikes, I think we would be completely isolated until the country had settled down.'

'You mean until large numbers of the population had died?' said Evan.

'I'm afraid that would be the case. As Tanya has so eloquently put it, the objective is survival firstly of self and family. When that has been achieved, we can help the wider community. If we don't survive we will not be able to help anyone.'

'It seems very selfish. Is there no way the whole community could be involved so that more people survive?' asked Patricia, always concerned with other people as much as herself.

'No, that's a government job and none of the democracies are managing to convince anyone to make sufficient sacrifices … '

Mark rudely interrupted, 'We've had many amusing discussions dealing with the ineptitude of governments and how they waste our money. I need to be convinced this isn't just a load of bull encouraging us to invest in some wild scheme in the bloody boonies while the rest of the world gets on with living their lives.' He glared at everyone, daring them to challenge him.

'I believe if we do nothing then we will all end up as victims,' said David, almost as if he didn't hear Mark. 'There may be others who are thinking like us and other so-called communes around the country that survive; they could be the basis of a continuing civilisation.'

'Will it be like Aboriginal tribes occupying parts of the country and clashing occasionally with each other over territory?' asked Mark, seeing his dream of leading the bank disappearing if this dire prediction came to pass.

'Hopefully not. We do all speak the same language. Once the disaster is well and truly over it ought to be possible for the survivors to cooperate and gradually rebuild, having learned some of the lessons of the past.'

The conversation continued into the night. Initially, everyone was anxious, but all settled down and applied themselves to the problem at hand.

Tanya tapped Patricia on the arm as dawn broke, 'Come, let's get breakfast, while they continue to argue.'

Watching Tanya while she drove home, Mark asked, 'Why didn't you want to discuss your own findings? Dad's are much the same as yours.'

'Just being cautious. It's too soon. I don't know what I think yet and what we should do about it. I'd assumed your dad would be on the side of the deniers; how wrong I was. Do we really want to be a part of his mad scheme? Thank God I kept my mouth shut. All our options are still open. Your challenge would have exposed any doubts he may have had, so I don't think he has any.'

'I didn't say it just to challenge his thinking, I'm having great difficulty in believing it all.' He glanced at Tanya, but she said nothing further.

CHAPTER FIVE
The Search

Two weeks later, David had an unexpected call from Tanya. 'I'm coming to see you,' she said without any preliminaries, 'When would suit?'

'Well, this afternoon would be fine, say three?'

'Okay, three. Could you keep the rest of the afternoon free? There's a lot to discuss.'

David was left guessing. *It obviously has to do with Saturday night,* he thought. She had given him no clue as to whether her reaction would be positive or negative. The other night she had participated in the discussions, but had been non-judgmental about the science and his solution. No other members of his family had brought it up since, except Chloe.

Tanya was shown into David's office, having helped herself to a cup of tea. She was well acquainted with the place as David and his partners had engaged her to deal with several legal issues. Impeccably dressed in an expensive black pant suit, set off by a cheerful, brightly-coloured scarf, she pecked him on the cheek in a daughterly way as she sat down.

At first they talked neutrally about the previous Saturday night.

'A lovely evening,' she said generously. David just nodded. 'I have done some of my own research on global warming,' said Tanya, looking at David to see what his reaction might be.

David looked at her uncertainly. Maybe she was here to give him the big thumbs down and say that nothing was going to interfere with her path to the top. He briefly thought of Mark's hostile remarks from that night.

'I am having a great deal of difficulty in believing the world will collapse in the way you outlined the other night.'

David looked at her again, wondering why she was questioning him. Why not Mark, or Joe and Patricia?

'Let's go through the detail,' he said after a moment, 'I have it all here.' He took his laptop and they both moved to a round conference table in his office.

It took two hours, much of the material already familiar to Tanya. What surprised both of them was the way they worked together and the sense of trust they were developing.

'So there it is,' said David. 'It's undeniable. We have the New Zealand scientists, the British Antarctic survey, and now the Pentagon all saying much the same thing.'

'The Pentagon? I missed that one.'

'Their conclusions were on the Internet. For some reason there is no sign of the thirty-eight page document anymore. Unfortunately, I failed to make a copy of it. I believe the document was suppressed and I suspect, if asked, they would deny it ever existed.'

'Mmm, the bloody Pentagon,' muttered Tanya disbelievingly. 'I still can't believe our world will be destroyed. It can't all just fucking disappear.'

David was mildly surprised at his daughter-in-law's language, but it seemed to him she was gradually reaching the same conclusions.

'You mentioned you had a plan to build something in the Blue Mountains, or somewhere. Can I see those plans? Mark and I have some resources … if we determine this to be credible and not just a load of bullshit.'

'There is no big plan as yet. First and foremost we need to find a place that can be made self-sufficient. Chloe and I are going to spend every weekend from now on hunting for the ideal property, instead of playing golf.'

'If you are comfortable doing that on your own, I will do some more thinking and talk to Mark.' Tanya looked speculatively at David. 'If you happen to find something that is hopeful, would you let me know?'

David laughed. 'Of course.'

'How much do you know about farming?' asked Tanya out of the blue.

David laughed again. As always she seemed to be a step ahead of the pack. 'Not a huge amount. I thought we would just muddle along. Some things will work and some won't.'

'I can help with research. There is a massive amount of information on the Internet, which will give the project some hope of starting off with things that might work instead of just taking a shot in the dark.'

'Yes, of course that would be very useful.' David began to feel hopeful. 'I have tried looking for that sort of information, but I find the exercise rather tedious. I have also been wondering about the legal side of things … but I'm getting ahead of myself. We need to find this place first.'

'By the way what does Chloe think about all this?' asked Tanya.

He hesitated briefly, thinking, *Honesty is the best way forward*. He said, 'She will go along with it all. But she hopes the science somehow is wrong and that, without our doing anything, planet Earth will magically provide a solution. I also believe she thinks the project will be too big and difficult for us to go on with.' He glanced at Tanya uneasily. He wasn't used to talking about his feelings with anyone, even his much-admired daughter-in-law.

'If the Ice Shelf collapses,' Tanya said thoughtfully, 'for a period the settlement will be like a separate country. It will be completely isolated and will need its own laws. The world will recover on a much smaller scale, and so will Australia and the survivors will need to be able to fit in.'

David looked astonished, 'I really hadn't thought that far ahead, but you're right. Maybe during the period of isolation we'll have time to think about what sort of society we want to live in. The first step is finding this property, then we can make a plan.'

Tanya sat for a few more minutes, sipping her tea. She got up, gave David another daughterly peck on the cheek, returned her tea cup to the kitchen, and left.

In the intervening weeks David had spent much time talking with Chloe. In particular, he showed her his sources, all highly reputable.

'Why isn't there more publicity? If this is about the survival of the world, why aren't people shouting from the rooftops? What you told us was a complete surprise. Are you sure it's not just a pile of bullshit peddled by some lunatic, fringe busybodies?'

David laughed despite himself. Chloe had always been impatient with people peddling fancy theories. She was much happier doing practical things. 'No, I think the research is genuine. Those aware of the research must hope some sort of magic solution will save us all in the nick of time. Also governments seem to have no idea how to deal with the situation without causing panic.'

'So what should we do first?'

'This weekend, instead of playing golf, we'll start an exploratory tour of the countryside, mainly New South Wales, to see if we can unearth such a place. We could even play some golf out there, stay in decent places; it should be fun.'

'You mean a series of dirty weekends for the next, however many weeks it takes to find this unlikely place.' She sidled up to him and put her arms around him.

'Most certainly,' said David. 'I'm sure we'll find some very isolated places where the only possible spectators will be the occasional wallaby, who'll run like hell when you start to make your "I'm coming" noises.'

She cuddled up a little closer, 'I was thinking more along the lines of nice comfortable beds. It's a very long time since we made love on a river bank.' She added wistfully, 'Patricia was conceived on a river bank.'

'Well, hopefully there will be beds and river banks.'

They didn't make it beyond the carpet in the lounge.

David and Chloe spent the next six months exploring the countryside. They inspected a number of potential properties listed with real estate agents. One or two were almost possible, but either had an inadequate water supply or could not be completely isolated. However, they enjoyed the various places they stayed in from the luxurious in the Blue Mountains and Pokolbin to the more basic in Lithgow and further West; they often managed a game of golf, always playing for a decent bottle of wine. Chloe won more often than not.

Despite the fun they had, Chloe was becoming more and more despondent. Some of the properties contained little cottages. In days gone by, they had obviously been someone's unfulfilled dream, with overgrown gardens and, once, two unmarked, child-sized graves. She thought the amount of work that would be needed was beyond their resources. She tried comparing those horrid little places to her beautiful North Shore home; there was no comparison.

'I have been talking to my friends about our project,' she said to David one evening after a fruitless day's search. 'They've been wondering what has happened to us over the past months. When I tried to explain what we were doing they were all quite incredulous, and wondering if we have completely lost our marbles. Once they realise we are serious, they change the subject. Are you really sure the Ice Shelf will collapse?'

'Yes, the latest scientific study has just been published and it reinforces everything I told you six months ago.'

'These weekends have been marvellous, but we haven't seen anything that remotely suits,' observed Chloe quietly.

'There is one tomorrow that sounds more promising.' said David defensively.

Chloe shrugged.

After three hours, sweat pouring off them in the uncomfortable heat, they were carefully finding their way along a poorly-defined track in the four wheel drive. To Chloe's irritation they had made several wrong turns, involving difficult and dangerous manoeuvres. Both Chloe and David were trying to help direct the driver.

The agent threw up his hands, 'I don't think I can find this place, we need better directions.'

David walked off to see if he could find the track. He came back, excited. 'Let me drive, there is something a little further along here.'

They emerged into a glade a few hundred metres down the uneven track and there was the usual decrepit two bedroom cottage that Chloe was becoming used to. David and the agent had gone off to look at the stream that was running through the property, so Chloe thought she would give the cottage a once over despite its poor condition. The place was largely covered in brambles, but she scrambled up the rotting wooden steps and onto the small verandah. There to her horror was the largest black snake she had ever seen, coiled up in the doorway. It raised itself up threateningly; Chloe stood there, completely frozen.

David had seen her walk to the cottage and was about to tell her to watch for snakes when he saw her reaction. He quietly moved up the steps and tossed a light stick onto the massive coils. The snake hissed and slid away down the verandah and into the nearby bush. Chloe collapsed into David's arms, shaking like a leaf.

They sat down on the steps. 'It's okay, just a red-bellied black snake; they are generally quite shy and not aggressive.'

Chloe just shook.

David left her on the steps with the concerned agent and went inside the partly open cottage door. 'Oh my God!' he shouted. He came out as white as a sheet. 'Dead … there's a dead body in there. It looks as if it has been there for weeks, if not months.' David and the agent peered into the gloom. 'Don't touch anything. We need to call the police.'

They tried the mobile phone but, inevitably because of the terrain, there was no signal.

'Let's just get out of here,' said Chloe, still shaken. 'Do you think he died of snakebite?'

'We don't know whether it's a male,' said David. 'I think it's improbable the snake had anything to do with it, but we'll find out.'

David took over the driving and, at her request, dropped Chloe off at their hotel before reporting to the police.

'It's too late to do anything today, but we will need you both to accompany us tomorrow morning,' they were told. 'Please arrive by six.'

David, the agent, three policemen, and a pathologist, in two four wheel drive vehicles, arrived at the cottage by nine thirty.

'Just be careful of the snake,' warned David, but there was no sign of it.

'Male, aged about fifty,' said the pathologist. 'One bullet wound to the head. I would say he has been there about six months. There is no sign of any firearm. His feet and hands are bound.'

'Looks like murder then,' said the inspector.

David and the agent made statements back at the station then David and Chloe returned to Sydney.

Chloe was unusually silent during the drive home.

'Although that place is no good, the agent now has a really good idea of what we want. He says there is a place about a day and a half's hike into the mountains just beyond where we were today. I thought we could try to go there next weekend. We have all the hiking and camping gear,' volunteered David insensitively.

Chloe bit her tongue. She was tempted to shriek at him that a snake and a dead body was enough for one week, but she kept her cool. 'I think you had better count me out,' she said. 'Anyway I'm not sure I'm fit enough for a three day hike. There's a decent competition on at the club this weekend, maybe I'll try to find a place in that. Mark may be able to go with you.'

David looked at her closed face and said no more.

Mark was unable to go due to a big deal at work, but Tanya had said, 'I'll go with you. It's a while since I had a good bushwalk. So it'll be you, me, and the agent or owner?'

David had kept Tanya up-to-date with some of the places he and Chloe had seen; it seemed the likelihood of finding anything suitable was diminishing with every passing week. The party had a four hour journey down a very rough, partly overgrown track in the agent's four wheel drive and then walked for a good six hours. The agent was worried about Tanya and kept asking if she was alright. At the end of six hours, Tanya was marching confidently ahead leading the way, with the bedraggled agent, streaming sweat, barely keeping up at the rear.

David and Tanya became more and more excited as they walked. They were following, sometimes with difficulty, an old track alongside a clear, fast-running stream. Both David and Tanya were familiar with the generally silent Australian bush, the sunlight flickering through the leaves of the tall trees. They knew that most snakes would sense them and move away quickly. There was the occasional thump-thump of a surprised wallaby or kangaroo fleeing, and from time to time there were flocks of birds—cockatoos, lorikeets and more, attracted by the water. Towards dusk they entered a narrow gorge where they camped the night.

David and Tanya slept next to the fire while the agent pitched a small tent a few feet away.

'It depends on what we find once we are out of the gorge,' said Tanya. 'If there is a large, cleared area, this almost looks possible. The problem is going to be the cost of building a road, but access could easily be blocked here.' She pointed upwards to the almost sheer sides of the gorge on both sides. I bet they've been trying to unload this place for years. It would be too out of the way for most people.'

David had collected wood and made a fire and Tanya helped him cook the dinner. 'Have you heard anything from the police?' David asked the agent.

'Absolutely nothing.'

～✎

The next day, after a difficult five hour hike along the stream, they found themselves in a valley with an extensive flat, almost treeless area extending as far as the base of the mountains on both sides of the stream and reaching upriver into the mountain as far as the eye could see. The agent sat under a lone tree while David and Tanya walked to the end of the flat.

'It must be at least a thousand hectares, just the cleared area!' David was unable to keep the excitement from his voice. 'Maybe a glacier or other freak of nature dug this valley out millions of years ago. It has not actually been cleared, or we would see stumps. It looks as if no trees have ever grown here, only on the mountainside. We need to get soil samples and some idea of the carrying capacity.'

'I will get a proper survey done and perhaps you could get an estimate of the cost of building a road. I'll check all the deeds,' responded Tanya, trying to keep it all businesslike. But she was also more and more excited by the whole idea of David's settlement.

They took a look at the small cottage, unobtrusive on a hillock strategically overlooking much of the site. David beat the outside with a large stick before they went inside. 'Snakes,' he explained.

'Chloe told me.'

The cottage was old, dusty, and full of spider webs and much of the timber used in the construction was rotten. There was no sign of recent occupancy; not a saucepan, bed, or chair.

'This is prime position,' said David. 'The cottage will have to go of course; we can build something more suitable.'

Tanya looked at him and said pointedly, 'We mustn't get too far ahead of ourselves, the place looks great, but we have to do our homework. Property, road, and then we can worry about houses.'

Tanya and David spent half an hour standing on the dusty deck of the cottage trying to get a feel of the place, 'It's almost as if it was made for the settlement you have in mind,' observed Tanya, letting down her guard for a moment. 'It's already isolated, surrounded by pristine virgin forest, with those steep rock walls on all sides. It's also very beautiful, with that tinge of blue from the eucalypts. And there's no noise at all, except for the breeze in the grass and the bird calls. And being quite high up in the mountains, although not as high as Katoomba, means it won't get ridiculously hot in the height of summer.'

A jet plane silently flew over, still very high, reminding them that Sydney with its four and a half million people, was not that far away. David remained silent, if he had dreamt of the ideal place this would be it. A few kangaroos came out to graze in the late afternoon, then a dingo came past, scampering off when it saw the humans.

'What did people do here?' asked David over the camp fire that night.

'No idea,' responded the agent, 'This is the first time I've been here. I understand people lived here for a few months at a time, but it's just too hard and isolated. You are the first people to have shown any interest in the place in ten years. We apparently had a religious group before that wanting isolation, but it was even too much for them.'

The agent had pitched his tent, retiring to his bed early in anticipation of the long hike home the next day. He thought he had probably wasted three days.

He couldn't understand why anyone would want to live in such a god-forsaken place.

David and Tanya talked until late; both were excited.

'At first glance it's ideal for the settlement you have talked about.' Tanya kept her voice down, not wanting the agent to overhear. 'But we have to be very careful. I will have a look at the legal stuff next week. The road is going to be expensive and we need to find a house builder. If we can find someone who buys into the idea we may get good rates. We should come back in a week or so with surveyors, and take some soil and grass samples.'

'You are not going to ask them to walk in here are you?'

Tanya laughed quietly. 'Stuff the walking! Once we have lined all the people up, we can hire a helicopter and be in and out of here within a few hours. I now have the coordinates.' She waved her GPS device. 'Buggerlugs over there will be none the wiser.' She jerked her thumb in the direction of the agent's tent. 'If we had come in here by helicopter this time the owner would have thought all his Christmases had arrived at once. We need to continue to keep their expectations low.' She hesitated for a moment, 'If you don't mind, if we decide to proceed, I would like to be in charge of negotiating the purchase price. I have a strategy I think will work. You can handle the building and road costs.'

David was thankful for her insights. He liked Tanya, but despite some suggestive glances from the agent, he saw her only as his daughter-in-law. There was absolutely no hint of any kind of sexual attraction between them. With Tanya's help, they might be able to pull off something which even the previous weekend was looking to be a rather forlorn dream.

A dawn breakfast cooked by David saw them packed and ready by seven. Between them, Tanya and David kept up a steady pace back to their vehicle, with the agent struggling behind. Arriving well after dark, David drove to the estate agent's office to collect his car.

Glancing back at the sleeping agent, Tanya said quietly, 'I had a chat to our friend. He thinks we're not interested, so I will leave him for two or three weeks while we do all our homework and then I will deal with him.'

CHAPTER SIX
Chloe

Chloe was utterly despondent. She could see herself spending years living in some hellhole, working herself into an early grave, looking after chickens and sheep, and fighting off large black snakes. She didn't like or know anything about chickens and sheep and was terrified of snakes. She was unconvinced about the science and all her friends and acquaintances dismissed it out of hand. 'Load of bullshit,' was the general consensus.

Patricia supported David's view. 'Joe and I have looked at all the references. They are all well respected. We think he is right.'

'What are you going to do?'

'We will see what Dad comes up with, but if it is half sensible, we will probably join him.'

'Even if that involves selling up? Joe giving up his very good job and moving to a perilous future in some remote, undeveloped bush retreat? What about the kids' education?'

Patricia laughed, 'Joe is not sold on his job and I can educate the kids at least as well as any school. Anyway, there is no purpose in them being educated just to die of starvation or something worse. Joe is very interested in technology and has been researching all he can about solar power. He thinks he can install solar in the settlement's houses. We've even heard about farmers in Australia and North America running their tractors on solar. He has signed up for a course to become an accredited solar power technician.'

Mark was too busy to think about ice shelves collapsing. When Chloe cornered him, he said, 'I just don't know, I thought it was all bull, but Tanya seems to be more and more convinced Dad is right, despite her misgivings. A couple of people in the office think the science is sound; others think its all crap. So I'm reluctantly accepting what's been dredged up might just be right. I wish to hell it wasn't and that we could all just get on with what we are doing. It's interesting none of the so-called climate change investment opportunities have seen the light of day.'

He and Tanya had many, often heated, discussions. 'What happens if Dad's conclusions turn out to be a whole load of rubbish?' Mark said to Tanya one day. 'We will have put all our funds into a fucking great white elephant in the Blue Mountains. Not to mention we will have spent some of the best years of our lives slaving away up there when we could be travelling the world, or just enjoying ourselves here in Sydney.'

'If you don't accept the science, maybe you should do your own research. You say that the brightest in your office tell you the science is sound. If that is so, what the hell are they doing about it?'

'They may intellectually believe in the science, but as the saying goes, "follow the money". Not one of them has made a move in the direction we are going. I am quite sure if the bank was asked to invest, the proposal would be laughed out the door. '

'So, what are they going to do when the Ice Shelf collapses, drown or starve? Those appear to be the two options if nothing has been planned.'

'Much of the funding for the settlement will need to come from us. I'm having real difficulty in believing all our efforts over something like the next fifteen years will go into building this settlement, and it may all be unnecessary.'

'What sort of legacy will we leave our children when we have them? They will probably be in their early to mid-teens when it collapses. If we do nothing, we might have indulged ourselves but they will just die.'

While Tanya believed in the science, she still had overwhelming doubts about the lifestyle change that would occur if she accepted David's proposal. If she channeled all her ambitions into developing The Settlement, she would have to forget about anything else in her life. She vainly hoped that Mark would come up with a different solution, so that she could forget about it altogether.

Mark responded by taking her in his arms, 'Children, you say, maybe we could practice … ' He started to undress her. He decided to stop expressing his doubts to Tanya, hoping to avoid more forceful arguments.

∼

Evan was busy moving to Europe. He joked with his mum, 'If it's true then I will drown with a whole load of Poms. Seriously I just don't know, but I have this opportunity and I am going to pursue it.'

∼

Jonathan was quite straightforward with Chloe, 'Dad is right. When it happens I will be in the army and we might be able to do some good. I shall certainly be keeping in close touch with Dad and you all to see what is going on and will help when I can.'

The weekend when David and Tanya were in the mountains, Chloe joined in a mixed four-ball at the golf club, partnered with Alan. They both played well and came close to winning the competition. 'I think I will skip the drink,' she said to Alan and the others in the four-ball. 'I'm just going down to Freshwater Beach for a quick dip and then I'll be on home.'

'Come and swim at Manly,' suggested Alan. 'You can change at my flat on the beachfront.'

'I'll join you at Manly, but I think I'll change here. Give me five minutes.' She rushed off.

Chloe at five foot six was a slim, natural blonde and knew, even at fifty, that most men found her attractive. She followed Alan, parking near the beach. She skipped across the road, slipped out of the shirt covering her bikini, and gingerly stepped into the light surf. Alan found her as she was drying off.

'I could do with a cup of coffee. Maybe over there.' She pointed to a café just off the beachfront.

'I have a flat nearby.'

'Is that where you live?'

'No, it's just an investment.'

Chloe wondered why he hadn't let the place. They talked and joked easily for more than an hour, ordering another coffee, Chloe finding the good looking Alan increasingly attractive.

Chloe looked at her watch, 'Is that really the time? I must be going.'

'Are you going home like that? Just in your bikini? What happens if you have an accident or have to stop for petrol? You could easily pop over and change at my flat, it will only take a few minutes.'

Chloe looked at him enquiringly, decided there was no harm in his suggestion, and said, 'Yes that makes sense, thank you.'

'What a lovely place,' Chloe said as Alan quickly showed her through the penthouse flat, 'facing the sea, but not noisy since it's so high up.'

'It needs some decent furniture,' said Alan. 'I've only had it a few weeks.'

He showed Chloe to a spare bedroom. She changed into a plain shirt and tight-fitting black jeans, showing her slim figure off. She had taken trouble with her make-up. Alan looked at her admiringly.

'Thanks,' said Chloe, smiling. 'I'm a bit late now, but I'll see you at the club in a couple of weeks. Maybe we'll win the comp this time.' She pecked him on the cheek as she left, with Alan thoughtfully touching the place where she had kissed him. He was sure they had both felt the electric charge at the gesture.

On the way home, Chloe thought about the nightmare of the settlement for the first time that afternoon. When she thought of Alan and the upcoming golf tournament, a slight frisson of excitement flowed through her. She quickly suppressed it.

David talked about the place he and Tanya had seen and Chloe took a cursory glance at a few pictures on his digital camera. 'We'll be going up there again in a week or two,' said David, glancing at her. He added hurriedly, 'This time by helicopter, with a seat for you. The place seems ideal.'

Chloe nodded, 'Okay. We'll see when the time comes.'

Tanya hired a helicopter from a client and they made several, unannounced trips over two days. The first trip took Tanya and two surveyors into the site. Two hours later the chopper returned with David and Fred Costas, a well-established small time builder and a friend of David's.

David and Tanya persuaded the pilot to fly around the whole property in order to properly assess its isolated location. The western side was pristine forest, protected by massive rock faces through which there was no apparent gap; the North was much the same. The South, they knew, could be accessed by walking through the narrow gorge. David asked the pilot to fly slowly across the eastern aspect. The whole place seemed perfect to him. He thought it was quite beautiful; the bluish tinge in the atmosphere from the eucalypt oil in the leaves of the gums wafted into the atmosphere. He loved how untouched it was.

'There are a couple of possible gaps to the East,' Tanya pointed.

'The additional access may be useful, but we will have to make sure they look inaccessible from the outside.'

David tried very hard to encourage Fred Costas to be part of the scheme. He knew that over time many houses would have to be built. There would be ongoing construction work if The Settlement was to succeed.

Fred listened politely. 'This all sounds rather farfetched. We have had many dealings over the years, but this is a way out scheme. Anyway, I can do nothing until you have built a road. We can talk again after that.'

'The road will only be a single track, but it will be tarred,' said David.

'It needs to be able to take a large truck, say a load of twenty tons.' He hesitated, half of him intrigued and half of him wanting to have nothing to do with it, but he added, 'I have a mate who may be interested in building the road. I'll talk to him if you like?'

David managed to get Chloe to come on one of the later helicopter trips. She was nervous and felt nauseous during the one hour journey. After two hours tramping around the place, Chloe could see it was ideal for what David had in mind. It was indeed a beautiful place and on the day of the visit the sky was clear and there was a fresh southerly breeze blowing, keeping the temperature down.

The fast flowing stream was clear. David knelt down and sipped the water. 'It is beautiful and sweet, try it.'

'Yes, very sweet,' she said unenthusiastically. She still couldn't see herself living there.

'When the road is built, how long will it take to drive to Sydney? I presume we won't always have access to a helicopter?'

'Probably not. Three hours or so by car.'

David did not register the negative feelings emanating from his wife. He was completely obsessed with his impossible dream coming to fruition.

'What do you expect me to do here?' asked Chloe. They were perched on the verandah of the tiny cottage on the hillock.

'Well, we'll need to encourage the right sort of people to join us.'

'What do you mean by the right sort of people? Millionaires and such?'

'No, God forbid. We want practical people who will contribute—builders, teachers, people who understand this environment, perhaps the original inhabitants. Apart from that, you could start a horse breeding programme.'

David knew that in her youth Chloe had been a very good and keen horsewoman. The practicalities of owning and riding horses in Sydney as well as bringing up four children meant she rarely rode any more.

'Horses? What would you do with them?'

'Several things. After the Ice Shelf collapses, we will not be able to use any of our vehicles. We'll need horses to get about and perhaps seek out other communities like this one.'

'You think there will be other communities?'

'Yes, I expect so. But there will be recreational uses for horses, like gymkhanas and polo.'

'All young people want to do is play games on the Internet and sleep with each other.'

David smiled, 'The Internet will collapse, perhaps forever. Riding horses will give them an alternative. If we have a decent stable we may be able to trade horses with other communities and we will need horses for regular patrols.'

'It sounds like a return to the dark ages.'

'For a few years it may be like that.'

'What do you envisage, a sort of hybrid between the Zulus and the Mongolians, with you as either Shaka or Genghis Khan?' she said playfully and then more seriously, 'Do you think you are going to be some sort of dictator here?'

'No. I had always assumed we would have an elected council and the leader would be chosen by the council. But, I haven't really had time to think it all through. You could help.'

'Okay, Genghis, horses it will be. I'll probably enjoy that. When should we start?'

'We purchase the property within a month or two. Then build the road, over six months to a year. We will need to build a few houses … But you could do some research, think about what sort of horses would be suitable …'

'You mean there are alternatives to four legs and a tail,' said Chloe with a straight face.

Despite himself, David laughed. He knew he needed to lighten up a bit, especially with Chloe.

Chloe allowed herself to be hugged. 'Oh yes, the bloody house. I will be involved in designing that if I'm going to live in it. I presume we can dispense with black snakes on the verandah and dead bodies in the lounge.'

'I have started to talk to an architect. All the houses here will use little energy. They will have solar power and face the right way.'

'What about air-conditioning?'

'Only nature's air-conditioning. The design of the house will make the most of it.'

'How big will it be?'

'Not very big. I think we will spend much of our time outside. There will be community facilities within walking distance. We don't need a competition to see who can build the biggest house.'

'Khrushchev, not Genghis,' muttered Chloe. She was having difficulty taking the whole thing seriously, it was just so far removed from her current reality.

Chloe, despite her negative feelings, started to research horses and spend time with David's architect on house design. If one believed in climate change, everything David was doing made sense. She just was not prepared to accept her world would change quite so catastrophically. She continued to play golf with Alan. They usually had a swim afterwards and Chloe often changed in his flat. She felt more and more comfortable in his company.

On one of the weekends when David was away at The Settlement, she played golf with Alan in one of the club competitions. She had hit her ball into a deep patch of rough out of sight and Alan had come to help find her ball. He accidently bumped into her, when suddenly and unexpectedly they were passionately kissing. Chloe was amazed at the strength of her physical response to Alan's deep kisses.

'We had better stop this,' she said shakily as she tried half-heartedly to push him away. 'Careful, or we'll be missed,' she said breathlessly after another deep kiss. They found their way separately back to the fairway. 'No luck, it's too thick in there,' she said shakily to the other couple, who had not noticed anything amiss.

As usual they went for a swim after the game. Alan said, 'Come up to the flat, you can have a shower there. I have bought some special coffee.' Chloe thought of the kiss and nodded.

Halfway through her shower Chloe called out to Alan. He nervously peered around the door carrying a tray with two cups of coffee. He nearly dropped everything when he saw her naked body through the shower door.

'Join me,' she said more boldly than she felt, 'forget the coffee.'

He needed no second invitation and was out of his swimming costume in a few seconds. They washed and dried each other thoroughly and then dived onto the bed. It was warm so they made love on the top of the soft clean sheets. Then they made love twice more.

As dusk arrived, Chloe dragged herself off the bed, dressed, and kissed a drowsy Alan as he watched her every movement. As she was leaving, Alan pressed something metallic into her hand.

'These are the keys to the flat. I will call you during the week.'

Chloe thought she would feel guilty. But instead she felt liberated from the nightmare of The Settlement. She relived and savoured every moment of her lovemaking with Alan. To say she had enjoyed it would be an understatement; it was kind, gentle, and very inventive. She knew she would go back to see him. In fact, she almost turned around there and then, when she was halfway home.

David was pleasantly surprised at Chloe's sunny demeanor when he returned. Mistakenly, he thought Chloe was finally on board.

Tanya had soon established the precise dimensions of the property for sale and the rights attached. 'There are no restrictions on water rights,' she told David. 'That means the dam you suggested for the top of the property is possible.'

'I have established a basis for building the road and have worked out roughly what it would cost.' David showed Tanya his costings. 'There is a twenty percent contingency in those figures and Fred has given me the cost of building two and three bedroom cottages. Again, I have added some contingencies, but I think I will be able to get him down once he comes on board.'

Tanya spent thirty minutes on her laptop manipulating figures. 'If the property can be bought for almost nothing then it looks as if one would be able to build the road, five three bedroom cottages, with some money left over for the dam, provided Mark and I join the scheme.'

'How are you going to get the property for nothing?' David was anxious about the two big unknowns. Acquiring the property for nothing was surely a dream and Tanya and Mark's commitment was still unconfirmed.

'Just watch me,' she smiled.

'Do you want help?'

'Not with what I have in mind. I will have that little shithead all tied up in knots within the next week,' she said, referring to the agent.

Tanya made an arrangement to see the estate agent, which she changed twice. She was deliberately late when she did eventually arrive for the appointment. The agent was agitated, but had obviously made an effort with his appearance. Tanya started off by listing all the problems with the property.

'Building that road is the killer.' She mentioned a cost figure almost double the one David had given her.

The agent blanched, but undeterred he mentioned a purchase price. Tanya started to pack her things away. The agent looked nervous; he had hoped this was his big chance.

'Look, we'll have to get real about this property. Maybe we should have dinner together.' Tanya told him where she was staying. 'I will see you there at seven thirty.'

Tanya made the most of her natural beauty and wore a very short skirt. The agent's eyes nearly popped out of his head when he saw her. During the dinner she talked to him in an intimate manner and made him feel he was the most fascinating person in the world.

'What are your real expectations about the property? It is useless to the owners, they never go there. In order to use it, a road will have to be built. What do the owners want? Would free access be any good to them?' asked Tanya.

'What about cash?'

'Forget cash. If a road is built, for the first time ever, access will not be a problem,' said Tanya.

'Access?'

'Yes, people will actually be able to go there.'

'Who will build the road?'

'We will, once the property belongs to us,' said Tanya.

'How would the owners benefit?'

'Access.'

⌁

They continued arguing for the next half hour. Tanya could see David's dream becoming a reality. Despite the excitement, she kept her head and was completely ruthless in her dealings with the agent. 'Look you'll have to speak to the owner, if we build the road for the first time ever he will be able to go there; if he then builds a house there he can either use it or he may be able to sell it. I can't do better than that,' said Tanya firmly but courteously.

A deal was finally concluded. The property would be transferred into the name of "The Settlement", and the new owners would be responsible for building the road. At the seller's expense, The Settlement would build a house to an approved design, to which the sellers would have the right of occupation for one hundred years. There would be no other considerations, cash or otherwise relating to the transfer.

'Give me the full name of the owner please,' asked Tanya as she made some adjustments to the agreement on her computer. She showed him the draft.

'It seems okay,' said the agent uncertainly.

'I would like to know tonight. Can you call the owner? I will just get this printed off, then we can sign it and have a drink to celebrate,' said Tanya.

Tanya returned twenty minutes later with two copies of the agreement, having settled her bill. The agent read the agreement and asked for two small changes, which they altered by hand and initialled.

'You have authority to sign this?' asked Tanya.

Yes.'

They signed.

'Okay, let's get those drinks.'

The agent tried to put his hand on her leg when they sat at the bar.

Tanya shook her head. 'Sorry, that was never part of the deal,' she muttered, gave the surprised agent a kiss on the cheek and left. 'I'll be in touch in a day or two.' She did not return to her room, but went straight back to Sydney.

~

'How on earth did you manage all this? They are actually going to pay us to take the place,' said David quizzically. He had glanced at the agreement and then read it more carefully, when Tanya proudly presented it to him the next day.

'It's amazing what the thought of a bit of fanny will do, unfulfilled of course,' said Tanya, without even the hint of a blush. 'The road still has to be paid for.'

It was David who blushed. He certainly didn't want any further discussion on how Tanya had manipulated the situation with the agent.

'Of course, but we were going to do that anyway. Build the road I mean.'

For Tanya, securing a deal on the property was the final piece of the jigsaw. They could now create a place where they might survive the apocalypse. This was the new reality. *All I need now is to convince Mark to help fund the place.*

She asked him to keep the next weekend completely free, 'From Friday evening to late Sunday. I have a surprise for you.'

'What's this all about?'

'It's a surprise, trust me.'

'You're up to something,' he said suspiciously.

'I'm always up to something,' she smiled.

~

Tanya had booked one of the best restaurants in Sydney. He relaxed as they talked about innocuous things. Halfway through the meal she said, 'I need to show you what your Dad and I have been doing in the Blue Mountains.

He looked at her suspiciously.

Entirely from her head, Tanya took him through all the science of what had been forecast. Even Mark was impressed at her grasp of the subject.

'The evidence for it is irrefutable.'

'Okay, but this idea of Dad's is virtually impossible. How would it work?'

'I'll show you tomorrow. We need to leave home at five am.'

The next morning, Tanya drove them to Bankstown Airport.

'Where are we going?'

'All will be revealed,' she smiled.

Mark just shook his head as they clambered out of the car at the airport.

Tanya had, the day before, arranged for camping equipment and food to be packed into the helicopter. They were in the air by six thirty.

Landing close to the decrepit little cottage she, David, and the agent had visited a few weeks earlier, Tanya, helped by Mark and the pilot, unloaded the helicopter and carried the equipment to a grassy area near the stream. When Tanya was satisfied she had everything she needed she said to the pilot, 'See you tomorrow around three.'

Mark helped to erect the tent and set up camp. They collected wood for a fire.

'I'll show you round,' said Tanya.

'Is this the place you and Dad walked to? I wondered what had happened. The subject went off the radar somehow.'

'We needed to make sure all the homework was done.'

'It is an amazing spot.'

'We need to do a bit of walking,' answered Tanya.

They explored everywhere over the next day. At various vantage points, Tanya showed Mark where she thought houses could be built, how they could block access from the South, where the cultivated area would be. Within half a day, Mark started to participate and he made a number of suggestions about the potential development of the place.

'The place is completely deserted,' he marvelled.

They stripped off and swam naked in the stream, then made love in the soft grass next to it. After a dinner cooked together they were sitting companionably near the fire, enjoying the warmth. A few kangaroos had emerged to graze in the evening.

Mark said, 'This is a wonderful place. It looks like it would cost a bomb though. I doubt we could afford it.'

'Would you like to know how much it cost? Nothing. All we have to do is to build the road.'

'What? You're having me on.'

'No, read this.' She handed him the purchase agreement for the property.

By the firelight, Mark read and reread the agreement. 'Who arranged this deal? It's fantastic, unbelievable.'

'I did. It makes the whole project a reality. We already have the funds to build the road and a few houses.'

'What can I contribute?' asked Mark.

Tanya smiled. 'Commitment, energy, brains, cash, in that order.'

Mark moved closer. They made love on a sleeping bag next to the fire.

The next day they continued walking, Mark animatedly discussing the potential developments.

'Security—are we sure we will be able to isolate the place when the flood happens?'

'Yes,' said Tanya. 'The southern road can be blocked if we collapse the gorge on either side. There is no access from the West or North. The East is not quite so secure. We can fly around it when the helicopter arrives.'

By the end of the weekend Tanya felt sure she had Mark on side and he committed himself to mortgaging the Mosman house to the hilt and putting all the funds at the disposal of the project.

The property was transferred into the name of "The Settlement Pty Ltd", the shareholders listed as David Bower, Chloe Bower, Tanya Bower, and Mark Bower.

Before they all signed the agreement, Tanya questioned Mark again. 'We both need to understand this is a major commitment, it will change our lifestyle completely. I have spent months trying to establish an argument against the science, hoping we would be able to forget your father's mad idea, but have found nothing. So I'm committed to putting every ounce of my energy into developing The Settlement so that the people living there will survive. Are you equally committed? Are we in this together?'

'Absolutely, we have no choice.' He looked away. Confronted by Tanya's intensity he felt powerless to say otherwise, regardless of any other feelings he might have had.

~~

A year later, the four of them, together with Patricia and Joe, drove down the completed road. It was only a single track, but it had a proper foundation and was tarred, so could be used in all weathers.

Tanya excitedly pointed out various landmarks, 'We camped just over there when David and I walked in here, more than twelve months ago.' She waved at a place hidden in the trees.

Mark grunted, thinking, How much of this fucking road did I pay for?

Chloe had been joyfully dreaming about her latest assignation with Alan, when she was woken from her reverie.

'Well, we've got this far. Now the real work starts,' said David.

Chloe's heart sank.

CHAPTER SEVEN

The Settlement

2012 TO 2016

While the road was under construction, David and the reluctant Chloe spent months arguing about their planned house in The Settlement. Chloe was eventually resigned to a house with three generous bedrooms and two bathrooms, but had managed to arrange for the lounge to have large picture windows facing down the length of the property, making the most of the magnificent view.

'It's not facing the right way,' David had argued unsuccessfully. 'We need to be facing north not south to make the most of the sunshine, especially in winter.'

Chloe just ignored him and made certain the house was built to her specifications, still a far cry from what she was used to.

A few weeks before the house was completed David broached the subject Chloe had been dreading. 'I was wondering when you thought we should move to The Settlement and sell here?'

'Jonathan still has eighteen months to go before he finishes university and goes into the army. Shouldn't we leave it until then?' She hated the idea of moving to what she now thought of as the wilderness.

'We really need to get on with developing the place and recruiting more settlers, otherwise we won't have done enough to survive. Jonathan can live with Mark and Tanya.'

Chloe was silent. The wheels of David's project ground inexorably on.

David continued, 'I will start discussions with my partners next week. Once I sell my share there will be no reason to remain in Sydney.'

'Will we be coming back to Sydney until your precious Ice Shelf collapses?'

'Of course, we can stay with Mark and Tanya.'

'Can't we just keep this place?'

'No. Tanya and I are presently setting out some rules for people moving to The Settlement. One of the rules is that they become fully committed. Having a bolt hole, such as a house in Sydney, will be against the rules and they won't be allowed in.'

'What about Mark and Tanya? I presume that doesn't apply to them.'

'No, financially they contribute far more than anyone else to the project, so their status will be explained to anyone who asks. They will stay in Sydney until the last possible moment and legitimately milk every cent possible from the bank, so we can ensure The Settlement is fully developed and sustainable.'

Chloe did not even attend the auction; she was too upset. She arranged to spend the day with Alan.

'Will you still be able to meet me here?' asked Alan anxiously when she explained the situation.

'Oh yes, I will be coming to Sydney regularly. I really don't think I could face being up there otherwise.'

Chloe thought about her own position. She seemed powerless to do anything or even slow down the move to the mountains. *I have my family, the horses are fun and interesting, and now I have Alan. I'm not bloody well giving any of that up.*

David had not told his business partners anything about The Settlement, so it came as a surprise when he told them he wanted to retire and sell his fifty percent share.

'When do you want all this to happen?'

'Soon.' He gave brief details of The Settlement, but left out his doomsday forecasts. He knew they wouldn't be interested and would wonder about his sanity.

He consulted Mark and Tanya and after two months of negotiations came away with a very good deal, payable over three years. David had arranged to share in the earnings of the business during the two year period his partners had negotiated to fully buy David out.

'It also suits the cash requirements for The Settlement,' Tanya said as she read the final agreement. 'They pay you for half the shares at once and then the rest in two portions over the next two years. It will boost the building program so we can get more people in sooner. But, you'll need to be onsite.'

'We have arranged to move before the end of the month. I think we should all have Christmas there,' responded David.

David decided to leave the move to Chloe, once the dates had been agreed. This fell in with Chloe's plans. Some of their furniture went to the Blue Mountains, but the house was too small to accommodate it all so Chloe quietly shipped many of the more valuable things to Alan's flat in Manly, removing some of his more tawdry pieces in the process. Tanya agreed to take most of the rest; she hated throwing things away or wasting anything.

The Manly flat became a home away from home for Chloe where she was surrounded by many of her most precious things. David would neither notice nor care if certain familiar items were no longer visible.

Chloe had been surprised at how much she had enjoyed thinking about building up a stable of horses. David had been delighted with her apparent enthusiasm. Shortly after their move she told him, 'I have bought six Arab mares for the stables. I have been riding one or more of them most weeks back in Sydney and although they are quite lively they are very well trained, so they'll be suitable for beginners. They're also more sure footed and smaller that your typical thoroughbred. I can show you where I think the stables should be, but all we need is a fence to keep them in for the time being.'

'Stables!' said David.

He had not planned for stables, but he had enough sense to keep his mouth shut. He arranged to build a horse paddock and in time the stables were erected where Chloe wanted them, uphill and east of the planned village.

Chloe contrived to spend a day or two every fortnight in Sydney. Much of the time was spent with Alan in the flat, although if she stayed overnight she always spent it with Mark and Tanya. Her relationship with Alan was based on sex, although they did share a few confidences and they had an occasional casual meal together. Both of them enjoyed the sex, but neither mentioned making the relationship more permanent.

Just before Christmas, Patricia and Joe moved into The Settlement. As hoped, Joe was now an expert on solar energy and had been responsible for installing all the solar panels. There was no other source of power in the houses, not even wood fires.

Joe had also acquired two old tractors and was in the process of converting them to run on solar energy with the help of two Australian and one American farmers' advice. 'Once both tractors are running on solar, we will never need fossil fuel for them again. I will also convert ordinary cars for use in The Settlement, but I'm not sure they would be legal on the roads.'

As members of the family Joe and Patricia had been granted shares in The Settlement Pty Ltd.

Patricia was also keeping busy. 'I will teach the children in the morning and then I'm going to set up a full curriculum and lessons for every class from pre-school to university entrance. No need to worry about local agendas and their vested interests and not the real needs of the pupils. Within three years, I hope to have the most modern, up-to-date curricula in the world, with the help of the Internet.'

'What about your children?' Tanya asked. 'Do they have enough of your time?'

'I give them a good four or five hours in the morning and they get on with their homework in the afternoon, under the watchful eye of their mother.' She smiled. 'They will be better educated than their peers within a year or so. At present they are not having much interaction with other children, but that will change as The Settlement develops.'

Fred Costas, the builder, had reduced his prices to a minimum since he and his family had committed to moving to The Settlement. Fred was the first non-family member, apart from the original owner, to be granted rights. As with the original owner, he had the right of occupation for one hundred years and had to pay a similar amount in rates. He had built his own house at his own cost.

'We really want commitment from the settlers,' said David. 'We should stop new arrivals owning anything outside.'

'Respectfully, that proposal has no chance of working,' responded Tanya. 'People will find more and more ingenious ways of hiding outside assets. It will push people away. And we would need a massive bureaucracy to monitor the situation. I think, the fewer rules the better. If The Settlement is an attractive place to live, people will commit.'

'I convinced Chloe to sell our Sydney house on that understanding.'

Tanya shrugged. Water under the bridge as far as she was concerned.

David saw the sense, but thought, *I've let Chloe down*. He still felt the move to the mountains was in their best interests. *Nothing, nothing is going to stop me from making this place viable anyway*. Thinking about his wife of thirty years made him guilty, so he put her out of his mind.

Tanya and David spent many hours determining the rules for allowing non-family members to join The Settlement. They came up with a simple set of rules.

- One hundred year right of occupation transferrable to approved settlers.
- The new settler would pay for construction of their own house to an approved plan.
- Dwelling maintenance, responsibility of the occupier.
- If a house was abandoned for more than five years, occupation rights would be cancelled.
- An impost of twenty percent of the cost of the dwelling payable to The Settlement Pty Ltd for construction of central facilities—community hall, recreation facilities, watch house etc.
- Annual rates.
- The Settlement Pty Ltd would act like a local council but with more powers.
- Miscellaneous rules—no privately owned weapons, no generators, no air-conditioning.

'Very few rules,' observed David.

'Yes, in time we may need to give people more of a stake in the place.'

'What do you have in mind?'

'Businesses may need to be owned by individuals, not us, the family.'

'At present few businesses would provide a living. We will have provided all the seed money.'

'Of course, but it might be smart to sell them off once they become viable,' said Tanya, looking at him for a reaction.

David shrugged, 'Let's get the operations set up first.'

Tanya's son Chas was born a year after David and Chloe had moved to The Settlement. Tanya took a week off from work, 'What the hell would I be doing buggering around here? We have a very good nanny who knows more about kids than I will ever know,' she responded when questioned by Chloe.

'Aren't you going to feed him yourself? It's better for him.'

'Of course. I have my milking machine thing that I drag around with me so I can express all bloody day. I have more than enough to feed two babies, so he's going to get my milk whether he likes it or not. It's caused a few awkward moments in the office, but they are getting used to it,' she joked.

Chloe just shook her head. She doted on the child and his birth gave her more excuses to be in Sydney; her relationship with Alan continued to thrive.

Over two years, The Settlement gradually took shape. David managed to persuade a doctor to participate. Like many of the settlers he spent two or three days a week in the mountains and the rest of the time outside. As the demand for services increased, the time individual settlers spent at The Settlement increased.

The first attempts at growing vegetables and planting fruit trees were thwarted by the depredations of the kangaroos and other wildlife.

'We are going to need a fence high enough and strong enough to keep the roos out,' David announced one day to Tanya.

They spent several weekends riding around the property marking out the dimensions of the fence, with Tanya sometimes carrying Chas in a sling across her front.

As they put markers down, David looked quizzically at Tanya. 'Hold on,' said David. 'The boundary is here.' He pointed to the marker

Tanya took no notice and put a marker down well into the bush. 'If we are building a fence, we should look to the future. I'm not sure the current acreage is big enough for all the people we are planning to have here. This gives us a chance to extend the boundaries a bit.'

'The markers you have placed will just about double the size of the property,' reflected David.

'Yup. We've never seen any kind of field officer, the terrain is just too difficult. The additional area is all thick forest, so we'll easily be able to disguise it by leaving one hundred metres of bush untouched. We may never need it, except maybe for farming. We should plant trees round all the fence posts in the new area to disguise them. If one has enclosed an area for a certain length of time one can claim ownership anyway. '

'The things you think of,' he said. He had always played everything right down the line, but went along with it even though it made him feel slightly uncomfortable.

The fence was built, enclosing the new area as well. Tanya and David were the only people who really understood the boundaries, so no questions were asked. After that, vegetables thrived and an orchard was planted.

~❦

David purchased a small herd of shorthorn cattle, suitable as both dairy and beef stock. He managed to find a family able to tend the stock and they encouraged the purchase of some merino sheep, for both wool and meat. He stocked the dam with trout, encouraging settlers to fish. He asked people to return smaller fish back to the water, rather than taking them for food.

~❦

Chloe was still leading her double life, spending at least one morning or afternoon every fortnight with Alan in Manly. David was obsessed with Settlement developments, for which Chloe shared no interest, so instead she thought of Alan. Sharing confidences with him was easy, 'I do not believe in the science at all,' she told him, early on in their relationship. They were lying together, comfortably naked in her bed after athletic and passionate lovemaking. This session had taken them excitingly all over the flat, culminating ecstatically in the bedroom.

'Explain it to me. But don't take too long,' he joked. 'I'll be ready to go again, very soon.' So she did, while holding his growing erection. 'Sounds barmy,' he agreed before they made love again.

While they spent most of their time together in bed, they still shared a love of golf. But then they found a common interest in horses.

'Horses!' exclaimed Alan when Chloe told him about The Settlement's extensive stable. 'I used to be a very good horseman; let's go out to the stables and go for a ride.'

From then on, the stables became a regular meeting place. The owners thought Alan was Chloe's husband and she didn't disabuse them. The second time they went out riding Chloe led them to an isolated glade near a pond on the pretext that they needed to water the horses. She tied the horses up so they could graze. Then, to his surprise and pleasure, undressed Alan so they could make love on the soft grass in the sun.

'What happens if someone comes?' asked Alan languidly in the warmth.

'Only two people come here,' Chloe laughed, 'you and me. Come any time.' She rubbed her ample breasts against his face.

~❦

Chloe often spent the night in Sydney, staying with Mark and Tanya on the pretext of seeing more of her grandson Chas. Sometimes, she was able to spend the night with Alan, telling David she was staying with Margaret or Eva, both colleagues involved in various charities. Chloe thought she was in love with Alan, but her family was too precious, so she continued to teach the growing number of Settlement children to ride.

Once, when she and Alan discussed their relationship after they had made love, he said, 'I have four beautiful children. They are all doing well at school, but they still need me there. I could never change that. This time with you means everything to me though. Long may it continue.'

Chloe was relieved, but pretended to be upset, 'So I am just a convenient fuck?'

Hoisting himself up on an elbow, he could see from her expression that she was joking, 'Bitch!' he exclaimed, smiling. 'Well I had better make the most of it then.' He rolled her onto her back.

'It's the same for you, from all you have said. You don't want to change anything,' he said afterwards.

Chloe nodded, 'Tell me if your feelings change, won't you? But I am thrilled to be here with you.'

Their relationship continued for three years. Together they were always easy and lighthearted, with many jokes and wonderful sex. Her usual text, ahead of time, read, "How would you like to find me?"

He always delivered a saucy reply. On that fateful day, it read, "Starkers, sunbathing on the balcony."

Chloe was expecting him before noon and when, for the first time ever, Alan did not arrive she tried him on his mobile. It went to voicemail. When she tried his office number, she was put through to a secretary

'Who is speaking please?' asked a tremulous voice.

'My name is Chloe Bower. I'm a friend of Alan's. It's a personal call.' She had never before called his office. The secretary hesitated, then burst into tears. Chloe waited, apprehensively.

'Alan was killed in a car accident at eleven o'clock this morning.'

Chloe went into complete shock. He had obviously been on his way to see her. With a valiant effort she managed to control herself. There seemed to be nothing that she could usefully say, but she did manage, 'Oh my God, how terrible. Is there anything I can do?'

'No, there is not much you can do,' said the tearful voice. 'I suppose he was on his way to see you.'

'Could you text me the funeral arrangements, please, when they have been fixed?' She gave the secretary her mobile number.

When it all sank in she wept bitter tears. She spent the afternoon in the flat trying to recover her composure and it was a very subdued Chloe who unexpectedly went to stay with Mark and Tanya that evening. She went to bed early feigning a headache, where she cried herself to sleep.

Chloe had never felt so alone in her life. The relationship with Alan had been fun, but it had also created an outlet for her during the misery of the move to the mountains. She would desperately miss her time with Alan and there was absolutely nobody that she could confide in.

After some thought she decided not to attend the funeral, but sent flowers anonymously and spent an hour in the flat at the time of the funeral thinking about Alan and the fun they had enjoyed. She knew she would visit the gravesite when she could find out where it was.

Months later she received an unexpected package from a firm of solicitors. Alan had left her the flat in Manly, completely unencumbered. Chloe wondered what to do as she no longer had any need for it. She called the solicitors to find out who had signed the note.

Having identified herself she said, 'I was surprised to read that Alan left the Manly flat to me.'

'Alan was very explicit in his instructions; he made the change to his will more than a year ago.'

'Oh, it is most unexpected. Can you answer two questions? Firstly, is the family aware of the bequest and secondly, can you tell me if the family has been well provided for?'

'The family had no knowledge of the bequest or indeed of the existence of the property and I can assure you the family is very well provided for.'

CHAPTER EIGHT
Floods

David spent many weeks worrying about water storage. He had never seen the stream dry-up, but he wondered what would happen to the dam they had constructed at the upper end of the property when the occasional deluge engulfed the area.

'We are not talking about heavy rain for only a few days,' he told Joe and Fred. 'There have been occasions in the past twenty years when something like five hundred millilitres have fallen in a week. Will the dam hold up? How much water should we release from the dam in advance of the rain? Will the rising water threaten our houses? What should we do with the livestock? And when we blow up the mountain to isolate this place, how big will the pipe have to be to carry the stream when the place floods? It's not much use saving ourselves from the flood caused by the collapse of the Ice Shelf only to be drowned by a flood in The Settlement caused by our own ineptitude.'

When heavy rains were forecast, David galvanised the community in moving all the livestock to higher ground and all their equipment under cover. So far, every threat had been minimal.

It caused grumbling in the community. 'Another overreaction. Next time, I won't participate. The houses are far away from the stream and water has come nowhere near the built up area,' was one reaction.

'It is better to be cautious,' advised David. 'We are still trying to understand the environment we live in. One day there will be a big storm and we will be glad of the preparations we have made.'

Weeks later, forecasters warned of "a major cyclonic event" approaching the Sydney region and Blue Mountains. Such events were infrequent, but often managed to restore levels in Sydney's major water storage facilities.

David circulated his usual warnings to the community. 'I suggest you stay in Sydney until this is over,' he told Mark.

'We should release all the water from the dam,' Joe advised. 'I'll see to it.'

The rain started slowly. David had made certain that all livestock were well out of reach and was doing his final rounds when Joe ran up. 'I can't open the sluices to release water from the dam. A connection is broken. I will only be able to repair it once the storm is over.'

'It'll have to be done manually,' said David. 'Come on.'

Driving the one conventionally-fuelled vehicle in The Settlement, Joe raced towards the dam. As they drove through the increasingly heavy rain they saw two teenage boys in swimming trunks running towards the stream, carrying a surfboard.

Joe stopped the truck and David ran over to them. 'Go back home. Surfing in the stream now would be very dangerous. The flood from the dam will be huge and you'd both drown. Go home now and I mean now.'

'Dad said it would be okay,' said one of the boys.

'It won't be, please go home,' David entreated.

The boys reluctantly turned around and started off in the direction of their home. Joe drove on.

'Damn,' said David, turning around and peering through the storm. 'Those stupid little fools. They just waited until they thought we were out of sight and now they're on their way back to the stream.'

'We can't wait,' said Joe. 'If I had been able to release the sluices automatically the dam would be almost half empty by now. If we wait any longer the water may start going over the top of the wall. It might even cause it to collapse.'

David briefly considered making sure the boys were safe. He decided he could get the sluices open and then make sure of the safety of the boys.

They parked above the nearly full dam. After an hour, five sluices had been opened using two large wrenches. 'We'll wait to see if that is enough, we may have to open all ten of them,' said Joe.

'I am concerned about those kids. The stupid little shits will drown if we open them all. We will have to rescue them before we open any others.'

'The wall may collapse … '

'So? We can rebuild the bloody wall. You can't replace a drowned child. We know what the silly buggers are up to, it's our responsibility to rescue them. Then we can come back and open more sluices.'

Joe drove carefully towards where he thought the boys might be. 'I must keep the truck well away from the stream … My God, look!'

The stream, usually only two or three metres across, was already almost fifty metres wide and broadening every minute. 'If those boys are in this, they will be in real trouble.'

'Look,' David pointed. 'There, in the middle. Holding onto a sapling. Quick.'

David tied a long length of rope around his middle, making certain it was secure. Joe tied the other end to the tow-hitch in the vehicle. David waded in, oblivious to the danger, losing his footing and then regaining it several times. He was completely out of his depth by the time he reached the boys clinging to their tree. The stream rose ever more quickly and he made a forlorn grab for a branch. Joe saw what was happening and drove the truck dangerously close to the edge of the boiling mass of water, once their peaceful, benign stream.

David managed to grab the tree. He wrapped the rope around both boys as well as himself, signalling to Joe to pull them out of the frigid, rushing water. Joe could see that David was on the verge of collapse. Using low ratio and first gear he managed to get the truck going on its own, very slowly. Leaping out of the cab, he grabbed the rope and pulled himself towards the struggling trio. Reaching them within a few minutes, he pulled David to his feet. With the help of the still, slow-moving truck it took them fifteen minutes to reach safety. Joe pulled the boys into the cab and then helped David.

'Hospital,' said Joe.

'No, no, we must open the rest of the sluices,' insisted David in a weak voice. 'The boys can help.'

Joe drove furiously back to the dam. They all watched helplessly as water started to flow over the top. 'There is nothing we can do now,' said Joe. 'Just wait and see if the dam holds.'

It didn't.

At first they noticed a few lumps of concrete flying off the top of the dam. Suddenly, there was a great crash and an enormous, ever-widening hole appeared, the water gushing down the valley. The dam emptied quickly. All that was left of the wall were two huge jagged edges.

They raced back to the village. By now the stream was nearly one hundred metres across. People were beginning to gather in consternation to see if the water would flood the village.

'We need to get them away from there,' said David.

Joe managed to persuade people there was nothing to be done and that the village would not be flooded. They noticed that some of the stock, despite David's precautions, had wandered too close to the flood and been swept away. Some of the vegetable area had been flooded as well.

David and the boys were all admitted to The Settlement hospital and spent a few days there. 'You all have mild hypothermia and we don't want that to develop into pneumonia,' the resident doctor told them.

A furious row erupted over the incident, with some blaming David and Joe for not opening the sluice gates in time and others blaming the two boys and their family. From his hospital bed, David realised emotions would get in the way of facts so he engaged one of the resident lawyers to conduct an enquiry. It was published as David left hospital, concluding that Joe and David would have been able to open the sluices if it hadn't been for the boys.

Insurance paid for part of the rebuilding of the dam, but all settlers were slugged with a large, very unpopular levy payable over two years. One or two families immediately thought of leaving The Settlement and there was a great deal of grumbling.

David had no inkling what was about to hit him. A week after the flood had struck, he had visits from a half dozen of the people he had considered his most promising settlers.

The first came in, saying, 'Look David, we were having severe doubts about the wisdom of moving here. All our friends think we are stark raving bonkers. The Government is doing nothing about this theory of yours and this flood has frightened all of us. I just don't think we are cut out for this life. It's all work as we don't have the resources to dash off to Sydney every five minutes. When we see the lives of our friends are leading, this place seems ridiculous. We want out. I have been offered my old job back and I am inclined to accept it.'

'What will you do when the Ice Shelf collapses?' asked David.

'Fuck the bloody Ice Shelf! I just don't want to believe that claptrap any more. Your smooth talking conned us into selling up and coming here. It's all bullshit!'

'What do you want to do?' David was quite taken aback by the man's vehemence.

'I just want out. You got us into this mess, you find a solution.'

David phoned Tanya. 'This is a real threat. Three people have come forward with much the same story; one was very aggressive and one admitted he made a mistake. I don't know if there will be others, but even three is a blow. We only have twenty-five families.'

'I will work something out,' she said.

David had always spent time with each settler family to deal with any concerns but, at her request, he left the difficult discussions to Tanya. Over two weekends, Tanya saw the now six disenchanted settlers separately. She always started with a detailed review of the science and the projected consequences. 'This is why you originally decided to join The Settlement. You seemed so enthusiastic. Can I understand why you have changed your mind?'

After lengthy discussions, two of the families changed their minds again and agreed to stay. 'We were genuinely frightened by the ferocity of the flood, but the science is still compelling. We will tough it out and make certain we can cope mentally with any future emergencies.'

'My wife is seriously ill, so we have decided to move back to Sydney and the best treatment. Settling here requires high-energy pioneering types, which is not us at present,' one man said.

'Will you return when she has recovered?' asked Tanya.

'The priority is her recovery. We'll worry about ice shelves collapsing after that.'

'What do you want to do with your investment here?'

'I don't know. Do you have any suggestions?'

'You could keep it and rent it out to new settlers while their property is being built. You could leave it unoccupied for the time being or you could sell it to a new settler. We can help with the first and last option.'

'You wouldn't consider buying it from us?'

'No, we can't afford that, it merely takes money from funds allocated for general development,' said Tanya firmly. 'Besides, what we need is commitment. Buying your place creates a precedent, so in future people may think they will always have an easy way out if things don't work out.'

'The best is to try to sell it to a new settler and rent it out in the meanwhile.'

The other three leavers collectively tried to intimidate Tanya with excessive demands. They visited her in her small office next to David's, on the upper floor of the community centre. She seated them in comfortable upright chairs. 'Would you like tea or coffee?'

There was an impatient gesture from the spokesman, a large, well-built man named Harold. He ignored her, aggressively waving his arms about. 'We've all had about as much buggering around as we can stand, so let's get on with it. The science is all bullshit. You and your pseudo-sophisticated father-in-law conned us into coming here, giving up our jobs, and our well-ordered lives. We all sold perfectly good properties in Sydney which have since increased in value.'

Tanya said nothing.

'Don't you have anything to say to all that, you tight-arsed bitch?'

To the utter amazement of Harold and his two companions, Tanya laughed. 'Come on Harold, you can do better than that. Why don't you try again?'

Harold stood up, brought his fist down on the desk making his two companions jump, and yelled, 'If you don't sort this out, now, I'll burn the whole fucking place down.'

Tanya coolly picked up the phone, 'Hello, emergency. Police please, urgently.' She gave them the address.

Harold and his friends looked shocked.

Tanya stood up, 'This discussion is over. The police will be here in a couple of hours, you'll have to explain your actions to them. Threatening to burn the whole place down is a serious criminal offence.'

Harold's companions shuffled to the door and waited, but Harold stood his ground. Eventually one of them gently took him by the arm and he left the office. 'You won't get away with ...' he yelled as he was jerked away.

The police arrived and took statements from Tanya, David, and two others who had overheard the conversation as well as the three protagonists. Tanya gave the police a recording of the conversation. Harold was arrested, charged, and released on his own recognisance.

'Round one to us,' said David anxiously.

'It is possible the whole issue will go to court, but I would be surprised if they have the wherewithal to mount a substantial challenge. The bullying tactic was trying to force us into a quick deal,' advised Tanya,

'Do you think calling the police was smart? We have certainly made enemies of all of them.'

'They were enemies already. They can't go around threatening to burn the place down and expect no consequences. I expect the next communication will be more civilised.'

'How long will all this take? If we have to suspend settler recruitment it will put a strain on our finances.'

Tanya, sitting across the desk from David in his meticulously tidy office, looked relaxed with her arms resting on the chair. 'I see no need to suspend recruitment. I'll give you a new agreement that all prospective settlers will have to sign. I've strengthened the clause stating that the settler understands the science and challenging it does not give them reason to sue us.'

The next communication came from a lawyer in Sydney claiming misrepresentation and demanding on behalf of the three protagonists—

- Complete refund of everything they had invested in The Settlement.
- Loss of earnings during the period they were residents.
- Loss of the increased value of properties sold to invest in The Settlement.
- A general compensation demand.

After Tanya told David of the development, she said to him, 'They are spending more on legal advice than the issue is worth. There is something else going on here.' There was an edge to her voice. She did not feel quite as in control as she normally would.

The following day an article in one of the major Sydney dailies informed readers that the Blue Mountains development initiated by The Settlement Pty Ltd was based on fraudulent claims of disaster based on climate change.

Tanya immediately issued a writ in the high court for damages of thirty million dollars against the paper. The panic phone call that followed from the paper said the authenticity of the article had been checked with a person who claimed to represent the company.

'Who did you check the article with?' demanded Tanya.

'We don't actually have a name, just a phone number.' The caller gave her the number. Harold answered the phone and Tanya replaced the handset without saying anything.

'That is someone purporting to be a representative of the company. He isn't and never has. I will be issuing a writ claiming damages from him as well,' she told the caller from the newspaper.

All the owners of the three properties wanting out of the scheme received a writ the following day to their individual residences in The Settlement claiming damages for willful misrepresentation.

Tanya explained the developments to David. The Sydney newspapers had now picked up on the story, publishing several sensational stories.

David said anxiously, 'This publicity is doing us no good at all. All prospective settlers have withdrawn. If this issue is not resolved soon we will run out of cash and the whole project will be threatened. Can't you settle with Harold and his accomplices and we can then get on with building this place up?'

'We will win all our court cases, I'm sure. We need patience.'

'And in the meanwhile we declare bankruptcy? For Christ's sake! The cash position is getting very tight. With all this publicity, borrowing is out of the question,' said David, a touch of anger in his voice.

Tanya called George, her ex-Cabramatta friend in the police. He had access to a great deal of information on individuals within the community and had often helped her with issues relating to her legal practice. Her access to the information he provided her with had materially helped in some of the cases she handled. Up till now, she had never used this facility on Settlement matters, knowing she would have to fully brief him on The Settlement before he would divulge anything useful.

She phoned George with her heart in her mouth. It was a private number, answered immediately.

'George.'

'It's Tanya here.'

The voice softened, 'So nice to hear from you. What can I do for you?'

'I need some very sensitive information.'

'Why else would you phone me?' he laughed.

Tanya gave him a detailed account of The Settlement and the reasons for its existence. George listened intently.

I have been given some information involving some sort of development in the Blue Mountains. I had no idea you were involved. Most interesting. Anyway, how can I help? Everything you are doing seems above board.'

'Yes, it is,' responded Tanya quickly. 'I need some information on a Harold Monckton.' She explained the reasons. 'Their legal costs are already higher than any gains they might make. And they seem to have effortlessly got the attention of the Sydney press. It doesn't add up.'

'As it happens, I have had some dealings involving Harold Monckton, within the last few months actually. The Government uses him to prosecute, in his own name, certain cases which they do not want to take on publicly. Some of those cases relate to climate change issues. It seems he has been quite successful in previous actions.'

'Why would the Government want to take action against us? We are completely legit.'

'I don't really know, but your theory and its apocalyptic forecasts will scare the shit out of Government. I expect they are afraid your theories might create an unwarranted panic in parts of the population. Whereas a small development in the Blue Mountains unobtrusively going bankrupt would probably attract no attention at all. They can then safely continue to ignore the issue.'

'How the hell do I deal with that?' wondered Tanya.

'I can't help you there. I merely provide information. There is a man, called Nicholson, previously with ASIO. Now in charge of dirty tricks in the Attorney General's department in Canberra. I will post details of three similar cases he has been involved in.'

'Thanks, that is most helpful,' said Tanya.

'No problem.'

Tanya always asked this question. 'Is there anything I can do for you, George?'

'No, I've told you before, I've pledged to fight the low life, not to join them. Although, I appreciate the donations you make to the home.' His brother, a victim of a vicious bank robbery lived in a vegetative state in a home for invalids; George had sworn he would look after him for as long as he lived. 'There is one other question though … '

Tanya knew what was coming, George often asked this.

'Is that bed of yours still occupied by that money-making machine?'

Tanya laughed. 'Yes, thankfully and he is not getting any smaller.'

'Oh well, I live in hope.'

She knew he was happily married with several children, but it helped them end the conversation on a lighter note.

Despite the commitments he had made, Mark had continued to have genuine doubts about his involvement in The Settlement. No one he knew even mentioned climate change and here he was pouring his life into the project. He worked tirelessly at his job and he was doing the same thing in the Blue Mountains over weekends. Meanwhile, his work colleagues had overseas trips with their families and enjoyed their lifestyle in Sydney.

He knew further discussion with Tanya would be fruitless. She was totally committed to the project and spent all her spare time helping to build it up. While he had accepted she would be taking the lead with regard to developments in the Blue Mountains, he found it galling to always appear to be trailing in her wake. From the time she had acquired the property, he had begun to feel inadequate. Neither of them ever said much about their careers, partly because of the confidential nature of the content. But Mark found Tanya's success and competence at work and at The Settlement intimidating. He was one of the brightest and most dynamic of the younger people at the bank, but Tanya's evident ability made him wonder if she would overshadow him in the bank environment as well.

Initially, he had put his considerable earnings into financing the project. Now he privately put some of his earnings into other investments. He bought a small cottage in Tuscany and soon had a reasonable nest egg of his own outside The Settlement.

The court cases dragged on with David taking more and more desperate measures; stopping all building and delaying as many payments as he dared. As a result, the inevitable happened; he received a notice of foreclosure unless a debt to an external builder was paid within two weeks. He phoned Tanya and Mark together in desperation. 'This means the end of everything we've built up, unless we can do something very quickly.'

Tanya was still surprised it had gone on so long and told them so. No notice was taken of her observations.

David phoned Mark, 'Look, you and I are going to have to deal with this ourselves. I'm going to keep Tanya out of it wherever possible. Frankly, she has really screwed up this time. Her aggressive behaviour has put the future of the project at risk.' David still believed Mark was fully committed; he had no idea Mark was quietly casting a bet both ways.

Mark had known the seriousness of the situation, but had not registered that the end of their dream was as close as two weeks away. *This is where I can make a real contribution. Whatever my doubts, I am not ready to walk away from my investment.*

Mark took a day off and drove to The Settlement. He thought he had left Tanya behind in Sydney, so was irritated to see their recently acquired helicopter. The helicopter was another source of frustration; before they acquired the machine Tanya had been quietly taking flying lessons, so was already licensed to fly it. Mark had done nothing.

Mark, now fully acquainted with The Settlement's position, offered David a solution. 'I have a deal at the bank, coming up in a few weeks. I will put all the funds from that into the project, but we do need to take a different approach with the court cases. The publicity is killing us. We need to stop it. Dad, I suggest you give the creditor a cheque, post-dated by six weeks, on the understanding that he withdraws his action. I will go and see Harold and his mates and cut a deal. If we come out ahead on those two issues, I'll handle the newspapers.'

Tanya was hurt. She knew she was being excluded from dealings with Harold. She tried to ask David the reason, but uncharacteristically he waved her away. 'Leave it all to Mark; he has a deal at the bank allowing him to give us more funds. That will help.'

But Tanya had noticed Mark's financial contributions reducing significantly in recent months. She thought, This is bullshit. Mark has no deal, but he may have funds. And we need his money wherever it comes from. So she said nothing. My only interest is making sure the bloody project survives.

With Mark and David now engaged, without her, in trying to rescue The Settlement, Tanya knew it was time to play her most valuable card—information she had gleaned from George.

From their cottage, Tanya phoned the Attorney General's department in Canberra, asking for Mr. Nicholson.

'There is no Mr. Nicholson in this department.'

'Oh yes there is. I spoke to him the other day.' She quoted an extension number given by George. He had warned her that Nicholson's existence might be denied. There was silence for a few seconds, followed by a few clicks.

A woman answered, 'Hello.'

By this time Tanya was becoming suspicious and furious. 'I would like to speak to Mr. Nicholson, please. It's about a man calling himself Harold Monckton.'

'We don't … '

'I know Mr. Nicholson works there. Please don't insult me by denying his existence.'

There was a brief silence. 'He is busy at the moment. Can he call you back?'

'In view of the difficulty I have had in trying to reach him, it seems this is just another ploy on your part to deny me access to Mr. Nicholson. You had better understand that unless I can speak to him, I have arranged for a series of articles to be published in various newspapers that give chapter and verse on what you people have been up to in recent times.' She gave the woman three names.

There was a deep intake of breath at the other end.

'I have considerable detail on your nefarious activities. If they come to light, I have no doubt anyone involved will spend many years in court and then in jail, including you, probably.'

Tanya was suddenly put through.

'Nicholson,' a curt voice answered.

Tanya explained who she was. 'It's about your agent, a man called Harold Monckton, who, funded by you, is trying to bankrupt our small … '

'I know nobody of that name.'

Tanya became angry, 'I suggest you listen to me very carefully, Mr. Nicholson.' She reiterated her threat.

'Where did you get that information?'

'I have no intention of discussing that with you. I know the information is one hundred percent accurate and so do you.'

'This is blackmail,' yelled Nicholson.

'No, all I have told you is what information will appear in newspapers starting tomorrow. You know exactly what I want. I will give you one telephone number of a person who will read you exactly what they are going to publish regarding your activities. I will wait on the line, while you make the call.' She gave him the number.

'I will call you back,' said a desperate Nicholson.

'No, I will wait on the line.'

Tanya was able to catch a few words of the call. Five minutes later, a very nervous-sounding Nicholson came back on the line. 'Okay, what do you want?'

'You know,' answered Tanya. 'Again, I will wait on the line while you make your call. This time I want to hear both sides of the conversation.'

Nicholson called Harold Monckton at The Settlement.

To start with Harold was full of bonhomie, 'We've got the bastards running, in a couple … '

'No,' said Nicholson harshly. 'You've really fucked up this time Harold. You are to pull the plug, now, today. Those legal bills you sent me, none of them will be paid. Just get out of there as soon as you can.'

'But, but, at last I have that fucking bitch on the run … I'm dealing with Mark now. He knows much less than the bitch Tanya. I will have that bloody place shut down in a couple of months, no more peddling that climate change bullshit … '

'No buts, just pull the plug,' yelled Nicholson. 'Tell me when you have done it. I don't want to hear another word on this subject, not today, not ever. Do you understand?'

There was a brief silence. 'Yes, yes I will pull the plug,' muttered Harold, 'Can you tell me what has changed?'

'No, I can't, just do it and get out!'

'Satisfied?' Nicholson asked Tanya angrily.

'Only when Harold has finally stopped all his nonsense and left The Settlement. I will ask the papers to hold those articles for the time being. And one other thing, Mr. Nicholson. Stay away from us. Don't ever come near The Settlement again.'

David was surprised to see Mark back from a visit to Harold so soon, 'They will be back over here in an hour,' said Mark, looking less comfortable than when he left for the meeting. 'While I was there Harold took a call. There seemed to be a lot of shouting. I don't know what he's up to.'

'I phoned the builder. He wants a part payment and will accept a post-dated cheque for the balance. If the cheque is honoured he will cancel his action,' said David uncomfortably.

Tanya appeared in the office. Mark and David looked up like two naughty schoolboys. She was on tenterhooks hoping her phone call to Nicholson had resolved the issue. 'I need two minutes of your time,' she said.

'Can't it wait?' said David irritably. 'We're trying to sort out the mess you've left us in.'

'I have highly pertinent information that will help resolve the issue,' she said evenly, knowing she had to remain calm. Any kind of heated discussion would result in disaster. 'Only a couple of minutes.'

David looked at her impatiently, 'Okay, what now?'

'I am now one hundred percent sure that a third party is funding Harold's case. I am also certain that the third party is from the Government. Their only objective is to close us down. They don't care what it costs. Do whatever you like, their objective is to bankrupt us.'

David looked at her with distrust, 'How the hell do you know that? You are just trying to justify your actions.'

Tanya wondered why their brilliant working relationship had suddenly gone so sour. She could see his panic. David was clutching at straws and somehow Mark had convinced him he could sort the situation out. She said quietly, 'The information is correct. I have a source in the police. I take full responsibility, maybe I was too harsh, but whatever we did would have made no difference. I have a strategy now I know will work.'

Mark wondered whether Tanya had yet again pre-empted him.

Tanya said to him, 'The funds you mentioned are critical.'

'I have a deal … ' he said unconvincingly.

Tanya thought they could now probably manage without Mark's additional funds, but she wanted him to further commit to The Settlement.

David relented slightly, 'Okay, they will be back here shortly.'

An hour later, Harold and his accomplices knocked on David's door. 'We would like to talk. We want you in the meeting as well.'

The visitors were made comfortable and were served with tea and biscuits.

Mark began, 'You all want out, you are in trouble with the police, and you have a large claim against you for willful misrepresentation. We can do something about all of that under certain circumstances.'

'You misrepre … ' Harold started.

'We are aware of the content of your claims,' said Tanya quietly.

'Ah, the bitch is allowed to speak,' said Harold, smirking. 'I thought I was dealing with the first team, but I see the reserves are still included.'

Tanya was surprised by his apparent confidence. She expected his case to collapse immediately. Maybe Nicholson had uncovered her subterfuge and had instructed Harold to continue. She tried not to betray her anxiety.

Mark stood up, took Harold quietly by the arm, and went outside, returning ten minutes later with a shaken Harold. 'Tanya, I apologise, my remarks were unnecessary.'

'Right, where were we?' said Mark.

'Our belief is The Settlement is virtually broke,' blurted out one of the other claimants, to Harold's amazement.

'If we go broke, how does that help you? You may end up with nothing,' said Tanya.

'Other people have left without all this fuss. We can do the same for you,' said Mark

'What's the deal?' asked Harold thoughtfully.

Tanya admired his gall. She was hopeful that shortly he would have to capitulate, unless Nicholson had called again, reversing previous instructions.

'You own three houses between you. You can rent them out to prospective settlers and perhaps sell them to those settlers in time. We can help and won't charge anything,' said Tanya. Nobody had ever been charged for such a service, but Tanya didn't think Harold was aware of that.

'We don't want any more buggering around. We just want out,' said Harold.

Mark pushed three envelopes to the claimants, 'These are cash offers for your individual properties, payable on settlement, which could be any time in the next week or so provided you withdraw all your legal actions.'

In the few minutes prior to Harold appearing, Tanya had insisted, forcefully, that they make ridiculous offers for the properties. 'I am certain Harold will capitulate and accept a very low offer. Then we can deal with the others. Hopefully, they will agree to stay or, if they still wish to leave, will agree to rent their properties out.'

There were looks of horror on the three faces opposite on opening the envelopes. Harold's face went puce, but he was restrained from saying anything by his colleague, who said, 'Give us an hour.'

'What did you say to Harold when you went outside?' David asked.

'That I would knock the living shit out of him if he made one more rude remark to my wife. Apart from immediately stopping all negotiations and continuing with our suit for misrepresentation, I also reminded him he still had a court case coming up with a possible jail sentence. I suppose he has behaved like this all along?'

David said anxiously, 'We're pushing them to the edge again. Is this wise?'

'Just watch, I promise if this doesn't work I'll bale out altogether. I mean that.' Tanya glared at them both.

Mark and David were shocked. They both knew The Settlement would be much worse off without her.

The triumvirate returned within an hour. Harold said, in a more conciliatory way, 'These offers are very low, far less than the houses' cost to build. Is there any way they can be improved?'

'We are now short of funds. Due to the publicity generated by your actions, several promising new settlers have decided not to sign up. If we are to purchase those properties we may have to hang on to them for months before we are able to sell them … We can deal with each one of you separately,' Tanya said. She watched Harold speculatively, knowing what his instructions were.

Harold drew a sharp breath. He could see he was being manoeuvred into a corner. Tanya was now clearly in the ascendancy. *Whatever happens here, bitch, I will get you one day*, he thought.

'Any individual agreements would have to remain confidential,' added Mark. 'Before anything happens, you will all have to withdraw your court cases.'

They negotiated three separate deals. Harold accepted a cash offer, only slightly higher than the first and the Bowers withdrew all the evidence they had submitted to the police. The other two claimants accepted the arrangement to rent their properties with a view to selling them when possible. Both were angry and felt they had been let down by Harold.

'You never know,' said Tanya, to one, 'you might get a good price in a few months' time, when we get back on track.'

All the court cases between the parties were withdrawn. Tanya breathed a sigh of relief once the arrangements were finalised. She did not mention her conversation with Nicholson.

The newspaper was told that all legal action involving The Settlement had been dealt with out of court. The newspaper agreed to publish a series of articles relating to The Settlement on the understanding there would be no further legal action against them.

The editor hesitated when Tanya produced four articles written by her. 'We write our own,' he said.

'These have all the facts stated correctly,' insisted Tanya. 'Change them if you have to, but please send me the amended articles prior to publication. It also might be helpful if some of you came up to the Blue Mountains to see what we are all about. '

Over the next few weeks, a number of positive articles appeared in the Sydney press after two journalists spent time with David in the Blue Mountains.

David, Mark, and Tanya had time for a full review of the crisis, during one of the younger Bowers' weekend visits.

A contrite Tanya said, 'I went about things the wrong way and put our future at risk. It won't happen again. But I am certain whatever we did would have made no difference. In the end, it was the Government withdrawing support from Harold that forced him to capitulate.'

Both David and Mark were uncomfortable about Tanya's secret source of information. They wondered if they had been told the full story.

'Mark, we should have involved you in the detail sooner than we did,' said David, trying to move the discussion on. He was embarrassed by what he now saw as his betrayal of Tanya. 'The remarks Harold made to Tanya were unforgivable.'

Mark felt slightly inadequate for not coming in earlier to support Tanya. He admired Tanya's acceptance of the blame for the fiasco and wondered if he would have had the courage to do the same. Part of him felt he had now gained something in his undeclared competition with Tanya for ascendancy. Another part felt even more inadequate. If their roles were reversed, he thought Tanya would have supported him to the bitter end and not tried to gain the advantage.

The rest of the board were horrified. 'Why didn't you involve us sooner?' asked Patricia. 'We are all part of this too, working our backsides off. And what about all the settlers who have put their faith in us?'

'I agree. My fault,' said David.

'I am concerned about Harold,' Tanya told the meeting. 'He certainly bears a grudge.'

Chloe was furious, but decided to say nothing. She was glad of her flat in Manly and her charities.

David tried to calm things down. 'The newspaper articles have generated a number of new enquiries for settlement. However, we need to accelerate the process. The best settlers have always been people with personal introductions from the family. I will talk to each of you individually about this over the next few days.'

~

Mark's reputation in the village was substantially enhanced by his actions in saving the community, via the additional funding. Most people thought Tanya had overreached and should have asked for help sooner. She said and did nothing to change that view.

Tanya was now reasonably certain Mark had been salting some of his earnings away privately, but did not raise the issue. *Who gives a fuck what he was doing,* she thought, trying to justify her inaction. *We've now got the money, where it belongs, back in Settlement bank accounts and Mark is more committed than ever to the project.* In her heart of hearts she knew she should tackle him on the issue, but never did.

~

Weeks later, Tanya told David the details about George's information and the telephone calls with Nicholson. 'I was pretty certain Harold would pull the plug, but there was still some risk. But I also wanted Mark's full commitment and the extra money. He feels he played a leading role in rescuing us from bankruptcy and so has taken a bit more ownership in this place. I have not said a word to him about what I did and never will … There is one other thing. My information about Nicholson is completely kosher. The fellow was and is a bastard. But all that stuff I told him about newspaper articles was pure fabrication. I certainly wrote the articles, but the phone number was one I set up.'

David looked horrified, 'What would have happened if he'd checked?'

'Because of his position he was never going to take the risk of doing that. If he had and been found out, the consequences would have been disastrous. It was far easier to do what he did and so he lives on, somewhat to my regret. Anyway, that was the reason I couldn't tell you more at the time.'

David knew he would never have been able to bring himself to take such a risk.

Once the crisis had settled down, David turned his mind to the dam. He spent months working out how he should cope with floods in the future. As well as rebuilding the main dam, he decided to build two smaller dams further down the valley, one almost opposite the village. The dams were re-stocked with trout. It became a favourite picnic spot in the hot weather, once a lawn had been established.

'The pipe carrying the stream will have to be much bigger than I first thought,' David told Mark. 'It will need a grid on the front so children won't play in there and I will grow trees and bushes in front to hide the unsightly view.'

Two short years after the birth of Chas, Tanya gave birth to another boy. 'We'll call him Didier,' said Tanya, without consulting anyone. As before, she was back in the office a week after the birth. This time nobody questioned her. Her children thrived under the expert tutelage of their nanny, and looked forward with much excitement to the almost weekly trips back to The Settlement.

'Didier?' David questioned Mark.

Mark shrugged, and said, 'Tanya,' by way of explanation.

CHAPTER NINE

The Settlement 2016

2016

David, accompanied by Spike, his Kelpie cross, would often stand on a hillock conveniently overlooking The Settlement. Today, he had asked Joe and Fred to accompany him. 'It helps in the ongoing planning to have it all visible in front of me,' he explained. The main dam had been completely rebuilt and the two smaller earth dams were in the process of construction.

Holding an area plan and facing northwest, David pointed out the forty houses clustered on the eastern side of the creek, settled on a gentle slope up the hill. There was room to build approximately sixty more dwellings. The stock, vegetable gardens, and crops were on the west side of the stream. They all knew there was enough of a slope between the village and the stream that even with the most extreme weather event the houses would never be threatened by flood. Chloe's horse paddock was just up the hill from the houses.

'The central parking area is working. Keeping vehicles away from The Settlement is the right thing. It keeps the dust down and the wide, grassed pathways between the houses are attractive, almost medieval in appearance. Plus, cars will be useless once we are isolated,' said Joe.

'Should we not spread the houses out a bit?' offered Fred.

'Theoretically it might be safer if there was a fire, but we need to make this place productive, so on balance limiting the housing area makes sense. If we have to defend ourselves in the future, the smaller the area, the better,' said David.

'We won't be able to buy petrol or diesel for years after the collapse. So we have set aside funds to buy a million litres of each. Where should we site the tanks?' asked David.

'As far away from the village as possible and we need to have easy access for cars, helicopters, and tankers,' said Joe.

'Would we ever think of starting another village in the bushland area we enclosed?' asked Joe.

'No,' was David's firm response. 'Looking after one village is difficult enough and what we have still has plenty of room to grow.'

The forty dwellings on the property housed about one hundred and sixty people. The Settlement had become self-sufficient and David anticipated that the speed of development meant they would be at capacity by 2020. The finances were now in good shape, despite rebuilding the dam and Harold's lawsuit and they had cash in the bank, most of which would be spent by the time the place was fully settled. In any event, David thought the banks would disappear once the Ice Shelf collapsed.

Each member of the Bower family had had their own house for some years now. David had insisted that none of the Bower houses were in any way remarkable and they blended in perfectly with the rest of the development. Jonathan had a small two bedroom cottage and David had personally funded a cottage for the absent Evan. Both of them were treated as a Settlement asset and were used often enough not to fall foul of the abandonment rule.

Tanya and David were very cautious with the funds belonging to The Settlement and ensured there was no hint of money being used for private Bower matters. None of the Bowers received any income for their work in the community.

Patricia had started the school with just a handful of pupils. There were now some eighty children in all classes from kindergarten to university entrance. David had recently encouraged the highly-respected headmaster of a high school in Sydney to settle. His wife, also a teacher, and their family would accompany him.

'We all feel you have done a wonderful job setting up the school ...'

Patricia smiled, 'Dad, I always thought someone like this would join us. I will gladly hand the school over to him. To be quite honest with you, it now needs a long term professional to take over. I can still help if required, but I think there is something else I can do for the community.'

'Oh!' David was pleased. He was expecting some resistance since Patricia had put her heart and soul into the school.

'I would like to engage the youth in developing life skills such as bush craft, animal husbandry, growing crops, and so on. Useful knowledge for their future after the Ice Shelf collapses.'

'It all seems very serious,' said David.

'It must be fun to ensure participation. Mum is doing great things with the horses, all the kids love that. I would like to organise other activities. For example, Joe could get the technically minded to understand how the solar power systems work. He thinks he can build a computer and involve the kids. We could have a young farmers' group who can help the people already running arable areas and the dairy. We could encourage more sport.'

'And you want to do all that?'

'Mostly I see myself as a catalyst. Once something is set up I will let them get on with things and they can come for advice as needed.'

'Perfect! When do we start?'

'Joe is ready to go once he gets the tick of approval from you. We may need a small amount of funding for computer parts and fuel for visiting neighbouring farms.'

'Go for it. School first, with these activities as an added dimension. This will only improve the attractiveness of the place.'

~

David found he had to deal with many issues he had not envisaged when vetting prospective settlers.

Don Weatherspoon, a recent settler, came to him one day. 'This is obviously a Christian community ...'

'We have many Christians in the community, plus the Jewish grocer whose brother is joining us within a few months, and a Muslim family whose house is presently being constructed. He is a very skilled carpenter, or rather a craftsman,' responded David.

Don looked discomfited for a moment, 'Your family are Christians?'

David hesitated, 'Although my wife and I were brought up in the Christian tradition, none of my family are practising Christians. Why?'

'We need a church for our services.'

'You can certainly build a church, but it will have to come from your own funds and be approved in the normal way for building projects.'

'We don't have any money. I thought a Christian community would provide the funds.'

'Would the church be available to all the Christian denominations in the community?'

Don looked uncomfortable. 'We had envisaged an Anglican church actually,' he said rather lamely.

'But we also have Catholics and Presbyterians,' said David.

'Well, they can look after their own communities, we will look after ours.'

'You knew before you agreed to settle that there will only be about three hundred people here. There are already many diverse beliefs here and I expect that to widen. We don't have room for every religion and their denominations to have their own place of worship and we certainly can't fund such a programme.'

'You should restrict new settlers to people with Christian beliefs.'

'Don, do you mean Anglican Christian beliefs?' said David kindly.

Don fidgeted, avoiding the question, 'I prefer to be called Donald.'

'Donald, there are practical reasons for having a wide cross-section of people here.'

'I don't like the Government's current immigration policy; that was one of the reasons for coming here.'

'Would you prefer the White Australia or Apartheid style of society?' asked David quietly.

'Well I wouldn't put it quite as strongly.'

'There is no possibility of having such a society here. Do you know why?'

Donald went on doggedly, 'They will not have our values ... '

'Please let me tell you one of the most basic reasons. The Ice Shelf will collapse in ten or fifteen years, after which this community will be isolated.'

Donald nodded uneasily.

'We have no idea how long the isolation will last, but whatever happens it will take many years for the society to develop and become integrated again. Probably two or more generations,' said David to emphasise the point.

'Yes,' said Donald impatiently.

'Donald, have you any knowledge of cattle or dog breeding?'

Donald looked angrily at David, 'No, I am a builder and lay preacher, but what on earth has that got to do with building a church?'

'If we restrict our small community to one racial group, which is what you are suggesting, the society will become inbred, have a very restricted skill base, and become much more susceptible to disease. We will be weakened and possibly not survive. Talk to the doctor or vet if you don't believe me.'

Donald flushed. 'You want my daughter to marry a Roman Catholic or a Muslim?' he said heatedly. 'She will marry a good Christian or not at all.'

David shrugged, 'Can I change the subject?'

'No more of this claptrap about dog breeding, we are God's people and He will look after us.'

'If you need somewhere to hold services, you are welcome to use the community hall. Just book it through my daughter Patricia.'

'It's not consecrated.'

'I'm sure the local bishop will have a solution. Better than not having anywhere at all.'

'I came here for help and have got an unwelcome lecture. We need a church and you should be willing to help us build it.'

'Donald, I am sure you are fundamentally a good man. If you are serious about a place of worship, talk to some of the other denominations here and see if you can come up with a solution. If you came to an accommodation with some other faiths maybe the Muslims could use a jointly-owned facility on Fridays, the Jews on Saturdays, and you could have the use of it on Sundays.'

The man's face went purple. 'I can't believe I'm hearing this! You want me to share my church with a bunch of heathens?' He stormed out, banging the door behind him.

Patricia came in just after Donald had left. 'What was all that about?'

'He wants us to build him a church, but just for the Anglicans. He has some very bigoted ideas. I told him "no go" and suggested he book the community centre for his services.'

'His wife came to see me last week on a similar mission. She has booked the community centre every Sunday from eleven am for two hours. I wonder what his reaction will be.'

'Don't know, but I suppose he will preach.' David grinned. 'I also gave him a lecture about inbreeding. He now has visions of hordes of Muslims coming to seduce his daughters.'

'Naughty!' said Patricia.

'People need to understand the community will be diverse.'

'Yes, but you are not running a cattle farm, you are dealing with people who can express their feelings.'

'Okay, perhaps I was a bit hard on him. But I won't be building churches for him or any other religious groups.'

Mark sometimes talked to Tanya about his friends' exploits outside The Settlement. 'Rooney has bought a mansion in the south of France.'

'What the hell is he going to do with that?' asked Tanya laughing, 'He gets tired of his latest shag after one weekend. If he invites a girlfriend to the south of France, I doubt the relationship will last beyond the flight over.'

'He has been with his latest girlfriend for more than a year,' answered Mark defensively.

'The south of France will flood, it's a pointless investment,' added Tanya.

～♪

Mark had become more committed to The Settlement after the children were born, especially his second son, Didier. *I suppose we are building something for the children's future as well as our own,* he reflected. All his life, Mark had found himself in leadership positions, at school and now at the bank; he was even tipped to be managing director at some time in the future. Intellectually, he accepted that Tanya, together with David, were the driving forces behind The Settlement and that he, Mark, should play second fiddle to her in that regard. This was despite the fact that he was the largest contributor in financial terms. Emotionally, he continued to find it difficult. He was inclined to try and take over any initiative, finding he had to consciously hold back, sometimes with difficulty.

His relationship with Tanya seemed more distant since moving to The Settlement. He thought he was still in love with her, he regarded her as his intellectual equal, and he admired her energy and beauty. They made love less frequently, but Mark thought that was probably normal. After all, they had two healthy, bright children and busy careers.

～♪

Talking one evening with Tanya in their Mosman home, Mark said, 'Security is going to be one of the biggest issues we face. I would like to be responsible for it. I have spoken to Jonathan and he thinks he will probably be able to provide military personnel to help with some training, if that is what we decide. I told Dad I would put something in writing and we can take it from there.'

'You must find it frustrating not to be in charge … '

Mark unsuccessfully tried to dismiss the thought with a wave of his hand, 'I don't have any more time to put into The Settlement. I accept you and Dad are the driving forces behind it. Give me the security responsibility and that will keep me out of mischief.'

Tanya could see he was making a real effort. 'What do you have in mind?'

Mark wondered what she was really thinking. He responded, 'To create a very high quality group within the community, something all or most settlers will aspire to. There will be no discrimination between the sexes.'

'You cope with playing second fiddle to me at The Settlement now because of your position in the bank,' said Tanya holding his hand. 'How will you deal with it when our world is reduced to three hundred or so people? But I think the security initiative sounds intriguing. I would love to belong to something like that. I am sure there will be support from the board. It's surprising nobody has thought of it before.'

Tanya's perceptiveness never failed to surprise Mark. He gently squeezed her hand. In his heart of hearts he knew she had put her finger on an issue that was likely to continue to come between them. He had no idea what to do about it.

Discussing the security proposal during the next board meeting, Tanya had rarely seen Mark so enthusiastic. 'I will spend a week in Canberra with Jonathan. He has set up a whole program to train a high quality group for any settler to join.'

'Both sexes?' asked Joe.

'Yes, there is no discrimination.' He smiled good humouredly, 'Anyway I don't see how we would keep Tanya out. I suggest a form of military training for all settlers over age thirteen. This would involve basic discipline, marching drills, and weapons training. Participants would have to be proficient on horseback and able to fire rifles accurately in a variety of situations. Horse riding lessons would be necessary before the age of thirteen, so participants gain enough skills to join the program once they turn eighteen. We can rely on Mum for that; most kids under her tutelage are already good horse riders.'

'Would this be voluntary?' asked Chloe.

'Yes, but if we get it right we will have more people than we can cope with trying to join. I am hoping it will be seen as an elite program. Jonathan has suggested calling it The Academy to reinforce that.' Mark paused to think about what he was going to say next. 'It needs to be taken very seriously. This will not be a game. I can foresee a situation, once the Ice Shelf collapses, where deadly force may be necessary to defend ourselves. The training will have to reflect that. With no rule of law, The Academy will be the one group that can help to uphold individuals' rights.'

The board members silently absorbed Mark's presentation. David thought, My intention was to create a peaceful place. I hadn't planned on an army.

'What about the older people?' asked Chloe.

'I'll have to think about that,' answered Mark carefully. 'The main group will have to be very fit and active, difficult for some of the older people. During a real crisis, it may be important to have people at home to defend the place and run regular patrols. Others can extend operations beyond The Settlement.'

'A home guard!' observed Chloe with a mischievous grin on her face.

At first there were less than a dozen participants, including Mark and Tanya. David provided uniforms while Mark designed and arranged the building of a gravel parade ground, about one hundred metres square, also used as a landing site for the helicopter. For six months, Mark also spent every weekend building a rifle range large enough for eight participants with a range of up to three hundred metres.

Soon they had two squads of eighteen people, one group over eighteen and one under. A third group of people over forty-five focussed on weapons training and parade ground drills, with less emphasis on elite physical fitness. Tanya was the only woman at first, but her participation encouraged others to join. Within months, enlistment was competitive and not everyone was accepted.

Jonathan had managed to purchase forty 30.06 Savage rifles. 'They will have to do for now. In time, I will try to legitimately get the same weapons we use in the army, the short-barrelled F88 Austeyr. They will be easier to use on horseback. But if people become used to the Savage rifle, using the army weapons will be a breeze,' said Jonathan.

Mark had returned from his week in Canberra full of plans and enthusiasm. 'I am proposing to set up a command and discipline structure. Some people, including me, will do courses in Canberra, arranged by Jonathan. We will bring in Army people every weekend to help with training. Even if it is a long shot, we aspire to the standards found in the Australian Army. Within the ambit of The Academy, any transgressions will be dealt with in the same way as the military.'

'What do you mean by that?' asked Chloe.

'Each person enlisted will sign an agreement to abide by The Academy's disciplinary arrangements while on Academy business. This may involve physical punishment for transgressions regarding their appearance, the condition of their weapons, how they deal with horses under their control, and so on. In bad cases, individuals may have to be expelled from The Academy.'

'You are talking military mumbo-jumbo,' said an irritated Chloe. 'What do you mean by physical punishment?'

'Captain Andrews recommends long runs in full battle gear or running round the parade ground holding a rifle above their head,' said Mark evenly.

'No lash then?' said Chloe, amid laughter from the rest of the board, including Mark.

Mark continued, 'We can't have people running around with guns and ammunition not knowing what they're doing. Now the armoury has been completed, we can reinforce the existing policy of not allowing anyone to keep weapons at home.'

The first time weapons were issued to Academy participants, Mark made them line up and sign for their selected weapons. Most were quite happy to comply, although one man in his early forties, Lance, objected, 'I have been around guns all my life; this rigmarole is just a lot of nonsense. I don't see why I can't keep the rifle and ammunition in my house.'

'Most people here have no knowledge of weapons at all. Can't you see it would be extremely dangerous for everyone to have weapons and ammunition at home? There are children about, and the houses are close together. If we did what you suggest there will be an accident,' Mark replied evenly. 'You either comply or you will be expelled from the programme.'

Lance signed with bad grace and almost snatched his weapon away.

During the first sessions with the weapons, the army training officer, Steve Gregory, explained in detail how the weapon worked. He made all the participants strip and clean the weapons and then reassemble them, firstly sighted and then blindfolded.

'I'm having trouble with Lance,' he confided in Mark after a few sessions. 'If he was in the army he would be on report by now and possibly in detention. That fellow is trouble and an accident waiting to happen.'

'Put him on report then, and I will deal with him. All Academy members have agreed to be subject to strict discipline.'

Mark made the rest of the group stand at ease on the sidelines while Lance was put through his paces. As well as his rifle, Lance was made to carry a full pack weighing twenty-five kilograms.

'Atten-shun!' Mark had waited in front of the hapless Lance till he complied. 'As you were,' he yelled. 'I can make this painful if you want me to, or you can choose to leave The Academy right now.'

Lance just glowered at him.

'Atten-shun! Right turn. Rifle at high port—that means hold the rifle above your head. At the double—that means run,' yelled Mark.

Lance fell over after five minutes and collapsed after fifteen.

Mark signalled for two of Lance's colleagues, and they revived him with some water. 'Take him to the hospital, then back home. I'll deal with the rifle.'

Mark went to visit him a few days later, preparing to be conciliatory until he was confronted at the door by a hostile Lance.

'You either cooperate or you will be expelled from The Academy,' said Mark firmly.

Lance said nothing.

'Well?'

Lance slammed the door in Mark's face.

'That answers my question,' said a bemused Mark.

Meanwhile, a number from The Academy approached Tanya after failing to find David. 'We are concerned at the way Lance was handled the other day,' said a spokesman.

'In what way?' asked Tanya.

'He was made to run around the parade ground until he collapsed.'

'So I heard.'

'It seemed to be a very harsh approach.'

'We are not running The Academy for fun,' said Tanya. 'When the community becomes isolated we almost certainly will have to defend ourselves. We need a well-trained, disciplined group of people. You saw how Lance was behaving. He does not fit in.'

'Defend ourselves against what?'

'The rule of law will cease to exist, so there won't be any police to come to our rescue. There will be people outside The Settlement who, in order to survive, may see us as an easy target. Mark is responsible for security and discipline within The Academy. Lance either behaves or leaves. The Academy is voluntary and if anyone wishes to join then they have to accept the discipline involved. That applies to all of us, including me. I have no influence over Mark's running of the security operation, and nor do I wish to. '

Later that evening, Tanya mentioned The Academy members' visit.

Mark started to bridle.

'Just listen to me for a moment ... '

'Don't interfere, it's my business.'

'I have no interest in how you run The Academy, but I do have a suggestion to fix all this lily-livered bullshit forever.'

'That's my girl.'

'You know that I can do all of what you asked Lance to do yesterday, and more.'

'Yes … '

'Put me on a charge. Make me run around the parade ground or whatever. That will really stop this crap and then people will start to understand what it is all about.'

'Extraordinary. Are you sure? What sort of a charge did you have in mind?'

'Of course I'm fucking sure, and I have no interest in what the charge is, you'll have to use your imagination.'

A few days later, as part of the parade discipline, the trainees were made to open the breeches of their rifles for inspection. To her consternation, Tanya found there was a round in the breech of her rifle, which she knew was dangerous and wholly against regulations.

Steve Gregory looked at the round in horror. 'Tanya Bower, a live round.' He held it up for all to see. 'I have no option but to put you on a charge. You will report here in full battledress, including your rifle, at five this afternoon. The rest of the platoon will attend as witnesses.'

At the appointed time Mark appeared. 'Lieutenant Gregory is unwell so I will conduct this afternoon's parade. Tanya, step forward. The rest of the platoon may stand at ease.'

There was a whisper from the rear, 'Bet he will give her an easy time, nothing like Lance.'

'If anyone else wishes to join Tanya, just say the word,' said Mark, hearing the whispers. 'Atten-shun!' he yelled and Tanya stood crisply to attention.

He gave her all the same instructions as he had given Lance a few days earlier, with Lance leering from the side of the parade ground. Tanya jogged around the parade ground with the rifle above her head for fifteen minutes. Then, Mark made it more difficult. Still keeping her rifle aloft, he made her run, lifting her knees to the parallel for another fifteen minutes. By this time, half the village was watching and Tanya was pouring with sweat. Mark made her frog hop for five minutes and then run around the parade ground for another fifteen minutes holding the rifle aloft. The final ten minutes she was made to run holding the rifle above her head and lifting her knees to the parallel. Lance was nowhere to be seen. 'Halt, fall in.'

Tanya returned to her place in the squad, sweating profusely and breathing hard.

'Are you alright,' whispered a voice.

'Of course I'm fucking alright,' said Tanya out of the side of her mouth.

'Tanya, step forward, talking on parade.'

He made her run for another ten minutes with the rifle above her head. 'Platoon, Atten-shun! Platoon Dismiss.'

Once all the rifles had been safely returned to the armoury, the whole platoon crowded around Tanya after Mark had left the parade ground. 'Are you alright? Can we help you in any way?'

'A jug of water and a beer,' Tanya responded. 'I'll be okay, I feel a bit wobbly though.'

An hour later an anxious Mark opened the door of their cottage to Tanya. The children had already gone to bed and nanny had made herself scarce. Mark ran to her and held her for a minute. 'You were marvellous. How are you feeling?'

'I'm in desperate need of a shower, otherwise okay. I seem to be some sort of hero though, so I had a couple of beers with them. You'll be pleased to hear there was absolutely no suggestion that the situation was contrived. I suspect if anyone is put on a charge in future, it will be a matter of honour to be able to complete the punishment.'

Lance was conspicuously absent from any further Academy training, much to everyone's relief.

'Are we allowed to have what amounts to a private army?' asked Tanya one day.

'Probably not,' answered Jonathan, 'but who is going to know. Many schools run army cadets and I don't see any difference to that, but I will try my best to legitimise the situation.'

CHAPTER TEN
Demetriou!

Tanya made certain she met all the new people coming into The Settlement. Recently, Fred Costas had persuaded David to take on a Charles Smith as Fred said he owed Charles for unspecified favours done in the past.

'I'm not sure about your friend,' said David. 'He seems uninterested in the science, and his wife has no knowledge of anything rural. Why do they want to come here? If I didn't know you better I would suspect they are running away from something.' David missed Fred's sharp glance.

Tanya knocked confidently at the door of the Smith house. When the man named Charles opened the door, Tanya stood there for a few seconds with her mouth open.

'Ah, little Tanya,' said Demetriou. 'I wondered when I would bump into you again. I see you are a part of the Bower mob. I confess this was the last place I expected to find you.'

Tanya was transported back more than fifteen years to her youth in Cabramatta. She really thought she had left it all long behind her and now here was this person, calling himself Charles Smith, bringing it all back. She had not seen him since her escape, although her father had visited Demetriou once in jail. Despite herself, she felt weak at the knees and her loins went liquid as the memories of their lovemaking flooded back.

Tanya needed time to think. She was certain Demetriou would be up to no good as she had heard rumours of further criminal activity and worse. There was no possibility he would be a genuine settler, so he must have some other motive. She said, 'I will return later to see your wife.'

Mark and the family knew the broad parameters of Tanya's background, excepting the more lurid details of the drug deliveries, and Demetriou. Both her parents had recently died and she had provided for them until the end. Of course, the family all knew Cara. She had visited The Settlement and knew there was a place for her there if she ever wanted it, but she preferred her own life and friends, just checking in on Tanya from time to time.

Tanya knew Demetriou's presence was a threat. She found David in his office. 'What do you know about Charles Smith and his family?' she asked without any preliminaries.

'Not all that much, Fred more or less insisted on bringing him in. Charles has some explosives experience, which will be useful for building the fuel storage facility.' David was curious. He knew Tanya did not ask idle questions.

Tanya wondered what to tell him, but thought of the trust between them, 'His name is actually Demetriou Smith. He changed his name for very good reasons. I'm going to do some checking.'

'How do you know his previous name?'

'I just do, ask no questions … Just be careful. It seems the normal checks were not done on Charles.'

Tanya visited Demetriou's wife, when Demetriou was out in the Settlement. 'I just thought I would introduce myself,' she said. Fiona at first appeared to be the ordinary wife of an ordinary working man, but after a few minutes Tanya came to a very different conclusion.

Fiona would not answer any questions directly. When asked where she came from, the answer was non-committal, 'Sydney.' Even when pressed, she was vague, 'In the West.'

Over a cup of coffee Fiona asked a number of pointed questions about the origins of The Settlement so Tanya gave her the spiel, explaining the expectations and responsibilities of new settlers.

'What levies?' asked Fiona.

'You have to pay twenty percent of the value of the house to the central fund plus an annual levy, like council rates. Everyone pays.'

'We know nothing about any levies,' said Fiona firmly.

Tanya looked at her shrewdly, 'Who paid for the house then?'

'Fred, he owes us.'

'Fred! What does he owe you for?'

'Stuff.'

'What stuff?' asked Tanya in an offhand manner.

Fiona shrugged, stonewalling her.

They talked about the children and their education before Tanya left. She decided it was unlikely Fiona knew anything of Tanya's history with Demetriou.

～๑

Tanya had planned to go for a ride on the Sunday before returning to Sydney, but first she sought David out. 'I had a word with Fiona, Demetriou's wife. The whole situation is dodgy. The Smiths seem to have something on Fred. He has paid for everything so far and will probably continue to do just that. I will check in with my police contact.'

David looked worried. 'I will have a word with Fred.'

Fred was one of his mainstays; regarded as a friend and confidant. David had thought Fred would always put the interests of The Settlement first but Tanya's comments worried him. She did not make idle statements.

～๑

Tanya walked the short distance to the stables and saddled a mare Chloe had recently acquired. After taking some of the smaller jumps erected near the stables she cantered off into the far reaches of the now very active settlement. The horse was a bit skittish, so she concentrated hard on keeping it quiet and under control. Despite her preoccupation, she soon became aware of another horse galloping furiously towards her. It was Demetriou. *Bugger. This can't be good news.*

She cantered quietly off a wooded area and waited. When he had seen her, she continued on her way. Her plan had been to hide in a nearby copse and when Demetriou had gone past, to quietly return to the stables. But an unaccountable impulse made her wait for him in full view.

Within minutes, Demetriou arrived with his horse all of a lather. He roughly pulled the animal to a stop and gave her his charming smile. Tanya let her guard down briefly, admiring Demetriou. Handsome and well-built, he looked the picture of health, resulting from heavy physical activity in The Settlement.

'At last, you are on your own. We had such good times back in Cabramatta. Somehow you escaped and here you are, with your bum in the butter. I ended up in jail of course. Can't we just spend a few minutes catching up, for old times' sake?' Demetriou dismounted. 'Let's tie the horses up.'

Tanya felt as mesmerised as the inexperienced teenager she used to be. She knew she was making a mistake. Demetriou was still big trouble, but the old attraction resurfaced. She thought, *There is no harm in a chat* while her more cautious side was urging her to get out while she still could.

The situation was taken out of her hands as Tanya was helped from the saddle and Demetriou tied her horse up with his own mount. She meekly complied when he patted a heap of leaves next to him as he sat down. 'I spent nearly three years in jail, and somehow you got away scot free?'

Tanya felt guilty. 'I asked my father to visit you, but I had to be careful or I would have ended up in jail too.'

'How did you escape?' He put his arm around her. Deep down, her stomach tightened with unwanted desire. The excitement of life with Demetriou, the deliveries, and their lovemaking came back to her with a jolt. There had been nothing like it since.

She explained how she hid in the garage roof. 'I went to live with my aunt and never went back to Cabramatta. My parents always came to visit me.'

Demetriou leant over and kissed her. She was unable to resist and the kiss deepened. He undid her riding breeches and put his hand into her now wet pants. All sense left her; she tore his trousers off and discarded her riding gear and knickers and the rest of her clothes. He mounted her and she wrapped her legs around his muscular body. It was just like it had been all those years ago and she came again and again as his seed burst into her. They held each other for a few minutes. Tanya described some of her success at school and work, but made no mention of Mark. Lying naked on a bed of leaves in Demetriou's arms, she had completely relaxed.

'You always were beautiful,' observed Demetriou. 'But even better now. You've filled out a little.' His eyes feasted on her hungrily.

Temporarily forgetting her severe doubts, perhaps due to the guilt of their different lives, she uncharacteristically burst out with, 'I found that shirt in the laundry basket. It was covered in blood. The shirt got all mixed up with my own clothes and I hid it in the garage … Unless the house has been cleaned up, I suppose it's still there.'

Demetriou nodded, 'Mum lives there now.' Tanya didn't notice the slight frown on Demetriou's face.

'I took the car and dumped it so that there was no association with you,' added Tanya in a further attempt to assuage her guilt. 'What was the story with the shirt?'

Demetriou didn't answer her directly; they made love again.

~∘

Tanya scrambled back into her clothes and watched as Demetriou did the same. The excitement never wavered. 'There is a cross country course here. It goes round and then back to the stables,' she pointed, grinning. 'I'll race you.'

Tanya waited while he remounted. 'Okay, go.'

She galloped off with Demetriou just keeping up, making all the jumps with ease. He disappeared and suddenly reappeared ten metres in front. They raced for another ten minutes, with Tanya edging Demetriou out in front at the finish. Pulling the horses up, still blowing from their exertions, they were still in the forest and not visible from the stables.

'We should return to the stables separately,' Tanya suggested. 'You can go back directly and I will return through the forest.'

'That was fun,' said Demetriou. 'You always were a randy little bitch; we should do that again soon.'

Tanya pulled away slightly, 'I have to go back to Sydney this afternoon. I'll be back at the weekend I expect.' She cantered off into the trees, beginning to feel guilty.

~૭

Tanya called George as soon as she arrived at her office on Monday.

'George.'

'It's Tanya here. It's about Demetriou Smith. He's turned up again.'

There was a sharp intake of breath at the other end. 'Jesus Christ, you do choose them.'

Tanya explained her concerns. She went on to explain his arrival at the Settlement and that Tanya thought he was up to no good.

'You will probably be right, but there's more to our friend than meets the eye. He was in the army for a while and became an explosives and demolition expert.'

'That's one of the reasons he's with us, for a little bit of demolition work,' she said and immediately wished she hadn't.

George said nothing, but Tanya knew that piece of information would be stored away for some future use.

Why would a commune in the Blue Mountains need the services of a demolition expert? 'Okay,' said George, 'have you got a large piece of paper with you?'

Tanya wrote for a good ten minutes—the original conviction, serious drug running prostitution, assault. 'He was charged for murdering a prostitute, but got off. During his time in the army there was a rumour he killed his platoon sergeant. The army investigation decided it was "friendly fire". Tanya, you will have to be very careful. He will want revenge on you and fate has delivered you into his hands.' Then there was a sharp intake of breath. 'Oh, my God, we are in real trouble now.'

'What?' asked Tanya. She was beginning to realise the tryst with Demetriou was a terrible mistake.

'He's an unofficial ASIO agent. They employ people like Demetriou to get in close to the underworld.'

'And that pays them off?'

'Oh yes, without doubt.'

'Why would ASIO be interested in The Settlement?' asked Tanya. This really was uncharted territory.

'Someone probably purchased a large quantity of explosive.'

'Anything else?' asked Tanya.

George laughed, 'Isn't that enough?'

'Do you have any information on where Harold Monckton has gone?'

'Nothing. But then I haven't really looked. Nicholson is still in place, so I think you can expect he is still involved with Harold in some way. His clash with you was one of his few failures; he will certainly be seeking revenge.'

After he rang off, Tanya spent a few minutes reflecting, *Jesus, I really am in the shit now.* She wondered how she would be able to deal with the situation.

A few days later Tanya called Jonathan. He had just been promoted to Major in the Australian Army. 'What do you know about ASIO?' asked Tanya.

He laughed, 'Probably nothing I can tell you.' She had expected this. 'Why do you ask?'

'They have planted an agent on us, unofficially.'

'There must be a reason.'

'David purchased a large quantity of explosive for some development work and for blowing the gorge when the Ice Shelf collapses. They are going to find out about our military training program.'

'ASIO people are mostly decent, you shouldn't have to worry. Also I registered the training program as a legitimate cadet corps.'

'Decent people? Not in this case. I had some acquaintance with this man in the past and he is an unsavoury piece of work.' She thought about her tryst with Demetriou in the forest. 'He is up to every trick in the book—drugs, murders, prostitution. And, we have people in the training program above the age of nineteen, the maximum age for participation.'

'Is your information from your secret police source?' Jonathan had used the source, via Tanya, for background checks as well.

'Yes.'

'Can you give me his name?'

'Demetriou Smith, now known as Charles Smith. He is married to Fiona Smith. Check her too.'

'I need to come up to The Settlement again; it's a long time since I was up there. I will cadge a lift in the 'copter when you next pick up the trainer.'

Jonathan told her he would have time to visit The Settlement in three weeks.

Tanya tried unsuccessfully to avoid any contact with Demetriou during the family's intervening weekend visits, but couldn't forget the memory of their lovemaking. All that was needed was a raised eyebrow from Demetriou and she took another ride one Sunday afternoon into the forest. Her whole life was work; there was no time for fun. So, without much thought her wild streak took over and she plunged headlong into another adventure with Demetriou. Tanya completely disregarded the risks; she knew what she was doing was foolhardy but was unable to stop herself. Although shivering in anticipation, a small part of her wanted to hesitate at the entrance to the wooded area, so she waited for Demetriou under a large gum tree still mounted. When he arrived he looked at Tanya eagerly.

'I'll race you again, bit longer than last time. Twice round the circuit,' she pointed, with a grin. He moved his horse nearer to Tanya's to kiss her, but she anticipated the move and deftly rode onto the well-defined track, ready for the race.

Demetriou smiled, 'What's the prize for the winner?'

'All in good time. Ready?'

Demetriou answered by galloping down the path. Tanya charged after him. She caught up with him, but whenever she rode up he made his mount swerve violently so she had to pull back to avoid a collision. They continued on with their wild ride for another few minutes, Tanya trying to pass Demetriou at intervals and Demetriou blocking her. Neither of them paid any attention to their own or their animals' safety. They often came across fallen trees, requiring both riders' considerable skills to negotiate.

Tanya was sure Demetriou wouldn't know about a little path that would take her out on to the main track a few metres ahead of him. She took the path and soon came out in front. But then she couldn't hear the sound of the horse's hooves behind her. Looking back, there was no sign of him. But she wasn't going to let him beat her; the thrill and excitement of the race continued. She urged her horse on excitedly, whooping as she caught up with him again. Veering off the main track again, with only a few hundred metres to the finish, she ducked a branch and seconds later heard a yell and a crash. Demetriou had followed her and not seen the branch. Tanya made a grab for Demetriou's horse's reins as it galloped past, quickly bringing it under control. Demetriou had been knocked out of the saddle and dragged along the ground for thirty metres, foot stuck in the stirrup, before Tanya managed to bring both horses to a halt. She saw his leg was twisted at a very awkward angle. Dismounting, amidst Demetriou's shouts of pain, she managed to release the foot.

'Oh, shit,' she whispered, breathing hard, 'broken leg I think.' Holding the reins of both horses, she gently tried to straighten out Demetriou's leg. He shrieked in agony. Quickly, Tanya tied the reins of Demetriou's horse onto the saddle, making sure the horse was unhurt, and gave it a pat on the rump. Still blowing hard, it cantered off in the direction of the stables. 'Maybe that will bring some help.' Tanya knelt down again, asking him, 'What happened?'

'I didn't see that branch and the bloody horse scraped me off against it and here I am. You must have known about the branch,' he said in a weak voice.

Tanya wondered what to do. 'Okay, this is going to hurt like hell, but I need you to try to stand on your good leg so I can get you onto my horse. We'll have you back at the stables in no time.'

He shrieked as Tanya got him under the arms and lifted.

'You have to help me. Come on, you are very heavy.'

Demetriou almost fainted, but they managed to get him standing up. He was grey with pain and sweating profusely.

'With the help of your sound leg I am going to try to lift you into the saddle.'

On the third attempt he was seated, only to faint and almost fall off again. She put his good leg into the stirrup.

'Okay, I am going to mount the horse behind you and then we will walk back to the stables.'

The horse was a little reluctant, but took the double weight without too much trouble.

Despite his pain, Demetriou smiled, 'That was all fun, if it hadn't been for this,' he pointed at his leg. 'You are still a wild little bitch.'

Demetriou almost lost consciousness more than once on the three kilometre ride back. As they approached the stables, a gaggle of people including Chloe, Mark, and Fiona came rushing out to help.

'We need to bring the stretcher from the hospital. He has broken his leg, so it needs stabilising. Get the doctor and I will get the helicopter going, to take him to Sydney.'

'What happened?' asked Chloe.

'Don't really know,' she replied with a straight face. 'He said the horse scraped him off on a branch, I went out on my own.'

When the doctor arrived, she rushed to complete her pre-flight checks on the helicopter. She removed most of the seats with Mark's help. Wracked with guilt, Tanya could barely look at her husband. By this time there were plenty of helpers and the stretcher was manoeuvred into the aircraft.

'He is sedated,' said the doctor, but if there is room I will come with you. I have already arranged for him to be admitted to Royal North Shore Hospital.'

'I don't think I will be back here tonight,' Tanya told Mark. 'I will need to go to Bankstown to refuel and by then it will be too dark to fly. I'll return in the morning.'

~·~

There was a crew of doctors and nurses waiting as Tanya touched down on the nearby sports ground that served as a landing pad for the hospital. 'I can pick you up in the morning,' Tanya said to The Settlement doctor. 'I'm sure they'll need you here for the time being and I can't wait. They'll want this place for other emergencies.'

'I'll call on the mobile when I know what's going on.'

~·~

The following weekend David quizzed her about the escapade with Demetriou. She told him what she had told Chloe and in view of their relationship he asked no further questions. He was vaguely aware of an animal attraction between the pair, but now that Demetriou was out of the way perhaps any issues would disappear.

Tanya asked about security and the amount of explosives purchased. On horseback, they went to the site of the planned fuel depot. 'Why did you buy so much? Clearly it has attracted the attention of ASIO. They probably think we're a bunch of terrorists.'

'I didn't even consider ASIO. I got a good price and the bureaucratic rigmarole I had to go through to get the order accepted was such that I thought that I would buy all we might need for now and the future. If properly stored they don't deteriorate.'

Securing the horses at the site, David proudly indicated a wooden door cut into the rock. He started fiddling with a large bunch of keys, but before he had found the right one the door swung open. David looked puzzled. 'Did you open that or was it already open?'

'I opened it,' she waved a piece of wire at him.

'Where did you learn that?'

'My misspent youth. I learnt all sorts of useful things when I was a wild teenager.' She grinned at him.

David shook his head. 'Well you won't have any trouble with the next one; it's the same type of lock.'

Behind the wooden door was a very substantial steel cabinet. David was right, Tanya fiddled for a few seconds and the steel door swung open. 'Quarter-inch steel,' said Tanya admiringly. 'How'd you get this in here? It must weigh several tons.'

'Your friend Charles, or Demetriou, helped. We couldn't have done it without him.'

'He recommended the locks I suppose?

David scratched his head. 'Yes, I think so.'

'Well he certainly has free access to all these explosives. He taught me how to pick locks in the first place. This security is worthless now. When we get back to the village we'll need Joe to get us something better.'

'Are you sure Charles is what you say he is? He seems a perfectly decent person to me and he is very competent.'

'Oh, I'm sure he's competent; he's very smart and an expert in certain fields. We know about his ASIO connection. He has also been involved in drug dealing, prostitution rackets, and a couple of unproven murders,' said Tanya.

David stood there with his mouth open. 'Murders, how do you know all this?'

'My contact. Have you been able to get anything out of Fred about the Smiths?'

'No, he has avoided all my questions.'

'I'll bet he has.'

'Why would ASIO employ a crook like that? Surely they have done their background checks. They would know what you know?' asked a puzzled David.

'I suppose it suits them to maintain their leads into the underworld.'

'Don't they think of our security? Making appointments like this could compromise us,' said David angrily.

'ASIO thinks of The Settlement as a potential security threat thanks to the purchase of this very large quantity of explosives.'

'Why don't they just come and ask, instead of this elaborate charade?'

'Just put yourself in their shoes. They would hardly go blundering around asking daft questions with a potential Al-Qaeda threat, would they?'

'But … ' David started to understand. 'I know I'm not a terrorist threat, I am white skinned, but I can now see some of the things we do, including the military training, could create suspicions.'

'Brown skin, white skin has fuck-all to do with it,' said Tanya aggressively. She glared at him.

'No, no, I suppose not,' he said quietly. He wished he hadn't said that. He guessed Tanya had suffered her fair share of discrimination because of her origins.

David carefully checked the quantity of explosives, nothing seemed to be missing. With Joe's help he arranged a very elaborate electronic security system, supported by solar power, which would certainly foil the skills of the Cabramatta lock pickers. He, Joe, Mark, and Tanya were the only people who held the security codes.

The following weekend, having dropped Mark, the children, and their nanny at The Settlement, Tanya flew to Canberra airport and refuelled. Standing with Jonathan she noticed an attractive lady officer, sporting Captain's pips.

'Captain Virginia Andrews. You must be Tanya.'

Tanya shook her hand and looked her in the eye, causing Virginia to blush slightly. Suddenly, it dawned on Tanya. *This is the famous Captain Andrews.* All the references Mark had made suddenly made sense. Tanya's mind raced. *The bastard has been shagging her on his trips to Canberra.* She immediately felt a whole lot less guilty about her tryst with Demetriou.

Having no idea of the drama playing out between the two women, Jonathan said, 'I could have arranged for you to come to the military facility, but I think you have attracted too much attention already. I didn't want to exacerbate the situation.'

'What do you mean?' asked Tanya sharply, as they walked towards the aircraft.

'The purchase of explosives and ASIO's interest. Thankfully, there has been no mention of our cadet program. I have heard their agent met with an unfortunate accident and is now recuperating in a military facility here in Canberra.'

Tanya glanced at Virginia, who appeared not to be listening. 'Must be more than an informal agent if they have moved him to Canberra. I suppose they have taken the opportunity to fully debrief him,' Tanya observed anxiously.

'Yes, there are also some other issues. It seems that Mark's bank is somehow involved in money laundering.'

Tanya looked at him disbelievingly. 'Does Demetriou know anything about money laundering?'

'I believe so. He needed some outlet for all the money he handled from the drug trade.'

'If he made a lot of money from the drug trade what the hell is he doing at The Settlement?' asked Tanya.

'I don't know the answer to that.'

That evening the Bower family had one of their now quite rare family dinners. No business was discussed, they simply enjoyed each other's company. Virginia had wisely accepted an invitation to a meal with a group from The Academy, but Tanya noticed Mark kept popping out for a few minutes at a time, she presumed to check on Virginia. To her relief, no one else had noticed anything amiss.

'There will be a meeting at ten tomorrow morning for family and spouses,' announced David at the end of the meal.

'I was going to go for a ride,' said Patricia.

'Too bad,' said Tanya brusquely. 'All family members must attend.' Tanya was still sensitive about her apparent mishandling of the business with Harold, particularly that the rest of the family had only been involved after it was over. She was determined not to repeat the mistake. 'It's critical you are there, I will explain why tomorrow.'

Patricia nodded. Although she trusted Tanya, she was sometimes irritated by her forthright manner.

David opened the meeting. 'There have been some serious developments.'

'Not more people leaving, having come to their senses,' said Chloe, more as a statement than a question. Everyone understood Chloe was still skeptical.

'Not this time. It's more serious than that.'

He now had everyone's full attention.

He explained about the explosives. 'Not unreasonably they have put us in the potential terrorist category. There is an ASIO agent here, Charles Smith, a man with a criminal record as long as your arm. His real name is Demetriou Smith.'

'Charles Smith?' asked Joe. 'Are you certain? Before his accident he was very helpful with a lot of technical stuff.'

'We are quite certain,' said Tanya. 'I have explained my rather wild youth. He was part of the group I belonged to and the reason I left. We have tracked him via our sources and he has a long criminal history. How did he help you Joe? We think he is creating opportunities for sabotage and probably blackmail, linked to his ASIO role or privately. If he left ASIO, technically he could still stay here. He is self-funded, as far as we know.'

Tanya looked around the well-known faces in the room; her family now. She wondered what they would think if they knew anything about her recent encounters with Demetriou, including the forest race and his accident. It didn't bear thinking about. She had always been so careful around them, suppressing her wild side. However she felt about the short, renewed affair with Demetriou, her only objective now was for The Settlement to be rid of him; anything else would spell disaster.

With the rest of the family open-mouthed, David explained about the inadequate locking on the explosives store, now fixed.

'How did you tumble to the locking devices scam?' asked Chloe.

'In the dim, distant past Demetriou taught me how to pick locks,' said Tanya.

Everyone silently thanked their lucky stars for Tanya. They could see themselves being blown sky high, never mind the Ice Shelf.

'I have learned more from ASIO,' said Jonathan. 'The Government is concerned about the growing number of communes. They are aware of about forty.'

'Forty?' said David in disbelief. 'Are they all worried about the Ice Shelf?'

'No, none of them. Some are religious, others growing marijuana, or just wanting the Government to let them alone. They are all regarded, including us, as part of a lunatic fringe needing to be shut down. They all have or will have an ASIO plant among them.'

They all looked at each other uneasily. None of them had ever fallen foul of the law except for the occasional parking ticket. To think they were regarded so negatively by the authorities was upsetting as they had always believed that laws and governments were there to protect them and their communities.

Jonathan continued, 'There is another threat. They believe Mark, or more specifically his employers, are involved in extensive, large-scale money laundering. They are claiming this place has been constructed using illegal funds.'

'Bollocks,' said Mark.

'Maybe,' said Jonathan. 'But we need to put all our efforts into disproving it.' He hesitated. 'Perhaps Demetriou has been informed and is putting himself in a position to blackmail us if we manage to prove we are entirely legitimate. They didn't realize my connection to this place at first. Now they do, so we need to get after it otherwise we are in for big trouble.'

'How many companies or anything else has your bank registered in its name?' Tanya asked Mark.

'Five hundred or so I expect, why?'

'Can you get me a list of those names, correctly spelt within the next few days?'

Mark nodded.

'Anything else?' asked David.

'There have been a few, I thought, inconsequential issues, or pinpricks, from the authorities recently. I thought they were unrelated, but they may be part of a campaign to undermine our efforts here. I have only realised the potential relevance based on Jonathan's input,' said Tanya.

'Could you be more specific?' asked Joe.

'Questions regarding water rights, after the new dams were built. The original deeds are quite specific and the query was quite unnecessary. And somebody has been scratching around checking boundary markings. The person wasn't very thorough and didn't find that we have fenced in additional land. We have never had forestry department interest before. There have also been a few tax queries, which I thought were routine. I think it all fits.'

'The police were here a week or two back,' added David. 'They wanted a list of residents. They mentioned harbouring known criminals, but wouldn't respond to further questions.'

'We will handle the serious threat of the money laundering first,' said Tanya. 'Everyone please report anything untoward to me or David. We need to have a complete picture.'

The meeting broke up in a very thoughtful mode.

Tanya and Mark participated in Virginia's training exercises over the weekend. Jonathan had decided to stay on at The Settlement for the week, so Tanya took Virginia back to Canberra on her own. Both women were wary. Virginia broke the ice, mentioning the trumped up charge and the punishment Tanya had endured. They both laughed.

'I do at least two sessions similar to that each week in Sydney,' explained Tanya. 'Now it is a matter of honour that they accept the punishment and deal with it.'

They chatted about family and backgrounds. Tanya even found herself enjoying Virginia's company.

On the way back to the mountains, Tanya thought about what David would say or do if he knew about her and Demetriou. She almost wept. Everything she had built up over the past fifteen years would be in jeopardy if any of that came to light. And why did I mention that shirt, still there where I left it? That will certainly come back and bite me on the arse. She shuddered at the thought.

CHAPTER ELEVEN

The Settlement, Continued

2016

Determined to make up for what she recognised as a relic of her juvenile infatuation with Demetriou Tanya now saw it was her duty to rescue the Settlement from the accusation of using illegal funds for development and then to get to the bottom of what Demetriou was actually planning.

Tanya spent days searching through the names Mark had given her. She then asked him for the accounts and annual registration details of eight of the companies. They all had peculiar names, not easily noticeable, where the order of certain letters had been changed. Only one of the companies had undertaken any significant activity in the past five years.

She called George with her theory that she suspected the names had been changed slightly so they could be used as vehicles for substantial money laundering activities. The "new" names were not registered anywhere and when the authorities started to look, all they could come up with was the names of the companies in the portfolio of Mark's employer.

'It is a form of identity theft,' Tanya said. 'Demetriou must be involved and has specifically targeted us.'

'You will have to leave all the details with me. Phone back in three days.'

When Tanya told Mark, he was truly shocked. 'I will have to brief management.'

'But they can't do anything yet. If they start to deregister some of these companies ASIO will see it as evidence we are trying to hide something.'

~

George was all business. 'It is what you suspected. Someone has moved a few letters around in these names and used them to launder large sums of money. They have made it appear that the companies in question, belonging to the bank, are the so-called money launderers. I'm posting the information to you.'

'Did you find any companies that I haven't mentioned?'

'No, there are thousands of names. It would be impossible.'

Tanya breathed a sigh of relief. She could now see a way out of this particular problem.

'You never told me what you did with the information I gave you on Harold Monckton,' said George, interrupting Tanya's reverie.

'He left and we haven't heard from him since.'

'I need to know what you did with the information?' George persisted.

She told him about her phone call with Nicholson and the eventual outcome as far as The Settlement was concerned. She did not tell him anything about her subterfuge regarding the newspapers. 'Do you know what happened to him after he left us?'

'No, nothing, but I will follow up.' George was unusually reticent.

'Is anything wrong?' asked Tanya.

George hesitated, before answering, 'My brother died two days ago. I have to go to the funeral today.'

'I am so, so sorry,' said Tanya. 'Is there anything I can do?'

'Not really, we always knew he would die young, he was so crippled. There are others like him in that home though.'

'I know, I will continue the donations.'

'Thanks. I knew I would be able to rely on you.'

Tanya waded through all the information that arrived the next day. Within a week she had all the evidence she needed. She called Jonathan. 'I've got to the bottom of the money laundering malarkey,' she told him. 'I need to confront ASIO. Can you make an appointment to see them?'

Jonathan attended the meeting in Canberra with her, but remained silent. She went through all the facts twice, needing to repeat her story to two senior staff.

'How did you come by this information?' she was asked.

'I know it is accurate. I have no obligation and no intention of compromising any of my sources.'

'It seems to be very thorough and, subject to our own checks, appears to be accurate,' the man conceded. 'Is there anything else?'

'There are some procedural things you can help me with. Firstly, my husband's employer will want to deregister all these companies. They are waiting for clearance from me to avoid arousing suspicion. Can you e-mail me the names and the fact that deregistration will not result in any further action on your part?'

The man nodded. 'And your other question?'

Tanya smiled. 'Are there any companies we have missed that still arouse suspicion on your part?'

'One,' a piece of paper was pushed across the table with a name on it.

'What do you want me to do about this? I can do what I did for the other companies or I can leave it to you.'

'You need to do it all, and then the matter will be closed.'

Tanya silently retrieved the piece of paper. She was just about to leave, when the senior man asked, 'How well do you know Charles Smith?'

Tanya hesitated for a few seconds before answering, 'I have only just become reacquainted with him since he moved to The Settlement. I knew him many years ago when his name was Demetriou.'

'He says you were responsible for his horse riding accident.'

Tanya laughed and did not rise to the bait. 'Sounds like his style. Anything else?'

'You have nothing to say about that accusation?'

'Ask the silly bugger who picked him up off the ground, who got him onto his horse, and who flew him to hospital in Sydney. He was on an operating table within three hours of the accident. I did not plan on spending my day doing any of those things. Anything else?'

There was embarrassed silence.

Tanya now took the opportunity to go on the attack. 'Look, Demetriou is a very nasty piece of work. While I understand you thought we were up to no good, we have proven otherwise. Demetriou's cover is blown anyway and he is a most unsuitable settler. Maybe you should consider moving him somewhere else.'

'Why do you say he is an unsuitable settler?'

'He doesn't believe in the science and his wife is the most unrural person I have ever come across. She is terrified of snakes and until she joined us she thought that milk came out of cardboard cartons.'

'What wife?'

'Her name is Fiona. She has two kids.'

They looked at each other, and changed the subject. 'What science?'

Tanya explained the concept behind The Settlement. 'So we set up this place, funded by the family. When the Ice Shelf collapses we will be in a position to isolate the community. We are already more or less self-sufficient, and we have a plan in place to survive. When the wider community, which we think will be much smaller by then, is ready to re-engage then we will be able to open up again. We are about half full at the moment, but there are people coming in every month.'

'And if the Ice Shelf fails to collapse?' The smirks around the table betrayed their scepticism.

'It will. Maybe quicker than we think,' said Tanya. 'Look, if you have any real interest come up for the weekend and we can show you round. I can pick you up in the helicopter.' She didn't expect a rush to accept her offer.

As Tanya was collecting her papers she asked casually, 'Do you know of a man called Harold Monckton?'

Quickly, before any of the others could say anything, the senior man said, 'No, we have never heard of him.'

The others all looked away and pretended not to have heard.

'What was all that about?' asked Jonathan, once they had left.

Tanya explained what she meant, 'We know there has been a concerted effort by the Government to discredit us. They want to close us down. Harold and Demetriou are strings from the same bow. I just wondered who was really running the show. I'm still not sure.'

Within a week, Tanya had provided the information to ASIO. A month later, Tanya received the promised e-mail. Demetriou, with his leg still in plaster, returned to The Settlement to recuperate. Tanya visited him and his family on one occasion. As always he was quite charming and Tanya almost forgot how dangerous he was. Tanya had turned to talk to Fiona. In an unguarded moment, she glanced back in his direction and caught Demetriou glaring at her with such pure hatred it was almost as if he had struck her. Shaken, she left quietly saying that if they needed anything just to ask.

The Smiths all left late one night a few weeks later. They did not even inform Fred.

'I wonder if we really have heard the last of them,' mused Tanya. She phoned Jonathan. 'If you can, see if you can find out where they went.'

'Could we do a check on our explosives?' Tanya asked David. 'I don't trust Demetriou just to walk away. He will have left some sort of footprint here and he will want to exact his revenge.'

Over two weekends, David and Tanya did an extensive check. All seemed to be in order until they reached the very last boxes in the store. They seemed complete until they were opened, but when scrutinised, they found each of the last one hundred boxes had one pellet removed.

'Fifty kgs of high explosive. That'll blow a mighty hole in anything. I wonder where the bastard has put it. Let's check his house and ask Fred,' said Tanya.

Fred knew nothing; Demetriou's disappearance was as much a mystery to him as anyone else. Jonathan sent a sniffer dog to Demetriou's house, but there were no signs of explosives in the house.

'I have managed to track Demetriou down,' Jonathan told them.

'Oh, good, somewhere in North Queensland I hope?' answered Tanya.

'No, he is with your immediate neighbour.'

'Oh, shit! Two days' ride away. We've never contacted them before, but we'll have to pay them a visit and find out what has happened to the missing bloody explosives.'

Tanya spent extra time looking for the explosives. She concentrated on the area where the fuel depot was planned. It took several weekends of painstaking search, but eventually she unearthed some wires and, digging down a metre, found one of the missing pellets attached. Covered in mud, she hurried back to find Mark, David, and Fred.

'There are another ninety-nine of these little buggers buried here. When Demetriou hears we have installed and filled the fuel store he will come here and, if we don't submit to his blackmail, he will set off the charges. We need to find all of them.'

The four of them dug and dug.

'We must keep all this to ourselves,' advised Tanya. 'We don't want the community worrying. We'll tell them if we find anything.'

'Here,' said Mark excitedly. 'I can see some sort of pattern. It looks as if the charges have been laid around the future base of the tanks. The bastard! His intention is to destroy the village and all of us with it.'

After another two weekends of searching, the four of them had found a total of ninety-eight charges.

'I wonder what the hell he's done with the other two charges? When the fuel tanks are full, one kilogram correctly laid could do just as much damage as all these.' She waved at the pile of explosives. She had noticed Fred searched less enthusiastically than the others, but tried to disregard her unease.

Without Fred, who made an excuse, they spent another fruitless weekend looking for the missing charges. David returned the well-preserved explosives to the store, separating them from the detonator. All had been enclosed in individual waterproof plastic bags.

Mark and Tanya carefully planned an expedition to the neighbouring property.

'We need to find out whether Demetriou is actually there and also to find out how secure their establishment is. If it is secure and well-funded then it will provide an eastern buffer. If not, we may have to find a way to help them.'

They thought of going by road. 'We must establish a route through the bush,' said Mark. 'Once we're isolated it may be important.'

They selected four men and four women to accompany them.

'Not Fred,' Tanya said to Mark firmly.

He wondered why she was so adamant.

All ten, well mounted, set off with provisions for a week. They left one person at the eastern gate of The Settlement with provisions and his horse. All the members of the group were armed with the 30.06 Savage rifles.

Tanya and Mark had decided to stay in the background, so Mike and John were sent ahead as an advance party since neither of them had had anything to do with Demetriou.

'The person who set this place up is called Bill McLoughlin, according to Jonathan,' said Tanya. 'Ask for him. Jonathan says he is a reasonable person just wanting to be left alone, so he may be a bit prickly to start with.'

They rode into a scattered array of buildings, seemingly deserted, not even a dog was visible. Unlike The Settlement, all the buildings had a different configuration and cars were scattered about. Mike dismounted and slowly walked over to the nearest house, knocking at the door. There was no answer. John then dismounted and tried another house, with the same result.

'There must be someone here,' said John doubtfully. 'The place is obviously well cared for.'

'Hello,' shouted Mike, 'anyone home?'

Ten men walked out of the shadows, all armed and pointing their rifles at the pair.

'What the fuck do you want?' asked a large bearded man, who seemed to be in charge.

'We are looking for Bill McLoughlin.'

'Who wants him and what is your business?'

'We are your neighbours and just came to make contact.'

'We know who you are. We have been following you since you crossed the boundary. You have been where you are for more than six years, have built a fucking great fence to keep all and sundry out, and have made no attempt to contact us before. Why now?' asked the bearded man.

John shrugged, 'We had nothing to offer. We have been very busy creating our own settlement.'

'What do you have to offer now?'

'Technology perhaps; I see you have no solar power. We might want to trade horses, or sheep, or even medical facilities.'

The rifles were lowered. 'How'd you learn my name?'

'Dunno, the boss out there told me.'

'Maybe you should call the rest of them and then we can talk.'

Mike went off to call the others.

John approached Bill McLoughlin and said quietly, 'A person who left our place under a bit of a cloud was rumoured to have come here ... '

'We've had no new people here for more than a year. Who told you that?' Bill said, rather too sharply.

They were invited to unsaddle their mounts and leave them in a nearby paddock. The horses all rolled in the soft grass and had a long drink.

'Very good stock,' observed Bill.

He showed them around. There were about thirty dwellings, as well as well-bred cattle and sheep. The vegetables garden seemed to be feeding the local kangaroos as much as the human population.

'We built a fence to protect our veggies,' said Tanya.

She was ignored.

Then Bill said to Mark, 'We kept an eye on what you were doing until you built that fence. Since then we don't know what you've been up to.'

Mark replied, 'Tanya actually designed and had the fence built.'

They were invited into a large open area with a thatched roof and no walls; the floor was rough concrete. It was evidently used as a community centre. A semi-circle was created from tables and chairs. Women started to lay out cups and saucers and a cake.

Bill said pointedly to Tanya, 'The ladies are over there.' He indicated a small hut fifty metres away, from where it appeared refreshments were being prepared.

Tanya tipped her hat back, looked Bill straight in the eye, and said, 'I and all the women in our group will be quite comfortable right here, thank you.'

Mark went over to Bill and said within everybody's hearing, 'Tanya is a director of our company and frankly without her we would not be as far along as we now find ourselves. She is the most senior person here.'

Bill looked surprised and uncomfortable. 'Where does David Bower come in then?'

The local women were smiling and fussing over Tanya and the other women in the visiting party, making sure they were served first.

Tanya waited for the women to finish. 'David sends his compliments and wishes you well. We would like to explore mutual cooperation. There may be some areas where we can genuinely help each other. If not, we can hopefully continue to coexist as we have done.'

'How do you think you can help us?' asked Bill.

'We can tell you about our place for a start. If you are interested, you could pay us a visit.'

'Tell us about your place,' said Bill.

Tanya spent fifteen minutes talking authoritatively. 'Of course if one believes in the science, we will block the road we built, preventing access until we are ready to re-engage with the wider community.'

Tanya noticed the local women had all quietly joined the group and were listening intently while she was speaking. She was assailed with questions.

'Who runs the school?' asked one of the women.

'My sister-in-law started it. We now have a headmaster from a leading school in Sydney. What do you do here?'

There were some wary glances. 'I run the school, but it's not really up to standard. I took it on because nobody else wanted to, but I am not a teacher,' said one of the women. Bill looked uncomfortable.

'Well you could come and have a look at what we have and we could transfer what is appropriate over the net,' replied Tanya.

'We don't have any Internet here,' said Bill aggressively.

'No matter, come and tell us what you want. We can make copies for you,' said Tanya, without looking at him.

Bill was surprised. He was expecting a lecture on the merits of the Internet.

'What about this solar power?' asked Bill.

'All our houses have no other source of power. We also have several tractors and a couple of utes which run on solar,' said Mark. 'We only allow fires for barbecues, and the wood is provided by The Settlement. We do not want people running around chopping down trees at will.'

Bill grunted disapprovingly.

'What happens when it is cloudy?' asked a voice.

'We have cold baths,' said Mark good-humouredly. 'It almost never happens though. Brother-in-law Joe is an expert on solar energy.'

Bill was now determined to show off some of his achievements, so he happily showed everyone around "The Bandstand" as they had named their place. Mark and Tanya were really impressed with the cattle and sheep.

'These seem to be better than anything we have,' said Tanya. 'Perhaps we could swap breeding programs.'

'Yes, of course. You help us with the solar stuff and the education and we could certainly help with the breeding programs,' said a now more expansive Bill.

The atmosphere had relaxed.

'I'll show him Demetriou's photograph,' said Mark, looking at Tanya for approval.

'Okay.' Tanya pretended to be looking at something that one of the women wanted to show her.

'Just wondered if you had seen this man?' asked Mark.

Tanya noticed a brief flash of recognition on Bill's face. He pretended to take a close look. 'Nope, we get very few people round here, I would recognise any visitors.'

Bill tried to change the subject, but Mark said, 'This man is very bad news—murder, drug running, money laundering, you name it. He now works for ASIO.'

Bill shrugged as if it was of no interest, but he unwittingly gave the impression that he knew a lot more than he was letting on.

Tanya walked off with one of the women towards the school room and Mark engaged Bill in a subject with which he was entirely comfortable—cattle breeding.

～ͻ

Tanya saw a house in the process of construction. 'New settler?' she asked, making conversation.

'Yes, someone called Smith, and his wife and two children arriving within a couple of months. We've not had any new people in here for more than a year. He's been around for a couple of years, helping us with some of the financial issues I think, but is now going to settle here.'

Tanya proceeded calmly, but her pulse quickened. *The plot thickens*, she thought.

The group had naturally scattered around the property and most of the visitors had learned something which they thought would be helpful when they returned home.

'We don't have anywhere to put you up,' said Bill, 'but if you would be happy to camp out, you are welcome to stay.'

They had a very jolly evening using some of the provisions they had brought with them, but, noticeably, there was no alcohol. They were all in their sleeping quarters before ten in the evening.

Tanya woke at three. She had heard a familiar activity in one of the sleeping bags at the far end of The Bandstand. Earlier, Tanya had noticed the youngest member of the party from The Settlement, James, barely eighteen, making eyes at one of The Bandstand girls. She waited until the activity had stopped and then crept over to the sleeping bag. She tapped them on their shoulders and they both looked up like frightened rabbits.

'Shh, maybe you should go now,' she said to the girl. Looking around the sleeping forms, she said, 'I'll take you back to your house.'

The girl looked up gratefully. 'It's okay. The house is just over there.'

Tanya waited until the near naked form disappeared through a window into the nearby house.

'Did you use a condom?' she asked James. He shook his head. 'Well there is nothing we can do about that now. I will not say anything, but there may be consequences. I hope you understand that.' The boy just looked terrified.

The group woke before six. Their new friends were busy herding cattle in for milking. They had a hasty breakfast and disappeared into the bright fresh day, heading back to The Settlement.

As they made their way carefully down the steep slopes from the eastern gate they were able to admire the picturesque cluster of houses nestled close to each other, with the stream just beyond. Further away to the west, cattle grazed comfortably in a large paddock of planted pasture with an extensive horticultural area nearby. Tanya took in the scene with a fierce pride.

After seeing to the horses and their own ablutions, Tanya held a meeting for all the settlers. 'We will see what happens, but we can use their stock breeding skills and help them with their school, solar power, and a few other things.'

Privately, Tanya and Mark told David that Demetriou would almost certainly be settling next door. 'Bill McLoughlin didn't want to admit it, for some reason. But one of the women confirmed it and I saw the house they are building him. One other thing, I found young James in the sack with one of their girls. He did not use a condom so we may have an unexpected event in nine months or so.'

'How did you know he didn't use a condom,' asked Mark.

'I asked him,' she said rolling her eyes in amusement. 'By the way nobody else knows.'

CHAPTER TWELVE
Sabotage?

Tanya never found the final missing explosive charges. In the end she decided that Demetriou still had them with him. Under David's supervision, sufficient rock had been blasted and three tanks had been delivered; one large enough for helicopter fuel and two smaller ones for regular petrol and diesel.

Tanya watched progress and concluded if Demetriou was going to act it would have to be soon. There had been two visits from selected Bandstand people and useful information had been exchanged, but Tanya was still suspicious of Bill McLoughlin's motivation. She knew Demetriou had established himself at The Bandstand but he hadn't appeared in any of the visits and when Settlement people visited, there was no sign of Demetriou or his family.

Tanya arranged with Mark, as head of security, for a twenty-four hour watch on the eastern entrance gate nearest The Bandstand. Tanya's initiative irritated Mark. He felt he should have come up with the plan himself.

Apart from her stunning looks, he had originally been attracted to her intelligence and apparent vulnerability. He had always understood her background and to a degree credited himself with rescuing her from the gutter, although he would never have dared to whisper a word of his feelings in that regard to her. He hated himself for these sentiments. He had always been a positive person, in control. Fits of jealousy were for other, weaker people. He remembered their first sexual encounter with a degree of disquiet as she had led the engagement, not him. He sometimes wondered whether it was his destiny to follow in her footsteps, forever. It was an unwelcome thought.

After four months of rigorous discipline, the surveillance was rewarded. Young James had been on the watch. In the middle of the night one weekend he came to Tanya's window, knocking quietly.

'Yes, what is it?' asked Tanya in a whisper. Mark was still asleep beside her.

'Two people have just come through the fence from The Bandstand. They left their horses at the gate and are walking down here.'

Tanya was now on full alert; this was what she had been expecting. 'Okay, go back to the gate, tie the horses up on the inside of the fence, and then lock the gate. Were you seen?'

'No, I'm certain of that.'

'Did you see who they were?'

'No, not really. I just made sure I kept out of sight. But I think one of them was Bill McLoughlin.'

'Were they armed?'

'They both had large backpacks, no rifles.'

She woke Mark, dressed, and ran over to alert David, Fred, and two others. 'It looks as if our man has arrived at last. Two of them, Bill McLoughlin and one other, probably Demetriou.'

They all wore dark clothing, had powerful torches, and carried their 30.06 rifles. David had a handgun. Their familiarity with the terrain helped the party make their way rapidly and quietly to the site of the fuel installation, which they approached carefully. All had planned positions, so without a word moved into place. The full moon had just appeared over the horizon.

'Make no move until I say so,' was Tanya's final whispered instruction. They waited ten minutes, thirty minutes, one hour. Tanya wondered anxiously if there had been some mistake and that the target was somewhere else on the property.

A stick broke, sounding like a thunderclap in the silence. Tanya kept very still and hoped the others had enough sense to do the same. A torch was switched on and there was Demetriou pulling something from his rucksack with Bill looking on. They had obviously waited for the moon to rise to give enough light to see properly. They seemed unaware that they were not alone.

Tanya crept closer. When she was just a few metres away she could see Demetriou fitting what looked like detonators to the missing explosives Bill was holding. They then moved to a position underneath one of the tanks and Bill started to dig a hole. Surprisingly, they spent no time looking for the other charges previously laid. Maybe the people from The Settlement were meant to find them.

As Tanya was preparing to take action, a rifle shot rang out. She saw some mud kicked up a few feet from the pair. They dropped everything and ran. Aiming at their legs, Tanya managed to get two shots off as the men disappeared into the bush.

The others emerged from their hiding places. 'I'm sure I winged one of them at least,' said Tanya, 'so we'd better start a search. And I want to know who fired off that shot.'

They found Bill twenty metres into the bush, clutching his leg as it bled profusely.

'Demetriou will be on his way back to the gate,' said Tanya. 'We need to be quick. Young James is there on his own and he is unarmed. Someone fetch the doctor and get this animal back to the centre. But please don't touch anything here, leave it just as it is, the police or ASIO will need to be involved.'

Tanya took David aside, whispering, 'Keep an eye on Fred, I'll bet you anything it was him that fired that shot. It was a warning. There is something between him and Demetriou.' Louder, she said, 'So, remember, don't touch anything and please leave two people on guard.'

David shook his head, 'I will try to find out about Fred but... '

Mark and Tanya ran, scrambled, and crawled their way to the gate, as best as they were able by the light of the moon. Mark's knowledge of the rough ground helped.

'Hopefully we can get back to the gate first. Unless he studied the terrain while he was here, we should be quicker,' said Mark. When they arrived at the gate some time after Bill had been shot, there was no sign of James or the horses. After five minutes, a very nervous James emerged from a nearby bush.

'Are you alright? Have you seen Demetriou?' asked Tanya.

'I'm alright,' said James shakily. 'Demetriou went through the gate, on foot, about ten minutes ago. He was in a hurry and kept looking behind him.'

'Did he take the horses?'

'No. I heard some faint rifle shots, a while ago now, so I took the horses and hid. Demetriou looked for them, he was running around swearing, obviously in a hurry but gave up pretty soon. I think he picked the lock.'

'You did very well, James,' said Tanya admiringly, patting him on the shoulder. 'He knows we are armed and he may not be, so he will be getting back to The Bandstand as fast as his legs will carry him. I think we should go after him.'

They found the horses grazing quietly where James had left them, and saddled them.

'Let's just think about what we should be doing,' said Mark, quietly trying to take the initiative. 'We have Bill wounded and probably in the hospital, Fred, whose behaviour is unpredictable, and bloody Demetriou running about in the bush. I think James and I should try to get to The Bandstand as quickly as we can. With the horses we should arrive there before our friend. Tanya, you should return to The Settlement to call the police and Jonathan.'

Mark had suddenly realised that from the beginning of the incident, Tanya had effortlessly taken control. Without thinking, the rest of the group including himself and David had done what they had been bid by Tanya.

'Okay,' Tanya responded, too late recognising Mark's need to be in charge. She glanced at him to see if he was irritated, but he was giving nothing away. 'I will be on hand if the helicopter is needed for anything and will try to make certain the police have a reception committee waiting for Demetriou at The Bandstand. Here, James, you take my rifle.'

Tanya walked back home, tired and filthy. She immediately sought David out, and they briefly exchanged news. 'Was it Fred who fired that shot?' she asked.

'Yes, he said it was a mistake and I am inclined to believe him.' David always wanted to believe the best in people. He was reluctant to even contemplate that his friend had deliberately put The Settlement in jeopardy.

'I don't believe him for a bloody nanosecond. Fred is very competent with a rifle and wouldn't make a mistake like that. I saw where the shot hit, for Christ's sake, and it was not close to either man. It was intended as a warning. I think Fred was surprised I managed to wing Bill. There is more, much more to our Fred than meets the eye. Perhaps I should interview him and his wife to see what I can find out. First, we phone the police and Jonathan so they can pick up Demetriou at The Bandstand.'

David was taken aback at Tanya's vehemence.

Jonathan responded quickly. 'I will advise ASIO, please do nothing until you hear from me.'

He rang back in ten minutes. 'ASIO will pick Demetriou up, but they have no interest in Bill. Call the police for him.'

'I don't like the sound of any of that,' responded Tanya. 'They will isolate Demetriou and deny he had anything to do with the explosives. We will end up defending a charge of unlawfully wounding Bill. Bugger ASIO, I am going to call the police to both places.'

Privately Jonathan agreed with Tanya.

'You okay with that, Jonathan?'

He remained silent.

'I get the picture,' said Tanya and hung up. She called 000 and persuaded the police to attend both places. 'I will be at The Bandstand,' she told them.

'How are you going to get there?' asked David, somewhat bemused by the rapid pace of developments.

'Helicopter—it's the only option, first thing in the morning. It will take Mark the best part of two days to get to The Bandstand and the same with the police. Demetriou will take longer. I will take three armed people with me. You need to make sure Fred's statement is accurate.'

Exhausted, Tanya spent the day recovering. She completed some basic checks on the helicopter and they arrived at The Bandstand early the following morning. 'Demetriou won't be back, but I expect the police to be there when we arrive,' she told her companions.

On arrival they were immediately surrounded by anxious people wanting to know what was going on.

Tanya said to one of the leading women. 'Please find Fiona and don't let her leave.'

There were some surprised looks.

'Go on,' said Tanya sharply, 'we've known they were here since before our first visit.'

People scuttled off to the newly-constructed house and after some shouting Fiona was dragged into the meeting.

Tanya detailed her suspicions about the missing explosives and laid charges. 'We have kept a watch on our eastern gate for months now and two nights ago we picked Demetriou and Bill up as they came through the gate and followed them. We caught them red-handed, installing a detonator into the stolen explosive charges and attempting to bury them under the tank designed for our helicopter fuel.'

There were sharp intakes of breath and looks of disbelief on the faces of her audience.

'They clearly intended to do us a great deal of harm, although no fuel has been delivered yet. The police were called and yesterday started on the lengthy process of taking statements in The Settlement. Other police were coming here. Have they arrived?'

'Last night, but we haven't seen them this morning,' said a woman, introduced as Caroline. Tanya knew she was Bill's wife.

'We think Demetriou is on his way back here on foot so he may yet be a day away. Bill was shot in the leg and is in our hospital, he's in no danger.'

Caroline said, unexpectedly, 'Pity you didn't shoot the bastard in the head.'

Fiona looked up sharply, but remained stoic, despite questioning glances from her fellow settlers.

Tanya asked one of The Settlement men to keep an eye on the Smith cottage. 'We can't let Demetriou scarper when he sees us and the police.'

Tanya had prepared a statement for the police when they finally appeared. But still there was no sign of ASIO.

Mark and James arrived well after dark. They also prepared statements for the police.

Mark whispered to Tanya just as they were all about to turn in, 'I'm worried about the police plans to apprehend Demetriou when he arrives. I'm taking one of our people down the track to block it and wait. Keep an eye on the Smith cottage, I saw the senior policeman having a private word with Fiona.'

As before, the visitors camped. Mark went with one of the men from The Settlement and dragged a tree across the access road, blocking it. Unbeknown to any members of The Bandstand, the other Settlement people, with Tanya taking one of the shifts, set up a watch on the Smith cottage. The police had retired to their own cottage.

Shortly after midnight a furtive figure dashed out of the bush and crept into the Smith house. Within thirty minutes, Demetriou, Fiona, and the two children emerged with suitcases which they packed into the car. They quietly drove off, using parking lights.

The two people keeping watch ran to Mark's position about five hundred metres away. The car was stationary at the road block, with Demetriou shouting and gesticulating at Mark, who had his rifle pointing at him. Soon he was surrounded by four Settlement people with rifles.

'Demetriou, you are surrounded. Get out of the car and come with us before anyone gets hurt.' The children started crying.

'Fuck you, I'll get you one day,' said Demetriou as he got out of the car. They tied his hands behind his back. They walked everyone back to the Smith cottage.

'Where are the police? What the hell did they come here for? We had better try to find them. Could you wake Tanya please?' said Mark to one of his colleagues.

Tanya went for Caroline when she heard the news. She answered her door almost immediately on Tanya's knock, 'We stopped Demetriou from leaving, but the police are nowhere to be seen,' said Tanya aggressively, 'Do you know where they are?'

'They were supposed to be watching the Smith cottage.'

'We watched it ourselves. They were nowhere to be seen. If it hadn't been for us, the Smiths would have driven away.'

'I will show you where they are staying.'

They went to a cottage on the outskirts of the property and banged on the door. 'Where the hell have you been?' asked Tanya. 'We have just stopped the whole Smith family from leaving. Weren't you wanting to arrest him?'

'Where is he?' asked the senior officer.

'At his cottage,' answered Tanya.

The two policemen dressed and accompanied Tanya and Caroline to the Smith cottage.

'Okay, we'll take over now,' said one of the policemen.

Mark and Tanya exchanged glances. 'No, I don't think so. You,' she said to the younger policeman, 'can take Fiona and the two kids by road to the police station in Parramatta.'

'I would like to leave the kids here,' said Fiona.

Caroline said firmly, 'No, you can't.'

Addressing the senior policeman, Tanya said, 'I would like you to accompany me in the helicopter to the Parramatta police station with Mr Smith. We take off at first light. The car can go now.'

The senior policeman shook his head imperceptibly at his colleague. 'Thank you, I must make one call though.' Accompanied by Caroline he went to make the call, returning a few minutes later.

While they were waiting Mark took Tanya aside. 'Maybe there was something going on between the police and Demetriou. We've certainly stymied any plans.'

'There will now be a suitable reception committee waiting for our friend,' said the unsmiling policeman on his return. To his colleague, 'Take Fiona and the kids to Parramatta, I will be there when you arrive.'

They loaded Demetriou into one of the rear seats of the helicopter, tying his hands and legs, and then bound him into the seat. 'If you make a sound, I will shove a gag into your mouth,' Mark told him.

Tanya produced a canvas bag. 'All firearms go in here while we are in the air.' The policeman put his service revolver into the bag. 'I said all firearms,' she repeated. He tiredly leant down and removed a small derringer from his right sock and without looking at Tanya, dropped it into the bag.

Demetriou was taken into custody on arrival.

Another police officer approached Tanya and said, 'Mrs Bower, you are under arrest and anything you say … '

Tanya had noticed the senior policeman from The Bandstand smirking as the officer approached. 'Oh really, what is the charge?'

'Malicious wounding. It is a very serious charge. There are also other issues in your background that require some further investigation.'

'I agree the malicious wounding is indeed serious. But if you choose to proceed with this nonsensical charge it will be vigorously defended.' She wondered about "the other issues". *Did Demetriou tell them something?*

The officer shrugged. 'I will have to take you into custody.'

'What would you like me to do with the helicopter in your car park?'

'Not my problem, you are under arrest.'

Tanya turned to Mark. 'You will have to make your own way to the office. Could you please phone my boss, John Chambers, urgently?' She kissed him as he left.

The officer was about to lead Tanya away when she said, 'Are you about to deny me the right to make one phone call?'

The officer hesitated before handing Tanya the phone. She made one private call, before being led away to the cells.

Towards evening, Tanya managed to attract the attention of the senior officer in the police station, 'Either charge me or release me. You can't just hold me a prisoner here,' she said to him forcefully.

'We can hold you for twenty-four hours without charge. There is an investigation underway.'

'I can assure you, officer, that if you step one bloody millimetre over the line I will throw the book at you. Your people failed to actively pursue and apprehend Demetriou Smith after he attempted to blow us all up. The dereliction will be reported in full to the senior police command. The charge of malicious wounding will not stand up to any scrutiny. I would advise you strongly to release me and concentrate on the main game. There is obviously something going on between this station and Demetriou Smith. I will have no choice but to investigate the issue personally. If you care to understand something of my background, you will very quickly come to understand that I am not to be trifled with.'

The officer walked away.

In the early hours of the morning, a shaken junior officer returned to the cells. 'Mrs Bower, all charges have been dropped. Orders from the very highest level.'

'This won't be the last you hear about this. The charges were exceptionally stupid. You should be ashamed of yourself.'

'I was just following … '

'Save it,' Tanya glared at him as she retrieved her possessions.

'We would like you to move your helicopt … '

'You people really are stupid. Where on earth to? If you want to be any use at all, bring me a cup of coffee. I will leave at first light.'

She was given a cup of coffee.

As the sky lightened, she flew towards The Bandstand, determined to find out the real story behind the apparent ill-will towards her precious Settlement. James and the others had returned to The Settlement on horses, some borrowed from The Bandstand.

Caroline greeted her in a friendly way. 'Is there anything we can do for you? I am slightly surprised that you returned.'

'Perhaps a meal and some sleep,' said Tanya tiredly. 'The reason I returned here is to have a chat, perhaps tomorrow. But first I must phone Mark, privately.'

'Where are you?' he asked.

'At The Bandstand.' She explained briefly what had happened at the police station. 'Most of these people seem perfectly decent to me, but some of them must have known of the plan hatched by those two morons.'

'I have just spoken to your boss. He says ASIO and the police got their wires crossed and you were arrested.'

'I hope to have nothing more to do with any of it, but I'm sure there is more to the story than you suggest. I think that bloody senior policeman arranged my arrest when he made the phone call. Are Bill and Demetriou safely locked up? Once that is assured I can find out what the hell is going on here.' She didn't mention anything about the policeman's remark regarding her background. *Demetriou must have told them something about that shirt and tried to put the blame onto me; well best of luck with that.*

'At the very least you will still be asked to give your side of the story to some sort of enquiry.'

'Okay, but I have better things to do than screw around with a lot of incompetents looking after their own interests.'

The Bandstand story emerged after much probing by Tanya. 'This place was always short of money,' said Caroline, an attractive, no-nonsense, buxom brunette, in her mid-thirties. 'Bill had said not to worry, that he would be able to fix it. We were introduced to Demetriou something like three years ago. He seemed nice enough, but we realised quite quickly he was into all sorts of illegal stuff. Anyway, he provided much needed funds and before we knew where we were he had us by the balls. He then moved to your place. He had no idea about The Settlement or that you were there, but his behaviour changed altogether then. He became obsessed with revenge.' She looked at Tanya curiously.

Tanya thought it was far too early to share any confidences. 'So what is the real situation here? We would like to think there is a strong, independent, and viable settlement and we'll help anyway we can, once we know if anyone else here harbours bad will towards us.'

There were some discussions among the local group while Tanya spent her time taking a critical look around. Eventually Caroline found her. 'We can show you all the figures. Luckily, I've been keeping the books so I know exactly what is going on.'

Halfway through the process David arrived on horseback. 'We were wondering if you were alright, since we hadn't heard anything.'

'I'm glad you're here. Take a look at this. The cash is all being taken up with interest payments. If it wasn't for the interest the place is viable.'

'Who do you make all the payments to?' asked Tanya.

'Just the bank,' said Caroline.

'Who owns this place?'

'I do. Bill had some idea it would be better if the property was in my name. There are some mortgages though and there is another document here which I have refused to sign.'

Tanya quickly read the document and then looked at her in admiration. 'That has probably saved your bacon. Give me two weeks.'

There was a look of uncertainty on Caroline's face.

'Because of some loose ends that Demetriou has left, if you let me I can arrange that the property will remain in your name free of any mortgage.'

'There are some operational things that can also be done, which will improve your cash position. I will also help by making suggestions for improvements,' said David.

There was still a look of distrust on Caroline's face.

'What was your dream in coming here?' asked Tanya.

'Just to be left alone to get on with life as we saw fit, without all this interference from governments.'

'I am sure we'll be able to achieve that for you.'

'I need to talk to the others. Can we reconvene in an hour?' said Caroline.

When they were alone Tanya said, 'Nobody will talk about the raid on The Settlement, not even Caroline. They all claim they knew nothing. They were aware that Bill and Demetriou had gone off, but not where. I am uncomfortable about that.'

David shrugged.

They spent time talking to five locals in their management committee. Caroline tended to defer to a tall, good looking man whose name was Rolfe. Tanya watched Rolfe and wondered if he was trustworthy. He seemed to want more than a working relationship with Caroline, but she seemed quite unaware of his interest.

The meeting broke up leaving Tanya with a brief to unscramble their finances. She flew backwards and forwards between Sydney and The Settlement over the next three weeks, the bank insisting they could do nothing until the new mortgage deed was signed. But, because of the disgraced Demetriou's money laundering activities, ASIO was persuaded to cooperate. Between George, ASIO, and Tanya, they were able to concoct a scheme whereby it appeared the bank had been actively engaged in money laundering.

Tanya had persuaded Jonathan to put pressure on ASIO to cooperate, 'All along they have misinterpreted the situation,' she argued vehemently. 'It was those fuckers who sent Demetriou, a known and dangerous criminal, to spy on us. His unofficial actions could very easily have destroyed us altogether. I know Government hoped to close us down, but burning the whole fucking place down in a helicopter fuel fireball would be a little over the top. If someone senior finds out … and all that horseshit with Harold, they must bear some responsibility.'

'Okay, okay, they will cooperate, don't worry.' Jonathan was amused by Tanya's passion.

'I will come down myself if I have to,' said Tanya, more calmly. She was surprised by Jonathan's confidence and apparent authority. *He must be more senior than I thought.*

'No. I understand your need to support The Bandstand. The ASIO people will cooperate, I promise you that.' Jonathan admired Tanya, although he was distrustful of her background. *I'm bloody glad I'm not married to her though. Poor Mark. It must be like having a tiger roaming round the house, day and night. No wonder he strayed with Virginia, stupid bugger.*

The bank did not want to be associated in any way with possible money laundering. When Tanya delivered all the paperwork to a still suspicious Caroline, she, Rolfe, and several others spent two days examining it. Tanya noticed Caroline had started taking more care with her appearance since David had been visiting from The Settlement.

A contrite Caroline returned. 'I am sorry I've been so suspicious, but we have been let down before. We could never have achieved this ourselves, so thank you.'

'No problem,' said Tanya, taken aback. She was expecting some questions at least.

'There is one other thing. We would like to pay you to run all the finances and legal affairs for The Bandstand.'

'We can work something out.' Tanya thought this would help keep The Settlement secure. *No more bloody Demetrious,* she almost said out loud. 'How has Rolfe reacted to that idea?'

A shadow crossed Caroline's face, 'He left this morning. He wanted to deal with it all, but I can handle the management and I now know I can trust you with the legal and financial issues. I think Rolfe saw this place, without Bill and Demetriou, as a major opportunity. But, he would have landed us in the same mess you've just rescued us from … We've trusted the wrong people.'

'I still don't understand how not a soul here knew anything about what Bill and Demetriou were up to that night. Caroline, you have to come clean with me.'

Caroline burst into tears, 'You have to believe me; none of us knew. Bill and Demetriou were becoming more and more secretive. They often went off without telling anyone. I know Bill was desperately worried about the financial situation. I only know what Rolfe said, that Demetriou had let slip he "had something" on you people and that would help solve the problem. Rolfe didn't know much; Bill wasn't sure if he could trust him.'

Caroline broke Tanya's silence, 'What's going to happen to Bill and Demetriou?'

'I expect they will spend most of their lives in jail,' answered Tanya.

'And if they are let out?'

'Well, if they come anywhere near here or The Settlement I will shoot them,' said Tanya vehemently.

Caroline smiled, 'Unless I get 'em first.'

Tanya changed the subject, 'I told you there were a couple of issues. Firstly, young Jane. If she isn't pregnant now, it won't be long before she is.'

Caroline's eyebrows raised a notch, thinking that dealing with a teenage pregnancy was mere bagatelle compared to the recent events, 'What has Jane been up to? I have been so preoccupied I haven't been keeping my eyes open.'

'Well she and James seem to spend every spare moment in the sack. From the first time we visited they haven't been able to keep their hands off each other.'

'They are very young, maybe just a good solid lesson on birth control would solve the problem for the time being.'

'One solution could be James living here or Jane coming to The Settlement,' offered Tanya.

'I will speak to her parents. What is the other issue?'

'Security,' said Tanya. 'We chose our location so that when the Ice Shelf collapses it will be easy to make inaccessible from the outside. While your place is quite isolated, when people are trying to escape Sydney and the surrounding towns they will soon find their way here and you will be overwhelmed.'

Caroline asked to hear about the projected disaster again.

'You don't need two access roads,' continued Tanya. 'You should plant one of the roads up with some fast-growing trees. The other road could be narrowed considerably by planting trees on the verges. The trees can be cut down over the road, blocking it for a couple of kilometres. People may still be able to walk in, but what I have suggested makes you more secure.'

'What are you planning at The Settlement?

'To blow up a whole mountain. That is why we purchased the explosives.'

'A whole mountain?'

Tanya nodded. 'Obviously the more secure you are, the more secure we are and vice versa.'

'I don't see why we can't plant trees. It makes sense.'

Tanya returned to The Settlement by helicopter, with Jane in tow, who was to live with Joe and Patricia. Monthly reciprocal visits between the communities were arranged.

Tanya also had regular discussions with George, 'On another subject ...'

George had responded laughing, 'Another curve ball I expect.'

'What do you know about Fred Costas?'

'I have something on that name perhaps, I'll dig and let you know.'

The next time they spoke George said, 'You asked about Fred Costas?'

'Oh, yes, I almost forgot,'

'That must be a first,' said George laughingly. 'Fred is Demetriou's half-brother.'

Tanya sucked in a deep breath, 'You're joking!'

'No, same father. Otherwise he is completely clean, not even a parking ticket. He has tried to protect Demetriou from time to time though, some sort of family bond.'

'Shit, I knew there was something. If Demetriou ever gets out of jail, I suppose Fred will continue to support him.'

CHAPTER THIRTEEN
Fred's Trial

Tanya had a quiet chat with David about Fred's affiliation with Demetriou.

'What do you want to do? Fred has been one of the mainstays of this place. I don't know what we would have done without him.'

'We would have found another builder,' was the acid response from Tanya.

'Well, what do you want to do?' repeated David tiredly.

'Confront him. You must agree, whatever his relationship with Demetriou, it is unacceptable to have people on the inside conniving to destroy this place. Come on David, can you imagine it? If the fuel tanks were blown up the whole place would have become a fireball. Despite our insurance, we do not have the resources to completely rebuild the place. We would be left with the option of committing suicide or dying of starvation like the rest of the population, the last six or seven years' work for nothing. He bloody well has to go.'

'Then we will have another enemy on the outside knowing our secrets. Isn't there another way? Anyway, you exaggerate; the tanks are far from here. '

Tanya was silent. She was determined nobody was going to threaten The Settlement, now as much her dream as David's. Because of her thoughtless encounter with Demetriou, she also had another reason to be rid of Fred. If he didn't know already, she was certain he would be told in time. 'If all the fuel we plan to store in those tanks was blown up there is certainly a danger that fire would spread to the village; they are only five hundred metres from here. We have insulated the tanks from bushfires, but if the tanks are blown up our precautions have no effect.'

'We could involve the police.'

'The police?' said Tanya contemptuously. 'In this situation they would be about as much use as two tits on a bull.'

David laughed. 'What about getting him to sign something acknowledging his relationship with Demetriou and that he has actually endangered the lives of people here as well as possibly destroying the whole project.'

'And then?' asked Tanya. 'He will still own his position here. What do you think the rest of the community will think if they find out about Demetriou? And what Fred did to protect him? We should speak to him first, but I really think we have to consult with the community. People have put their faith in us. If Fred managed to do something in the future with Demetriou's help and the community finds out we were aware all along, they would go ballistic.' Tanya was furious. 'As soon as the Ice Shelf collapses the authorities will have to empty the jails. Those two hyenas will make for this place, especially if they know that Fred is still here.'

'After the Ice Shelf collapses we will have to have our own legal system and run trials,' said David thoughtfully. 'Maybe this should be the first issue to consider.'

Tanya hesitated for a moment. *This really is the solution,* she thought.

'Brilliant, quite brilliant! If we manage this correctly we will avoid the mass hysteria a story in the newspaper might generate. We must speak to Fred, soon.'

'There are some lawyers already in the community. We should appeal to them and make sure everyone understands what we're doing. We should distance ourselves and just appear as witnesses.' Any brief feelings of animosity she might have felt towards David had dissipated as she applied her mind to the issue.

The two lawyers were approached separately. One agreed to act as prosecutor, the other as defence. They brought in a colleague from outside to act as judge. It was agreed that a jury of six would decide whether Fred was guilty or innocent. The external judge spent days in the community contemplating what sort of punishments could be appropriate under the circumstances should Fred be found guilty.

He was arrested and questioned by Tanya with David attending. They presented the lawyers with all the evidence they could muster.

David briefed the community newspaper that Fred was to be prosecuted for willfully endangering the existence of The Settlement and the people living in it. He told the editor that this particular trial would create a basis for dealing with offences against the community once the place was isolated.

Many of the residents struggled to find seating in the small community centre where the trial was held. The prosecution opened by stating they would prove that, because of misguided loyalties, Fred had endangered the community. The defence opened by stating that Fred had been a model citizen, had built a lot of the houses in the village, and had done far more good than harm in the community. There was general applause from the audience at this point.

The judge banged his gavel looking benignly over the large gathering, before he said, 'I realise there is enormous interest in this case, but I must insist you keep quiet during the proceedings and that you don't try to influence the jury in any way. If this happens again I will regretfully have to clear the court.'

The prosecution called David Bower to the witness stand. David explained Fred's contributions and trusted status.

'Would you say he had a privileged position in the community?'

'Certainly. He was one of the first settlers and was consulted on all building projects.'

'Do you think he has made a great deal of money doing what he did?'

'Probably not, his quotes are always very competitive, but he made enough to keep his head above water. In any event, no settler comes here to make money. Almost without exception, the people who come here share the vision to build a community that will survive the forthcoming disaster.'

'Do you think the defendant shared this vision?'

'Yes, I had many conversations with him on the subject. He was always very positive and made many constructive suggestions helping us become more self-sufficient.'

'And you say he was trusted?'

'More than almost anyone else outside the family.'

'Who was responsible for recruiting the settlers?'

'Mostly me. The family, particularly Tanya, agree on the skills required and the type of people we think will fit in. Then I go out and find those people. Although family members have introduced people who have successfully settled here. In almost every case, I conduct the final interview.'

'What is the purpose of the final interview?'

'To ensure the prospective settler buys into the vision, understands the standard of living may well be lower than what they are used to, and that they would have to take on certain responsibilities for the benefit of the community.'

'Did you or anyone else interview Charles Smith?'

'No.'

'Why?'

'He had been introduced by Fred, whom everyone trusted. Fred knew what we were about and understood the process. We attempted to arrange interviews, all of which fell through. I now think this was a deliberate move on Fred's part to shield him. So Charles and his family just arrived once his house had been built.'

'When did you realise Charles was not what he seemed to be?'

'Tanya knew him when she was growing up. She told me his name used to be Demetriou Smith. Further digging revealed his criminal record and time spent in jail. Tanya also found out Fred had funded Demetriou's arrangements here; he paid for the house, for example.'

'What did you do when you found out?'

'I tried to talk to Fred, but he avoided all questions. Demetriou was quite useful. He was an explosives expert and helped us with some blasting to install storage tanks. So we left it. Then he had an accident and we found out that apart from his criminal record he was also an agent for ASIO. He left very shortly after recovering from his accident, much to our relief. We thought that was the end of that.'

Under further questioning David explained about Demetriou's connections with the neighbouring settlement and where most of the missing explosives were found.

'Most of it?'

'There were two pieces missing, enough to blow the fuel depot sky high once the tanks had been filled. Tanya was concerned, so she arranged a watch on the gate. One night two men came through the gate carrying heavy packs.'

'What happened then?'

By this time the roomful of almost one hundred people was absolutely still. Nobody could believe what they were hearing.

David told the court how he, Tanya, Fred, Mark and two others had gone to pre-prepared positions near the tank installation. How they had seen Demetriou and Bill, in the moonlight, digging a hole underneath where the tanks were to be installed. 'They were fitting a detonator to the missing explosive. We had been told not to move or fire before Tanya gave the order. As she was getting into position to arrest the pair, a shot was fired and they fled. Tanya winged Bill in the leg as he escaped.'

'Who fired the first shot?'

'Fred.'

'Are you sure?'

'Yes, he said it was a mistake.'

'And you believed that?'

'I was inclined to believe that, but not Tanya. She thought it was a warning shot. She saw where the bullet had struck, far away from the pair. We didn't yet know about the relationship between Fred and Demetriou.'

'How did you find out?'

'Tanya has some contacts in the police and after some delays she was told that Demetriou was Fred's half-brother. They have the same father.'

There was a brief hum among the audience. The judge looked up and it all went quiet again.

'And then?'

'We decided we needed a judicial process to ensure the rule of law would be applied in The Settlement now and in the future. So Fred was arrested and questioned and this is the first case to be heard under this system.'

'Please continue.'

'Fred, at first, vehemently denied it was a warning shot. When we told him we knew they were related and had proof, Fred broke down and admitted everything in a written statement.'

'Why did Fred continue to support Demetriou?'

'He gave us a garbled explanation, but I think due to a sense of family loyalty. It seems Demetriou took advantage of the situation. Demetriou is a violent man and there was a suggestion some of Fred's other relatives might be harmed if he didn't continue to cooperate.'

~

When the judge called a break, everyone began talking at once. Most of the settlers had no idea of the drama with Bill and Demetriou. Sentiment varied about Bill's punishment.

~

When the court reconvened the defence asked David to remain in the witness box. 'If Fred was such a trusted member of the community, why wasn't he a shareholder and a director?'

'I started the company with my own money and individual family members have contributed capital, mainly for development. All the other settlers have paid for the construction of their own houses, but have only contributed to general development through a levy on their houses. This applied to Fred as well.'

'Isn't this just a device for the Bower family to maintain control?'

David was genuinely taken aback. 'No,' he tried to remain calm. 'The rules are explained as settlers arrive. Anyway, without the money my family has put into the project it wouldn't exist.'

'So although you state that Fred is a trusted member of the community, he is not a member of the inner circle, so to speak.'

The prosecution intervened. 'Objection, this line of questioning is going nowhere.'

'Objection sustained,' said the Judge. 'Please stick to the point.'

Nevertheless the defence had made its point; Fred was like a trusted employee, not a member of the inner circle.

'You keep mentioning Tanya. What is your personal relationship with Tanya Bower?'

There was an angry murmur among the audience at the unfounded implication. The judge looked up sharply.

'She is my daughter-in-law. She and I independently came to the same conclusions regarding climate change. Together with my son Mark, her husband, they have put every cent they own, a considerable sum, into this project,' said David calmly. He looked about the court. He was certain everyone present thought his relationship with Tanya was completely above board. His calm demeanour and his willingness to listen had earned the trust of almost every individual in The Settlement.

'No further questions.'

The prosecutor called Tanya to the stand.

She stood, lovely and immaculate, in jeans and a red blouse. At this stage in the proceedings, she felt secure and confident.

'What is your role in this community?'

'I am on the board of The Settlement Pty Ltd. Believing in the science, I have basically spent every spare minute helping to make this place a reality.'

'Every spare minute?'

'I have two children and a full time job in a law firm in Sydney.'

'What is your relationship with Fred?'

'He was one of the first settlers here and has built many of the houses. I make a point of getting to know all the settlers, Fred and his family included.'

'How well do you know Demetriou Smith?'

'I was part of a teenage gang in Cabramatta when I was about fifteen years old. Demetriou was the leader of the gang.'

'Why did you leave the gang, if indeed you did?'

'Many of them joined criminal gangs when they matured. I decided I could do more with my life.' She was still confident, but becoming uncomfortable with the direction of the questioning.

'What was your reaction when you found Demetriou had been accepted as a settler?'

'Horror. I was sure he couldn't be a benign settler. I knew he would have some scheme which would undermine the community.' Tanya explained her contacts with the police and their confirmation of her suspicions regarding Demetriou. Under questioning she told much the same story as David.

The prosecutor had one further question. 'Mrs Bower, you talked about your membership of a teenage gang in Cabramatta.'

'Yes,'

'Can you tell the court why you suddenly left the gang?'

'I came to my senses and decided to make something of my life.'

'How old were you?'

'Fifteen,'

'How old was Demetriou?'

'About eighteen.'

'No further questions.'

Tanya was asked to remain on the stand while the defence questioned her.

'You left the gang because you came to your senses?'

'Yes.'

'Was there an incident that provoked this?'

Before the court case started, Tanya had considered that her teenage relationship with Demetriou might be exposed. Fred probably knew the details, so she had decided, if the question arose, she would have to tell the truth. But she had needed to talk to Mark first, a discussion she started the previous evening:

'Mark, you know about my youth in Cabramatta,' she said quietly.

'Yes,' he said, disinterestedly, continuing to read a business paper.

'With this court case tomorrow some issues may emerge … ' she hesitated, 'I may have to explain some details that I have never told anyone, not even you.'

'Oh?'

'Demetriou and I were lovers.'

She then had his full attention. His reading material was discarded. 'Holy shit! Why didn't you tell me before?' He suddenly thought this was an opportunity to assert his authority over Tanya, but quickly dismissed it. He wasn't an unfair man.

'It wasn't relevant. When we met you knew I wasn't a virgin. I never discussed any previous boyfriends with you or anyone else. We never discussed any of your previous girlfriends either.'

Bitch, he thought. *She knows perfectly well I never had much in the way of previous girlfriends.* He was briefly reminded of their first sexual encounter. 'Why didn't you mention it after Demetriou arrived here as a settler?'

'My mistake, I should have and I'm truly sorry. There are some other issues.'

'Yes?' he said warily.

She explained how she had hotwired cars and acted as Demetriou's driver while he made drug deliveries. She gave him a detailed account of her narrow escape from the police who had come to arrest Demetriou. 'He was convicted and served a three year jail term,' said Tanya.

Mark stared at her, mouth open.

'Aren't you going to say something?'

'What can I say? Anyway that is all in the past now. It makes no difference to our relationship.' Mark knew Tanya had a tough start. A life his sheltered upbringing in the middle class Bower household had not prepared him for. Her revelations added a new dimension to his understanding of that time. He was torn by his admiration for her subsequent escape from her disadvantages and not wanting to hear any more about a past he was powerless to influence.

'We have a good relationship and a successful marriage, but since we are talking, isn't there something you need to tell me?'

'What the hell are you talking about?'

'Virginia Andrews.'

'What has she got to do with anything?'

'You find her attractive.'

'So?' he said uncertainly.

'You're screwing her aren't you?'

'No!' Mark was all of a sudden on the defensive. *How the hell did she work that out?* He had been very discreet. To his irritation, now he was on the back foot and it was no longer about Tanya's misdeeds. He would never admit to the affair. It would be too humiliating and put him in an even worse position with Tanya.

'Bullshit, all those extended visits to Canberra. And when she visited us here you were like a cat on hot bricks.'

'I have not touched her. You are becoming paranoid. You are trying to divert my attention from your previous relationship with Demetriou,' said Mark unconvincingly.

'You need to be straight with me Mark. I have a very difficult day ahead of me tomorrow and I need to know you are telling the truth.'

'I am telling the truth.'

'So you have never slept with her? Not once, ever?'

'No.'

'I would like to believe you, but I saw you together. I'm ready to let sleeping dogs lie, but you need to come clean with me.'

'I have nothing to come clean with you about.'

'Think about it Mark.' Tanya asked calmly. She wanted to believe him, but he held her gaze for only a few seconds before looking away. He was lying, much to her disappointment.

Mark was furious and embarrassed at the turn in the conversation, suddenly having to defend himself. The fact that she was right about the affair made it worse.

Tanya quietly went to their bedroom and locked the door.

Mark dejectedly found his way to the spare room.

'Yes, there was an incident that helped me change my mind.'

'Can you please tell the court about it?'

'Yes, but you have to understand I have never told anyone about this before so it will come as a shock to most people.' Tanya was determined to be honest and upfront, she did not want it dragged out piece by piece.

'Go on.'

'Demetriou and I were lovers.'

There was a gasp of astonishment from the audience.

'That doesn't explain why you left the gang.'

Tanya explained how she had hid in the garage roof.

'Police cars?'

'They had come to arrest Demetriou. He was eventually convicted of drug dealing.'

'And you had no knowledge of Demetriou's activities?'

The prosecutor intervened, 'Objection, Mrs Bower is not on trial here. She has explained why she left the gang.'

'Sustained,' said the judge. 'Any further questions?'

'Nothing further.'

The rest of the hearing consisted of other community members testifying for and against Fred in almost equal numbers.

The prosecutor finally called Fred to the stand. His version of events agreed with the testimonies of David and Tanya.

He was quite calm when he described his role in the community. 'I helped to design and then build many of the houses. They are all environmentally sound, complementing the landscape and atmosphere here,' he said proudly.

'How did you arrive at the design concepts that were eventually adopted?'

'David helped with the specifications. Mark and I always talked in detail with prospective occupants,' and then dismissively, 'with some input from Tanya.'

The prosecutor noted the thinly-veiled hostility towards Tanya.

'You and Demetriou are half-brothers. Why don't you have the same surname?'

'I took my mother's name and he has our mutual father's name.'

'What made you ask Demetriou to join the community?'

'Demetriou has always been in some sort of trouble. Over the years I have helped him extricate himself from many scrapes.'

'Scrapes! He was involved in some terrible crimes—drug dealing, murder, money laundering ...'

'He was never convicted of murder,' said Fred sharply.

'Nevertheless he was convicted of other very serious crimes.'

'He is my brother,' said Fred with the hint of a tear in his eyes.

'Why did you invite him here?'

Fred was silent for a moment. 'He invited himself.'

'But you paid for the construction of his house and all the levies and taxes.'

'Yes.'

'Why?'

'He has no money of his own.'

'Why didn't you tell David about the situation? You hold a position of trust in this community.'

'David would not have accepted him if he had known about his background. Also, Demetriou told me he was an agent for ASIO and I couldn't tell anyone.'

'If you knew he was an ASIO agent why did you pay for everything? Surely ASIO was paying him.'

Fred fidgeted in the witness stand as if he was struggling with something. 'Well?'

'ASIO paid all the costs,' Fred eventually whispered.

'Please repeat that so everyone can hear.'

'ASIO paid all the costs,' repeated Fred more loudly. There were gasps of astonishment from the audience.

'And you still didn't tell David anything, your trusted friend and confidant?'

Fred shook his head.

'Why? You have jeopardised your whole position here.'

'I knew everything was above board here and Demetriou would find nothing. I hoped he would report that to the people at ASIO and then move on. I would have helped the community and hopefully helped Demetriou a bit as well.'

'Why didn't you confide in David?'

'I thought I could do it all on my own. When it was established the place was in the clear there would be no need for anyone else to know.'

'Alright. Did you know of the history between Tanya and Demetriou?'

Fred nodded uneasily.

'Surely you would have realised when Tanya saw Demetriou the game would be up and she would tell David? And that they would look into his criminal history knowing his background?'

'Everything had gone too far by the time I thought of that.' He said dismissively, 'I know nothing of Tanya's contacts anyway.'

'That beggars belief. What is your relationship with Tanya?'

'She is a director here. I suppose she has done some good.' There was no mistaking the hostility in his voice. The audience reacted imperceptibly. Tanya was generally very popular among the people in The Settlement.

'You don't like her.'

Fred remained silent.

'How do you feel about her role here in The Settlement?'

'She behaves inappropriately for a woman.'

'Meaning what exactly?'

'She charges round this place as if she owns it—flying helicopters, taking part in The Academy, galloping round on her horse.'

'This place would not exist if it were not for her contributions both financially and otherwise,' said the surprised prosecutor.

'A man would've done better.'

There was a growl of disapproval from the gallery, resulting in a sharp glance from the judge.

'A man such as you?'

Fred remained silent.

'If you remain silent, I will have to assume that you saw Demetriou's arrival as a chance to somehow diminish the role Tanya plays in the community. Is that the case?'

Fred looked down.

The prosecutor paused to let the information sink in among the jurors. There was a hum of conversation from the gallery.

'Could you please explain what happened on the night Demetriou and Bill McLoughlin tried to plant some explosives in the area where the fuel tanks were to be installed?'

Fred relayed the events of the night.

'Did you know they were going to be there and what they intended to do?'

'No, I have not contacted Demetriou since he left The Settlement,' Fred said firmly.

'I have a statement here, signed by you, that you deliberately fired a warning shot just as Tanya was about to arrest the pair.'

Fred remained silent.

'Well, is this your statement?'

Fred nodded. 'Yes it is.'

'Could you explain your intentions? If the pair had succeeded, the damage to the community would have been extensive.'

Fred flushed angrily. 'That stupid bitch Tanya had taken over again, issuing all the instructions. It was a military operation; she shouldn't have even been there. Mark is responsible for security, he should have been running the operation.'

'So you fired a warning shot allowing your brother to escape.'

'Yes.'

'If your brother had not been involved would you have fired the shot?'

Fred remained silent.

'No further questions.'

The defence had no questions and couldn't wait to get Fred off the stand.

In summing up, the prosecution said that Fred had used his position of privilege in the community to clandestinely introduce Demetriou, an act of family loyalty. 'The suggestion that he acted as he did for the good of the community is an afterthought and should be dismissed. He endangered people's lives, particularly the party that was about to apprehend Demetriou and Bill. If the charges had been successfully laid many members of the rest of the community would also have been put in harm's way. I ask the jury to find him guilty on all charges and that he should be given an appropriate sentence.'

The defence argued that he had been a loyal member of the community for many years and had done a great deal of good in the community. He had perhaps been misguided in helping his brother, but many others would have acted the same way if they had been in his shoes. 'I ask the jury to find him not guilty on any charges; especially since no actual damage was done to anyone.'

While the jury was considering the verdict, Tanya had a brief conversation with David. 'Maybe we should ask Fred what he wants to do. I'm not concerned about the personal comments he made towards me, but his position here is now untenable; and we have other builders. If he opts to leave it may ease the pain and he won't be quite as hostile as he might otherwise be. We will have to come to some arrangement regarding his house, but that shouldn't be difficult.'

David looked at her in astonishment. 'You would offer him that after all he said about you?'

Tanya shrugged. 'I am thinking about The Settlement. Fred's wife might even choose to return here on her own one day. When the Ice Shelf collapses, Bill and Demetriou will be released from jail along with all the other prisoners. The fewer people out there hostile to this community, the better. We can't sentence Fred to imprisonment since we have no prison. He might even be persuaded that what is being suggested is actually his own idea.'

Tanya was genuinely concerned about the future of The Settlement, but she also wanted Fred out of the way. She was still deeply ashamed about her affair with Demetriou; she had risked putting power in Demetriou's hands thus endangering the future of the project. She desperately wanted to hide her indiscretion. Getting Fred out of the way would reduce that risk.

David approached the prosecutor, who then convened a meeting with the judge. Before the jury had concluded their deliberations Fred was approached; he was amazed at the benign nature of the proposal. He was obliged to sign a legal document, drafted by Tanya, acknowledging his guilt on all counts and agreeing never to live in or approach The Settlement again. The document made it clear that the restrictions did not apply to his wife and children and that ownership of their house was transferred forthwith to his wife.

The agreement was published in full in the community newspaper, with most settlers supporting what had been agreed. Tanya hadn't wanted any credit so most people assumed, wrongly, that the judicial process had arrived at the solution. Fred and his family left one night under the watchful supervision of David.

Fred had the grace to say to David prior to leaving, 'Thank you. If it wasn't for you I envisaged being locked up somewhere.'

'Thank Tanya,' he said, trying to keep the anger from his voice. 'It was her idea, despite the unjust things you said about her. She even drafted the agreement you signed.' He was determined somehow to make it up to Tanya.

Fred looked shocked, saying nothing, but climbed into his car and drove off with his family all of whom were crying. Months later, David received a letter from Fred spelling out the details of Tanya's misdeeds as a teenager in Cabramatta. Nothing was left out. David had not known about the drug dealing, but he was not altogether surprised. It was the final paragraph of the letter that shocked him.

"David, you may like to know that the sexual liaison between Tanya and Demetriou continued after Demetriou arrived in The Settlement. Tanya was also responsible for Demetriou's riding accident. It is not surprising she was so keen to be rid of me."

Tanya's not so perfect after all, he thought.

For months he wondered what to do with the letter. *Should I tell Mark?* He concluded that Tanya was more important than anyone to the development of The Settlement, even the honour of his son. A few months later, he burnt it.

Mark was surprised by the arrangements made for Fred. He could see that Tanya had come up with a very good solution. Again he wished he had thought of it himself. He had never stopped hiding a portion of his income from Tanya and investing it secretly. Virginia had accompanied him on one short business trip overseas, where they spent a few days in his Tuscan hideaway. Yet he still longed for more control at The Settlement.

The Bower family decided to establish a number of principles under which justice would be administered based on the acceptance of the first "local trial". They would consult the community to establish what the new laws would be and how they would differ from Australian law. However, Australian law would apply until isolation occurred.

They made it clear at the outset of the consultation that The Settlement would have no jail or police as the resources did not exist to maintain those institutions. Under these circumstances, other punishments would have to be administered for crimes that would normally be the subject of a custodial sentence.

Punishment for a variety of crimes including theft, firearm offences, assault, wilful property damage, and mistreatment of animals would include a combination of the following—naming and shaming; counselling; bans; premise searches. A repeat offence or more serious crime would result in public flogging with a cane. A major offence or repeat offender could see the guilty party expelled from The Settlement. In aggravated circumstances, in the case of rape or murder, the death penalty, by firing squad, could be imposed by the court.

There were several days of discussions in the community hall relating to the laws that would apply when they became isolated. The community was wholly engaged in the process. 'Why are we unable to just keep all the laws we have presently?'

'We have no jail and no police,' answered David, 'and don't propose to invest in either of those institutions.'

'Why?'

'Can you imagine a jail here, especially if someone was being held for a long period of time, for murder or rape for example? It would just hang over the community.'

'We could send them to jail in Australia.'

'We don't know that any jails will exist in Australia. It's possible that when the Ice Shelf collapses all jails will have to be abandoned and inmates released to fend for themselves. Anyway, isolation means isolation. We will not have any contact with the outside world.'

There was silence after the last comment.

After much discussion there was general agreement on the more minor offences. There was some grumbling about the introduction of corporal punishment, but in the end it was agreed that the application of corporal punishment would be exceptional and that processes existed to minimise its use. There was considerable opposition to the introduction of the death penalty for rape and murder.

'Along with most of the Western world we abolished the death penalty years ago. Surely this is a backward step,' argued someone.

Tanya had remained quiet up to that point. 'We will be returning to a more primitive existence,' said Tanya. 'We have military training now for a reason. The possibility exists that we will have to defend ourselves. Other communities may run short of food and try to take what we have by force. Anyway, the court can order the expulsion of anyone found guilty of rape and murder, but I think it should have the option of imposing the death penalty in extreme circumstances.'

'What is meant by extreme circumstances?'

'Let us assume a child was abducted, and murdered by a member of the community. Would anything less than the death penalty be appropriate in those circumstances? We don't want individuals taking the law into their own hands. If we allowed that to happen this community would descend into anarchy. The ability to apply the strictest sanctions is warranted in extreme circumstances.'

'Who would apply the death penalty?'

'Our Academy,' answered Mark. 'It would be their duty to implement any sentence imposed. There are well-established methods of concealing the identity of individuals firing the fatal shots.'

'Expelling people from the community is almost the same as implementing the death penalty.'

'Maybe,' agreed Mark. 'We are here to nurture and protect our own. Anything that threatens us should and will be severely punished. We may not survive otherwise. Currently, in the wider Australian community, when a person is sentenced for a crime he or she commits they are sent away and the wider community remains largely unaffected. That does not apply here. We will be facing people convicted of offences day in, day out. With minor offences we will be able to live with that, but I don't think anyone would be willing to associate on a daily basis with a person convicted of a major offence. Under those circumstances, people may take the law into their own hands.'

'Expelled people might hold a grudge and try to take revenge.'

'Possibly, yes,' agreed Mark, 'but we can't execute everyone. We will be strong enough to take our chances in that regard.'

CHAPTER FOURTEEN
The Pool

2017 TO 2021

Tanya had thought she would be the main contact between The Settlement and The Bandstand. But very quickly, she realised David had made it his business to run the relationship. She didn't really mind, but was curious about the reason and sooner or later she knew he would come and tell her. Tanya thought about how the situation would change if David ever found out about her indiscretion with Demetriou, remembering how he had briefly turned on her during the Harold debacle.

'I still think others at The Bandstand would have known about Demetriou and Bill's raid. Keep your eyes and ears open to see if someone lets anything slip. I'm sure they are all hoping we will let sleeping dogs lie,' said Tanya.

David privately thought Tanya was flogging a dead horse. With Bill and Demetriou out of the way, any individual's ill will would have long since dissipated.

~෨

Tanya knew all was not well between Chloe and David. Chloe had never really accepted the move to the mountains and spent far too much time in Sydney. However, she was dedicated to the stables and the riding school and was keen to instill in the youth a sense of adventure as well as the ability to look after oneself or a group without outside assistance. She had already established a difficult cross country course, but it was confined within the boundaries of the larger settlement. Among her pupils, Chloe had always had the record time for completing the course, but there were two young boys in their mid-teens who were now challenging her.

'I have been speaking to Mark and, as an adjunct to the military training, I have agreed to take some of the better riders out of The Settlement for a week on horseback,' she told Tanya. 'Just ten of them from here and maybe some from The Bandstand plus me. They're going to do everything themselves.'

'Shouldn't you have one other adult with you, in case of an accident? Imagine a kid with a broken leg and you are out of mobile range. How would you handle that? Anyway, are you comfortable with such an expedition? I thought you hated the bush?'

'I actually quite like the bush, in small doses,' said Chloe quietly. 'I asked Mark to come, but he is too busy. Maybe you could come with us.'

'I could, but who would fly the helicopter if it were needed?'

'When Australia was colonised they didn't have helicopters,' responded Chloe acerbically.

Tanya grinned, 'Touché. Okay, I'll come with you. I'm actually owed a very large amount of holidays.' But Tanya never did anything without consideration. *At the least, I'll find out what's going on in Chloe's life.*

There were seven teenage boys and seven teenage girls, plus the two adults. The teenagers had planned everything—the route, each meal, the quantity of horse food they would carry, and where they would camp. The horses would have to be tied up at night since there were no paddocks, so they planned appropriate watches through each night.

'We have fourteen teenagers, all with their hormones raging. What do you think we should do about that?' asked Tanya before they set off.

'Dunno, it is so long since I had to deal with anything like that.'

'I have some condoms and will talk to each girl individually. I don't want to encourage them to do anything they wouldn't be doing anyway, but we don't want any unwanted pregnancies. Some of the parents will have dealt with this issue but not all.'

When Tanya spoke to each girl, two of them were quite open and actually showed her the condoms included in their luggage. Three were grateful for the discussion and took the condoms on offer. The last two were just embarrassed.

'I know this is a sensitive and personal subject,' said Tanya, 'but if you need any advice please come to me. We will all be very close for a week and will learn a lot about each other.'

There was a great send off from The Settlement. Travelling north, each participant rode one horse and led another, carrying their own food, horse food, and cooking utensils. In addition, each person carried their own clothing and toiletries and was provided with a cape that could be made into a two man tent when buttoned together with another. Chloe had brought a large amount of first aid equipment to deal with every possible eventuality. Tanya had brought her own 30.06 and her twelve bore shotgun. Two of the boys were each allowed to carry a 30.06.

Before they set off, Tanya had insisted that the three of them carrying firearms had a brief inspection, making sure each weapon was clean and that none of them was loaded. Tanya took the first inspection and thereafter they took it in turns, morning and evening. The boys enjoyed being treated as adults. Four of the group were from The Bandstand, so the route was planned to drop them off on the way home.

The first day was slow, but uneventful. Chloe and Tanya just let everyone get on with things and deliberately gave little advice; eventually, one of the older boys, Roger, took charge. After they had stopped for the night, some people were directed to collect firewood, some were put in charge of the meal, others tended the horses. Deciding who was to share each tent took some time. Neither Chloe nor Tanya checked on who was sharing with whom.

'I am sure it will change over the week,' said Chloe in an aside to Tanya.

Tanya checked that all the horses were correctly tethered. One camper had to come back and learn how to tie the beast up properly.

'If a horse gets loose and canters off, the others will become restless and we will end up losing half of them. They might also injure themselves if they escape.'

'Thanks, I was coming back to check, but there just seems to be so much to do.'

'Simple rule,' said Tanya, 'horses first, people second.'

The girls had taken charge of the meal and soon produced something simple and tasty. Gradually, the relationships sorted themselves out; some people did more than was expected of them and some less. There was a lot of chatter but by nine o'clock most of the group had retired.

'Tanya and I will take the first watch,' said Chloe. 'Two hours.' They chatted about inconsequential things, but it was noticeable that Chloe avoided any discussion related to The Settlement.

I will get to that over the next few days, thought Tanya.

At eleven, two girls emerged sleepily from their tent. Tanya went around the horses with them making sure they were all quiet.

'Keep a small fire going,' she advised, 'it helps in the morning. It will also keep dingoes away. I have hung all the spare food up in the trees so they will not be able to reach it, but they may sniff around. Don't under any circumstances feed any animals.'

Chloe was asleep when Tanya crept into her own sleeping bag.

The last watch woke the camp up at five, just before dawn. 'Eat well,' urged Chloe. 'There will just be sandwiches on the move.'

They packed up the camp. By nine o'clock they were all ready to move. Tanya and Roger took a turn around the site making certain the fire was out and buried and there were no signs of rubbish anywhere.

They made better progress the next day and by three o'clock they had arrived at the next campsite. They all stood in a semi-circle to admire the spectacle; a spray of water creating a twenty foot waterfall flowing into a deep, beautifully clear pool. There was a grassy bank where they were standing and sheer rock walls on the other side.

Chloe said, 'Horses first ...'

'People next,' chorused the group.

Tanya watered and fed her horse and found a spot near the pool to dump her and Chloe's equipment. She then stripped everything off and stepped gingerly into the pool as if she was completely alone. Her nipples puckered in the cold water as she splashed a little water onto herself. As the boys' eyes almost stood out on stalks, Tanya slipped into the water, swam across the pool and back, and yelled, 'What are you all waiting for? It's beautiful.'

She ran to where her clothes were, picked up her underwear and a piece of soap, sat on a rock in the pool and proceeded to wash herself and her clothing. She made no attempt to cover herself. She knew she was beautiful, with her slim body and long legs culminating in the small dark patch between them. She hoped if they all followed her example then they would soon ignore each other's nakedness and just see each other as people. Gradually the group followed her lead, first Chloe and then the rest of them. One or two thought they would swim in their underwear, but as soon as they did there was a cry of 'off, off, off.' Within ten minutes, the pool was a boiling, splashing, yelling place of teenage fun.

Tanya pulled on her calf-length riding boots, hung her now clean underwear on a nearby bush, and went to check on the horses, quietly grazing. She checked each one of the thirty-two horses. With the help of two of the now unselfconscious but still naked girls, she looked at the hooves of every horse, picking their feet up and getting rid of the small stones with a hoof-pick she had in her baggage. As she was about to return to the pool, she saw five Aboriginal people standing in the shade, dressed in animal skins; two men and three women. They had obviously been there for a while but had only just decided to show themselves. Tanya was quite calm, although the girls drew a deep breath.

'Hello,' said Tanya, uncertainly.

There was a brief acknowledgment from the older man, who then said something to the youngest member of the group in his own language.

'He say this is sacred site,' said the young girl, translating.

'Oh, we didn't know, it didn't look as if anyone had been here for many years.'

The man said something urgently, waving his hand at the naked figure of Tanya.

The girl translated, 'He says you do sacred site much honour by swimming naked first in the pool and then making all your children swim after you. Much honour.'

Tanya was expecting to be told they would have to move. 'Oh, thank you. It is a very beautiful place.' Tanya was uncertain what to do next but she asked the group if they would like to join them.

The Aboriginal group had a brief discussion, one went behind a bush and appeared with two wallabies and a possum, apparently their next meal. They made it clear they would eat their own food but would like to be part of the group.

Tanya retrieved her now dry underwear from the bush and put on a tee shirt.

The Aborigines skinned the creatures they had hunted, building a big fire; pieces of wallaby and possum were placed on the coals once the fire had died down. In the meantime, the riders had started to prepare their own meal with both groups watching each other curiously. Chloe offered the Aboriginal group some of the food they had cooked; hesitantly they took some lamb chops and the young girl said, rubbing her stomach. 'This meat is okay. The rest of your food makes us ill.'

They cut off small pieces of wallaby and handed it around. The boys ate it with relish; some of the girls were a bit tentative.

'Just think of it as Skippy,' said one of the boys unkindly.

'You had better make the most of it,' said Rachel, one of the older girls, who had now taken charge of the catering and food supplies. 'We have no more meat after this and the rest of the rations will have to survive this heat.'

There was a brief discussion among the Aboriginal group. 'If you come with us tomorrow we can show you two things, a place that no white people have ever visited and also somewhere where you can hunt birds, wallabies, and maybe goanna. That is our special place,' the young girl translated, now much more confidently. After dinner, some of the riders started to go to bed.

'Wait,' the leader said firmly, 'we have something to show you.' They waited for half an hour.

'This is why we have come here at this time,' the young girl translated. 'The moon will rise soon.' She pointed to a sharp pinnacle now clearly visible in the night sky. 'Our ancestors told us we should wait for a young white woman who would cleanse the pool by swimming around it, naked, and now these predictions have been answered,' she said indicating Tanya. They waited a few more minutes and a shaft of light from the moon lit up the centre of the pool. The Aborigines all knelt in front of Tanya, performing a dance, and then asked her to go to the pool which was only a few metres away.

'He wants you to go into the pool again, and stand on that rock in the middle,' the girl translated.

'This is weird,' said Roger, but Tanya did not hesitate. Without a word she stripped all her clothes off, waded into the now chilly pool, swam to the rock, and climbed it facing the group. As she stood up the light from the moon emerged from behind the pinnacle of rock and gradually lit up her naked beauty from head to foot. She stood there, in silence, for ten minutes. Then she dove in, swam around the pool twice, and then hopped out of the water.

The Aboriginal man's speech was translated. 'Our ancestors predicted a female god, standing naked on the rock in the moonlight, an older woman, and the beautiful young people, all white. We have come here now for seven years waiting for this to occur and now it has.'

The man hesitated for half a minute and the girl continued, 'There is a second prediction. Big waters will rise, from where we do not know, but there will be hunger among all the people. Our ancestors have told us to protect you "White Goddess" and all your children. We will return every year to renew this belief.'

There was absolute silence for a further ten minutes. All the riders, of course, knew and understood the science behind The Settlement, but here was an outsider, who could not possibly know or understand it, making precisely the same prediction.

Tanya spoke slowly, so the young girl could translate. 'Some seven years ago, my husband's father, called all the family together and made the prediction you have now talked about. He then found the place we call The Settlement, two days' ride from here.'

'The place with the big fence,' said the Aboriginal man. Tanya nodded.

'We have made it self-sufficient, so when the big waters rise we can block it off and hopefully survive until all is settled again, which may take many years.'

'Our ancestors have told us we are to help you survive and then our traditional lands will be returned to us, so that we can look after them. The new community that will emerge will be a mix of the old and the new. We will not let the country be destroyed like it is being destroyed now,' said the Aboriginal man firmly, translated by the young girl.

Tanya got up and embraced him. 'Let's declare ourselves blood relations.' She cut her palm with a sharp knife and the man did the same. They mixed the blood, hand to hand.

'What about AIDS?' asked the ever-practical Chloe.

'We don't have AIDS in our community and these people have almost no contact with the so-called civilised community, so the chances of any of us contracting aids is about zero. However, this is voluntary.' Soon everyone had mixed the blood, including the somewhat reluctant Chloe.

The Aborigines settled around the fire as the rest of the party went to bed.

'There is no need to run the watch routine tonight,' said Chloe. 'Our new friends will make sure no horses escape.'

Tanya and Chloe were far too animated to retire so they just sat by the fire and chatted. 'That business with the light striking me while I was standing starkers on that rock … '

'Yes,' said a rather doubtful Chloe.

'That was no accident.'

'Oh,' said a very surprised Chloe.

'You see that pinnacle in the sky over there.'

'Yes.'

'Well, a few minutes after I stood on the rock, the moonlight shone directly on me and the rock. I bet, due to planet movement, this particular event can only happen annually. They must somehow have got all the maths right even if they can't explain it in precisely those terms. Our Aboriginal friend knew exactly what he was doing.'

'Good heavens. You don't really believe in all this mumbo jumbo surely?'

'Well yes, I do. He reached the same conclusions that David and I, using all the science available to us, quite separately arrived at. It is quite extraordinary, it actually backs up our beliefs and from a source we had no knowledge of.' After a thoughtful silence, Tanya said gently, 'You have never really believed in what we have been doing in the Blue Mountains, have you? It must be very difficult for you. I have often wondered how you cope, with David having obviously found his life's work.'

'I have never discussed this with anyone else, but I feel I can tell you now. This whole business has upset me, has destroyed my world, if you like. I was more than happy with our life and I have a great deal of difficulty believing in the research. I know of nobody else who believes it. David and I spent months looking for a place and we came up with blanks, much to my relief. I thought the whole thing would just go away. Then you and David found The Settlement and within months it was all a terrible reality,'

Chloe paused, gathering her thoughts. 'I met this fellow at the golf club, Alan. It took a few months, but we eventually became lovers. He had a flat in Manly and we used to meet there every two weeks or so.' Chloe's face was lit by the light of the moon, now high in the sky. She looked happy, contented for a moment. 'The relationship was mainly based on sex. And it was exquisite, delicious. He made no emotional demands on me and vice versa. Agreeing a date and time to meet was the easiest thing in the world. He had a wife and four kids and I had you lot. We discussed our situation at length on several occasions, neither of us wanted to change anything.' Chloe wiped away a tear.

Tanya sat quietly. She had always wondered whether there were greater depths to her mother-in-law. 'You keep saying "had", as if it was all in the past.'

Chloe wiped away another tear. 'He was killed in a car accident three years ago, on his way to see me. I didn't go to the funeral but spent many days in mourning; I still miss him.'

Tanya thought there was much more to Chloe's feelings than just sex.

'Most unexpectedly Alan left me the flat. Apparently he had changed his will about a year before he died, but he never mentioned it to me. So I now have a flat in Manly and David knows nothing about it.'

There was another reflective silence.

'I have had other lovers since,' offered Chloe. 'One was looking for a mother substitute and another thought he could two-time me. I put a stop to all of that double quick. There is someone in the wings at the moment though. I don't rush these things.'

'Does David know anything about this?'

'Not really. He is in love with The Settlement and I am expected just to play second fiddle. We had a real home, which he sold.' She laughed mirthlessly. 'I spent the day with Alan while he was busy selling it. He may now think of The Settlement as his home, but it certainly isn't mine. The nearest thing to a home for me is the flat in Manly. If he ever thinks about it, he must wonder about my absences.'

They watched the fire, enjoying each other's company.

'I have never told a soul about this, not a soul,' said Chloe. 'Thank you for listening to me. I have never felt any guilt, much to my surprise.' She squeezed Tanya's arm.

The Aborigines waited patiently while the camp was struck and packed. They would just have picked up their few possessions and left, having buried the fire. Eventually, the caravan started moving at eight thirty, a good half hour earlier than the day before.

The Aboriginal man came with the young girl. 'Call me Derain.'

Tanya had heard the word before, it meant "of the mountains".

The group rode on with Derain, on foot, leading.

They appeared to be approaching a sheer rock face, became more and more overwhelming with no apparent exit. Derain said nothing, continuing confidently on his way. Although the group had started to trust the Aborigines, there were some uneasy glances.

Derain eventually stopped, his words, translated by the girl. 'Everyone will stop here, and unsaddle the horses. You can come with me,' he said, indicating Tanya. 'I will show you. Bring your two horses.'

They led the two horses, disappearing into some thick bush. Within five minutes, they were on a very narrow path with a steep drop on one side and sheer rock walls on the other. Tanya tried not to look down. The horses somehow understood and walked unconcernedly along the path, following Derain. After about a kilometre, the path broadened and they emerged into a glade. It was an earthly paradise, with tall grasses and a stream running through. There were glimpses of kangaroos and wallabies and at the far extent there was a small settlement, with a few untidy looking huts made with rough sticks covered with grass and animal skins. A group of about twenty Aborigines crowded around shyly while Derain made a short speech. They all bowed down before performing some sort of ritual dance.

This must be something to do with the White Goddess, she thought. 'What about the others?' asked Tanya nervously, indicating the way they had come.

Derain waved her concerns away. 'Soon, soon,' he said smiling.

He showed her where her group could camp, then Derain and many from the Aboriginal village disappeared. An hour later, much to Tanya's relief, Roger and Rachel arrived leading their horses. Then, at ten minute intervals, the rest of the group arrived, helped by the people from the village. They all gradually assembled, Chloe bringing up the rear.

Derain came over and made a short, translated speech. 'We must bring you here first as the White Goddess. Then we bring all the others slowly so as not to frighten them or the horses. If you want meat, the boys with rifles can go with some of the people from the village; to find kangaroos, wallabies, even goannas.'

The group spent an untroubled three days in the village. There was lots of swimming naked in the streams. Two of the boys hunted with their compatriots and there was much amusement when the white boys attempted to use the heavy hunting boomerang, missing by metres, not even frightening intended prey.

The two girls who had been embarrassed in the face of Tanya's safe sex speech shyly approached her. 'Do you still have some condoms?'

Tanya nodded, fished in her luggage and handed over some packs. Looking them in the eye, she said. 'Don't be forced into anything you're not sure of.'

They rushed off, giggling.

During the visit Tanya had questioned Derain why no white people had ever been to their village before. 'You can see it's too difficult, people must have guide to come here,' he had answered. She was unable to get any more out of him than that.

After three days, Tanya sought Chloe out as she was sunbathing naked on a flat rock. By now, everyone was quite unconcerned about their lack of dress.

'We need to think about finding our way back. We said we would be about a week. I don't want anyone to be getting worried.'

'I had really lost all sense of time. I could happily spend another week here.'

'Is this the Sydney girl speaking?'

Chloe laughed.

'I'll talk to Derain, but one of us could go ahead to tell them we are on our way and then the rest follow at a more leisurely pace,' said Tanya.

'Okay, but to your original point, if anyone gets hurt what do we do?'

Tanya returned in ten minutes. 'They'll send somebody, today, so we can pack up at leisure and leave tomorrow. Derain will show us a way that takes three days to get to The Bandstand.'

When they eventually left the village at midday the following day, Chloe took stock of her charges. The transformation was almost complete. From the shy, uncertain group who had left a week earlier, she now had a group confident in their bush craft, able to cook and camp, confident in their sexuality, and more certain of their relationships with adults.

They were all laughing and joking and said to their Aboriginal counterparts. 'Come and see us at The Settlement and we will we back next year when the White Goddess has to stand on the rock again in the moonlight.'

Derain took them a different way with another steep, narrow footpath where they all had to dismount.

'Derain says, to leave a ten minute gap between groups in case anyone gets into trouble,' Tanya told the group. Derain and the translator alone remained to assist as they negotiated the difficult descent from the village.

From various vantage points they were able to admire the endless vista of the pristine forests, always washed with the blue tinge from the eucalypt oil. There was the occasional landmark, mainly of sheer, golden brown rock faces. Then they rode down into the bush again, where the visibility was down to a few metres with the sunlight peering uncertainly through the leaf canopy.

They camped for the next two nights. On the second night, the boys shot two kangaroos. Derain watched them butcher the prey for a few minutes. Satisfied, he signalled to Chloe to come with him.

They stopped in a clearing, Derain showed Chloe a large black snake sunbathing in the last light of the day. Chloe tried to withdraw, but Derain held her arm, preventing her from moving. They stood still and silent, watching the animal for ten minutes. Chloe thought they were leaving, but Derain held her by the arm and brought her closer. He picked up a large stick and lifted the snake up with it, much to Chloe's consternation. He showed her the various markings before gently putting the animal on the ground where it slithered away.

'Snake, more frighten of you,' he said.

Chloe was still quite frightened, but her fear was not as great as before.

On the evening of the third day, a jubilant but tired group arrived at The Bandstand, full of stories of their adventures, including detailed stories of the White Goddess and the Aboriginal village. Tanya was relieved there was no sign of David.

Tanya made sure she sat next to Caroline during the evening meal, asking if they had received the message about their delay.

'Yes,' she said noncommittally. 'As soon as we received it David phoned The Settlement to let them know. He left this morning.' She flushed slightly, and went on to more mundane subjects.

Tanya's suspicions were confirmed. It was apparent David and Caroline had become an item. She hoped he would deal with the issue sensitively.

Tanya gave Derain a key to both the western and eastern gates of The Settlement. 'You may come and go whenever you wish.'

'And you will come to the sacred pool in the next year for the celebration of the White Goddess?' he asked through the translator.

'Of course.'

They embraced.

~~~

The children invited the community to a presentation on their trip within days of returning home. There was immense curiosity, which grew as the participants told their various stories to parents and friends.

The photographic display began by showcasing a naked image of Tanya standing on a rock in the moonlight. There was an immediate intake of breath and some fidgeting, but nobody left the room.

After the presentation, one woman yelled out, 'Pornography! Nothing but pornography.'

A few voices in the room agreed.

Chloe and Tanya kept silent.

Roger and Rachel continued with their presentation. 'We learnt many things during this trip,' said Roger. 'Most importantly, the Aboriginal people we met at the pool have the same vision as we do regarding the collapse of the Ice Shelf and the rising water levels. They explained it all in terms of what their ancestors had told them would happen. Interestingly, enough they have been visiting the sacred pool for seven years. They predicted our arrival at the site, it was part of their vision. They asked Tanya to swim to the rock you saw in the photo. Tanya decided, without being asked, to strip off, just as their ancestors had predicted, The naked White Goddess would stand on the rock bathed in moonlight. Within a few minutes, a beam of light appeared from behind a pinnacle and surrounded Tanya. We all feel we witnessed a very significant event.' He hesitated, 'even a revelation. Also, we now have an approximate date for the projected collapse of the Ice Shelf.'

'What is the date?' someone asked.

'It appears to be 2025, or maybe a year later, possibly during the ritual with the White Goddess at the pool.'

'Did Derain have sexual intercourse with the White Goddess?' asked an anonymous voice from the back of the hall. There was a deathly hush, some people in the community were truly shocked by the naked pictures of Tanya and the same question was also on their minds.

There was a spontaneous shout of 'No!' from all those on the trip.

'Did the Aboriginal people have sexual intercourse with any of the participants on the trip?'

Again a spontaneous and resounding chorus of, 'No!'
~~~

There was a short silence.

'We learnt other things on the trip too,' said Rachel, continuing. 'Firstly, not to be ashamed of our bodies. When we were in camp everyone walked around naked if they felt like it. We also learnt many things about camping in a hostile environment, preparing and maintaining the camp, and clearing away our presence before we left.'

The audience was still discomforted by the talk about nudity. People asked whether they could visit the village without the help of the locals.

'No,' replied Tanya. 'They would have to escort us in. It is difficult to find and access. We were the first whites ever to have been to the village.'

'Had they ever see white people before?'

'Yes, some of them spoke English,' replied Rachel.

Chloe spoke up, 'It seems there are some outstanding questions which could best be answered privately. I will be available to answer as will Tanya or any of the participants.'

The meeting broke up, but Chloe and then Tanya were assailed with questions.

One woman approached Tanya, saying, 'Thank you for reinforcing the safe sex message with my daughter. I don't know, and don't want to know, whether she uses the information or not.'

'She showed me the condoms you had given her. The last thing we needed from the trip was unwanted pregnancies,' said Tanya.

Another very nervous woman said, 'If I had known you were going to hand out condoms, I would have prevented her from going at all.'

'I didn't want to be a policeman on the trip and I didn't want to be responsible for any unwanted pregnancies, so I made certain that all the girls had some advice,' said Tanya evenly. 'At this age they all have hormones bouncing around in their bodies and I had no knowledge of what sexual education each of the participants had been given. When I was their age I was given no advice, so experimentation was the only option. It was just a question of luck that it all turned out alright. What sexual instruction have you given your daughter?'

'Well, nothing, we were just wondering what to do,' said the woman uncertainly.

'It is often better to have a third party give the instruction, with the parents providing moral guidance.'

'Could you do that?'

'Certainly, me or the doctor.'

'I would rather have a woman give that sort of instruction to my daughter.'

'I think that cleared the air a bit, it was right to have a completely open discussion. It will make participation in future trips easier,' said Chloe.

'It looks as if I will be giving sex education lessons to all the young girls in The Settlement,' said Tanya.

'Rather you than me.'

The excitement of the trip died down after a few weeks. The naked image of Tanya created a barrier between her and some members of the community, although many people still came to her for advice.

As The Settlement developed, Tanya persuaded David to sell many of the operations that sustained the community to individual settlers. 'The Bowers can't own everything, it makes us and the whole community very vulnerable. Funds we receive in this way can be used for further development and to make us more secure.'

'What do you have in mind?'

'Well, we could flog the cattle herd off now to the family who run it, the same with the sheep. We could encourage someone to set up a weaving shop and someone else to make clothes and so on. We should encourage business growth and issue licences so we have some ability to help and indeed impose sanctions in the rare cases where that may be necessary. At first they will have to abide by Australian regulations, but once the Ice Shelf collapses our licence will be the only one that has any validity. We could even sell the hospital,' said Tanya.

'How will all this be funded?'

'I have applied for a banking licence. There has been a bit of eggshell dancing on the part of Government, they still regard us with suspicion, but it should be granted shortly. So all the transactions should be through The Settlement bank.'

'Who will own the bank?'

'The family, there is no other option. But everything else should be owned by outsiders. Appropriate rents should be paid to The Settlement Pty Ltd for use of Settlement property.'

'Would the shareholders remain in the family?'

Yes, for the moment that makes the most sense. As things develop, it may have to change. Maybe when the next generation takes over,' said Tanya carefully.

'What about currency after the collapse?'

'When we are completely isolated, most of the transactions will be electronic. Joe has the capacity to build computers and maintain a suitable system. In time, we may have to print our own currency.'

At the regular board meetings, the board members agreed to an orderly sell-off of the operations previously run by the company. As Tanya had suggested, applications for licences for new businesses were encouraged.

'We need to ensure we are not unwittingly creating monopolies,' Mark suggested. 'If we are to sell the dairy herd, for example, it may need to be sold to two different people.'

'Are we going to have some sort of democracy?' ventured Patricia.

'What do you think?' asked David.

'Well, in time it would mean people other than current shareholders in the company would be part of this board. Our cosy board meetings would certainly take on a different flavour.'

David looked uncomfortable.

'At present that would be difficult,' said Tanya, supporting David, 'as almost all development funds have come from the family. We don't want other people muscling in.'

'There are something like one hundred houses here, and the funds for building them were provided by individuals. Those people are now being asked to invest further with the sell-off of assets belonging to the company. This is all very good for The Settlement and will make us much stronger, but sooner or later those people will want a say in how this place is run,' responded Patricia firmly.

There was a thoughtful silence around the room.

'I don't think we are quite ready for a one adult, one vote system at present,' said Mark. 'There is still a lot of uncertainty and possibly a need to act very quickly when the Ice Shelf collapses. Anyway, what you say makes sense Patricia. How about dividing The Settlement into wards of, say, twenty houses, where we can talk to the residents and generally understand their feelings and community concerns? Each ward would be the responsibility of one of us.'

'How would that work?' asked David.

'I would have a regular, say monthly meeting with all the adult residents in my ward. Any issues would be brought back to the board. I could personally visit anyone who didn't attend to unearth any concerns. It would provide our first formal consultation process.'

David said defensively. 'There is plenty of consultation now. I walk round the community on a daily basis and talk to everyone.'

'We all do that, but the community has grown. I think what Mark has suggested is a good step in the right direction. As the community becomes more confident we are going to have to involve more people in the decision-making process at a much higher level,' said Joe.

'I am seen as the leader in this place, so I don't think it is appropriate for me to be a ward representative. I will continue to do as I have always done.' Instinctively he felt uncomfortable with the possible democratisation. *The family have put up all the funds*, he thought. *Outsiders will not have the same sensitivity when handling individual situations.*

'I really don't think I can take on any more responsibilities, with my charitable work in Sydney and the horses, so please count me out,' said Chloe. Secretly, she wanted no more involvement than she already had with the Settlement.

Mark continued, 'Okay, we can divide the community into wards of twenty-five houses each. That's me, Tanya, Joe, and Patricia each with the responsibility for a ward. Dad, you have an intimate knowledge of all the people in the community, perhaps you could have a first pass at allocating the four of us to individual wards.'

'I will probably just do that on the basis of geography and then we can adjust some of the allocations where we think it is necessary,' he responded unenthusiastically.

Patricia had noticed her father's reticence, and said to him afterwards, with her arm around his shoulders, 'I know this is difficult for you, but in the end this place will have to be run on democratic lines to survive.'

He said nothing but reflected on one of his conversations with Chloe in the very early days where she had thought he wanted to be some sort of dictator. *She was right*, he thought. *I will always find it difficult to have anyone but the family in charge here.*

Mark knew bush survival would be an essential part of Academy training. While the trip to the pool had given people some idea of the challenges in the bush, he thought something more rigorous was needed. He saw the introduction of Derain into the community as a heaven-sent opportunity to hone the bush skills of all Academy trainees.

'I take a few people into the bush for a few days at a time,' said Derain, through his translator, once he heard Mark's idea.

'People need to be able to survive in small groups or on their own,' said Mark.

'Must understand bush first, otherwise will die. I will look after. In one year, or two, all will be very good in bush.'

David was concerned about the effect Derain and his people might have on two families with an Aboriginal heritage recently arrived at The Settlement. They had attended the presentation on Chloe's bush trip, but had made no comment.

'How do you feel about our contact with Derain and his people?' David asked Tony Dyson, the head of one of the families.

'Our families lost contact with our tribal cousins long ago and gradually adopted the values and lifestyle of the settlers. Although we have a few words from our Aboriginal ancestors, there was no common language, so we would be unlikely to be able to hold a conversation with Derain and his people in their own language.'

'What about Derain's vision?'

'We adopted the Christian faith many decades ago and no longer believe in ancestor worship. But we are from the city, so anything Derain can teach us about bush survival is most welcome.'

Derain's reaction, through an interpreter was, 'These people went away from their roots. Maybe we can help them find them again.'

CHAPTER FIFTEEN

David and Caroline

Tanya wondered what, if anything, she should say to David about his now obvious—to her at least—relationship with Caroline. She certainly would not have worried about any of the other residents in The Settlement, but David's contribution to the continuing development was critical. Especially now they had a clear deadline.

She was at the stables tending one of the horses with a loose shoe. Roger and Rachel were helping. After showing them how to heat the shoe and mould its shape, she cooled it down and, using nails, fixed it to the hoof. Seeing David nearby, Tanya handed over the equipment to the children and said, 'Finish it off and when you have done that come and show me.'

David and Tanya talked about mundane things when, uncharacteristically, David blurted out. 'I need to talk to you. You probably know enough about Chloe to have guessed that all is not well there.'

Tanya said nothing.

'But there is a further complication now … '

'Caroline,' said Tanya quietly.

'How the hell did you know that?' asked a perplexed David.

Tanya shrugged.

'I'm not sure what Chloe gets up to in Sydney, but she has indicated she is not happy here,' said David.

'So what can you do about it?'

'I don't know. And there is the complication of Caroline,' said David.

'I was relieved to see you made yourself scarce before we arrived at The Bandstand, after our trip. Chloe would have worked it out if you had stayed.'

'I don't know how you realised. You haven't even seen us together.'

'Look,' said Tanya firmly. 'You are the driving force behind The Settlement.'

'And you.'

Tanya held up her hand. 'Hear me out. You need to make up your mind whether you want to see this thing through. There may be another seven years before the Ice Shelf comes crashing down. That is much bigger than your relationship with Chloe or Caroline. Decide what you really want and we can work out a plan, and I can certainly help.'

'Tanya, since we are having this rather personal discussion I will tell you that I had a letter from Fred, after he left. He told me about you and Demetriou, while he was resident here. I burnt the letter, but do you have anything to tell me?'

Tanya's gut tightened. She was afraid of losing his respect. She briefly considered denial, but rejected it. She told David the truth.

'It's all quite true and I am utterly ashamed of what happened. It only happened once, which makes it no better, but I was infatuated with him as a teenager and I relived that in a moment of madness. I realised quickly all he was after was to destroy me.' She also explained she had initiated the reckless dash through the trees which had resulted in Demetriou's accident.

'Fred's letter implied the liaison continued for some time,' said David.

Tanya shook her head, 'No, just once. Fred either deliberately extended the truth or Demetriou lied.'

David was always inclined to believe the best in people. He could hear her shame and believed she was telling the truth.

'The worst thing,' continued Tanya, shamefaced, 'was that my actions put the future of the whole Settlement in jeopardy. I still have sleepless nights when I think about it.'

'Consider the matter closed, as I said the letter was burnt and I have told nobody.'

Tanya recovered her composure, 'Returning to the question of Caroline, you sort out your feelings and then I can help you. I don't want you to declare for Caroline and then find you have been cuntstruck and want to unravel everything.'

David looked shocked. 'Some of the expressions you use … '

'Only when they are appropriate.' She put her arm around him, saying more gently, 'We have worked well together. Neither of us could have brought this thing to where it is without the other. You are essential to its continuing development. Please recognise that. If Chloe gets really pissed off, it may raise the question of ownership of The Settlement. We can't afford to pay her out.'

David looked shocked, 'I don't think it will come to that. She doesn't want to cut herself off from you all. I can't see it happening, but I'll bear it in mind.'

'Mark and I are going to Sydney in a day or two and will not be able to return next weekend. Let's chat again then. Also we mustn't forget about potential enemies at The Bandstand.'

David shook his head, 'They all seem to be onside. And you are a hero over there after fixing their finances.'

She gave him a daughterly kiss on the cheek and went off to examine the handiwork of her two protégées. She was relieved that her indiscretion had not affected their relationship.

David paid regular visits to The Bandstand and was always greeted in a straightforward and open way by Caroline. He helped her with the business and they found, with his ministrations and her energy, they were making considerable progress. Their liaison was now accepted among the people there, so there were no questions when they retired to her cottage. David was enthralled with their lovemaking and the same applied to Caroline. She asked no more of David than he was able to give. From her point of view, the current arrangements suited her very well. She was in no hurry for further complications. It suited David very well too.

So he decided to try and speak with Chloe. It took a month before they were able to have a sensible discussion; either he was at The Bandstand or she was on one of her unexplained visits to Sydney. When Tanya tried to broach the subject he just waved her away.

Chloe had now had three dates with her latest friend, Clark, in the flat. So far, it seemed similar to the relationship she had with Alan, having made sure all he wanted was regular sex. Otherwise, he seemed to have a stable relationship with his wife and three children. They met once a week. Chloe was in charge of the flat, so she had the keys.

David and Chloe were having a quiet dinner in their cottage when David asked, 'I know we've been here seven years, but I've never asked you this before, although I think I know the answer. Is this what you want?'

Chloe didn't speak for a number of minutes. She was tempted to fling the dinner in his face. 'Yes, you know the answer,' she said evenly. 'While I understand the science and I can see you are succeeding, I really play no role here at all. You could do without me. Someone else could manage the horses just as well as I do. This is your life's work and I am irrelevant. We never make love anymore.' She desperately wanted to cry.

'What do you spend all your time doing in Sydney?'

She looked at him wonderingly. 'What would you do in my place? I've had a couple of lovers and that tends to occupy my time. I still spend time on my charities; otherwise I spend time here.' She was amazed at how civilised they were being. If there had been any emotion left in the relationship there would have been plates flying by now.

'How long has this been going on?'

'Oh, since before we moved here, six years or so.'

It was David's turn to be surprised. 'Six years?'

She nodded. And, much to his surprise, she held his hand. 'We had so much and then you went and destroyed it all. I understand the logic, but I am not engaged in it and never will be.'

'If you understand the science surely you realise we couldn't have done anything differently.'

'None of my friends are taking any notice of this threat. I think we will have sacrificed the last fifteen or twenty years of our lives, all for nothing.'

'The threat is absolutely real, I promise you that. Look at Tanya and Mark. They are smart and wealthy. Would they have made all the sacrifices they have made if they didn't truly believe they had to do so. She and Mark could easily have ignored me and done all the things the very wealthy do, like swanning round the world on luxury trips, buying fancy homes in Italy, and engaging in the high life of Sydney. Instead, their Mosman home is mortgaged to the hilt and all the funds have been invested here. They spend every spare minute here, despite their very busy lives. All our children, except Evan, believe in what we are doing. Jonathan has even convinced the military that our premise is correct, so they are likely to be the only government institution that will survive. Derain's tribe arrived at the same conclusions, completely independently.'

Chloe looked contemptuous at this last remark, 'I'm not giving up my life in Sydney, not for anything. This is your dream, not mine. And don't think Mark is totally onside with the science, he's not.'

David looked at her sharply. He had realised Mark had his doubts, but any withdrawal of his support would be another threat to The Settlement.

'What do you expect me to do?'

'We will carry on as we have been. If, and it's a very big if, your conclusions are correct, I will then make a decision to either come back here or drown with the rest of them.' She hesitated, 'I know about Caroline by the way.' She burst into tears and ran out of the room.

Chloe contemplated leaving The Settlement altogether and discussed it with Tanya. It was an anxious moment for Tanya as Chloe's decision might threaten The Settlement, but she kept her cool.

'Now that you both know about the other's lover, you really have the best of both worlds. There is now no reason why you can't spend as much time as you like in Sydney. If you left, it would put pressure on your lover to create something more permanent, which might destroy the relationship altogether. Then where would you be? Remember, you have many friends and much support here as well.' Tanya said nothing about the effect Chloe's departure would have on the financial affairs of The Settlement, especially if she wanted to be paid out for her share. She never said a word to David about the conversation and Chloe never raised the point again.

CHAPTER SIXTEEN
Bushfires

Derain took his bush craft training duties for The Academy personnel very seriously indeed. Every member of The Academy, including Mark and Tanya, spent up to a week at a time in the bush with him and a colleague. They came away with some understanding of the wildlife and how to deal with them, to hunt them if needed, as well as the food that was available, in the form of berries and roots. Most importantly, they were shown how to navigate their way through the bush, which to the untrained eye looked very similar from one place to another.

After two years of induction, Derain said to the often impatient Mark, 'Now we can put them to the test, each pair can go out with one of my people who will leave them in a certain place. They must find way back here by self. First test will be only one day walk from here. If no one get lost, then we can try two days walk and then three days.'

'And if they become lost?'

'We check. If really lost we help.'

'What about doing this on horseback?' asked Mark.

'People must learn to look after self first. If that okay, then they can learn look after horse and self in bush. This not easy.'

The first exercise was completed without any major mishaps. Tanya was accompanied by her eighteen year old niece, Kim. Both Tanya and Kim were very competitive and were determined to be the first of the forty groups to return.

Their Aboriginal guide left them at dusk. Camp was set up carefully. Tanya cleared an area for the two man tent knowing snakes would avoid open spaces, 'We'll leave a log burning overnight to keep dingoes away,' volunteered Kim.

'Any spare food should be hung up in a tree,' said Tanya.

Having struck camp and making sure they had left no trace of their presence, with Kim leading, they walked steadily back towards The Settlement, heading for the western gate. They had both made mental notes of the various landmarks on the way—a rock here, a tall tree there, a small glade. At one point they were in doubt as to which way to go and Tanya took the lead.

After about an hour Tanya said, 'This is wrong, my mistake, we need to go back.'

Arriving at the spot where they went wrong, Tanya said, 'Kim, you lead now, but if we are still to be first we need to get a move on, I've wasted two hours.'

Just before dusk they arrived at the western gate, manned by one of the older settlers who said, 'Mark was first. They came through about twenty minutes ago, but you are second.'

'Damn, if we hadn't made that diversion we would have arrived first,' said Tanya. In her heart of hearts she was relieved as she didn't want to keep beating Mark at his own game. All except one group returned within two hours of Kim and Tanya. The last group was eventually escorted into The Settlement by their Aboriginal guide at midnight.

'They walk wrong way, did not look at sun,' Derain explained to Mark the next day.

Mark didn't skite, but she could sense the relief in him that she had not beaten him home.

Derain was a regular visitor and had established a strong relationship with David. He had managed to learn some English. Sometimes he stayed for weeks on end and then he and whoever was with him would inexplicably disappear, to reappear again weeks or months later. The people in The Settlement became quite used to his visits and talked to him about the local wildlife and the weather.

Within the community, there had been a few less than successful attempts at hunting kangaroos to supplement the meat supply. People often went out, but only bagged the occasional animal.

David mentioned this to Derain, who said, 'I fix.'

In time there were many in The Academy who became skilled kangaroo hunters, even in the thick forests of the Blue Mountains. The meat became a regular feature on many dining tables.

David had offered to build him a cottage, but Derain preferred his humpy, claiming, 'Big house make us all ill.'

One day, a woman came screaming out of her home yelling, 'Snake, snake.'

Derain calmly went into the house with a sturdy stick and emerged carrying the live snake on the stick. He released the terrified snake near the edge of the built-up area.

Her husband, Dave, made to kill it with a spade.

'No kill, no kill,' said Derain gently, restraining the man. 'Snake go away now, not return. 'I show you how to treat snakes.' He took Dave into the nearby bush for a day, picking up snakes on a stick, much as he had shown Chloe. Dave was soon able to lift the snakes quite competently. He became the snake expert, in Derain's absence, and removed any snakes that appeared.

On another visit Derain sought David out. 'Big fire, this year.'

'What do you mean by that?' asked David anxiously; he had noticed the surrounding bush drying out. While there had been occasional small fires, easily dealt with, since the early days, David knew that periodically the Australian bush caught fire in the most dramatic and spectacular fashion. After such an event, the bush naturally regenerated itself.

'Very dry, big fires this year.'

'Okay, is there anything we can do?'

'Yes, start burn now before big summer heat.'

'Where?'

'I show you, first inside. Afterwards, maybe outside.'

David understood that to mean they should arrange a controlled burn at the northern end of The Settlement, at least to start with.

David held a meeting in the community centre, persuading everyone they would burn the one thousand hectares of bush they had enclosed.

Derain kept his interpreter nearby during the burn. 'Only start the burn after midday, the wind strength and direction is usually more settled in the afternoon,' she translated. 'The fire should be started with the wind behind the burn and there should be people behind the fire making sure it only burns in one direction. Then we must back burn towards the main fire. This means the fire will burn itself out.'

They selected a small area first, to practise. With one hundred settlers assisting, they successfully burnt an area of about one hundred metres by one hundred metres. Each fire-fighter had a damp sack, with people detailed to maintain a water supply from the nearby settlement fire truck.

On the next attempt, they chose a two hundred metre front and the aim was to burn to a depth of about one kilometre. This was done very successfully and by late afternoon the main burn and the back burn had met. As Derain had told them, the fires automatically extinguished themselves. People were left on duty to make sure all fires were indeed out and that no embers could escape into the unburnt areas.

One of the more active members of the community, Gervais, approached David and said, 'We burnt about twenty hectares today; how many hectares in this section?'

'About a thousand.'

'So it will take us fifty days or so to complete the exercise. Don't we need to move more quickly than this? Our participation rate will drop off if it takes too long and then we might be in trouble.'

So the next day they burnt an area with a front of five hundred metres and a depth of two kilometres. The wind was gentle and although the fire escaped several times there was no difficulty in containing it.

'That's about one hundred hectares,' said Gervais. 'Much better. Maybe we could extend the area again tomorrow to finish the job quickly.'

'Must watch wind,' said Derain. 'Too much wind then everything will burn, whoosh,' he waved his arms upwards, 'maybe some house too. Must respect fire, he very powerful.'

'We seem to have coped very well up to now. Aren't we being too cautious?' remonstrated Gervais.

'Better than burning people or houses,' said David.

Gervais grunted dismissively. 'The bloody houses are three kilometres away!'

'Fire jump many big distance,' said Derain heatedly, 'even right over village.'

Gervais ignored him.

The following day all one hundred firefighters gathered ready for the fray. Many had developed an unwarranted confidence from the little experience they now had and felt they could cope with anything. By midday, there was a steady and strengthening westerly breeze.

Derain approached David. 'No burn today. Too much wind.'

Amid some grumbling the burn was abandoned for that day and then the next. On the third day they were about to abandon the burn when Gervais said, 'This is nonsense, we agreed to controlled burns and I think we should just get on with it.'

'No,' said David. 'The situation should be easier tomorrow, and rain is forecast in a few days. It will be safer then.'

David returned to his office for a spell, then looked for Gervais to see if he could convince him they were doing the right thing.

'He's not here,' said his wife when David knocked on the door of Gervais' cottage. 'He didn't return with the rest of the firefighters.'

David was about to deal with other matters when he noticed a thin plume of smoke coming from the bushland area. He hesitated for a minute and then called Joe and several others. It was on occasions like this that he missed Fred. 'The stupid buggers have gone ahead and started a burn and the wind is getting up. We need some people here manning the hosepipes and keeping every house damp. The rest of us will go to the bushland area. Those people will shortly be in real trouble. How many of them are there?'

'Less than a dozen.'

David just shook his head.

About eighty people accompanied David back to the bushland area. Others remained behind to look after the houses in the village. David asked the doctor, a nurse, and the ambulance to accompany them.

'Wind change,' Derain observed, pointing. 'Those people will burn, we hurry.'

When the party arrived they could see a large area was burning out of control. There was no sign of Gervais and the others. Derain had a quick word with David and then ran into the bush on his own.

'We'll try a back burn from the area we have already burnt,' David instructed. The group spread out and lit the bush adjoining the already burnt out area. The heat was intense and two people had to be given first aid by the medical staff. There was no sign of Derain or Gervais.

David could see they were making some progress in the area where they were established, but the fire had leapt to another area. He left forty people in the original back burn area and took another forty to start a further back burn to try and block the new threat.

After several hours, David's team were exhausted. There was smoke everywhere, so visibility was down to a few metres. They had no idea whether they were making any kind of progress.

Derain appeared through the smoke. 'Two die, two burn bad, others maybe okay,' he told David. Someone appeared with a water truck. 'All gone hospital,' Derain added. He then directed David to change the focus of their attack on the fire and the other forty people joined them. They spent the night there, upright and continuing to fight while people brought food from The Settlement.

'Three houses burnt,' David was told.

'Anyone hurt?'

'No, I don't think so.'

Towards morning Derain emerged out of the smoke, smiling. 'Rain come, one hour or two.'

Within an hour, a heavy shower drenched all the firefighters and helped to put out the fires.

Derain said to David, 'You go, leave ten people here.'

David was greeted by a lot of very tired and disgruntled settlers when the firefighters returned to the village.

They told him Derain had run into the bushland where Gervais and the others were being overwhelmed by the fire. He made them pick up the two dead bodies and led the group of ten out of the fire area.

'We were trying to get away in the opposite direction. If it wasn't for him we would all be dead,' said one of the survivors.

Three houses had been burnt by embers and one had completely burnt to the ground. David could see it was Gervais' own cottage.

Divine retribution, he thought.

Gervais was one of those being treated in the hospital. He had been burnt on his legs and hands, but would survive. One of the others died shortly after being admitted to the hospital. The rest would live, although one was badly disfigured and would need a wheelchair for the rest of his life.

David asked the whole community to attend a meeting at the community centre. He stood on the small stage and waited for silence. His clothing was ragged and covered in burn marks, hair dishevelled, and face black with soot, much the same as most in the community.

'The community has suffered a great shock over the past twenty-four hours. Some people have lost their lives, others have lost houses and other possessions, and we still have to complete the project to burn off the northern bush area. Our deepest sympathy goes out to all those who have suffered losses, particularly of loved ones. Please do not make assumptions about what happened. I have already asked one of the legal fraternity among us to conduct an enquiry which will be completed within a few days. We can then take action. Do not, I repeat, do not take any action individually. It will just make matters worse.'

'It was that silly bugger Ger—'

David interrupted sharply, 'Wait for the enquiry to be completed. We can then take action. The community will be kept informed.'

'Will there be a court case like Fred's?'

'It's conceivable, I don't know yet,' answered David patiently. He was determined not to prejudge the situation and not let anyone else make the same mistake.

The enquiry report was published three days later in The Settlement newspaper. It found that Gervais and several others had deliberately ignored instructions from David and had endangered the whole community with their actions. The enquiry named all the people involved, including those that had died as a result of their own foolishness. As a footnote, it praised the role Derain had played to mitigate the disaster. Gervais and two others were still in hospital and would remain there for some weeks. Gervais' family were staying with friends in the community.

David wondered what action should be taken. Tanya had been absent during the controlled burn, but said when consulted, 'This is almost as bad as the business with Fred. They did not mean deliberate harm, but there was considerable damage to the community through wilful disregard of instructions. If we take him to trial what sanctions can be imposed?'

'We could expel him, indeed all of them, the same as Fred. We could impose some sort of community service. That's about all.'

Many in the community expected Gervais and the others involved just to leave the community once they had been released from hospital. None of them did.

The Settlement's second trial drew another large crowd. Many in the community were angry with Gervais and his friends and wanted them expelled. Everyone was astonished when Tanya appeared as the advocate for the defence.

There were seven people in the dock. The prosecution opened by stating the offence and referring to the details of the enquiry. 'I will show that the actions of all the accused resulted in the deaths of three people plus considerable damage to the community. I am going to demand they be expelled from the community and forfeit all their assets in The Settlement.'

Tanya asked if she could read out a statement signed by all the accused.

The prosecution and defence were requested to approach the bench, where followed an animated, whispered conversation.

Tanya then read out the following statement. 'We,' she read out all the names of the people involved, 'collectively recognise that we deliberately ignored instructions, that we caused the death of three people, and unnecessary damage to the community. We unreservedly apologise to the community for our actions and we submit ourselves to the mercy of this court, whose jurisdiction we accept.'

The prosecution looked nonplussed. 'Is that a guilty plea?'

'Yes,' answered Tanya.

The six jurors were dismissed.

The prosecution went through his case briefly. 'This plea changes nothing. I still demand all the accused and their families be expelled from The Settlement and that they forfeit all their assets to the community.'

There were some worried looks among the accused.

Tanya then stood up and, one by one, she spent up to thirty minutes for each defendant detailing how they had contributed and what the community would lose if they were expelled. 'While the people in the dock are guilty as charged, I am telling the court that if we expel these people it will be us, the community, that will lose as well as the accused. We all know them. They are not evil and they have expressed contrition for their misguided actions.' She hesitated and the court was hushed. 'In mitigation, I ask that any sentences imposed be suspended for five years. If after that there has been no further infringement the sentences will be cancelled.'

The court then rose.

'Sentences will be passed tomorrow,' announced the judge.

Tanya had a brief conversation with Gervais and his fellow accused, who were very concerned. 'We have exercised the only real option available to us. I don't think the judge has any option but to accept your plea.'

'We just rolled over,' complained one.

'If you had fought the case more aggressively then you and your families would all be out on your ear within days, with absolutely no recourse,' said Tanya firmly.

The next day the court assembled to hear sentencing. 'All the accused have pleaded guilty and I have determined that their sentences will be expulsion from The Settlement, with their assets forfeited.' There was an astonished hum from the spectators. The judge banged his gavel.

'These are very serious crimes! But in the interests of the community I am persuaded some mitigation is in order.'

The courtroom was silent. Even Tanya was nervous, although she felt confident of the outcome.

'The sentences of the following people,' the judge read out six names, 'will be suspended for six years, if any further misdemeanours occur during that period then this court has the jurisdiction to carry out the sentences imposed.'

There was jubilation and disbelief on the faces of the six. The judge banged his gavel again.

'As for the sentence imposed on Gervais Jones. What you did was inexcusable. You recklessly disobeyed instructions, the consequences of which we are all aware. I have pondered long and hard over the proposal presented by your defence counsel. Frankly, I do not think you deserve any consideration whatsoever.'

Gervais hung his head.

'Having said that, and taking account of the needs of the community, your sentence will be suspended for twelve years. The same conditions apply as with the other sentences imposed today by this court.'

Pandemonium broke out in the court. Some were pleased; others thought that no suspensions should have been granted.

'What does all this mean?' a somewhat bewildered Gervais asked Tanya.

'It means you may go about your life as if nothing has changed. If you fuck up again, the court has the authority to expel you and confiscate all your assets here.'

'You mean it's like a yellow card, except it lasts twelve years.'

'Yes. Maybe in six years, it may pay to ask the court to have the time period reviewed. I will be able to help you with that. All you have to do is to behave. You could also consider contributing over and above your basic responsibilities to the community.'

'Like what?'

'Anything. You will find something. Derain is a good example. If it wasn't for him you would be dead and the rest of us may have been burnt to a cinder.'

Gervais looked utterly confused and ashamed, up until then he had barely regarded Derain as human. It had certainly not occurred to him to thank him for saving his life.

Tanya felt a deep sense of satisfaction at the outcome; and The Settlement was the winner once all was said and done. She also now had many more loyal allies within the community who had witnessed her even handedness.

David completed the controlled burn in the northern area within the following two weeks. They then helped the settlers at The Bandstand with their own burn off.

Afterwards Derain advised David. 'All this mountain, big burn this year,' he said pointing to the pristine forests surrounding The Settlement, 'danger not over. There will be lightning strike, many strike maybe within one month. Area very dry, will burn very hot. Need to have people ready to fight fires. Much training needed, must be ready.'

'Should we have a controlled burn out there?' asked David.

'No,' answered Derain, 'too big, too late.'

David, Mark, and Joe organised fire teams throughout The Settlement and they had twice-weekly drills. This time there were no dissenters and the whole community participated enthusiastically.

As Derain predicted, a month or so later, a massive electrical storm engulfed the mountains. While there was some rain it was insufficient to dampen the now tinder-dry bush. The fire started on the western slopes of the forest facing The Settlement. The community had been organised into shifts by Mark, still absent in Sydney, and Joe, so that there were three shifts of eight hours each. One shift on duty, manning all the equipment; one shift providing food to the duty shift, and trying to keep The Settlement functioning; and one shift hopefully sleeping.

At first the fires started slowly and didn't seem to pose a big threat, but within a few hours several fires had joined. David and many others in the community watched the growing spectacular firework show, flames leaping thirty metres and more into the air and showers of sparks flying high. To the community the fires were amazing, but looked distant and non-threatening. But the wind rose rapidly and the unearthly noise of the fire roaring across the tree canopy at high speed highlighted the danger they were facing. A few embers started to fall among the houses, which were quickly extinguished by the well-prepared firefighters. The cattlemen and helpers were keeping the herds calm and constantly spraying them with water.

'Be careful, snakes,' advised Derain. 'Wallaby, kangaroo, maybe dingo stopped by fence, but not snake or goanna.'

The first night the wind died down, but fires continued to burn hungrily, consuming thousands of hectares of forest. The community thought they had everything under control. Once the wind had died down there were no more ember attacks.

David frequently visited the teams of firefighters. 'The temperature has barely dropped tonight and tomorrow the forecast is for highs of over forty degrees. So the situation is going to become really ugly, much worse than today.

Make sure everyone drinks plenty of water and sticks strictly to the routines. This crisis will likely last for some days. Keep all skin covered from ember strike.'

David always appeared calm, however he sometimes felt,

I came here to create a haven for the family and some others to survive. I really had no idea what I was taking on. He gave nothing away, however, and even managed to call Chloe, away in Sydney. 'Don't come back for a few days. We are in for a terrible time with the fires, it's not too bad right now, but I think the next few days will be really rough.' The fact that she was probably seeing her lover no longer bothered him; he had no wish to see her hurt in any way.

Chloe for her part briefly considered the man she had married. *He's still considerate*, she thought wistfully. She took full advantage though and arranged for Clark to stay with her in the flat for a few days. *It's his dream, not mine*, she thought.

Nothing could have prepared the crews for what was to follow. The next day the wind rose early and the well-established fires in the west started to spread. The roaring noise was insistent and suddenly there were fires in the bush to the north and then the east. Visibility was extremely poor as the smoke swirled about the tightly-packed cottages. David rushed about telling people to cover noses and mouths.

'Dear God, the fire has jumped almost ten kilometres from one side of The Settlement to the other. We should be thankful for our controlled burn; there is very little left to burn on here.'

A team of four with a small fire truck was despatched to the north to deal with any small fires that might erupt in their own territory.

At one stage during the height of the inferno, fires started in two houses simultaneously at each end of The Settlement. The firefighters were quickly on the scene and the fires extinguished.

'Make certain the fire is unable to spread to other buildings,' the leader of each group told their crews.

People with burns, respiratory problems, dehydration, and exhaustion inundated the hospital. After being treated, any who were able returned to firefighting duties. The inferno lasted for several days. Once the fire had burnt the bush in the immediate vicinity it continued on its destructive path beyond. There were many small fires in the bush surrounding The Settlement, so the pall of smoke hung over everything.

David knew that he could not expect any help from the Rural Fire Service, the area was just too rugged and remote.

Ten days after the fires started there was a sharp shower and then it rained steadily for a few days, extinguishing all but the most resilient fires in the bush.

When it was all over the exhausted fire crews, with dirty clothes and blackened faces, all stood and examined their new vista. Instead of the pristine green bush, waving in the breeze all that faced them was a blackened, lifeless disaster on all sides. An occasional wisp of smoke could be seen reaching for the now azure blue sky. There was no sign of any life whatsoever, except what existed within The Settlement, which was to all intents and purposes untouched. The Bandstand had also survived.

'Thank heaven you helped us,' Caroline said to David by phone. 'We would have been in trouble otherwise.'

David held a meeting. Once he had quiet he said, 'We have survived the biggest potential disaster that has ever faced us. It looks terrible now and our mountain looks as if it will never recover. However, nobody here has been badly hurt, the five houses that were damaged can all be repaired and the insurance will pay for that. All our services are still intact, we have water, food, and all our stock have survived. The same firestorm is unlikely to happen again for many years and the bush will recover. It is time to make a few repairs. This is one of the biggest challenges we have faced and we have come through it as a community because we faced it together. There will be bigger challenges in future, but this should be an inspiration to all of us. We should also all thank Derain and his people for the advice they have given us. They saved our community.'

David was about to close the meeting when Donald Weatherspoon approached. Patricia had seen him edging towards the stage and had quickly alerted all the other denominations represented in the community and, much to Donald's astonishment, they all followed him and stood with David. Donald went bright red and was about to sound off, but David had been alerted by Patricia.

'Thank you Donald for reminding us all of our individual faiths. Perhaps our Thai friend, the only Buddhist here, would lead us all in a brief prayer of thanks for our salvation.'

In broken English, the Thai doctor gave a short speech giving thanks for the salvation of the community.

David said. 'I'm sure all the faiths represented here will wish to make their own thanks. I suggest you all meet outside to arrange that.' He ushered them off the platform.

'I was going to give an Anglican prayer,' sputtered Donald.

'You can still do that,' said David. 'You could even book the centre unless someone else has booked it ahead of you.'

Patricia said to him quietly, 'At least you didn't give him a lecture on cattle breeding.'

'He still has a bit to learn.'

Based on the experience of the flood disaster, now a few years back, Mark, Tanya, and David braced themselves for a flurry of resignations from the less-committed settlers. After the controlled burn, but before the big fires, Joe, Patricia, and David had identified and visited ten vulnerable families. Patricia was successful in calming people's fears. Her down-to-earth approach reminded people of the reasons for establishing The Settlement and the fact that the catastrophe was now likely only three or four years away.

'Do you still believe in the science?' Patricia was asked by one family.

'Certainly, I have never had a moment's doubt since we moved here ten years ago. The current research is ever more compelling.'

'It's very hard, now with all this hot weather.'

'Yes, but that is Australia. Climate change has made the situation worse. You have invested a lot coming here. We are talking about survival, not merely an alternative lifestyle.'

A few people had a word with David, but there was no major upheaval as there had been after the floods and nobody left The Settlement.

'There are more people now than at the time of the flood. I think it helps,' observed Joe. 'I expect our visits calmed a few nerves.'

CHAPTER SEVENTEEN

The Wedding

David and Chloe had kept in constant touch with Evan in London over the years. Through phone calls and Facebook, David learnt of Evan's longstanding relationship with an English girl named Beryl. He often wondered whether their relationship would lead to marriage and if Evan might eventually return to Australia.

On Christmas Eve 2020, the family had all gathered at The Settlement for the Christmas festivities. The usual call on Skype was made to the home of Beryl's parents, Charles and Elizabeth Browning, who in Evan's words owned a "pile" in Dorset, in a village near Sherborne, in the English West Country. The Australian contingent was more than usually exuberant as the call had to be made at the end of their Christmas Day in view of the time difference. After greetings and good wishes between all the family members, Evan, with the blushing Beryl beside him, was eventually able to say, 'Mum, Dad, Beryl and I are getting married.'

'Married?' David exclaimed loudly, halting the Australian end of the conversation. 'Congratulations! How wonderful.'

A slightly tearful Chloe took over. Her words were drowned out when Mark started singing, with the others all joining in, 'Hooray for Evan, Hooray at last, Hooray for Evan, he's a horse's ...'

He was unable to finish when Chloe uncharacteristically yelled, 'Quiet! Whatever will they think of us if you continue like that?' She had a few tearful words with Evan and then with the Brownings.

'June would be the best time for the nuptials. We can have the reception here. The garden will be looking lovely at that time of year. There is plenty of space so most of you can stay with us for a few days at least,' said Elizabeth.

All of Evan's siblings wanted a quick word.

'It could be useful for me, I have many contacts in the banking world in the UK. Are you up for a trip?' said Mark, looking at Tanya.

Tanya nodded in agreement. 'The kids will come with us.'

Jonathan added, 'We have constant contact with the British military, but some face-to-face would be valuable.'

Joe and Patricia were more hesitant. 'Maybe,' said Patricia, 'we'll have to see. I will have to put a whole lot of things in place here first.'

'I will go, but I'm not sure for how long. Things might go wrong if we are all away for an extended period,' said David.

'Well I think it will be a relief to get away for a while. I would like to come for something like three months,' added Chloe.

Some uneasy glances were exchanged. The rift between David and Chloe seemed to be widening.

~

Chloe left on her own two weeks before the wedding, which was to be on Saturday, June 19th 2021. She spent a few days with Evan and Beryl in their small flat in Hampstead and then at Elizabeth's insistence, joined her in Sherborne.

David arrived a few days before the wedding, driving down to Sherborne with Evan; Beryl had left for Dorset earlier to help her mother with the wedding arrangements.

'Do they really have enough room for all of us? It seems an awful imposition,' asked David.

'One needs a GPS system to navigate around the house,' joked Evan. 'I'm sure it won't be a problem, they wouldn't have offered otherwise.'

Evan continued to navigate his way from the M3 to the crowded A303. 'This takes us most of the way there,' he said. He pointed out Stonehenge with its small collection of visitors circling the ancient site like vultures.

'Does this mean you will never return to Australia?' asked David.

'One can never say never, but I am totally committed here to the music business and Beryl has a large extended family.'

'What about the Ice Shelf?'

'I haven't thought much about that, Dad. Other than people at The Settlement, nobody else even mentions it.' Evan had always thought the idea of an impending catastrophe was nonsense. He and Chloe had discussed it many times and he tended to agree with her position.

'Tanya and Chloe went on an exploratory trek with some of the younger people and they came across a small Aboriginal group who have precisely the same vision as we do about "great floods". They have even given us an approximate date for the catastrophe.'

'There has been a stunningly beautiful photo, all over Facebook, of Tanya standing naked on a rock in a pond. Is that the expedition you are talking about?'

'Yes. She goes there every year with a group of youngsters. It cements our relationship with the Aboriginal community. Those pictures of Tanya have been around for a couple of years.'

'The Facebook focus is about Tanya. The collapse of the Ice Shelf, although mentioned, has more or less been given a back seat.'

'So where do you stand on the science?' asked David gently.

'Much as I did when you first presented it. I just don't know. It seems to be a fringe belief,' he said politely, not wishing to upset his father.

'We still have a cottage for you at The Settlement, which we use for new settlers whose houses have not been completed. It's there for you if ever you want it.'

'I know, I've mentioned it to Beryl.'

They drove on in companionable silence, admiring the soft lines of the attractive English countryside. David felt sad so little notice was being taken of the science behind the development of his dream.

'You are only spending a few days here?' ventured Evan.

'Yes, there are more than three hundred people in our village now dependent on the family for support and leadership. The whole family is here, so I need to return to make sure that any crises are dealt with.'

'What sort of crises?'

'Bushfires, floods, dingoes, problems with the livestock, issues with the neighbouring settlement; there's always something.'

'Seems a long way from a small flat in Hampstead and this beautiful and mostly benign countryside here in England.'

David shrugged. He could see what was forecast would be difficult to imagine on a warm, pleasant summer's day in the west of England.

'Mum seems to be having an extended holiday here in Europe?' said Evan.

'Yes, she has never really accepted the change in our lives. I think she needs a break.'

'She has had a difficult time since you started The Settlement.'

'She has done a great job with the horses and riding school; she has her own way of dealing with things.' David was not prepared to discuss the deterioration of his relationship, even with his son. He wondered what the sleeping arrangements would be at the Browning establishment.

When they arrived, David was escorted into his own room by Elizabeth Browning. Chloe's things were not in the room. David was standing at the window admiring the large, well-kept garden, now with a marquee being erected in the centre of it, when there was a knock on the door.

Chloe stepped into the room. 'I am just next door, in case you were wondering. We will be sharing the bathroom.'

'This is a marvellous place. Is there really enough room for all of us here? Especially in separate rooms?'

'I told Elizabeth we usually slept in separate rooms. Being English she asked no questions.'

'Thank you. It will make life easier. I'm looking forward to the next few days.' He looked at her and realised his feelings for her were now those of friendship only. He guessed it was the same for her.

David played two games of golf with Charles, Mark, and an English friend followed by a night out at a local pub. He also spent one evening taking Charles Browning through all the reserach behind The Settlement as well as a selected number of photographs going from the bare undeveloped site to the thriving community that now existed.

'So there are three hundred people in the community?' asked Charles.

'Three hundred and twenty-one. By tomorrow probably three hundred and twenty-two with the latest birth. I am expecting an e-mail shortly.'

'And you really believe this?'

'Yes, Tanya and I, quite separately, came to the same conclusions years ago now. There is a neighbouring Aboriginal group who also have the same belief. Anyway, as Evan may have told you, he has a cottage there, so you and Elizabeth and any other members of the family would be more than welcome to come and stay for a few weeks or for as long as you like. Other parts of Australia are also worth seeing. Mark and Tanya still live in Sydney, but come over in their helicopter almost every weekend.'

'It's years since I visited Australia, I find the flight uncomfortably long. We may indeed take up your offer though.'

There was a minor argument about clothing for the wedding. 'I was just going to wear a suit,' said Mark.

'No you are not,' said Chloe firmly. 'All the Brownings are wearing formal morning suits, so that is what you'll all be wearing. We don't want anyone to think we are a bunch of rural peasants, whatever the truth may be.'

Tanya added, 'The local hire shop can kit out all the Bower boys. We girls will be dressed up to the nines. We don't want a whole lot of Aussie blokes with us looking as if they have just emerged from the cowshed.' She laughed. 'I have never had so much fun in my life. We are going to make a big splash.'

Thankfully, it was a nice sunny day. The service was held at eleven o'clock with a reception in the garden of the Browning house afterwards. Suitable speeches were made by David, Charles Browning, and Jonathan as Evan's best man.

Some of the guests recognised Tanya from the famous Facebook picture.

One of Beryl's male cousins, William, plucked up courage and approached her. 'Forgive me for asking, but aren't you the person whose image has appeared on Facebook—you were naked on a rock in the moonlight?'

Tanya answered without embarrassment, 'That's me. I have done the same thing three years in succession now, on the only date that the full moon lights up that rock.'

'That image is all over Facebook. It is brave of you to expose yourself in that way.' He was unable to keep the smirk off his face.

A small crowd had gathered to listen to their discourse and they were all quite taken aback by Tanya's total lack of sensitivity.

'Do you see it as just a photo of me standing naked on a rock?'

'Well yes,' was the hesitant answer.

'Can I tell you the story behind the photo? It's much more than just an attempt to compete with the page three girls in *The Sun*,' Tanya said confidently, with a laugh.

There was renewed interest among the people in the gathering.

'Please go on,' said William. The smirk had now disappeared.

'My mother-in-law and I took a group of teenagers from ours and a neighbouring settlement out into the bush for a week.'

'Settlement?' asked William.

Tanya briefly explained the reason for The Settlement. She explained about the pool, the Aboriginal group, and then the naked pose on the rock.

There was a hushed silence waiting for Tanya to continue.

'Is that it?' asked William.

'No, the most significant part of the whole incident was when I returned to the group.'

'Still starkers?' asked a sceptical voice.

'No, it was quite late at night by then and was becoming a little chilly,' Tanya responded calmly.

' Derain and his people told us of their vision, exactly the same as ours.'

'This just applies to Australia?' asked a hopeful voice.

'No, sea levels will rise by something between seven and seventeen metres worldwide. If you want to know how that will affect you personally, take a look on Google Earth.'

'And you believe in all the mumbo-jumbo?' asked William aggressively.

'My research supports the theory. The Aboriginal forecast is so interesting because they are illiterate and have no access to computers and yet can tell us the precise date each year that the moon will strike that rock. We go back to the pool every year. They call me the White Goddess.'

'Tell us more about The Settlement, how big is it?'

'What sort of investment is there in the place?'

'We have more than three hundred people and one hundred houses. We have recently estimated the replacement value of the site and it is well in excess of two hundred million dollars.'

'Are you sure of that?' asked an incredulous voice.

'As well as the houses, we have a community centre, swimming pool, library, hospital staffed by medical professionals, school, tennis courts, a polo field, shooting range, a large number of livestock and horses, and about eight hundred hectares under cultivation. We also have major water storage dams and a military training academy.'

'What's all that for?'

'We predict the Ice Shelf collapse will cause panic and pandemonium in Sydney. At that point we are going to isolate the community by blowing up a mountain to block the only road access.'

There was an uncomprehending silence for a minute or two.

'What do you do about electricity and fuel?'

'We run on solar energy, with some contingencies for emergency car and helicopter fuel, stored in massive tanks.'

'This is pure fucking fantasy,' said a disbelieving voice. 'Just bullshit, I'm not listening to any more of this crap.'

One or two people moved away.

Tanya continued telling the remaining group about their haven in the mountains. 'You should come and visit us. Evan and Jonathan have houses there that are often empty. Mark and I still live in Sydney, so we could meet you and take you to The Settlement in the helicopter. Come with the group to the pool next April and witness the ceremony for yourselves; it is life changing. I think the Brownings will come in September.'

'If this prediction is real, what should governments do about it?' asked a now contrite William.

'Most of the climate change initiatives have come much too late. There is nothing that can be done in time to stop the Ross Ice Shelf from collapsing into the sea. So governments should be creating infrastructure to cope with the impending flood, such as port facilities that can be used with higher sea levels and moving oil refineries to higher ground.'

'That will cost billions.'

'Yes.'

'Where are they going to find the money?'

'They should reallocate all their resources to quickly deal with the infrastructure issue. If they don't they will cease to exist anyway. Our belief is that there will be a worldwide catastrophe. Many societies will cease to exist.'

The mood was now sombre in the garden.

'I think I'm spoiling this joyful occasion, I'm sorry,' said Tanya quietly.

'We should throw Evan into the pool,' shouted Mark. Evan tried to escape, but was eventually captured and dragged to his fate.

Chloe looked on disapprovingly. 'Boys will be boys,' she said to Elizabeth.

'One, two, three,' yelled Mark as they threw Evan, morning coat, top hat, and all into the still chilly pool, with Beryl's cousins participating just as enthusiastically as his siblings.

Tanya smiled indulgently as a member of the group she had been talking to approached. 'What you are doing in Australia is most interesting.'

Tanya started to move away, 'I think I've said too much already.'

'No, no, just hear me out. My name is Sebastian.' The urgency in his voice made Tanya stop and listen. 'This whole issue needs more publicity. Use that Facebook image to publicise the environmental issue facing all of us.'

'We had hoped that would happen, but we were facing a major bushfire emergency at the time and spent no time on it. What do you suggest?'

'I use this technology on a daily basis. I am sure that within three months we can have one million followers on Facebook and Twitter. Once you get to that level it will just go ballistic. Governments will then have to take notice. Are you going to be here for a few days?'

'Mark and I are going up to London tomorrow and have meetings there all week. After that we have a plan to take the train to Paris before returning to Sydney.'

'Where are you staying?' asked Sebastian.

She gave him her mobile phone number. 'Most evenings we will be free, although we are trying to book a West End play or two if I can drag the philistine along. Maybe we should lock in a date now.'

CHAPTER EIGHTEEN
Shutdown?

Within three months there were, as promised, one million people worldwide following the Facebook postings relating to The Settlement. The emphasis gradually changed from the naked pictures of Tanya to the forecast collapse of the Ross Ice Shelf and its ghastly consequences.

Settlement community members sent Sebastian information to include in his daily update. Even David and Chloe sent things through, although usually her contributions were sceptical. Her disbelief added another dimension to the Facebook pages, helping to grow the audience.

When the worldwide audience reached fifty million, governments started to take notice. Suddenly, the price of land in remote areas in Australia and many other parts of the world escalated sharply, with people belatedly trying to imitate the developments in the Bower settlement.

When the weekend visitors reached more than one hundred in a weekend, Mark announced. 'We are unable to cope. From today, each visitor will require a coded pass to enter and exit at the front gates. '

They restricted the entry to fifteen visitors at any one time. It worked for a few months until some impatient visitors broke the barrier down, allowing a flood of people to inundate the property. It took the efforts of most of the community to persuade them to leave.

'We'll install a barrier with spike pads that will only be removed when the code is correctly entered,' said Mark. 'At weekends I think we will have to have armed guards as well. It gives us all some idea of the necessity for completely isolating ourselves when the Ice Shelf collapses.'

Jonathan warned David that there was increasing unrest in Canberra about the pages of comment on Facebook. 'They are receiving e-mails and calls from all over the world suggesting we should be closed down.'

'What do you think I should do?' asked David.

'Be prepared for a nonsensical initiative from Government. I don't need to tell you to stick to your guns, I'm sure you will do that anyway.'

More and more of the Facebook postings attempted to discredit The Settlement and the science behind it. Most of it was ill-informed and resulted in renewed interest in the topic.

Tanya spoke to David by phone during that period. 'There have been some odd things going on.'

'Such as?'

'I have been followed by the same car whenever I leave the house.'

'Coincidence, surely?' said a sceptical David.

'No, this has happened about ten times now.'

'Take the licence plate number and report it to the police.'

'The funny thing is I have reported it twice. The second time I made the report they said they had no record of the complaint. My tyres have also been let down a couple of times. Mark has had similar problems.'

'Did you report that?'

'Yes, they just laughed at me. It must have something to do with the huge social media following.'

'Yes, I'm pleased about that. It may influence Governments around the world to finally address the problem.'

'I'm sure they think of us as a threat. Have there been any unusual happenings at your end recently?'

'Lance was arrested a few weeks ago. The man you made an example of in the parade ground.'

'Oh, yes, of course.'

'They are now suggesting we should have realised he was a known criminal and may be charged accordingly.'

'Ridiculous! Lance's name was on the list of residents you gave the police a few years ago. There is no possibility they will be able to make that stick,' said Tanya angrily. 'I think they are trying to shut us down again.'

'Shut us down? We are much stronger than when they tried that earlier in the piece,' said a now very concerned David.

'We need to find out what they will settle for ... I don't like any of this. You may be asked to attend a meeting, in Sydney or Canberra, perhaps relating to Lance's arrest. Please don't go voluntarily. If they arrest you that's another matter. Something is brewing. Mark and I will move to the mountains until this nonsense has all blown over.'

Within the week, Mark and Tanya had made arrangements with their respective offices to work from The Settlement and they moved with the family to the Blue Mountains. The intimidation ceased and Tanya was hopeful that whoever was behind the pinpricks had given up.

She said to David, 'We should be careful, they may merely be planning something else.'

A week later David received an urgent call from a Canberra number. 'Mr Bower?'

'Yes,' replied David.

'My name is Nicholson, from the Attorney General's office.'

'Please give me a phone number where I can reach you. The call must go through an identifiable switchboard and then be put through to you.'

'Is this charade necessary?' said an astonished voice.

'Yes, I need to be certain this is not a hoax.'

'I promise you it is not a hoax.'

'There have been some peculiar goings on in recent months. I have to be certain the call is genuine.'

'What sort of problems?'

'The number please Mr Nicholson, or I put the phone down,' said David firmly.

There was a sigh and David was given a Canberra number.

David quickly called Joe and explained he needed a call to be recorded in a few minutes. He buzzed Tanya. 'It's certainly about this Facebook stuff. The Attorney General's department wants to talk to us. We need to be as hard as nails. Do not give an inch, but be polite.'

When Joe indicated all was ready David dialled. The call was answered by a switchboard, then a secretary, followed by Nicholson.

'That was quite unnecessary,' said an irritated voice.

Joe waved at David. 'The conversation is being recorded,' he mouthed.

'Hello Mr Nicholson, one can't be too careful, apologies for the delay in returning your call. I also needed to have my senior colleague with me as part of the conversation. Her name is Tanya Bower.'

'Good morning Mr Nicholson, you will remember a previous conversation with me, some years ago,' said Tanya.

There was no response from the Canberra end.

David looked at her curiously.

'Harold,' she mouthed.

He nodded his understanding.

'We know this conversation is being recorded at your end,' said David. 'I would like to inform you that we are also recording the conversation.'

There was a brief hesitation on the line and Nicholson said, 'I want to talk to you about all this Facebook nonsense. Do you know what I'm talking about?'

'I presume it has to do with the science of climate change,' said David.

'Well partly.'

David remained silent.

'I would like you to put a stop to all this sensational nonsense on Facebook about climate change and about the collapse of some lump of ice in the Antarctic that is supposedly going to cause mayhem around the world.'

'The science surrounding the collapse of the Ross Ice Shelf, Mr Nicholson, and the projected outcomes have been in the public domain for more than twenty years. Millions of relevant pages are available on the Internet. There is nobody who can put a stop to it,' said Tanya quietly.

There was a muffled conversation at the other end.

'The current publicity is making people panic. The US President, the British Prime Minister, and a dozen others have called asking us to stop this nonsense. There is no acceptance, in Canberra, that this analysis is correct.'

'The analysis is correct. What should be done about it is the real question. Many people will die as a result of the inaction of governments round the world. Respectfully, continuing denial of the science will just result in a bigger catastrophe,' said Tanya.

'I can't influence any of that. You need to close down the Facebook page.'

'The Facebook page is run from London, with postings from around the world,' said David.

'But it's all about your bloody place in the Blue Mountains. You have encouraged people to invest on the basis of a fraudulent, unproven theory. We could close you down on that basis alone.'

'I don't think so,' said Tanya. 'Every settler knows the science, but has accepted that the decision to settle here is theirs alone. You have tried this nonsense before. As I expect you know, there was an ASIO plant here for a few months. When he found everything was above board, he moved on.'

'Where is he now?'

'Goulburn prison.'

There was silence from Canberra.

'Have you consulted the federal environment or climate change people about the science?'

'No.'

'We have had discussions with both departments. It is well accepted.'

'The amount of publicity is embarrassing the Government. We could send in the police and close you down.' The tone was threatening.

'Remember, everything you say is being recorded. Unless you formally withdraw that threat within an hour this whole conversation will be posted on the Facebook site. That will probably double our following overnight,' said Tanya quietly.

'The department will not be pleased. I need to phone you back.'

'The first thing you need to do is to withdraw the threat you made, very specifically.'

'I withdraw the threat.'

'Not good enough, it needs to be very specific,' interjected David.

'My name is Nicholson from the Federal Attorney General's office and I formally and unreservedly withdraw the threat made to send in the police to close you down,' said Nicholson in a tired, irritated voice.

'Thank you,' said David. He attempted a conciliatory suggestion, 'If you have the time, it might pay you to visit us. You will find we pose no threat to anyone. I will arrange to fly you in here by helicopter.'

'Whose helicopter?'

'The Australian military's.'

'I will ring back later today.'

～♪

When he called back, Nicholson suggested David visit Canberra. Tanya, Joe, and Mark all shook their heads vigorously.

'To what purpose?' asked David. 'And please remember this call is also being recorded.'

'In order to explain the climate change science to all the parties involved here.'

'There are dozens of people in Canberra, considerably better qualified than anyone here, to explain all aspects of climate change. If you want to learn something fresh, pay us a visit.'

'So you won't come to Canberra?' said Nicholson.

David had nothing to add, so remained silent.

The phone was put down in Canberra.

～♪

There was a call from the gate to Mark, 'There are two police vans at the entrance, most definitely SWAT teams. They wouldn't say why they were there and they have no warrants. I have sent another dozen Academy people to the gate as reinforcements.'

'This is bullshit,' said Tanya forcefully. 'I think we should post the phone conversation on Facebook and be done with it.'

'When we escalated the crisis at the time of the floods, we came off second best. I think we should phone Nicholson back. I don't think the people in Canberra have any idea of the scale of The Settlement,' said Mark.

David called Nicholson in Canberra and was told he was busy.

The phone rang thirty minutes later.

'Have you changed your mind about visiting Canberra?' asked an aggressive-sounding Nicholson.

'No, quite the opposite. I'm sure you are aware there are two SWAT teams stationed at our front gate. They aren't communicating with us and have no warrants. You need to understand Mr Nicholson, that more than three hundred people are settled here, including a large number of women and children. SWAT teams imply violence. Can you imagine the press reaction if one of our children was hurt in an action by the police? Dealing with a few comments on a Facebook page would certainly pale into insignificance compared to dealing with that,' said David quietly.

'Three hundred people?' asked Nicholson, surprised.

'Three hundred and thirty as of yesterday. We have a school, a hospital and so on. We are wholly self-sufficient and pose no threat to anyone. Attempting to shut us down by force will get you nowhere. If you really wish to understand what we are about, please pay us a visit.'

'I will call you back.'

'Please remove the SWAT teams first,' said David.

The visit was arranged for a week later.

'It will include representatives from the environment and climate change ministries,' advised Nicholson.

The six civil servants, awaiting the military helicopter flight, were surprised to be greeted by, "Colonel Bower", as Jonathan introduced himself.

'Are you related to the Bowers at The Settlement?' asked Nicholson.

'David Bower is my father. I will give you some background on the way over,' he said.

The complete Bower fraternity formally greeted the visiting group.

'We have arranged a brief presentation of The Settlement and our achievements here. Then, we will give you a site tour in one of our solar-powered vehicles. We have arranged a lunch in our community centre, where you will meet many settlers, after which there will be time to discuss any issues you wish.'

The visit went very smoothly. Tanya made her presentation and David conducted the tour of the site, including the hospital, where the staff had just completed a major operation on an ill patient. The official entourage were shown the dams, stock, milking parlours, horses and cultivated area, as well as the recreational facilities, several houses, and school. There was no mention of The Academy.

Nicholson and Tanya avoided each other as far as was possible.

Tanya thought, This bastard has caused me more grief than anyone else I know.

Knowing the visit was critical, she said no more than was required of her. Nicholson found he was confronted by an obviously competent, very attractive woman. He was intimidated by the experience as Tanya had nearly derailed his career.

Patricia talked about the youth programs. 'Most of the young belong to various groups, some recreational and others teaching them essential life skills important to their long term future in the community. Many are learning trades here while others are at university, studying degrees such as medicine, veterinary science, agriculture, and forestry. We are working on a plan to continue university level training after isolation.'

'What about welfare?' asked Nicholson.

'There is no welfare as such and, as far as we know, nobody in the community receives Government welfare. However, we do have some people who have either had an accident or are otherwise incapacitated. They all have a function within the society; there is a hospital orderly who was born with Down's Syndrome for example. Families look after their own and the religious groups help in this regard as well,' Patricia answered.

'I see you've had an extensive bush fire,' one of the visitors observed, pointing to the still partially-blackened hillsides.

'Yes, the advice we received from our Aboriginal settlers was invaluable. It almost certainly saved the community and many lives. We were well-prepared,' David told him.

'You have Aboriginal settlers here?'

'They come and go, but they are very much part of us. They teach groups about the basics of bush craft and about local wildlife. We also have many faiths represented here. The Christians, Jews, and Muslims are in the process of building a joint facility for worship.'

'Astonishing!'

The visitors enjoyed a sumptuous lunch in the community centre.

'Everything you see here was produced in the community,' said Chloe. 'All the children are taught to ride. It forms a major part of the recreational activities.'

Nicholson said, 'Our impression of the place is good. You seem to have a clear plan. I understand, if this Ice Shelf collapses, you are going to isolate the place and wait for some sort of recovery?'

David nodded.

'What about the rest of us?'

'How many people survive depends on what the Government does to mitigate the situation,' said Tanya.

'We, and most nations around the world, are committed to policies that will reduce greenhouse gases materially over the next fifty years,' interjected the visitor from the climate change ministry.

'That is admirable and necessary, but unfortunately that will not save us from the current situation. The Ice Shelf will collapse.'

'What should we do then?' There was a chorus of frustrated voices.

'As fast as possible, you should build infrastructure that reduces the impact of the floods. Oil refineries will have to be moved to higher ground and ports need to be able to operate in the new environment,' said Tanya.

'But that will cost billions.'

'Trillions,' said Tanya unhelpfully.

'Where are we going to find such huge funds?'

'You could borrow from overseas. You probably won't have to repay much of it because many of the lenders won't be in existence within a few years. Also, cut every budget by a percentage and use funds from that.'

'I don't know of any other country thinking like this.'

'Not many are doing much, but check what the Chinese are doing. I'll bet you anything they are doing exactly what I've suggested.' Tanya didn't think any of them were absorbing what she was saying, it was just too difficult. 'They may even be thinking about what the new world order would look like. I expect that Australia may be part of their considerations.'

'They wouldn't dare come here, the Americans ... ' Nicholson's voice trailed off. 'The real purpose of our visit is how can we reduce the current panic and then put in place a strategy to deal with what we've learned today.'

'We won't post any new information on the Facebook page. I expect interest will slow down over the next few months.'

Several of the visitors made gracious speeches praising David and what had been achieved at The Settlement. Many watched as the helicopter took off and set a course for the southwest.

'I don't think they see us as a threat anymore, so they will take the pressure off,' predicted Tanya. 'They won't be able to get their act together in time. Any country taking the threat seriously will be keeping quiet, especially if they are installing infrastructure. Just watch out for countries borrowing heavily over the next three years. After the collapse, Australian mineral wealth will be worth two fifths of five eights of fuck all until the world starts to consume again in, say, five hundred years. Jonathan will give us a full briefing, but I think we can get on with our lives and our preparations for the catastrophe. Any bets one of that group will be an applicant for residence here? Whew!'

Jonathan reported a week later, 'There was some chatter about the visit on the way home, but they soon began to discuss other issues. In my perambulations around Canberra over the last few days, I believe you are right off the radar.'

CHAPTER NINETEEN

Rescue

Up to 2025

More than one hundred people were now participants in The Academy; all were very fit and proficient in handling their weapons, even the new short-barrelled automatic rifles Jonathan had legitimately acquired from the army. The two day exercise of trainees being left in the bush and having to find their own way back to the village had been successful both on foot and on horseback.

'We should now engage trainees in a real test,' suggested Mark to Derain. 'Maybe a three or four day journey back to The Settlement, on horseback.'

'Two group,' said Derain, holding up two fingers. 'Not enough people in my village to manage all at one time.'

Before any of these major exercises Mark always gathered the trainees together, emphasising the importance of The Academy. 'We will probably be compelled to defend ourselves. If you don't want to be killed, you may have to kill another person. We need to understand and deal with our environment. Yours and The Settlement's very existence may depend on your ability to survive on your own in the bush for extended periods. One threat we can anticipate is the emptying of the prisons. Remember Demetriou? He and some others in Goulburn prison hold grudges against us. He may try to come back to this place, most probably with hostile intentions. These exercises are necessary and will help to make us as prepared as we possibly can be.' He watched as his message gradually sank in.

Tanya was relieved to be in a separate group from Mark, so there was no competition between them. Since he arrived before her in the two day walk, she and Kim had beaten Mark and his partner by half an hour when the exercise was done on horseback.

Tanya and Kim were in the second group of people in pairs. An Aboriginal man, on foot, escorted them outbound for four days and as planned abandoned them to their fate. They had only been allowed to carry a small amount of food, meaning they had to forage for at least half the journey. It was the same with the horses, so each group had to plan on allowing their mounts to graze for part of each day. Tanya and Kim took it in turns. The first evening, Tanya had seen a large black snake sunning itself on a rock. She picked it up on a stick as Derain had instructed and, with a swift stroke from a heavy knife, cut off its head. Kim shot a possum the second day and a wallaby on the fourth evening.

After the guide had left, Tanya said to Kim, 'If we are able to find some berries or roots, maybe we could try to get back home in three days instead of four. We will certainly be back before anyone else if we manage that.'

Kim said cautiously, 'Is that necessary or wise? If we rush things we may lose our way and we don't want to hurt ourselves or the horses.'

Finally, Tanya's wild streak prevailed. They made good progress on the return trip, passing the third day's campsite just after midday. By four o'clock in the afternoon the pair stopped and Tanya said, 'I noticed this site on the way over, so we're on the right track. It has good water and grazing for the horses.'

'We don't want to flog the horses too much,' said Kim. 'Remember the penalty for bringing horses back in poor condition.' But, on inspection, the horses were okay. 'I have sorted one of the shoes on my horse, maybe you could have a look after our gourmet meal,' she laughed, enjoying the grilled wallaby.

'They'll last until we get home,' Tanya announced as she stood up and stretched, having carefully examined both horses. 'It won't help if we rest them for a day anyway, any damage has already been done.'

To everyone's surprise, they arrived at the eastern gate just before dark on the third day.

'There is a bit of an emergency,' the man at the gate said. 'I will alert them.' He rang on the makeshift telephone.

'Mark wants you at the hospital. I will take the horses.' Tanya was told. 'If you try to ride down there in the dark, you might break a horse's leg.'

'Not to mention our heads,' said Kim quietly.

They scrambled down the steep slope and, three hours later, arrived dirty and scratched at the hospital. Mark greeted them, saying nothing about the record-breaking journey home. 'One of the guides came in and told us a garbled story about a bad accident. We'll need the helicopter, I'm afraid, first thing in the morning.'

'Do we know roughly where the accident happened?' asked Tanya.

Mark managed to find Amaroo, the Aboriginal guide, and they were able to pinpoint the approximate area where the accident had occurred. Mark and Tanya, together, were at their absolute best in these circumstances. There was no hint of any rivalry and both were intent on finding a solution.

'Kim,' said Tanya, 'we must refuel and service the helicopter, remove seats to accommodate a stretcher, and install abseiling equipment in case there is nowhere to land.'

Mark made a move to help, but with a glance from Tanya he withdrew, understanding Tanya wanted Kim to be fully involved. In Derain's absence, Mark tried to quieten Amaroo's fears about flying. He spoke almost no English, but somehow Mark managed to convey to him that he was needed to help find the victim.

Before they took off, Tanya said to Mark, 'Kim has considerable medical knowledge, if we can find the place I will lower her and Amaroo down. I may then have to return here for more manpower.'

Taking off to the northwest, Kim tried to calm Amaroo's fears. To start with, Amaroo was unable to orientate himself. Tanya then took the helicopter as low as she dared and hovered slowly over the bush; suddenly, Amaroo became animated, having recognised a landmark. He was then able to quickly guide Tanya to the accident site.

'Can't land there,' announced Tanya. 'Kim, harness Amaroo and lower him to the ground, then go down with all your equipment. Take this GPS device so I can find you again.'

Amaroo was harnessed, but it took all Kim's powers of persuasion to get him to leave the aircraft. A few minutes later Kim scrambled into the harness, 'Make sure you are firmly strapped in,' said Tanya, 'one accident is enough.' Kim nodded impatiently and lowered herself to the ground.

Communication between the aircraft and ground proved difficult, but Tanya understood she should lower the stretcher. She did so with difficulty while trying to keep control of the machine. Heavy rain started to fall, making the operation more dangerous. Kim waved from the ground to raise her into the machine.

'One female with concussion and a badly broken leg,' said Kim as she crawled back into the aircraft. 'The patient was kept warm by her companion, Stephanie, but is in a bad way and needs hospitalisation. Stephanie put down one horse with a broken leg. Let's lift the patient up here. I will accompany you to the hospital. Amaroo, Stephanie, and the remaining horse will return home on foot.'

The stretcher and patient were precariously winched into the helicopter and strapped down.

'Is she okay by herself with Amaroo?' asked Tanya anxiously as they closed the door of the helicopter.

'Stephanie is young, but as cool as a cucumber. Our patient wouldn't have survived without Stephanie's ministrations. She'll be fine. I'm quite sure she trusts Amaroo.'

Landing at The Settlement thirty minutes later, the patient was examined, in situ, by the local doctor. 'We will deal with this here. Any delays will put her life further in jeopardy.'

The other groups struggled in over the next few days followed by Stephanie and Amaroo two days later.

'There needs to be some sort of medal given to Amaroo, Stephanie, Kim, and Tanya,' David said to Mark when it was clear the patient was out of danger.

'Count me out,' said Tanya firmly when consulted. 'All I did was pilot the helicopter, which is well within my comfort zone. The other three deserve the highest honour though. If Amaroo hadn't dashed back here, she would have died.'

David held a ceremony some days later. 'Due to the bravery of some of our own, we have decided to make the first Settlement bravery awards.'

'To Tanya, The Settlement George Medal for bravery in the face of danger.'

'To Amaroo, Stephanie, and Kim, the highest award for extreme acts of bravery, The Settlement Victoria Medal.'

The applause continued for ten minutes. Tanya had meant the emphasis to be placed on the other three, but many in the community noticed Tanya's attempt at self-effacement and their admiration grew.

'I don't want to spoil your party,' Chloe whispered to Tanya afterwards, 'but what the hell did you do to those horses? It will take weeks, if not months to get them right. Both have strained fetlocks and all the shoes need replacing.'

'I offer no excuses. Kim tried to slow us down, but I wouldn't listen. Maybe it was some sort of divine intervention, if we hadn't picked up the patient when we did I don't think she would have survived.'

'You were by far the quickest. I suppose it tells us what's possible in an emergency.'

CHAPTER TWENTY

Final Preparations

The Brownings spent three months in The Settlement staying in Evan's house, a place he had never seen, and another three months travelling around Australia.

On the eve of their departure, Charles made a rather formal farewell speech to David and Chloe, 'What you have done here is amazing. We are not sure about the forecasts and have decided, if necessary, we would rather face our demise at home in familiar surroundings. Anyway, at our time of life it is difficult to see what we could contribute here. So thank you for your hospitality and we will keep in touch.'

Chloe glared at David, nodding as if to say, 'Just how I have always felt.'

Others from Beryl's family paid visits, and one couple stayed. Several made a point of visiting the pool with Tanya and a new group of the young, now of all colours, being introduced to living in the bush. Chloe always led the expedition, with Tanya still playing her vital role.

For most visitors, the pool experience was transformational and they returned home as advocates for the science and further action.

When Derain was asked for a date when the Ice Shelf would collapse, in his improved English, he said, 'White Goddess always talk about Ice Shelf. We know nothing of it. Big waters will rise, where from we do not know.' He spoke in his own language then, translated as, 'I will tell you one year from when big waters will rise, ancestor will tell me then.' Derain also made a point of saying to the group, 'Ancestor pleased with White Goddess and Settlement and David and family. Very pleased with brown and black people now coming to Settlement. Ancestor say that when big waters rise much land will return to Aboriginal people so we can look after land again. We, much help to Settlement, maybe Settlement much help to our people.'

211

Kim had spent many happy hours helping out in the hospital from the age of twelve. She was now at university in Sydney studying medicine. 'I'm going to stay there as long as I can, in other words until the Ice Shelf collapses. I'll come back here as often as I can cadge a lift either from Tanya in the helicopter or Granma,' she told her mother.

'Keeping up-to-date with The Settlement is important,' advised Patricia, 'but not at the expense of your studies.'

'The Academy is pretty important.' Kim quietly added, 'I wonder if I will be able to kill someone if I have to, or if I will just wimp out.'

Patricia had always seen her daughter as being helpful and concerned with the welfare of others, despite her forthrightness. She couldn't bear to think of her having to fight a real war, 'Don't worry about that at the moment, focus on your studies,' she said sympathetically.

~

Jason, Joe and Patricia's second child, had almost completed several electric and electronic engineering courses where he could find them, mostly on the Internet. He had worked with his father on many projects within the community and was as proficient as Joe in keeping all electrical installations functioning. He had even helped Joe build their first computer.

Always enthusiastic, he bounced into Joe's workshop one day saying, 'I don't think I need to complete a degree, but I want to learn from some people overseas. I've been in touch with some I'd like to visit. This is a rough itinerary. If I don't do it now I'll never get the chance.'

Joe finished what he was doing, before looking at the itinerary, 'Probably a good idea … and maybe some more places too.' The pair spent a companionable hour revising Jason's itinerary.

~

'Business class travel?' said Jason smiling. 'The Settlement will pay.'

Joe smiled. 'Chancer. Nothing but the very back of the plane for you mate, and the cheapest accommodation. We need information, not lessons in fancy travel. I'll speak to David as he's sensitive about using Settlement money for family members. But don't worry, we'll manage somehow.'

Book Two

CHAPTER TWENTY-ONE
The Date

Derain accompanied Chloe, Tanya, and the group to the pool in the Blue Mountains in April 2025. Everyone wanted to be there. It was predicted to be a watershed event in the life of the now very well-established community.

'There aren't enough horses for everyone,' said Chloe. 'We could take about fifty people, but that's too many. Fourteen's the number, plus Tanya and me. We'll decide by ballot, apart from a few.'

Derain was asked his opinion. 'Same as first trip, too many people there last one, two years. Ancestor not like it so much.'

The Bandstand was asked to fill four places, as they did on the first trip. Roger, Rachel, and Kim were also allocated places. The other seven were allocated by age group ballot, so one person each from ages thirteen to nineteen were selected. There was some grumbling, but most accepted the procedure was fair.

David was asked if he wanted to take part in, perhaps, the last visit to the pool before the collapse of the Ice Shelf.

'There's no need,' he said. 'I've been there many times with Derain. He told me roughly what time the moon will emerge and strike Tanya standing on the rock. We can arrange a barbecue on the parade ground and be with you all in spirit.'

The group were now very experienced in the bush; setting off very early one morning, travelling light, since they were only to spend the night at the sacred pool. The sun was setting just as they arrived at the pool and camp was efficiently and quickly set up. Derain met a contingent of fifteen from his village at the pool.

There was an enormous air of expectation among the group.

'It would be smart to have finished dinner by eight thirty,' said Tanya.

Derain was quite unconcerned. 'Moon come up when moon come up, makes no difference if you eat then or not.'

Nine o'clock came and went. Then nine fifteen. By nine thirty there was some fidgeting among the contingent from The Settlement. At ten o'clock, Derain and the Aborigines performed a dance in front of Tanya, lasting about thirty minutes.

'What's going on?' asked Chloe.

Tanya concentrated on the ritual. Halfway through the dance she stripped off and swam to the rock. Effortlessly, she drew herself up on the rock, facing the group, as the moon emerged and bathed her nakedness in its unearthly, ethereal light.

The group silently watched, as the Aboriginal dance continued. Tanya was about to dive off the rock, when she saw the distinct shape of a crocodile in the water. She quickly looked over at Derain. He had his eyes closed and appeared to be in some sort of a trance. A feeling of intense euphoria came over Tanya as she realised there was no danger, so she dived off the rock and swam twice around the pool as she had done now for seven years in a row. There were some shrieks from The Settlement group as they saw the crocodile swim alongside her, but make no move to touch her. It then disappeared as Tanya emerged from the water to dry off and dress.

'My God, my God,' said Chloe, shivering, as she touched Tanya all over as if to make sure she was alive. 'I really thought you were done for! Didn't you see the croc?'

'Oh yes, I saw it all right,' answered Tanya, as the rest of the group gathered around. 'Somehow, I knew there was no danger.'

The Aborigines had all melted away into the night. There was excited chatter from the group, who were far too animated to contemplate sleep.

'Where have they all gone?' asked Rachel, expressing the group's curiosity.

'We should wait and see,' said Tanya. 'Most of this has never happened before. They will come back, probably at dawn. Tonight is obviously seen as a very special occasion.'

The chatter continued for another two hours after which they all fell into bed except for those on watch. Tanya shared her tent with Chloe. There was no need for supervision anymore as the group ran the camp competently.

'I think that having sixteen of their own people at the pool tonight was a sign of equality and a willingness to share this land,' Tanya said to Chloe. 'They believe the floods will completely change the fortunes of the wider Aboriginal community.'

'How on earth do you know all that?'

Tanya shrugged, 'I just do.'

'Does that mean trouble for The Settlement?'

'I don't think so. It is more of a live and let live sign.'

〜♪

They were having breakfast as the dawn broke when all sixteen of the Aboriginal group appeared out of the half-light.

Derain came to Tanya and said, 'Waters will rise three hundred and sixty-five days from today. This is the word of our ancestor.'

'That means April 25th 2026,' said Tanya.

'Anzac Day,' said Chloe. 'Extraordinary!'

'The Ice Shelf will probably collapse about a week earlier than that around mid-April 2026. So now we know,' added Tanya.

Some of the group surrounded Derain. They all knew him well from his bush craft expeditions.

'Crocodile?' said Derain in a genuinely disbelieving voice. 'There was no crocodile.'

'Yes there was. We all saw it swim around the pool with Tanya.'

'No, too much cold for crocodile here, definitely no crocodile.' He did not seem to be joking and was quite certain.

'There was definitely a crocodile swimming beside me,' said Tanya.

A confused Derain began an animated discussion within his group. They then came and prostrated themselves in front of Tanya.

'What's all this about?' asked Tanya as the hairs on the back of her neck stood out.

'This ancestor, not crocodile,' said Derain. 'Will look after you always. This very big sign. Maybe happen only once before, long ago, long ago.'

The conversation and arguments went on for some hours and the group decided to stay another night at the pool.

Derain and his people had left when Tanya emerged from her sleeping bag before dawn.

〜♪

At the community meeting the following day, Kim, Rachel, and Roger described all the usual and unusual events at the pool. Most people were by now quite used to the naked images of Tanya appearing after these visits and took no notice. But in all the pictures from the trip, there was no sign of the crocodile. The whole group, including Tanya and the ever-sceptical Chloe, swore they had seen it in the pool with Tanya.

217

'Anyway, we now have a date for the collapse of the Ice Shelf. We, as a community, must really focus on that and make absolutely sure we have done all that we need to help us survive into the future. There are community people regularly travelling to places outside, and we have people at university in Sydney and elsewhere. Individuals will have to make their own choices, but I would suggest the whole community should be safely back here no later than the end of March 2026. That will give some leeway for mistakes in the forecast.'

Over the next few months, Tanya tried unsuccessfully to persuade her police contact and friend George and her Aunt Cara to move to The Settlement.

Cara paid one visit but said afterwards, 'I'm too old to move to such a place. If it happens, then I will die here among people I know.'

George wouldn't even visit.

CHAPTER TWENTY-TWO

Icefall

APRIL 2026

David was sitting quietly in his office on April 16th, two days before the expected collapse of the Ross Ice Shelf in the Antarctic. He was busy ticking off the extensive list of things he and the community had agreed they should accomplish prior to the collapse; something he'd done a hundred times in the past few months. He knew Chloe was still in Sydney as well as his granddaughter Kim and some others. He hoped they would be back that day or no later than the morning of April seventeenth. Chloe had cut things fine all her life, and he wasn't particularly worried about her. He knew Kim was trying to complete a project and there was some discussion about a recalcitrant boyfriend. He phoned Patricia who told him not to worry.

A few minutes before midday he received a phone call from his youngest son, Jonathan, aged thirty-four, now a Brigadier in the Australian Army. A call which turned him absolutely cold. 'Dad, the Ice Shelf has just fallen into the sea. There will be an announcement on the ABC at noon. I had hoped to give you an hour or two's advance warning, but there is no choice but to issue a public notice.'

David was silent for a short minute.

'Dad, are you still there?'

'It's your mother,' he said in a desperate voice. 'She's still in Sydney. So is Kim. They were supposed to return today or tomorrow. Once there has been an announcement it will be too late. There will be pandemonium in the city and gridlock within hours.'

'Maybe Tanya could pick them up in the helicopter.'

'I will try.'

He quickly found Tanya and Mark. She immediately ran to find Patricia, telling her the news. 'If you can contact Kim, tell her to make for this address,' she handed Patricia a piece of paper with Chloe's Manly address. 'I will try to pick people up at Brookvale Oval at Manly.'

Patricia looked bewildered.

'Just get hold of her, it's the best hope she has. If we can contact Chloe, I might be able to pick them up together.'

Mark and David called an urgent assembly in the community hall.

David rang Chloe a half-dozen times in the few minutes he had before the gathering. He left several messages on voicemail telling her the news. They switched on the television set in the packed hall just as the news broadcast started.

There was the usual stuff, irritating David—a middle class welfare initiative, a grisly murder in Melbourne, a monetary scandal from a senior Government minister. The people in the audience moved restlessly wondering what was so important.

The fifth item on the news finally caught the full attention of the audience. David quickly pressed the record button on the TV.

'The Ross Ice Shelf in the Antarctic has detached itself from the mainland and collapsed into the sea.' There was a collective gasp from the audience as the news report included a summary on the Ice Shelf.

The Australian Prime Minister appeared on the screen and said, 'The Government is monitoring the situation together with a panel of experts here in Canberra. People will be advised what, if anything, they should do but I am advising calm. At the moment please do not take any action. There will be another address on this subject when we have something to report within the next few days.' The picture faded.

Pandemonium reigned for a few minutes, mostly from people who had family members and friends still outside The Settlement.

Tanya stood up, waiting for the room to quieten down. 'There are a few people who have not yet returned. Regardless of what the Government has said, Sydney will soon be in gridlock. The best chance anyone outside has of being rescued is to make their way to Brookvale Oval at Manly Beach. I will be leaving in a few minutes by helicopter. I will try to make a few trips. Please tell them to hurry. Manly Beach,' she repeated.

There was a flurry of conversation, but Tanya rushed out of the room, leaving others to field the anxious questions.

David requested people's attention and said, 'Please reassemble in two hours or so, when the gorge will be blown. I will have more words for you then.'

Tanya took off, having armed herself with a handgun and the defence force issue, short-barrelled automatic rifle. *Dear God, I really hope I don't have to use any of these things*, she thought.

An hour later she circled the oval and easily managed to land. Several people rushed towards the machine. At first she didn't recognise anyone and then three Settlement people emerged from the crowd, shoving their way to the front of the throng. Tanya waved the handgun and fired a shot into the air. The crowd backed off slightly so the three could climb aboard. She looked about in vain for signs of Chloe and possibly Kim.

'Anyone else there?' asked Tanya.

'Yes, but they are right at the back,' said a trembling girl.

The crowd started to move towards the machine again, so Tanya leapt into the pilot's seat and gunned the engine. 'Shut the door, will you,' she yelled as they took off, narrowly avoiding the big Norfolk pines lining the beach. 'Fasten your seat belts.'

As the machine gained height and flew across Sydney's tree-lined North Shore, they could already see there were cars blocking all the main thoroughfares out of the city; most suburban streets were also jam packed.

'We were called from The Settlement and told to hurry to Manly. We took the Cat from Circular Quay. I think we were very lucky; hundreds were left standing on the Quay.'

She dropped the passengers, checked there was enough fuel for a return trip and was about to take off again when David appeared.

'Is this wise? They said you had a problem with the crowds at Manly.'

'We did, but I'll manage. I'm hoping Chloe and Kim might be there this time.' She accelerated away as David backed off.

The crowd was even larger on the next approach to the oval. Tanya flew the helicopter very low over the heads of the people, twice, scattering the crowd.

Hurriedly landing with a bump, she hoped any Settlement people had seen her and would run to the machine. She thought she had less than a minute to land, load any passengers and leave, otherwise she would be swamped and the helicopter would be grounded.

There was absolute chaos on the oval as people tried to rush the machine. Tanya opened the helicopter door and fired a burst from the automatic rifle over people's heads. The crowd hesitated and four Settlement people sprinted towards the machine. There was a shot from someone in the crowd, felling one of the runners who clutched at his chest. Two of the four by this time were scrambling into the machine and the wounded man was being half dragged and half carried towards the helicopter, by his companion.

'Here, hold them off with this,' she tossed the rifle to a girl she had trained with at The Academy.

Some shots were fired from both sides as Tanya ran over to the wounded man. Picking him up with a fireman's lift, she ran the few paces to the helicopter and tossed him into the machine, covering everything and everyone with blood.

'Try to fix him up,' she yelled unnecessarily.

Leaping into the pilot's seat, Tanya accelerated the engine. But as the helicopter started to rise there was a man clinging on to one of the runners. The passengers looked on anxiously as Tanya gained height slowly and then flew over the beach and the shallows. She managed to jerk the machine and it suddenly rose quickly as the man lost his grip and fell into the sea.

'Hope he can swim,' said Tanya looking out.

Instead of making for home she made the mistake of turning the helicopter around, looking for the dropped person. She pointed to a clothed figure swimming strongly.

'There,' she said, relieved.

Then the helicopter's Perspex window shattered and Tanya felt an excruciating pain in her left shoulder. With difficulty, she managed to fly the helicopter higher, directing it to the northwest. There was blood pouring from the wound. One of the passengers rushed over, having seen what had happened, ripping Tanya's shirt sleeve open and applying a tourniquet, and then bandages, to stem the flow of blood.

'Stop the blood if you can, I will manage to fly this thing with one hand,' said Tanya shakily. 'Some idiot shot me. How is our other patient?'

'Bad, very bad, but we are dealing with him. You just worry about getting us home.'

'Try not to move about too much,' directed Tanya, 'it makes it more difficult to fly.'

Sweating and fighting off bouts of dizziness the hour it took them to reach The Settlement seemed like an eternity to Tanya. She somehow clumsily landed the machine on the parade ground and switched the engine off.

Joe saw the bad landing and rushed over to the machine yelling, 'Stretcher, bring the stretcher and the doctor. They might be in trouble.'

The wounded man was rushed to the hospital as Joe crawled into the machine to find Tanya in a dead faint at the controls. 'She was shot in the shoulder as we left Manly and has lost a lot of blood, but I don't think the wound is life threatening,' Joe was told. There was blood in the cabin and all over the controls and pilot's seat.

~⁰

David tried a number of times to phone London. On the tenth attempt, he made the connection. A very sleepy voice answered the phone, 'Oh, hi Dad,' said Evan, 'is this important? It's after one in the morning here'

'I'll be quick,' said David. 'The Ice Shelf fell into the sea a few hours ago. There is a fifteen metre tsunami heading this way at one hundred kilometres an hour.'

'Oh, shit,' said Evan now very much alert. 'Beryl and I have a plan to come home. We will try to call from time … ' the connection was then lost.

~⁰

While Tanya was involved with her rescue mission, David had asked Mark to blow the gorge. All the charges had been laid within the past few days.

Mark, accompanied by ten others, drove to the entrance gate. The guards there were instructed to lay all twenty nail pads that had been procured for the purpose, along the road from the gate for a kilometre. They erected a sign at the kilometre mark.

~⁰

EXTREME DANGER
BLASTING IN PROGRESS
DO NOT ENTER

~⁰

'Hopefully that should stop anyone coming in,' said Mark.

'What about the people who haven't yet returned from Sydney?' asked an anxious member of the guard.

'My mother and Kim included,' answered Mark grimly. 'Sydney will be in gridlock within an hour. There is no chance that people will escape by road if they haven't already done so. Tanya is picking people up at Brookvale, if they can get there.'

Mark and his group withdrew down the gorge, back towards the village. He instructed everyone except himself and one other to return to the village in the vehicle. 'There'll be rock all over the road once we blow this place up,' he explained.

Going to a small, reinforced concrete hut, Mark spent twenty minutes making the correct connections. His companion was asked to check everything.

'There are about three hundred charges laid. We need to be sure they are all connected correctly and that the mountain will indeed drop into the gorge,' he said, almost to himself. 'Ready,' he said to his companion.

The man nodded nervously.

Mark pushed the plunger.

There was a brief silence. And then mayhem. A massive flash was followed by a series of enormous explosions. The rumble caused by falling rocks lasted for more than ten minutes and the whole area was then coated in a mantle of dust. Mark looked out of his bunker. A few pieces of rock had fallen nearby even though they were some way from the gorge. 'Nothing much more we can do here,' he muttered. It took them more than two hours to walk back to the community centre.

The centre was bursting at the seams, with everybody anxiously waiting. When the vehicle returned from the gorge David called for silence. 'As we all know, we planned to isolate ourselves by closing the gorge once the Ice Shelf collapsed. Mark is about to do just that.'

Even prepared, the whole community jumped out of their seats when they heard the massive blast down the valley and the continuous rumble that followed.

'This is the new reality,' said David, once everyone had settled down again. 'We are now isolated. No more trips to Sydney, no more outside visitors. It will be very difficult to leave and virtually impossible to return. It will obviously take time for all of us to become used to the situation. Aside from planned meetings, please raise any issues either with me directly or with the Bower family representative in your ward. This is very important. We need to have everything out on the table.'

'My son is still out there,' said a panicky female voice at the back of the hall. 'Are there going to be any more rescues in the helicopter?'

'I'm not sure how practical that is,' said David. 'Chloe and Kim have also not returned and Tanya was shot and wounded during the last rescue. I think we were very lucky the helicopter didn't crash. Also communications are becoming difficult. How would we know where to find people?'

The woman burst into tears.

As the meeting broke up, a dust-covered Mark marched in. There was some desultory clapping. David said quietly, 'Tanya is back, she's been hurt and is in the hospital.' Mark rushed out.

Tanya woke with an excruciating pain in her shoulder, and an anxious Mark looking on.

She smiled. 'Look at you. You look as if you've been down a mine or something.' He gave her a dusty kiss. 'I've just blown the gorge.'

A slight frown crossed her brow. 'This is what we've been waiting for all these years,' she said quietly. 'Heaven knows what life will be like now.' She hesitated. 'It's pretty ugly out there. Any sign of Kim and Chloe?'

Mark shook his head sadly. 'I had better see to the kids.'

With the help of painkillers, Tanya was up and about within a day.

'Did you see anything of Chloe and Kim?' David had asked Tanya.

Tanya shook her head. 'The crowds make it too dangerous to try any more rescues with the helicopter. Apart from this.' She gestured towards her injured shoulder.

'How is the other fellow?'

'He's battling, we'll see in a day or two.'

CHAPTER TWENTY-THREE

The Escape

Kim had received the message from Patricia, but it took her several hours to reach Manly on foot. She had just arrived and was pushing her way through the panicking crowds when she witnessed the incident with Tanya's helicopter at the oval. With her heart in her mouth she saw a man clinging onto the helicopter runners, drop into the sea. She was relieved to see the machine apparently flying off safely to the northwest.

With difficulty she found Chloe's flat. On the way was a supermarket in the process of being looted. Knowing they might have to walk to the mountains, she joined in and filled two large bags with food, mainly bread, cheese, and fruit.

Kim was well-built and tall at nearly six foot. Although no classical beauty, with her mother's blonde hair she was buxom and pretty. She knocked confidently on the door of the penthouse flat. She knew her grandmother was there, having seen her parked car.

The third time she rang the doorbell and knocked insistently, the door of the flat was snatched open. Chloe stood there, glaring, dressed in a housecoat from her chin to her bare feet. She said, without any greeting, 'What the hell are you doing here?' Chloe was dishevelled and obviously naked under her gown.

Kim who had always had a warm, loving relationship with her grandmother was momentarily taken aback, but said hurriedly, 'Granma, the Ice Shelf has collapsed and the whole town is in chaos. Just look out of the window. We are too late for Tanya to pick us up. We have missed the boat, so to speak, so we need to make a plan.'

Chloe looked uncomprehendingly at Kim for a second, then the bombshell suddenly registered. 'You'd better come in. What are those bags for? And the backpack?'

'We are going to need food. The supermarket downstairs was being looted, so I joined in. I doubt if there is anything left by now. The backpack has sleeping bags and clothes. We may have to walk back to The Settlement.'

Chloe said shakily, pointing to the kitchen, 'Make yourself a cup of tea or coffee, I need to get dressed.' She hesitated. 'I have company, by the way.' She glanced at her granddaughter for a reaction.

The Bower grandchildren had discussed the possibility of their grandmother and a lover. All of them adored Chloe, lover or not.

Kim heard a male voice and some conversation down the passage. There was the sound of a shower while she boiled the kettle. She noticed the beautifully-appointed rooms and furniture. There were photographs of the family and some tasteful pictures on the walls. It really was a home to Chloe, she realised.

Within half an hour, a fully dressed Chloe emerged from down the passage, wearing jodhpurs and riding boots, followed by a tall, handsome, grey-haired man in his late fifties, dressed in a suit.

Blushing slightly, Chloe said, 'Clark, this is my granddaughter, Kim. Kim, this is Clark Mason.'

They shook hands rather formally.

'What's this about an Ice Shelf collapsing?' asked Clark.

'The Ross Ice Shelf in the Antarctic has collapsed into the sea. There is a massive tsunami heading this way. The whole city is in turmoil. Just look out of the window.'

'When did this happen?' asked Clark, looking out of the window. 'My God, look at all the crowds.'

'Earlier today,' she said impatiently.

'Oh yes,' said Clark. He was trying to keep the anxiety from his voice.

They quietly sat and drank the tea prepared by Kim, almost as if nothing was amiss.

Kim looked at her grandmother anxiously. 'Granma, we need to get moving. It's too late for the helicopter. I saw the last trip Tanya made. I had to walk here as no vehicles are going anywhere. The whole place is gridlocked.'

'Walk?' asked Clark. He was beginning to realise the seriousness of the situation. 'I should probably go; it will take hours to get to Roseville.'

'Yes, I suppose you should,' said Chloe reluctantly.

Clark moved to the front passage with Chloe, out of sight of Kim. She began looking for another backpack for Chloe to carry.

After ten minutes, Kim heard the front door close quietly and a tearful Chloe returned to the kitchen.

'What should we do?' asked Chloe.

'We have to walk back.'

'Wouldn't horses be a better bet?'

'Where'll we get horses?'

'There's a place north of the city in Terrey Hills.'

'Okay. We need to be careful what we take,' said Kim. 'Here's another backpack.'

They carefully selected items for each pack, with emphasis on food and warm clothing. They ate what they could from the resources in the flat, knowing food would be the biggest issue on the long trek ahead.

Chloe emerged from the bedroom, gingerly carrying a large handgun. 'I'm uncomfortable with this. David gave it to me some time ago and I haven't touched it since. With all your training, maybe it would be better for you to have it. We may need it.'

Kim took the gun, a .45 Webley automatic. She made sure the chamber was empty and noted the magazine was full. She put the safety catch on and tucked the weapon into the back of her trousers, so it was hidden by her jacket. Chloe passed over two boxes of ammunition.

They were almost ready to go when Chloe said, 'I can't bear to leave this place in a mess. Could you just help me tidy up please.'

So they made the bed and vacuumed all the floors. Chloe emptied the fridge, leaving the door open. She took all the garbage to the basement. Everything was left as if they would be away for a few months' holiday. Kim carefully cleaned the gun.

'I know this looks odd,' said Chloe, 'but this place has meant so much to me over the years. I need to be able to remember it like this now, even if I never see it again.'

Kim nodded. She felt much the same way about her home in the Blue Mountains. 'I understand Granma, I really do.'

Chloe whipped around the flat once more, finally switching off the electricity, and, wearing their packs, they went out, carefully locking the front door. It was now dark and all the streets were lit.

The crowds had grown in the three hours Kim had been in the flat, so they went down a side street and walked up the hill past Brookvale Oval. After less than a two kilometre walk, Chloe spotted a man on a motor scooter leaping off and joining in nearby looting. He had left the engine running.

'Quick,' she said, 'hop on. I had one of these when I was younger.' She clumsily engaged the gears and they drove off, whipping past the stationary traffic. To start with progress was rather unsteady, but after a few minutes, Chloe seemed to be perfectly in control.

'Better than walking,' she shouted into the breeze.

They wound their way slowly up the Wakehurst Parkway and Forest Way. The roads were all packed and hardly moving. Several times people tried to stop them, presumably to take the scooter away, since that was the only form of transport making any progress at all. Kim had the gun readily accessible and when one man became very aggressive she fired a shot at his feet and he scampered off. By ten in the evening, they were in McCarrs Creek Road.

'The stables are here, just around the corner,' said Chloe, as she drove up a narrow path and killed the engine. 'We'll wait here. I hope nobody else has the same idea and the horses are all safely asleep in their stalls. I was going to offer to pay, but I don't think that'll work. I'll leave them a note though. We'll wait until all the house lights are out.'

Kim could see Chloe had put the emotion of leaving her flat and her lover behind her and was now fully engaged in getting them both back to the Blue Mountains.

At midnight they crept into the stables. The horses were all quietly resting. Chloe shone her powerful torch around. 'We'll take three, one each and one for the packs. I'll select some while you try to find some sacking to muffle the sound of their hooves.'

Within thirty minutes, they had three horses fully tacked up and their packs were firmly strapped onto one of the horses, together with a bag of fodder.

Chloe was busy shining the torch around. 'What're you looking for?' asked Kim.

'Wire cutters. We'll have to cut fences when it's too difficult to find ways around.'

Kim, standing in the shadows, became aware of someone approaching. She waited in the dark behind a door while Chloe continued her search.

'Who's there?' said a male voice.

Kim tensed up and waiting, holding the gun, whacked the man on the head as hard as she could as he crept past.

'Ah, here we are,' muttered Chloe. 'What was that?' she asked anxiously, reacting to the noise of the man falling to the floor.

'Someone heard us,' said Kim. 'I'll tie him up, but we must move quickly before anyone else comes.'

'It's the owner, damn. I really have no reason to hurt him, but we must be quick,' said Chloe, shining the torch over the inert body as they tied and gagged him, propping him up against a sack of horse food. 'No note now,' she added.

Rapidly and noiselessly they led the horses out of the stables with their muffled hooves enclosed in sacking. In minutes, they were down the road and into the dark, where they were able to mount having removed the sacking.

Chloe said, 'I've ridden here quite a bit as I bought most of the original Settlement horses here and tested them in the park. We need to go southwest until we have passed Duffy's Forest Creek and then we can head northwest. There are many paths through the Ku-ring-gai Chase National Park. We'll have to keep going, even in the dark. With a bit of luck we will be over the Newcastle Freeway by about dawn.'

After making a few wrong turns in the dark, just as the sky was lightening up in the East they saw car lights, completely stationary, on Bobbin Head Road. The mostly sleeping people in the vehicles, barely noticed them. So they found a gap and all three horses were quickly guided over the road.

'It may be more difficult crossing the freeway,' said Kim. 'There will be panic and people may behave irrationally.'

Within two hours, the pair skirted alongside of the Ku-ring-gai Chase road with little interference from people in vehicles. They ran into trouble when they tried to cross the Newcastle Freeway at Mount Colah. Chloe, leading the pack horse, thought she had spotted a gap between two cars and was just about to ride through when the driver aggressively started his car and closed it. Kim realising there was no time for negotiations, or any type of nicety, drew the Webley and shot the car's two front tyres out. The driver emerged and started to protest, with his wife and small children screaming inside the car.

'Get into that fucking car,' Kim shouted, 'and move it back. You have ten seconds or the next shot will be into your thick head.' She pointed the gun. The man rapidly did as he was told. Kim fired three shots into the car's engine, which then stopped running, as they raced through the gap, crossing the other carriage of the freeway without difficulty, and disappearing into the surrounding bush.

'Whew!' said Chloe. 'Close one. Obviously we must avoid human contact where we can. It's cross country from now on anyway.'

Stopping at noon, and unsaddling in some trees they watered and tethered the horses, allowing them to graze. Two hours later they continued the journey, after indulging in a small snack from their limited resources. They rode through Galston and Kenthurst, an area consisting mainly of small holdings, using gates where they could find them. On one occasion they were unable to find a gate, so Chloe held the horses while Kim cut the barbed wire fence, folding all the strands back on themselves to protect any animals passing through.

If another human was sighted they immediately moved away, where possible, out of sight.

Finding a small copse as night fell, Kim said, 'There's a house a k or so away. I suppose we can risk a small fire.'

The horses were in a place where they could graze and were also given a little of the fodder. Kim cooked chops and boiled some vegetables, which she had rescued from Chloe's fridge. 'We forgot the tea,' Chloe announced, taking the kettle off the fire and hunting through their supplies.

'We must boil the water anyway,' said Kim. 'Leave the boiled water out overnight and I'll fill water bottles in the morning.'

The night passed uneventfully, with Kim crawling out of her sleeping bag now and then to check on the horses. They were on their way at dawn.

The routine continued for the next few days. There was some difficulty in finding a ford to cross the Hawkesbury River, but they were now moving into less-settled areas with larger properties and it became easier to avoid being seen.

'We'll be in the mountains soon,' said Kim hopefully.

Crossing one major road was a real headache. Many of the cars on the road had run out of fuel and it was clear people were panicking, having eaten all their food. Kim approached the road in hiding, watching for more than an hour before she returned to Chloe and the horses.

'We should go before dawn when most people are at their lowest ebb. It'll still be quite dark and we'll be well on our way before anyone notices anything. On horseback, we ought to be able to easily outrun any pursuit.'

'What about midnight?' asked Chloe.

'We could try that, but we get into thick forest shortly after we cross the road and I don't fancy wandering about there in the dark.'

Staying well away from the road, they spent an uncomfortable night worrying about the next morning. Both had trouble sleeping without the warmth and comfort of a fire. But they certainly didn't want to give away their presence.

At five in the morning, Chloe said, 'Come on, I'm sick of this, let's make a move.'

Packing up quietly, and making certain all their horses and equipment were in order, the little entourage crept towards the road.

Kim again went ahead. The vehicles were scattered everywhere, but everyone appeared to be asleep, staving off another dreadful day.

She chose a place with a decent gap between vehicles and while it was still dark they crossed over the road quietly and quickly, disappearing into the bushes on the other side. Finding a path, they had the horses moving at a fast walking pace.

'I hope we weren't seen,' Kim whispered, 'but I saw movement to our right. We'll go on a bit, until it gets light, and then I'll double back to see if we're being followed. Don't worry Granma, I won't be far away. Just putting into practice some of Derain's lessons.'

When it was fully light, Kim told Chloe, 'Keep going on this path, I'm going to double back. If there's anyone following they are going to get a very big surprise.'

She left the path and quietly rode her horse back to where, still hidden, she could see the path they'd taken; there she waited. Not more than ten minutes later, three men in their thirties came running along the path.

They were talking. 'I saw three horses. That's the way to go; there's no chance now with the car. We're all going to die on this bloody road if we stay here.'

'How many people?'

'Two women; should be easy meat. We'll fuck 'em and dump the bodies in the bush. Nobody will miss them with all this chaos around. They'll never be found. Maybe the dingoes or dogs will eat them.'

Kim had made sure the Webley was fully loaded and ready. Her blood was now boiling. She considered taking all three men out there and then, but it was too late and they had gone past. She made herself calm down and riding her horse, followed the men, keeping just out of sight. It took a few minutes before the men caught up with Chloe. She was quite serene, knowing Kim was on hand.

'A fucking granny,' said one of the men. 'Fancy fucking a granny!' He made a grab for the reins, but with Chloe's skill she managed to evade his grasp for a minute until two of them cornered the horse and one held the reins.

'We are having the horse and you,' said the apparent leader. 'Off or you will get hurt.'

'I don't think so,' said Kim, still mounted. None of the men had seen her approach.

The man just stood there grinning. 'You won't dare use that gun. I bet you don't have a clue how it works anyway.'

'I am going to count to ten,' said Kim through gritted teeth. 'If you are still holding the reins of that horse you will get a bullet between the eyes. One, two, three ...'

'Ah, bullshit, you couldn't hit a barn door at ten feet,' the man blustered.

'... eight, nine, ten.'

A split second's flash of apprehension crossed the man's grinning face as Kim calmly lifted the Webley, took aim, and shot him between the eyes. He was lifted up and thrown back a metre with the impact of the heavy bullet. The horses skittered, but were just kept under control.

'Jesus Christ,' shrieked one of the others, making to run.

'Stay exactly where you are or you'll both get the same treatment.' Kim fired another shot at one of the men's feet. 'Hands above your head.'

'We didn't mean anything. It was just a joke,' one of them pleaded.

'You mean, "We'll fuck them and leave their bodies in the bushes for the dingoes" was just a joke!' Kim retorted angrily. 'You,' Kim yelled at one of the men, 'undress, and get a move on. Yes everything. Off now!' The man hesitated. Kim fired a shot at his feet and he quickly stripped. Soon naked, he was shivering in fright.

'I just need my money and credit cards,' he pleaded.

'No you don't, not where you're going. Stand over there and if you move one inch you'll get one in the head.' Kim waved the gun in the direction of the dead man.

'You're a bloody maniac!'

Kim ignored him. 'Now you, the same thing. Quickly.' The second man complied and, like his companion, soon stood shivering.

'Put the clothes in a pile. Then both of you, strip your dead friend, and put his clothes on the pile too. Hurry up!' They jumped as Kim fired a shot next to them. 'Okay, now light the clothes.'

'There's no lighter.'

Wordlessly, Chloe tossed the man a box of matches. The pile of clothes was lit. Both men had crapped themselves and were crying as they watched for ten minutes as their clothes burned to ash.

'If I ever see either of you again,' said Kim, 'you'll get a bullet between the eyes. Now get the hell out of here.' She fired two shots just wide of the pair. There was momentary hesitation and then they ran, tearing themselves on bushes as they scampered down the path, naked and barefoot.

Kim, still holding the gun, slumped down on the saddle. 'Jesus, I didn't think I'd ever be able to do that. The Academy,' she explained, glancing at Chloe, while she reloaded the gun's magazine.

Chloe, shivering in fright at their close call, edged her horse over and put an arm around Kim, 'You saved our lives. Thank you. If I'd been on my own I'd be a goner by now. Those bastards, did they really say those things?'

'Definitely, I was only a couple of metres away. They were deadly serious.'

'We'd better get going. What are we going to do with the dead man?' asked Chloe.

'Nothing. If his friends don't fetch him, he'll suffer the same fate as they had planned for us.'

They continued along the ill-defined path, climbing steadily into the mountains, without stopping, putting as much distance between them and the road as possible.

CHAPTER TWENTY-FOUR
First Weeks of Isolation

Apart from Kim and Chloe there were two others who had not returned before the Ice Shelf collapsed. The families of the two absentees had badgered David to do something to somehow return their loved ones home.

'I've explained to you that Kim and Chloe are also missing. Patricia told Kim where to find Chloe, but we haven't heard from either of them since and mobile phone contact hasn't been possible. So we're in exactly the same position as you. The only hope is that they can somehow walk back here. If we don't hear anything within two months, we will have to assume they didn't make it and are dead,' David looked off into the distance, impatiently wiping away a tear.

'Do you have any idea of your family members' whereabouts?' he asked.

'We've had no contact since the day before the collapse,' David was told by Graham, the father of one of the absentees.

'Did they intend to return?'

'We think so,' was the uncertain reply.

David looked at them. Somehow they expected him to wave a magic wand and their loved ones would suddenly appear.

'Mark and Tanya are organising a number of horse patrols to go out in various directions from here. Speak to them and maybe join one of the patrols. In any event, make sure the leader of each patrol knows who is missing and what they look like.'

'What about the helicopter? Many others were rescued in that way.'

David shook his head. 'Tanya was wounded on the last trip. She's the only pilot and is out of commission for the moment.' He shrugged. 'I won't be making any further attempt to find Chloe and Kim, however tempting that might be. It would be a wild goose chase and put other people's lives at risk unnecessarily. I am desperately hoping they are alright and heading back here. But our job now is to look after the people here and ensure their safety and welfare. I know how you feel. It's desperate. I'd do something if I could.'

David saw a number of black looks, hearing a comment as they left, 'Bloody Bowers just look after their own. They don't care about the rest of us.'

David was infuriated by the unjust remark, but kept his peace. They were in Joe's ward and he would be briefed on the issue.

Mark had organised ten patrols with four members in each. They were equipped for a two week journey. Graham was eventually persuaded by Joe to join a patrol. 'It's the least you can do,' Joe told the man.

'You should be sending the helicopter out again,' said Graham.

'We have one pilot who can't fly. For heaven's sake, use your sense, man. What you are suggesting is like committing suicide. The helicopter almost crashed last time.' *If they wanted to return, why did they leave it so late? They were given a year's notice*, he thought. Joe was desperately worried for Kim and Chloe, but Joe knew Kim was resourceful and could manage herself as well as anyone in the bush. He had unsuccessfully tried to calm Patricia's fears with that thought. For weeks after the collapse of the Ice Shelf, Patricia cried herself to sleep in his arms.

Mark briefed the patrols before they left. They all knew the people that hadn't made it back. 'What we need is information, so just observe what you see. It may be tempting to try to rescue people. Don't try it. The likelihood is that you will be torn to pieces. Don't put yourself or your patrol at risk.'

Joe made sure Graham was included in his patrol. Virtually every member of the community, except the aged and infirm, had been through the training provided by The Academy, so Graham was a competent horseman and could handle a weapon. Tanya had planned each route with Mark's help and they were sent out over a two day period with Joe and his group leaving last.

Mark did not accompany any of the patrols. He, Roger, and Tanya planned to fly over the catastrophe about to engulf Sydney, making sure there was a full record of the event they were certain would destroy the spectacularly beautiful city. They had already watched in horror, while the TV was still functioning, the pictures of the dreaded tsunami roaring up from the Antarctic. As Derain and his people had predicted, the massive wave was due to hit the Australian coast on April 25th 2026.

On the appointed day, Tanya had woken with a start while it was still dark. After a split-second it hit her. Today was the day the world she had known would change forever. The fifteen metre tsunami hurtling its way towards the Australian coast at one hundred kilometres an hour would crash into Sydney, with a destructive force such as the world had never before witnessed—Sydney, beautiful Sydney, her home town, where she had grown up and flourished. She shuddered, wondering how she would cope.

Trying to create a sense of normalcy, Tanya woke the rest of the family—Mark and their two teenage children. She managed her usual ten kilometre run, with her injured shoulder causing little discomfort. Easing the helicopter from its base on the parade ground of The Settlement, she flew the machine easily with her usual skill.

Mark occupied the right hand seat of the machine, holding his camera carefully. Roger, in one of the rear seats, was in charge of a further two cameras. Circling, they all admired with pride their small Settlement, created from a raw piece of Australian wilderness. 'We'd better bloody well make sure all this survives and us with it,' Tanya muttered to her companions.

Mark was idly wondering how he would cope with the inevitable changes to his life wrought by the tsunami. Tanya smiled at him, trying not to display her nervousness at what they would soon witness. Slim and brown-haired, Roger's benign looks belied his competence. He had spent most of his life in The Settlement and was pleased to be asked to accompany his two much admired leaders on what was bound to be a life-changing experience.

Flying southeast, Tanya headed directly to the iconic harbour city into increasingly heavy rain.

'Does the weather have something to do with the tsunami?' Mark asked, looking nervously at Tanya.

'Probably, but it's going to take more than a few drops of rain to stop me,' said Tanya, anticipating Mark's point.

Mark remained silent.

The city was eerily quiet. All the major roads leading out of the city were completely gridlocked. It must have been that way for many days now. There were people standing around their vehicles. Many of them waved desperately.

Mark saw a man aiming a rifle at them, 'Look out,' he pointed, but Tanya had already seen the danger and swiftly manoeuvred the machine downwards and away to safety.

'Well, it hasn't hit yet,' said Tanya, as they circled the city centre. 'I'll head out to sea for ten minutes to see if we can spot anything.'

She directed the helicopter over the beaches and the grey Pacific Ocean. The machine was now being buffeted by high winds.

'Don't worry,' said Tanya, noticing her passengers' discomfort as the machine dropped suddenly and bounced back just as quickly, 'this thing can cope with much worse.' Mark and Roger concentrated on their cameras and tried to ignore the discomfort.

'Jesus Fucking Christ, look,' yelled Mark, fifteen minutes later, pointing through the rain-swept windscreen. And there it was, a huge wave, looking threatening and lethal even from the relatively safe vantage point of the helicopter; stretching from horizon to horizon.

'I'll follow it in,' announced Tanya as she carefully turned the machine around, hovering a few metres above the wave as the cameras whirred. Her apparent calmness belied the inner turmoil engulfing her. Although she and David had forecast this very event more than fifteen years earlier she, mentally, had to pinch herself. Speaking into the headphones, she said, 'This is real, it's almost too difficult to believe that we're not in some ghastly dream.' She glanced at Mark, who was giving nothing away, focussing on creating a clear record of the catastrophe about to engulf them all.

Minutes later the massive wave crashed into the coast, with a destructive fury difficult to believe. Tanya followed it as it swept through the famous Sydney Heads and into the harbour. The many small craft scattered around the shores were picked up and tossed about like children's toys, many of them smashing into each other and into buildings innocently lining the shore, ending up like so much matchwood.

'Look at that,' said Mark. All three watched in horror as one of the huge cruise liners, having taken refuge in the harbour, was picked up with the destructive force of the wave and dumped right into the Sydney Passenger Terminal. The vessel fell onto its side; many people on board, who had presumably thought they'd be safe on such a large vessel, were seen falling hopelessly into the churning waters.

'It's much worse than we could possibly have imagined,' said Tanya tersely as she piloted the machine, following the wave. 'Nobody and nothing will survive this.' In front of the wave still stood the beautiful, peaceful city, and behind it a mass of wrecked houses and boats, dead and dying people.

The water raced up George Street and the other streets leading away from Circular Quay—the place where Captain Phillip and the eleven ships of the first fleet had arrived from England with a load of convicts in January 1788. The few figures visible on the streets were tossed about like rag dolls, before being swamped.

'Almost two hundred and fifty years of history just blitzed away in a few seconds,' whispered Tanya.

Flying south through ongoing bursts of rain to Botany Bay and Sydney Airport, Tanya kept the helicopter as low as was safe. The wave had preceded them. The airport was just a tangle of wreckage with huge planes piled one on top of the other. Many of the hangars were no longer visible or were represented by grotesquely deformed pieces of concrete and steel. Several ships in the nearby Port Botany had been swept two or three kilometres inshore. On the southern side of the bay, the Kurnell Oil Refinery had been virtually razed to the ground, the few stacks remaining poking like sentinels out of the murky waters. Surrounding suburbs were completely inundated.

Mark said more calmly than he felt, 'The water will go some way inland, but will then retreat as the land becomes steeper, creating another wave of destruction. We should go to North Sydney and see what happens there.' He wondered how he had ever doubted the science behind what he was now witnessing.

As they flew back over the harbour they saw that a large cargo vessel had crashed into one of the pylons on the iconic Sydney Harbour Bridge and had created a huge obstacle there, with debris and other vessels piling up against the bridge. As they watched, the power of the flood moved a huge pylon. As if in slow motion, one by one the gantries of the enormous bridge fell into the harbour. Soon there was nothing left of the bridge that had stood there for almost a hundred years, but remnants of stone and concrete pylons and a few ghostlike pieces of steel sticking out of the water.

Mark was right. The power of the wave had swept far up the Warringah Freeway, one of the major arteries leading north out of the city. It had travelled up the Pacific Highway, past the skyscrapers of North Sydney and over Crows Nest and beyond the Royal North Shore Hospital. The water had smashed its way into all the little streets, which days before had housed innocent people going about their daily business. Almost all of these people would have either lost their lives in the flood or would be sitting in cars on one of the major arteries leaving Sydney going nowhere and gradually starving to death.

Within a few hours, the destructive force of the flood had slowed and the water had started to retreat with an equally vicious force, sweeping cars, houses, and any people that were left back towards the harbour.

The once majestic harbour was now a sea of death and destruction, bodies of humans and animals floating amidst the wrecked cars, buses, trucks, and other assorted debris. The wreckage of the bridge, the "coat-hanger" as it had been known, peered out from the filthy water.

'Look,' said Mark, 'somehow the Sydney Opera House is still standing.' He focussed his camera on the top half of the famous sails, poking out from the debris-strewn water now obscuring the lower half of the landmark.

'We'll have to refuel quite soon,' announced Tanya. 'We'll return home, refuel, and come back. I feel so helpless not being able to help anyone down there, including any of our own still left.'

On their return, Tanya flew south until they crossed the M4. She flew as low as possible in the persistent rain over what was now no more than a long term car park. Sodden-looking people emerged from their vehicles and waved desperately. Some cars had tried to escape the traffic jam and had ventured across country only to become bogged down.

Returning to the harbour, they saw the flood was still pouring down the steep slopes from the north, but they could see that water levels were settling down to around fifteen metres above where it had been before the catastrophe hit.

'We forecast this all those years ago,' said Tanya in disbelief.

'It'll be a couple of weeks before the flood reaches Western Europe and the Eastern Seaboard of the States,' Mark observed. 'I hope they now understand what's going to hit them.'

Making several circuits of the greater city, they could see the coastal suburbs had suffered almost total destruction, there was absolutely no sign of life anywhere now within several kilometres of the coast. Inland all that was visible were signs of panic. Tanya was able to manoeuvre the helicopter near one isolated supermarket, which had been completely trashed, the doors and windows broken.

'Comprehensively looted,' Roger observed.

'I've seen enough,' said Tanya. 'We have a reasonable record.' Mark and Roger signalled acknowledgment and she turned for home.

Not a word was said on the return trip to The Settlement.

Tanya briefly thought about how the day's events justified their work over the last fifteen years and more. But she quickly put those thoughts out of her mind, trying to focus on what needed to be done in The Settlement. She also had a moment to worry about the missing Settlement people, particularly Chloe and Kim.

Mark was relieved he had continued to support the development of The Settlement and tried unsuccessfully to put out of his mind the doubts he had about his role, with him playing second fiddle to Tanya.

Roger was generally not given to introspection. His future had always been tied up with The Settlement and the projections he had been brought up with had now come to pass. He fiddled with his cameras all the way home, not wishing to interrupt the silence.

The Settlement turned to the BBC and CNN for images, once the ABC and other Australian channels disappeared, via a receiver dish Joe had rigged up during the past year. After a few days those sources of information also dried up.

All the Bowers were busy visiting villagers, sympathising with those traumatised by the catastrophic images.

'The only thing we can do,' David told people, 'is to focus on what needs doing here. There is absolutely nothing we can do for the outside world. Ensuring our survival is how we can make a contribution.'

Mark organised two internal patrols, circulating daily inside The Settlement fence, to ensure there were no incursions.

Tanya also made sure the helicopter was fully serviced. 'We need to traverse the city and surrounds again, recording the situation for future generations, so the same mistakes won't be repeated.'

David and two others rode over to The Bandstand to make certain they were safe and secure. They returned within a week and reported that, so far, there had been no incursions there.

Within ten days, the patrols started to return. Tanya started to debrief them when she realised most members of the patrols were reluctant to describe their experiences. The scenes of horror gradually emerged—people fighting over scraps of food, gun battles between motorists, packs of dogs pulling dead people from cars, people dying of panic, thirst, and hunger everywhere.

One patrol failed to return.

Tanya and Mark mapped out the route they had taken.

'I will take the helicopter to see if I can find them,' said Tanya. 'Graham, maybe you could come with me.'

After two days of searching, Tanya spotted the bodies of horses lying beside a road. She flew low over the scene and some people ran away.

'They look like our horses being butchered for food,' observed Tanya. 'Graham, fire a few shots so the people keep away, I'm going down.'

Graham did as he was told, but when Tanya tried to land the helicopter she saw someone aiming what looked like one of The Academy's short-barrelled rifles at them. Luckily it jammed and Tanya quickly flew out of reach.

'We haven't got a hope,' said Tanya. 'If we go in there, we'll suffer the same fate as that patrol. We can assume they're all dead. People will survive for a few days on the horse meat, but it will putrefy and then they will die. We'll return in three weeks to see if we can recover any bodies.' She continued, 'We still have enough fuel for about two hours. Where do you think your son might be?'

'He was living in a house in Epping. I have the address.'

Tanya entered it into her GPS system and shortly afterwards had the helicopter hovering over the house.

'That's it, that's the place,' said Graham excitedly.

Tanya flew slowly over the area. There was no sign of anyone, just a few dogs wandering about, scampering away when the helicopter hovered overhead.

'What do you want to do?' asked Tanya.

'Is there any chance we could land just for a few minutes?'

'The garden is too small, but I can land over there.' She pointed to a football field about two hundred yards away from the house. 'I will have to keep the engine running. Hopefully, I can give you time to run to the house and back. You have to understand, though, that if I'm threatened I'll have to take off and may not be able to pick you up again. If we do get into trouble, I will land at that oval over there in thirty minutes. If you are there, I will pick you up, otherwise you're on your own. Understand?'

Graham hesitated, weighing up his own personal safety against the slim possibility of finding his son. 'Okay, I understand.'

They landed and Graham clambered out, armed with one of the short-barrelled Academy rifles. There was nobody about. Tanya, as promised, kept the engine running and watched Graham sprint across the grass and disappear into a side street. Suddenly a myriad of people emerged from the nearby houses and started to converge on the helicopter. She had no choice but to take off again. She flew over the house that Graham had identified and saw him smash down the front door and go in. Tanya hovered for ten minutes. People started to converge on the house as Graham emerged. He waved at the helicopter and pointed in the direction of the oval. Tanya was able to monitor his progress, but made as if to return to the football field so most of the now substantial crowd followed her there, allowing Graham to run to the oval, alone. As Graham ran across the oval Tanya landed only to see him being tackled rugby style by a young man Tanya hadn't seen. Unthinkingly, she leapt out of the machine and ran to the now struggling pair. She knocked the aggressor over the head with her own rifle and dragged a groggy Graham into the aircraft. She was just about to take off when the man appeared at the window of the helicopter.

He was clearly unarmed and mouthing, 'Help me, help me.' Tanya hesitated, then opened the door of the machine and pulled the youth in.

'Any trouble, and you will get a bullet and be tipped out. Strap him in, will you Graham.' They took off just as people started to scramble onto the oval.

On their way back to the mountains, Graham tearfully told his story. 'I found them all in the house; my son, his girlfriend, and two small children I've never seen before. We didn't even know they existed. They were all lying peacefully in their beds, dead. There is a note dated April 16th which says … here, read it.'

Tanya steadied the machine and read—

Dear Dad and Mum, you may never see this note in view of the impending disaster. But if you ever find it, we should explain that we cannot face living in the world that will now emerge, so we have taken the only option available.

None of us will have any pain. Sorry about not having told you about the children; we couldn't face your disapproval. Your loving son, Daryl.

Tanya handed the note back.

'We wondered why we were never invited to the house. Daryl was always so secretive,' a tearful Graham explained. 'My wife and I strongly disapproved of Daryl's relationship with his girlfriend. We thought it immoral. Maybe we could have been more accommodating,' he added quietly. A tear escaped.

'And who are you?' Tanya asked their unexpected passenger, who had remained silent and was looking around in a bewildered manner.

'Call me Silas. I lived a few doors down from Daryl, but I didn't know he had committed suicide. We've all locked ourselves away since the catastrophe and we've run out of food. Where are we going?'

'We live in a secure place in the Blue Mountains,' answered Graham. 'You'll be safe there.'

They flew unseeingly over the spectacular mountain scenery, each engrossed in their own thoughts. They landed safely within the hour.

Silas was taken in by Graham and his wife, Denise—a surrogate son.

A day or so later, Graham and his wife Denise visited David in his office, 'We have come to apologise for the things we said to you a few weeks ago.'

'There is no need,' said David. 'We live in very traumatic times. There is still no sign of Chloe or Kim and we are all beginning to fear the worst.'

'Tanya risked her life to try and help us,' explained Graham. 'She made no mention of Kim and Chloe, but selflessly helped me understand what happened to our son.' They were red-eyed and looking dreadful.

'I appreciate what you've said, although it is unnecessary. Maybe the boy you rescued will bring you some solace.'

David had been thinking about the capacity of The Settlement to provide for the people living there. He explained to Tanya, 'The last two or three years we've had reasonable seasons, but there's been little surplus production. We've consumed almost all of what's been produced. If the weather turns, we could be short of food and have to impose rationing, which would be a disaster. No one in the community overindulges. We should start to develop some of the forest area you enclosed all those years ago.' He smiled at the memory.

'Graham was once a forestry worker, I'm sure he'll take that on,' responded Tanya.

CHAPTER TWENTY-FIVE
Homeward Bound

After the ghastly incident with the rapacious men, Kim and Chloe made rapid and silent progress along somewhat ill-defined paths, always trying to steer a route to the northwest.

By late afternoon, Kim stopped her horse saying to Chloe, 'We'll camp somewhere here. With a bit of luck we'll have scared the shit out of anyone thinking about following us; we still need to be careful though.'

'It looks as if there's a storm brewing,' answered Chloe, looking at the black clouds building from the southwest. 'We need to have something to eat first and the horses are tired, so we need to look after them. I'm guessing we still have a long way to go?'

'Okay Granma,' said Kim, not answering the question. In truth, she had no idea how much further they had to go or how long it would take. 'Hang on to the horses for a few minutes and I will see what I can find.'

'Could you stop calling me Granma; we're in this together. I'm Chloe now.'

Kim nodded and handed the reins of her horse to Chloe. She returned fifteen minutes later. 'I've found a place. There's an overhanging rock and it's quite dry. It'll provide some protection. There's no water for the horses though. We'll have to share our own supplies until we find a stream and we'll have to mask our trail using one of Derain's lessons. The place is uphill to the right of the path, so we first go left and downhill. Then we should split with me going back towards the way we came and you going in the same direction. You should then cross the main path and head uphill. I will meet you about a hundred metres above where we are now. If anyone has followed us they will not see where I crossed the main path to go uphill.'

Chloe looked a little uncertain. 'It's okay Gr ... Chloe, just focus on what I said. When you think you've done all that, stop and I'll find you. It should take about an hour; the bush is quite thick.'

'Is this necessary?' asked Chloe.

'Maybe, desperate people will do desperate things; it's better to be safe. If anyone has followed us, we'll hear them long before they have an inkling we are anywhere near.'

They went off into the bush as Kim had directed and once they were some two hundred metres downhill from the path, Kim went left with two of the horses and Chloe turned right. Chloe found Kim's instructions easy to follow and within half an hour she was in place, as far as she could judge, about one hundred metres uphill from where they had originally stopped on the main path. She dismounted, loosened her horse's girth, and sat down with her back to a tree. Holding the reins, Chloe allowed the horse to graze while she waited.

Kim made certain she cut a swathe through the bushes that could be easily followed. When she turned back to cross the main path, she took one horse at a time, crossed the road, and tied the animal up. She took another route altogether with the second animal. Both routes were now quite difficult to follow, and as she crossed the main path she swept the path clear of all hoof prints.

It will take an expert to see that anyone has been here, she thought as she rearranged bushes into their original position and admired her handiwork. *Derain would be proud of me.*

Within the promised hour, she spotted Chloe, now sleeping quietly with her back against the tree. Kim thought she would have a little fun and as noiselessly as possible managed to lead her two horses into Chloe's small clearing, then sat on her haunches and waited. Soon one of the horses snorted loudly and Chloe woke with a start, looking wildly about her.

She smiled when she saw Kim. 'How long have you been there?'

'About ten minutes. You looked as if you were having a lovely dream.'

'I was.' She didn't elaborate.

~❦

There was room on the dry and dusty floor under the overhanging rock for both humans and horses. They unsaddled and Chloe gave the horses some water and fodder while Kim collected bundles of firewood. Then they cooked dinner from their now dwindling supplies. Just as darkness fell, the heavens opened with a vengeance.

During the evening meal, Chloe said uncertainly to Kim, 'I always had grave doubts about the science and The Settlement. It seems David and Tanya were right all along. Despite the horses, I've never really felt at home there. Now I don't know how I'll fit in, if we ever get back.' Chloe didn't mention David's involvement with Caroline. 'I'm very grateful you made the effort to find me though, the alternative doesn't bear thinking about. How did you know where to find me?'

'Mum gave me the address. I think Tanya gave it to her.'

'Tanya, always one step ahead of the sheriff.'

Kim didn't say much, busying herself with the food. She thought about Chloe's lover. *People do overcomplicate their lives, me included.* She briefly considered the boyfriend she had broken up with a few days before the news of the flood. *I would've been back at The Settlement if he had agreed to come,* she thought. *It seems like some sort of divine intervention that I was around to help rescue Granma.* Like most in The Settlement, she knew about David's relationship with Caroline. She wondered how Chloe was going to be able to cope without her trips to Sydney, but put the thoughts firmly out of her mind. *There is still a long way to go.*

Heavy rain continued to fall until the early hours of the morning. Kim popped out of her sleeping bag several times during the night, mainly to check on the horses and to keep a small fire going.

At first light Chloe emerged and said, 'I haven't slept like that since I was a girl. It must be because I unburdened myself to you last night.'

Kim wasn't sure how to respond, so said nothing.

Chloe busied herself in the dust near the fire with a breakfast of stale bread and some remaining marmalade.

'It's extraordinary,' observed Chloe. 'There can't have been a drop of moisture in this place for generations. How did you know it was here?'

'Derain again,' Kim told her. 'He said to look where the rain was coming from and go to the lee side of a rock and that would be the safest place.'

When they had finished the meagre meal, Kim asked Chloe to tack up the horses. 'I'm going down to the path to see that we're not being followed. Anyone who followed us would have had a hard time last night.'

Kim slipped and slid her way down to the main path. When she had it in sight, she waited and watched for a full fifteen minutes. As she was about to turn back, she heard a faint sound coming from somewhere downhill. Cautiously, she crossed the path and followed the sound. Within a few minutes she saw what appeared to be a blonde head rocking backward and forward. The sound she had heard was a continuous wailing. As Kim approached, she could see a teenage girl cradling a boy or man's head.

She made sure whoever it was could see her and then said quietly, 'What happened? How can I help you?'

The girl jumped up in absolute terror, yelling, 'Don't touch me. Don't touch me.' She started to back away.

'It's alright, I don't mean you any harm. Please tell me what happened and what you're doing here.'

'I'll go back. Please don't shoot me.'

'Go where? What makes you think I want to shoot you?' She held out her hands to indicate they were empty. 'How did you get here and what were you trying to do?'

'I should go back to the road, but Mick here,' she indicated the prostrate form at her feet, 'is dead, I think. I don't know what to do.'

'Why are you here?' Kim repeated.

The girl said shakily, 'We were stuck on the road, food was running out, and we had no fuel. We heard some garbled story about two women who'd crossed the road on horseback, so Mick said we should follow the path, that it was better than starving to death on that road. So we followed the hoof marks, you know, of the horses, which was easy. Some people were bringing a dead man back to the road. They told us he'd been shot by two women on horseback. We nearly turned back, but Mick wanted to take a chance. So we did. Then after a very long time, Mick said the horses had left the path up there. And just as it became dark it started to pour with rain. Mick was just ahead of me. He shouted, "Snake!" He was bitten, I think. Then he passed out and must have died. I stayed because I didn't know what else to do.'

'Do you have anything with you?'

'Mick had a sweater and a water bottle and there are some biscuits in the rucksack.'

The girl had calmed down a bit and handed Kim the rucksack. Kim had a quick look inside after she had checked to see if Mick was showing any signs of life.

'Mick is dead,' she told the girl gently. 'Look, with last night's rain all the hoof prints will have washed away. If you try to return to the road you will get hopelessly lost and die in the bush. We are camped up there,' Kim pointed, 'in a dry spot, and are making for a place in the mountains where you'll be safe. You can try to go back if you want, but we won't be going anywhere near that bloody road again. What's your name by the way?'

'Susan.'

'Okay, Susan, I'm not going to hurt you. Please understand that. Come with me to our camp to dry off and get something to eat. I will come back and bury Mick. Are you a Christian or anything? Maybe you'd like to say a prayer for him?'

Susan nodded nervously.

They found Chloe all ready to leave with the horses saddled and the fire buried.

She was surprised to see Kim accompanied by a dishevelled, wet, teenage girl wearing sandals, a skimpy pair of shorts, and a tee shirt. Kim explained the situation and introduced Susan.

'I'll go and dig the grave,' Kim told Chloe. 'Susan needs warm clothing and something to eat, so I'm not sure how soon we'll be able to leave. Could you assess the food situation? There are now three of us.'

Kim pulled the spade from their luggage and ran down the hill. She returned an hour later with all Mick's clothing. 'We are short of clothing so I rescued this stuff and his backpack. Can you conduct a burial service, Chloe?'

'Probably. We still have food for three days, if we are careful.'

'Let's pack up here, give Mick a decent burial, and then be on our way. I want to put as much distance between us and that blasted road as possible. Are you still with us Susan, or are you thinking of returning?'

Susan shook her head, 'I'll come with you.'

Chloe had already given Susan some vitamin C pills. 'You have just spent a night in the rain, this might help stave off a bad cold,' Chloe explained to a surprised Susan.

Susan was dressed in a spare pair of Chloe's jodhpurs and a sweater. Kim found her a pair of sturdy shoes in her own luggage. They were too big, but better than sandals. The horses were led down the path to the body.

Kim had already placed Mick in the deep grave and crossed his hands over his chest.

Chloe said what she could remember from a funeral service while Susan watched, dry eyed. She was persuaded to put a handful of earth on Mick's body, then Kim quickly filled the grave with earth and covered it with branches from nearby.

'Do you want to be able to find this spot at some time in the future?' asked Chloe.

Susan shook her head.

By midday, they were on their way with Susan riding quite comfortably behind Chloe. They chatted amiably.

'How long was Mick your boyfriend?' Chloe asked.

'He is … wasn't really a boyfriend,' Susan answered, hesitatingly. 'He lived next door, so I have known him for a long time. Just recently he started to take an interest in me. We had sex a couple of times.'

'Why did you run off with him?'

'Everyone in the street had decided to leave. My family car was full so I went with his family. Then we heard about you two, and Mick just grabbed me and said this was the only way out. Most of the people in the traffic jam were running out of food and fuel. They'll probably all die there. So here I am,' said Susan in a matter-of-fact way.

Chloe had already told her about The Settlement so Susan seemed relaxed about where they were headed.

'How do you know the way?' asked Susan.

'We don't,' said Chloe. 'We know that if we keep moving northwest we'll eventually arrive. It may take some time though.'

'I thought you said you only had food for three days?'

'Yes,' interrupted Kim. 'Tonight I will do something about that. There is plenty of food all around us if you know where to look. Please don't worry, none of us will starve.'

'What sort of things are you talking about?'

'Wallaby, snake, berries, leaves, goanna, you name it,' said Kim cheerfully.

'You eat snake?' asked a horrified Susan.

'Certainly,' interjected Chloe. 'Tastes a bit like chicken and it's much better than dying of starvation.'

Susan pulled a face. 'I thought snakes were poisonous.'

'Some snakes have venom in a gland in their head that they inject through their fangs. If you cut the head off, the rest of the animal is very good eating.'

'Two weeks ago I was eating a McDonalds hamburger in Blacktown with a few friends. Now I'm in some unknown forest riding a horse with strangers and will soon be eating snake to stay alive.'

'Snake is much better for you than any of that fast food rubbish,' observed Chloe.

Susan shuddered.

'How old are you?' asked Kim

'Sixteen, in July.'

～つ

They kept moving all day. In the evening, they camped next to a small stream. Kim showed Susan how to collect firewood. 'Just make a bit of noise and bang logs with a stick before you pick anything up.'

Chloe tended to the horses and Kim disappeared for an hour, returning with a medium-sized wallaby, which to Susan's horror, Kim started to skin and butcher.

Kim waved her pistol, 'Not the ideal hunting weapon, I had to creep up very close.'

'We're going to eat that?' Susan asked, as Chloe built up the fire.

'That's all there is tonight. Eat this or starve. I had the same reaction when we were introduced to it by the Aborigines. It's much better for you than beef or lamb, as it has a very low fat content.'

Susan was hungry and eventually was persuaded to eat some wallaby.

Kim kept a small fire going all night and regularly checked on the horses. Chloe allowed Susan to share her sleeping bag. When they woke, Kim's sleeping bag was empty. She returned just after dawn with a large, headless black snake.

'I will skin it later,' said Kim. 'I think we should keep going all day today; progress is quite slow now we're in the mountains.'

Susan ran to the side of the camping area and was sick. 'It's the snake,' she said.

Chloe shook her head and whispered to Kim, 'Pregnant; morning sickness.'

Kim's eyes widened and she nodded.

Despite everything, Susan ate a large breakfast, including some cold wallaby.

Progress was slow, but constant. Kim managed to keep the larder stocked with snake, wallaby, honey, and some berries. Susan soon became used to the diet and appeared to be blooming, even though she was always sick in the morning.

Chloe took her aside one day, put her arms around her, and said, 'My dear, this sickness in the morning means you're pregnant. It has nothing to do with the diet.'

'Pregnant! I can't be. What will they think at school? What will Mum say?' she started to cry.

'Susan, where we are going your pregnancy won't be an issue. Anyway, I will look after you,' Chloe told her. Then she added gently, 'Please understand that the life you had was destroyed by the floods. Your school is gone, and, I'm sorry to say, your mum may be dead.'

Susan glared at Chloe, disbelievingly, unprepared to accept her world had changed so drastically, 'This is just a pack of lies! I don't believe it. Are you taking me to be some sort of slave? Where there will be no escape?'

'No, not a slave. But sadly, everything else is true. More than anyone, I regret what is happening. It's ruined my life too,' said Chloe calmly. 'We didn't ask you to come into our lives and we certainly didn't plan on having someone like you around. It's made the whole situation much more complicated.' Susan glowered at her as Chloe continued, 'Come with us for now, if you still want to go back home down the track we will help. The Settlement has a helicopter that could drop you off, but you need to get used to the idea that everything has changed.'

Eventually Chloe folded Susan into her arms and hugged her. 'We'll look after you. Somehow fate has put us together and saved you from death. I can promise you, once we reach The Settlement, you and the baby will have the best possible attention.' Susan cried for a few minutes and then quietly helped to pack up the camp.

Kim could see the terrain was changing as they continued into the mountains. She told Chloe, 'These steep rock walls are worrying me a bit. I wonder if there's a way out. We have to climb to the top of that very steep ridge, and then I think we won't be very far from home. Getting up there is going to be a problem though.'

After several more days of painfully slow progress, the little party arrived in a well-formed valley with steep rock cliffs surrounding them and no apparent way out. It was six weeks since they had stolen the horses and escaped from Sydney.

'This is a very good campsite. We have plenty of food now, the horses need some rest, and there's water in the stream. What I'm proposing is that you two stay here and I'll find a way out. It might take a few days though,' Kim explained.

'Won't you get lost and not be able to find your way back here?' asked an anxious Susan.

'No, is the short answer. Just stay put. I don't think there is any danger and nobody's following us. I've been checking regularly.'

Kim was away five days. During that time, Chloe and Susan washed all their clothes and cleaned their equipment. Chloe showed Susan how to brush the horses with some suitable leaves, check their hooves and horse shoes, securely tether them, and move them to better grazing areas.

Although the nights were becoming colder as the winter season drew in, the days were still warm, so the pair spent many happy hours swimming in the stream and sunbathing naked on a nearby rock.

'No sign of even a sniffle,' Chloe observed, looking at Susan. 'You are either very lucky or have a very strong constitution.'

Susan shrugged, then said to Chloe, 'I'm sorry about my outburst when you told me I was pregnant. I was frightened. You and Kim have saved my life. I hope you can both forgive me.'

'You were forgiven long ago. But I was meaning to ask how long since your last period?'

'Two months now. Are you sure I'm pregnant? I've been late before?'

'Look at the little bump and your breasts are growing, aren't they? They look bigger to me. Six more months and you will have a bouncing baby.'

'Pregnant! And Mum wanted me to go to university,' said Susan wistfully.

'We have university courses at The Settlement. What did you have in mind?'

'Really? Some sort of engineering, I like fiddling with cars, bikes, even computers,' said Susan excitedly.

'Well, there's plenty of scope for that. My son-in-law Joe, Kim's dad, does all that now, but he needs all the help he can get.'

'Why were you stuck in Sydney?' asked Susan, during one of their increasingly personal conversations.

'I never really believed in the Ice Shelf theory, so I spent more and more time in my Manly flat.' She glanced at Susan and then surprised herself by saying, 'I was having too much fun with my lover and time got away from me. We didn't know the Ice Shelf had collapsed until Kim came and banged on the door. By then it was too late.' Chloe couldn't really believe she had shared this confidence with Susan, a sixteen year old girl.

'Kim was told to come and find me. It certainly scuppered her chances of being rescued. I feel a bit guilty about that. If it weren't for her I would probably be dead by now,' she continued matter-of-factly.

'She is very fond of you,' said Susan. 'She would've felt awful if she hadn't been able to find you. Who is this David you keep talking about?'

Chloe talked about her husband, their separate desires, and failing marriage. She even told Susan about David's lover.

'I find all that rather confusing,' said Susan.

'I expect you do, I have trouble understanding it all myself.'

Kim arrived dirty, sporting many scratches from her explorations. She was carrying a dead snake and some honey. She admired the orderly, tidy appearance of the camp and the little two man tent made from Settlement capes. Chloe had been sharing it with Susan.

'I'm happy to keep sleeping rough, unless it rains,' said Kim. She noticed that Susan and Chloe had developed a strong bond, almost like mother and daughter.

As they prepared the evening meal, Kim told the other two, 'I've found a way to the top, but there's a difficult climb where we'll have to be careful. Once we're at the top, it's only about a two day hike to our eastern gate. We'll have to let the horses go though. There is no chance they'll be able to get up the cliff face.'

'Let the horses go?' queried Chloe. 'Wouldn't it be kinder to put them down?'

'I don't think so,' answered Kim. 'There's plenty of grazing and water around; maybe they'll somehow team up with other horses.'

By evening of the following day, they were at the base of what looked like an impossibly steep climb up to the top of a cliff.

'I'll take all the equipment up there first, then take you, one at a time, roped together with me, to the top. There is no danger if we keep our heads and take things steadily,' Kim said.

'I'm really frightened of heights,' said Susan.

'No problem,' said Kim, more confidently than she felt. 'Just don't look down.'

Kim spent half the next morning carrying all their equipment up the steep climb. 'We'll leave the saddles and tack behind under shelter. There's no value in exhausting ourselves with something we don't need. If people at The Settlement want to come and fetch it all later, they can.'

Chloe announced, 'I've let the horses go. We took off their shoes first so they don't go lame.'

'Okay, Susan, you first. I'm going to climb up with the rope attached to both of us. Then you'll follow me to where I've secured the rope. Then I'll go further, and so on. The rope will be under your shoulders so we don't hurt the baby.' She smiled encouragingly, 'Remember, don't look down. Move slowly like I showed you, one hand or foot at a time and you can't fall. Wait till I tell you to move.'

The first two of the five climbs went without a hitch and Kim thought the rest would be easier. Having secured the rope around a large boulder, Kim looked down and said to Susan about twenty feet below, 'Okay, you are secured, just move slowly.'

Susan was about halfway up the climb when something made her look down and she lost her nerve. There was a shriek as she fell the three metres to the ledge where she had been resting and then slid off, the rope saving her. She wasn't injured, but was left dangling. Kim made sure the rope would hold and, with no thought for her own safety, climbed down to the ledge and managed to haul a terrified Susan back up.

'I can't do this, I just can't,' she whimpered.

'Oh yes you can,' said Kim firmly. 'I will come with you this time. Remember you won't fall as the rope is firmly secured. Okay, now one step at a time. That's great. Now move your right foot; now the left hand; now the left foot; now the right hand.'

It took about ten minutes to make the climb, but there were still two climbs to go. Kim called a rest for a few minutes. 'Now I will go up there, secure the rope and then I'll come back for you, okay?'

Susan nodded.

Half an hour later, an exhausted Susan was lying down on one of the backpacks sipping water. She heaved a sigh of relief and looked admiringly at Kim. 'I really couldn't have done that without you, I don't know how you do it.'

'Just wait till we get home, we can give you lessons then. Is the baby alright?' she asked anxiously.

'I think so, everything feels normal.'

'I'll fetch Chloe now. She's probably wondering if we're okay.'

An hour and a half later, Kim and Chloe appeared at the top of the cliff. 'We'll stay over there tonight.' Kim pointed to a large tree. 'I know exactly where we are now. The gate is a two day walk from here.'

By mid-afternoon, on the third day after the climb, the three of them came out of the bush and there, as if by magic, was the oft-mentioned gate. Kim picked up the old-fashioned handset which Joe had installed for regular contact with The Bandstand and wound the handle vigorously.

'Hello, who is it?'

'It's Kim and Chloe and we have a visitor. Could I ask you to let us in and please bring three horses?'

'Who? Kim?' said a disbelieving voice.

'Yes, we were stuck in Sydney, but now we're here.'
'We'll be there soon! This is unbelievable, everyone thought … '
The connection was cut.

~~~

'It may be dark by the time they get here. It's about a three hour ride from the stables,' Kim told Susan.

Chloe started fussing around. 'Dear God, look at us! We all look like nothing on earth. We should try and tidy up a bit. Whatever will they think?'

Kim laughed. 'Don't be ridiculous Granma. We look like we've been wandering through the bush for almost two months, which is exactly what we've been doing. At least we are all in one piece and healthy, especially little mother here.'

They all laughed, glad their ordeal was nearly over.

'Don't call me Granma. Here Susan, let me tidy you up a bit. I'll brush your hair and you can wash your face.'

Almost three hours later there was a cacophony of sound coming from inside the fence. It seemed almost everyone from the community had come out to greet them. Dozens of people came rushing through the gate—David, Mark, Tanya, Joe, Patricia, and all the children. Chloe kept a firm grip on Susan, making certain she was not drowned by the reception. There were hugs and kisses all round and Chloe kept introducing Susan, who after weeks of not meeting anyone was quite overwhelmed by all the attention.

Chloe found herself enveloped in David's arms. For a brief moment it was almost like old times. 'We're all thrilled you made it back. We'd almost given up hope.'

She looked at him, but could see nothing had changed. He would've said that to anyone who'd spent two months walking back here.

Three horses appeared and, with Chloe leading Susan's horse, they made their way to the village.

'There will be a bit of a reception in the community centre,' David told everyone within earshot. 'We had almost given up. What a day!'

~~~

Somehow they all managed to escape the crowd and went to bed; Kim to Joe and Patricia's house.

Chloe said to David, 'Susan will have to stay with us, probably permanently. I'll explain who she is tomorrow.'

Chloe had half expected David to say something about the validity of his predictions, but, to his credit, he never mentioned the subject again.

The community insisted on hearing the story in the centre the next day. Kim and Chloe told the full story, with Susan adding her part towards the end of the presentation as she grew in confidence. The community really took her to their hearts and there were never any questions about what she was able to contribute. Chloe adopted her and took her to the doctor at the first opportunity.

'Three months plus,' Susan was told after she had been examined. 'It is likely to be a fine, healthy baby; just eat well, don't drink or smoke, and come and see me every month. Chloe will make sure you join an appropriate exercise class if that's what you want. I'm assuming you want to keep the baby.'

Susan nodded.

A month or so later she talked to Chloe. 'I now sort of understand this place and have seen all those horrible pictures of the floods hitting Sydney and other parts of the world.' Susan shivered involuntarily. She looked entreatingly at Chloe, 'If it wasn't for you and Kim I would be dead. I know that. But I keep thinking about my family. I'd like to know what happened to them. I know Tanya has taken flights over Sydney. Do you think she would help me?'

Tanya took Kim and Susan on the flight, as Kim had the best knowledge of where they crossed the road; the place where Susan and her parents were stuck. They studied the map and soon came up with the coordinates.

When they flew over the area they could see that cars were still scattered everywhere, but there was absolutely no sign of life.

'If I fly low, will you be able to spot your family car?' asked Kim, looking at Susan, who was trying desperately not to be sick.

'Probably.'

They made several passes over the mass of vehicles looking for a bright red Toyota.

'There, under a tree,' said Kim. 'Does that look like the vehicle?'

Susan was sick all over the interior of the helicopter. 'Yes, maybe.'

'Do you remember the registration number?'

Susan gave her what she could remember of the number as they flew slowly past.

'That looks like it could be the vehicle,' said Kim. 'If we can land I will go and have a look.'

Tanya found a level area and landed the machine fifty metres from the car. Kim leapt out and said to Susan, 'You stay here, I will have a look. But please understand, there is no chance there is anyone alive in that car.'

Kim shot two threatening-looking dogs as she ran to the car. All the windows were closed and the doors locked. Looking inside, she saw the remains of two adults and three children. She shot the driver's window out and reached in to open the door and was immediately sick from the overwhelming stench of putrefaction. Holding her breath, with a valiant effort she managed to find the man's wallet in his jacket pocket. Driver's licence in hand, she ran back to the helicopter.

'Is this your dad?' she asked a very pale and shaken Susan, who nodded and burst into tears.

'There is a man, woman, and three children in the car. They have been dead for some time. I think your father shot them all and then himself. I'm really sorry.'

Susan said nothing, but tears continued to flow.

'Can I see them?' Susan asked eventually.

'I don't think that's a good idea, they are all in a terrible state of decomposition. Better keep your memories.'

Susan nodded after some reflection, 'Mum, Dad, and my three younger sisters,' she whispered.

'The best thing I can do is set fire to the car. We can say a few prayers like we did in the forest for Mick.'

Susan nodded tearfully. 'At least I know what happened to them.'

Kim and Susan said a few short prayers standing next to the helicopter. Susan returned to her seat and Kim took her short-barrelled automatic and fired a burst into where she assumed the car's fuel tank would be. Some fuel started to drip, but there was no sign of fire.

'Here, wrap this paper around a stone, light it, and then throw it at the car. Don't get too close.' Tanya handed her the paper and a box of matches. Once the paper was lit, Kim threw it at the car. Within seconds, the leaking fuel caught fire and the tank exploded, the car becoming a ball of flames. They sat and watched for a few minutes.

'Do you want to pay a quick visit to your home?' Tanya asked Susan.

'Yes please,' said a tearful Susan. 'I may be able to find a few photos and some clothes.' She gave Tanya an address in Horsley Park.

The helicopter was hovering over a house in a well-to-do street. 'That's the place,' said Susan excitedly; she wiped away her few remaining tears. The whole area appeared to be deserted and Tanya landed in the wide street opposite the house.

Kim and a rejuvenated Susan dashed out and ran to the house. Susan found the front door key under a flower pot and rushed into the house, which, although dusty and stale, was just as it had been left weeks earlier. Kim filled a bucket with water and went back to the still-running machine and cleaned up Susan's vomit.

Susan soon appeared with a suitcase. 'Just a few clothes and some photos. I could bring my laptop if there was room?'

Tanya nodded, 'You could bring sheets and blankets as well.'

Having cleaned up the mess in the helicopter, Kim made certain the electricity and gas in the house was switched off and that the garbage had been put out. She checked all the windows. 'The lights are no longer working, but at some time in the future the utility companies may start operating again,' she explained to Susan.

They filled the helicopter with Susan's luggage and a collection of sheets and blankets. There was no sign of anyone.

'The whole street decided to leave at the same time, there was no real plan,' said Susan as they took off towards home. She took the house key with her.

CHAPTER TWENTY-SIX
Their New World

Tanya and Roger, by now a competent pilot, flew the helicopter around Sydney and environs on several occasions making extensive video recordings. Central Sydney was almost completely flooded, and Circular Quay inundated. The huge skyscrapers stood like sentinels, knee deep in water. The Kurnell Oil Refinery was under water. There were long streaks of oil from the refinery on the south side of Botany Bay and from the airport on the north side. Several cranes, some suspended at precarious angles, was all that was visible of Port Botany. A ship's funnel poked out of the water on Southern Cross Drive, seemingly the ship had been lifted from its mooring at the port and driven the three kilometres inland to its current resting place during the first violent impact of the flood. The nearby Kingsford-Smith Airport was completely flooded, with a few tail fins of abandoned aircraft just visible. Very occasionally people emerged and waved desperately, but in general the city was deserted.

They landed on an oval close to Epping Road. The rugby posts on the oval were sticking out of knee high, unmown grass in anticipation of the next game, now never to be played. As with all the major arteries out of the city, the road was jammed up with cars not going anywhere. Tanya hopped out, leaving Roger at the controls of the machine. She disappeared for a few minutes and then Roger saw her being violently sick next to the deserted bus stop.

A very pale Tanya returned to the aircraft and sat silently for a minute. 'Dead people! Most cars have several bodies inside, although there were some on the pavement. It's too ghastly to think about. They all just died there. Many of the bodies outside the cars look as if they've been partially eaten by something, probably dogs. Let's go. There's nothing we can do for these people.'

After several of these trips, she said to Roger, 'I think we will leave it at that. We should show it all to the community though.'

Mark said to Tanya one evening over dinner, 'With all our recent patrols there was no sign of any direct threat to us here at The Settlement. But I'm still worried about Demetriou and Fred.'

Tanya nodded.

'Jonathan told Dad in a recent satellite call that all the jails were opened up to give inmates a chance of surviving by themselves. I just wonder how long it will be before we see them. '

Tanya said nothing, but her eyes widened . She hadn't given Demetriou a thought in years.

'There has also been some contact with Evan, so he is still alive. All the message said was "Rome" and then weeks later "Istanbul", according to Jonathan.'

Tanya forced herself to relax.

Jonathan was now the most senior surviving officer in the army. David had kept in close touch with him by way of a satellite phone for a while and then with a flock of homing pigeons both The Settlement and the army base near Canberra had nurtured for the past few years.

'We are surviving,' Jonathan told David, 'but have no capacity to help anyone. Our resources are concerned mainly with incursions from the North. When you are able, it would be helpful if you could secure the Port of Newcastle. You have the military capacity. My guess is you have two or three years to do it.'

'What about Sydney?' asked David.

'Nothing at the moment, but leave that to us.'

Over ensuing months, Mark and his brother Jonathan had set up regular meetings, sometimes in the now deserted city of Canberra and on alternate visits at The Settlement.

On one of his visits to Canberra, Mark enquired about Virginia Andrews.

'At the time of the collapse and before the flood hit, many of the people here returned home to see if they could help their families. I think Captain Andrews went home.'

During his discussions with Mark, Jonathan frequently referred to his battle with some of the military hierarchy who had thought his Ice Shelf obsession was ridiculous fantasy. However, he'd managed to maintain a budget and had copied many of The Settlement initiatives, 'What you did at The Settlement is now the basis of the survival of what's left of the Australian military establishment. I think, in time, it will be the basis of re-creating some sort of Government in Australia.'

There were ten thousand active military personnel on various bases as well as in ships and submarines scattered around the coast of Australia, plus partners and children. A food supply, schools, and hospitals were all being maintained.

'We are trying to establish the number of people and groups that have survived. We estimate there are about one hundred groups, such as yours, around Australia that survived the flood aftermath; The Settlement being the most highly developed. Our resources are stretched now maintaining the geographic integrity of Australia. In future, in cooperation with groups like yours, we would hope to be able to be a catalyst in rebuilding the Australian nation.'

At the time of the flood, Jonathan had taken the initiative to deploy troops to several bases in the continent's North. 'I had already secretly created infrastructure in Darwin harbour to cope with an increase in sea levels of fifteen metres, so most of the navy made it there. We managed to feed all the depots from Canberra at first, but most of them now have their own sources of food.'

CHAPTER TWENTY-SEVEN
Isolation, Continued

Graham was enthusiastic about his new project and encouraged several others to join him in clearing some two hundred hectares of the bush at the northern end of the property. 'I could make furniture from some of these trees, even the burnt ones,' he told David. 'If we had some proper tools it would help a lot.'

'Do you know anyone who stocked tools in Sydney?'

'Sure, plenty of places. I know exactly where to go.'

A few days later, Tanya, with Joe and Graham on board, set out to find the site of a major supplier of high grade tools in Western Sydney. They flew around the factory several times, but there was no sign of life, so Tanya set the machine down in the main fenced-in yard. Graham and Joe checked out the locked main door, then asked Tanya to pick it.

'Okay, but you two stand guard here. We never know who might appear from the shadows. Walking back home has no appeal.'

It took a few minutes to unlock and open the door.

'Only take relatively light objects,' she reminded them as she returned and waited in the pilot's seat.

Joe and Graham emerged with a trolley loaded with various objects.

'Extraordinary,' Graham said. 'The place has been left clean and tidy, almost as if they were expecting to return tomorrow. Anyway, now I can really get on and make some decent furniture. I will probably set up a sawmill in the forest to avoid shifting all the trees down to the village.'

Having set a precedent, every month or so, Tanya was asked to go on similar expeditions to find items that were desperately needed. Mostly, they went about their business unhindered. Once, several people armed with rifles appeared as they circled the premises. Tanya immediately backed the helicopter away and flew out of range.

'Phew,' she said, 'one can't be too careful.'

Chloe looked after Susan as if she was her own. She always attended the medical examinations and made certain Susan was eating correctly and had enough rest. She encouraged her to continue with her schoolwork.

David, although he had no objection to the pretty girl, became more and more lonely at home. He began to spend more time at The Bandstand and his liaison with Caroline flourished.

As Susan's time approached, Chloe said to him in a quiet moment, 'The baby will arrive soon and I'm committed to helping Susan look after it. But that's not really fair on you. So I was thinking, Jonathan's house is unused; one of us should probably move in there. It doesn't matter to me which one of us it is.'

Jonathan's house was well furnished and, without any fuss, David moved his belongings there. He had become quite used to fending for himself due to Chloe's frequent absences in Sydney. It also meant he could make trips to The Bandstand without having to explain his absences.

CHAPTER TWENTY-EIGHT
The Raid

2029

Three and a half years post isolation David, as always accompanied by his latest Kelpie, stood on the hillock, his favourite vantage point from the very early days. He was quietly confident. The community had pulled together far beyond his expectations. There was sufficient food, no violence, the school was operating as normal, and several people were completing university courses. So far there had been no sign of Fred, Bill, Demetriou, or Lance, all of whom held possible grudges. Two hundred hectares of the property's northern bush had been cleared and was now productive. The food store was gradually being filled, preparing for the possibility of leaner years.

The community was very active. Mark had maintained a high standard of readiness in The Academy; there were parties in the community centre at least monthly; and, the dramatic society always had one play in production and one in rehearsal. There were several pop bands and regular gymkhanas, supervised by Chloe and a very active sporting fraternity.

David, very fit for a seventy-four year old, was still active in the community, although he wondered from time to time when he should formally hand the leadership reins over to Tanya. There were also a number of the younger Bower fraternity who were capable of playing a wider role. And he still regularly visited Caroline at The Bandstand.

~

A boy was running up the hill to where David stood. He could see from his urgency that some new crisis needed his attention. David quietly walked down the incline; he felt ready to cope with anything, except what he was about to have to face.

'It's Caroline,' said the breathless boy. 'There's been a raid on The Bandstand. She's badly injured and Tanya has gone to help her.'

David went icy cold inside.

Some hours later a bloodstained and barely conscious Caroline was brought to the hospital, supported by Tanya and three others. 'Raid—Demetriou, Bill … another from here … dozens more. Bandstand men … dead, except one or two … escaped to bush. Women raped, taken away … buildings burnt. All stock taken. Will come here … next,' Caroline jerkily and breathlessly told her story as she was taken in for emergency treatment.

David was too traumatised to help much, so Tanya firmly took charge. 'I will take twenty Academy people, at least fifteen women to assist with the injured and traumatised women and girls. We leave in an hour. See if you can find Derain,' she said to Kim, 'I think we might need him.'

When Mark had been briefed, he declared, 'Code Red emergency, all able-bodied members of the community will be called up. A camp will be established near the eastern gate, and we will run regular patrols like we have planned.'

Tanya left him to it while she focussed on the readiness of her team. While she was apprehensive as to what she might find, Tanya was confident she'd be able to deal with it. They had trained for this. She was clear that this was no time for niceties and planned for ruthless action, eliminating any future threat.

Barely noticed by the rest of the community, busy making preparations of their own, the group clattered out of the yard. Derain had persuaded Chloe, over the years, to teach him the rudiments of riding a horse. He was still not particularly comfortable on horseback, but he could see the urgency of the situation and made up, with Tanya, the twenty-second member of the group.

Every person had had extensive military training; they were well dressed in hard wearing jodhpurs and riding boots, all had leather jackets and a bush hat. Kim, having completed her medical training, was the official doctor responsible for leading the pack horse with the requisite medical equipment. Food, horse fodder, clothes, and tents were carried by other packhorses. All had the short-barrelled, army-issue automatic rifle and a large, sharp bush knife. Axes, ropes, and saws were scattered through the group.

Tanya led the group at a cracking pace up the hill and through the gate, stopping to camp when it became too dark to see. They couldn't believe the sight that greeted them when they arrived at The Bandstand at noon on the third day after Caroline's arrival. There were bodies of men shot to pieces and just left where they had died. Many of the buildings had been burnt down and all the stock had disappeared. The vegetable garden had been trampled.

Tanya said in a business-like way, trying not to show her horror at the sight that greeted them, 'They have taken all the women, cattle, horses, and sheep, as Caroline told us.'

One of the men in the posse started a solar-powered bobcat and was in the process of digging a large hole slightly away from the houses. 'Mass grave,' he explained. 'Maybe someone should identify each person before we bury them.'

Derain had scouted ahead and returned by mid-afternoon. 'Maybe four hundred head of cattle, many sheep, and plenty horses. At least twenty-five men. Women be made to walk barefoot behind, thirty or more.'

During the day, ten Bandstand settlers emerged from the surrounding bush, both men and women.

A tearful woman recounted the horror, 'They came in the middle of the night, so we were completely unprepared. The men who resisted were just shot and some of us ran into the bush. Most of the women were raped, tied up, and marched off with the stock.'

The fifty bodies were gently placed in the mass grave after being identified. A short service was held before they were covered in earth.

'Did you see any of the raiders?' asked Tanya,

'Definitely Demetriou. And a man who was here for a few months called Rolfe. I thought I heard Bill's voice, but by then I had escaped. We had no chance. Has there been any sign of Caroline? I saw her riding away.'

'She raised the alarm, but is now in the hospital quite badly hurt,' answered Tanya.

'What do you want to do?' asked Tanya of the traumatised group. 'You can stay here, or we can offer you an escort back to The Settlement.'

'What are you going to do?' Tanya was asked.

'Catch up with that bunch of renegades and teach them a lesson they will never forget, if any of them survive. We'll bring all your women and stock back safely, I promise you,' she said fiercely.

'They already had quite a lot of stock with them. They must have raided other places before coming here.'

'Any other people?' asked Tanya frowning.

'Didn't see any, but we weren't really looking.'

'I wasn't aware of any other communities nearby,' said Tanya.

~

The Bandstand people decided to stay put. 'The raiders didn't find the food storage area. Thank God David insisted on us having it. We'll have to start thinking about rebuilding. How long do you think Caroline will be out of action?'

'Some weeks I expect,' answered Tanya. She looked at them in admiration. *They could easily have chickened out and retired to the relative safety of The Settlement.*

'Caroline will expect us to get on with things; we mostly know what to do.'

'We'll head off early. I'll send for some help for you, so expect it within the week. I don't think you'll be troubled again, but please be cautious. You should all sleep in one or two houses, and keep an armed guard on at night. It might take us a week or more to sort out the raiders and return the stock. Hopefully, we'll take them by surprise with our quick response.

Tanya asked Derain to lead the group as they started off the next morning.

'Track five day old,' he told them. But with the number of cattle, they were easy to follow. 'Stop here, one night, see all cowpats, move very slow.'

The posse moved quickly, and within two days, Derain was able to tell them, 'Cows only two, three hour ahead. I think will stop soon, maybe stay one, two day in that place. Rain, water plenty here.' He pointed up to a tree-covered mountain. 'Plenty grass as well.'

Tanya called a halt. 'Time to camp. Kim, if you could find a suitable place. Derain and six of us will go scouting. We want to mount a surprise attack. When we fully understood the situation, we'll strike. Our objective is threefold—one, rescue the women; two, kill all the raiders; and three, take all the stock back.'

'Shouldn't we take the raiders captive?' asked one.

'And then!' expostulated Tanya. 'We have nowhere to keep them, for heaven's sake! I want them all dead unless there are exceptional circumstances. You saw what they did to our friends. They showed no mercy and nor should we.'

Tanya and her group of scouts had a quick meal before following the stock's spoor.

'Maybe more than twenty-five men,' said Derain, pointing. 'I am counting forty women, see all footprint.'

Once they could hear the lowing and bleating of animals, Tanya called a halt. 'Derain, go ahead. We'll all wait here.'

Two hours later Derain returned.

'Will stop here for two, three days. People know cattle and are making sure all have water. Women told fetch firewood, but can't run away. Men have taken all clothes.'

'The bastards, just wait until I get my hands on them … ' said a female voice.

'I have plan,' Derain continued. 'These,' he waved a large bunch of deep green leaves, 'if put in boil water, maybe for tea, will make people sleep very deep. Maybe then we can take women away.'

Tanya thought for a moment, and then said, without any emotion, 'We must get these leaves into the hands of some of the women, but we don't want to frighten them or alert their captors. So three of us well known to the women will scout around and see if we can pass the leaves on. It's almost dusk, so we need to get a move on.'

Tanya ran rapidly through the bush. She caught a glimpse of an almost naked female picking up wood and approached carefully. The woman looked up, and was ready to flee, when Tanya grabbed her and firmly clamped a hand over her mouth. There was a fierce struggle.

'Natalie, it's Tanya! We're here to help you,' Tanya whispered. The struggles stopped as Natalie recognised Tanya's voice, almost collapsing into her arms. 'Look, you must be very brave. I need you to return with all this firewood as if nothing has happened. Then you must make tea for the men and put these leaves in the water. It will put them to sleep.'

Natalie looked at Tanya. 'They will rape us again tonight. You must help us before that happens.'

'How many men?'

'Maybe thirty.'

'How many of you women?'

'Forty-one.'

'There are twenty of us, so we won't be able to take them on directly. This way we'll make sure you can all escape and we can get every single one of them. There will be two other women with leaves. Try to make sure none of the other women drink any of the tea. When the men are asleep, we will be nearby. Try to escape in the direction away from the cattle and don't try to do anything to those bastards. I have a plan for them, but we need you all out of the way first.'

Natalie made a valiant effort to control her emotions. 'We'll do our best. Thank you for coming. Now we have hope.'

Tanya, well hidden, watched in the half light as Natalie brought a few more sticks towards a large fire now burning in the clearing. Other women were starting to return with bundles of firewood. The women, without being asked, were in the process of preparing a meal. She returned to the scouting group.

'We should aim to have all the women out of here and on their way home before midnight. Kim can try to treat any injured.'

'We don't have enough horses.'

'Oh yes we do,' said Tanya. 'They won't be needing any of theirs.'

'What are you planning?'

'You'll see, but none of those bastards will escape. Derain, check how many guards they have on the stock?' He disappeared.

They were now gathered within three hundred metres of the main camp. There were a number of ear-splitting shrieks over the next two hours as a number of women were raped. There was tension among the rescuers.

'Can't we just go and sort those mongrels out now,' growled one.

'Keep calm,' advised Tanya. 'The most important thing is to rescue the women, not get shot in a botched rescue attempt. Ahh, here come a few. Get them out of here quickly, two to a horse. A few more and a guide can move them out.'

Derain returned, 'Three guard, no more.'

Natalie arrived in the next group. 'Most of the bastards drank the doctored tea and are asleep. There are guards with the cattle and that animal Demetriou is still awake, he didn't drink any tea. He's shagging that little bitch Sarah, who seems to be enjoying it. She's gone over to their side, she was even ordering us around.'

'How long will it take for the rest of the women to escape?' asked Tanya.

'Twenty or thirty minutes.'

'How will we know when they're all here?'

'I can stay. Some of the others have had a hard time tonight and need treatment.'

While waiting for more of the women to arrive Tanya asked Natalie, 'Do you know where they're headed? They must have had some sort of plan?'

'They talked about a place in Barrington Tops, another three weeks herding the cattle. They were going to use us and the cattle as some sort of admission fee so they'd be welcome there.'

Tanya shook her head, 'That would be the start. Demetriou will have a plan to take the place over, I'm sure. Anyway, he won't be doing any of that if my plan works.'

The women were loaded two to a horse and sent off in groups of five or six with an escort. 'There will be a bit of a commotion here just before dawn, try to be well away from here by then,' said Tanya

'That's forty of us,' announced Natalie as she and a companion rode away with Kim as escort, 'Forget Sarah, she deserves everything coming her way.'

'That's all our horses gone, and thirteen of us left to deal with the cattle and the raiders. Derain, Tony, and I will nail the three guards. No noise! Then we make our way around the camp and gather near the water. No action! And keep out of sight until I give the word.'

The three of them crept around the camp and identified the three guards, overhearing one of them say, 'We should have been relieved an hour ago; maybe I'll see what's going on. I'm really looking forward to a piece of struggling fanny tonight,' he laughed as he walked off. Tanya saw Derain take his man down and Tanya silently ran up to her quarry, wrenched the man's head back and savagely cut his throat right to the backbone. There was no sound as Tanya dropped him like a lump of turd, muttering, 'No more anything for you chum, least of all fanny.'

Derain wiped his knife on the grass as Tony arrived.

'All okay?' asked Tanya.

Tony nodded.

The other ten arrived.

'One at a time, go and fix yourself up with a horse. Be as quiet as you can. It's possible Demetriou might still be awake as he and Sarah didn't drink tea. Fetch horses for Derain and me.'

Tanya and Derain kept watch; if they had needed to they would have taken Demetriou out.

On one occasion he called out, 'Is everything okay?'

But a female voice interrupted loudly, 'Come back to bed, I need your large cock.' They heard the sound of a female orgasm and then silence.

'Enjoy it,' said Tanya to herself, through gritted teeth, 'it's the last one you're ever going to get.'

As quietly as possible, they separated the sheep and loose horses from the bulk of the cattle and guided them to the rear of the very large collection of animals. The now apprehensive cattle were gathered close together to within two hundred metres of the sleeping camp; a screen of trees ensured they were not visible from the camp. Tanya's group, now all mounted, were strategically placed around the rear of the restless herd, helping to guide them forward. Just as the first light flickered in the East, Tanya waved. On cue, five of the group fired a full magazine from their automatic rifles into the air.

There was a bellow of sheer panic from the cattle and they took off, running as if the very devil was chasing them. Sixteen hundred hooves thundered through the trees and then right through the middle of the camp, scattering all in their wake. The remains of the fire were cast over nearby sleeping bodies, one or two of whom leapt up only to be flattened and crushed by the panicked herd. Tanya saw Demetriou jump up and race away to the edge of the camp. A naked female form tried to follow him, but Demetriou offered no help and she was caught on the horns of a furious cow and flung shrieking into the air, then crushed by the hundreds of hooves following.

Tanya galloped past the racing cattle. 'That bastard will not get away,' she yelled to no one in, intercepting Demetriou about a hundred metres from the camp. 'Demetriou!' she yelled. As he turned around to see who had called, after a moment's hesitation, she emptied the contents of her automatic rifle into his body.

The cattle thundered on. They were brought under control about two hours later by Tony and Rachel, who gradually turned the exhausted animals around and, with the help of the rest of the group, returned them to the water. The sheep had scattered, but were easily herded together again. The horses had disappeared. The Bandstand stock would probably return there, the rest would be scattered to the four winds.

Tanya looked at the wrecked camp. Every man had been trampled to death and was barely recognisable. Sarah looked like an abandoned rag doll. There was really nothing left at all. The group stood around and looked in horror and amazement at the mayhem they had generated. Two of the group were sick. The rescuers looked at Tanya with a combination of admiration and fear at her clinical execution of the ruthless plan.

'Collect everything, including what is left of the bodies, and pile them all up,' ordered Tanya unemotionally, although inside she felt some unease. 'We'll have a big bonfire; we need to leave some evidence of what happened here as a lesson to any other chancers like Demetriou and his ilk.'

'Aren't we going to give them a proper burial?'

'I'm not,' said Tanya firmly, trying to hide her emotions. 'Remember what these rats did to our friends and the sheer bastardry with which they treated those women. They'll live with that, and any consequences, for the rest of their lives. Say some prayers of your own if it would make you more comfortable. I'm just glad they've been eliminated.'

Tanya turned away and, unseen, shed a brief tear which she wiped away impatiently. Her tumultuous relationship with Demetriou was finally over. She wasn't really sure of her feelings, although she took solace that her precious Settlement was now safer.

Derain noticed. He put an affectionate arm around her when nobody else was looking, 'White Goddess did right thing, this Demetriou very bad for you, ancestor not like him.'

Tanya briefly leant against him and then gently pulled away. 'We still have to get all the stock back to their owners,' she said.

They spent the day at the camp tidying up and making certain the bonfire they'd lit was fully burnt out and extinguished. The cattle had calmed down and were ready to be herded quietly back to The Bandstand.

It took a week to return. The cattle were used to being herded for long distances, but many of the sheep died along the way.

On arrival, Kim greeted the remaining rescuers. 'I've sent half the women to hospital. I did what I could for them, but they are generally in a bad way. They lost husbands and sons and some have lost homes, as well as the trauma they suffered at the hands of the gang.'

The stock was herded into holding yards, separating the cattle and sheep.

'Many of these cattle didn't come from here,' Natalie told them. 'We brand all our cattle and about a quarter of the herd in the yard aren't. Also we mainly had merino sheep and there are other breeds in there. They must have raided at least one other place.'

'First things first, let's get this place back on its feet,' said Tanya.

'We're getting on with it, but we need Caroline for some of the bigger issues. We can't look after all this stock for one. There are far more than we had in the first place and we no longer have the manpower.'

'We'll take most of the stock to The Settlement,' said Tanya, after some thought, 'but we'll leave the milking cows here. You'll need to deal with any infected udders. We'll leave the sheep as well as they won't survive another long trek.'

'Our vet died in the raid, and could Kim stay here for a while. Some of our people are badly in need of ongoing treatment.'

'I'm okay with Kim staying,' answered Tanya. 'I'll get a vet over as soon as I can. Anything else?'

Kim nodded. 'Let The Settlement men stay too. We need muscle to start the rebuild.'

Tanya, Derain, and ten women from the rescue party took four days to drive the three hundred and fifty cattle to The Settlement.

Settlement people were slowly coming to terms with the developments over the past few weeks. Most had assumed they were perfectly safe in their isolated environment, but now realised this wasn't necessarily the case. The question was, how should they proceed from now on? The Settlement was strong and secure, but beyond their boundaries people worried what sort of bedlam reigned.

Tanya briefed the board and then the whole community on the developments at The Bandstand and how they had handled the situation. There was some disquiet among Settlement members when she described the stampede and its results.

'Couldn't you have dealt with the raiders more humanely? A simple execution would have been better. You seem to have reduced us to the level of those animals.'

Tanya was about to respond when a furious woman from The Bandstand yelled, 'My husband and son were brutally murdered by the raiders. Our house was burnt to the ground and I was repeatedly raped until Tanya came and rescued us. A different plan might have injured some of the women or even the rescuers. For Christ's sake, wake up. Those people deserved nothing but what they got and I for one applaud Tanya and the rescue party.' She started clapping and was gradually joined by the rest of the community.

'We now need to decide how we proceed,' said David. 'It's clear we can't just sit it out and hope the situation resolves itself. The board will discuss options and get back to you.'

Tanya had told the board how many of the stock weren't from The Bandstand. 'We believe the raiders attacked other places first. I think we need to find out what happened as it will influence how we act.'

'What do you suggest?'

'I'll take another party out. If we have Derain with us we'll be able to follow any trails left by the raiders, even if it is a bit old.'

'What about using the helicopter?'

'We won't be able to follow trails that way. Anyway, our fuel supplies shouldn't be overused and the helicopter is getting old. We either need spares or a new helicopter.'

David grunted, 'Okay. Plan to take another party out.'

'There is one other thing everyone should be aware of,' said Tanya. 'It's noticeable there's been extensive growth in the bush outside. Perhaps because of the heavier rainfall we've had since the flood. It may make getting about more difficult as time goes by.'

'Derain said something similar,' said David. 'We've noticed the better seasons here inside the property since the flood.'

Before the party left, David said to Tanya, 'I'm thinking of moving to The Bandstand. It may make sense for the two to be merged anyway. The people there are now in a very bad position and, anyway, we can't have more than four hundred people here.'

'Where does Chloe stand?'

'She's committed to helping Susan raise her child. I don't see much of her since I moved into Jonathan's place. She told me it would be a relief if I left. I think my relationship with Caroline is awkward for her even after all this time.'

'Who would run this place?'

'You would, with Mark as your deputy.'

Tanya's heart beat a little quicker at the last remark. While she had always known she would eventually take over from David, she was in no hurry for it to happen. In her heart of hearts, all she really wanted was for the current situation to continue. *I wonder how Mark will react.* She shivered involuntarily, knowing it would be difficult for him. 'I will think about it,' she responded evenly. 'What's Caroline's position?'

'She's keen, and sees no other option.'

Over the past three and a half years since her rescue, Susan had matured and, with Chloe's unwavering support, had nurtured her son.

'What are you going to call him?' asked Chloe, just after he was born. 'Mick after his father?'

Susan had shaken her head. 'I'll call him Barry, after my father. I'm sorry about what happened to Mick, but we would never have married and I don't want a daily reminder.'

With Chloe spending as much time as was needed looking after Barry, Susan was able to finish her schooling. Chloe also taught her to ride properly and she joined The Academy. By the age of nineteen, it was as if she'd spent most of her life within the community.

Susan's good looks attracted many male admirers. 'I'm not interested in any sort of boyfriend, not until I've finished my degree and contributed something to this community. I'm helping Jason and Joe with their technical stuff and I'll finish my electrical engineering degree in two or three years.' Then she added, 'Chloe, you've been like a mother to me. First the rescue and then the support you've given me. I sometimes wonder what life would have been like if I'd been rescued and then just left here as an outsider. It doesn't bear thinking about. It seems inadequate, but I thank you from the bottom of my heart and hope, someday, to reciprocate.'

Chloe looked embarrassed. 'It's pretty easy to do what I've done, just because of who you are and how you behave; it reflects well on you and your parents. Anyway, I'm doing some of it for myself. It has been my solace since the collapse and I look forward to it continuing.'

They embraced for a few minutes, with Barry holding onto them both clamouring to be included.

CHAPTER TWENTY-NINE
The Expansion

2029 TO 2031

Within days, Tanya led a new group of twenty out on the exploratory expedition. This time there were ten men, as well as the ever supportive Derain, and ten women. They were completely re-equipped and had fresh horses. Tanya was excited; she'd found it restrictive, always cooped up in The Settlement.

One night was spent at The Bandstand while Derain scouted around searching for possible trails. 'Hard,' he told Tanya, 'trail much old.' He smiled. 'But Derain will find, Derain always find.'

Derain stayed a few hundred metres ahead of everyone, so if he had to backtrack the trail wouldn't be ridden over by the remainder of the group. A day and a half later, Derain galloped his horse back to them. 'Body, there is body here on side of track. Tanya, you come.'

'Maybe Fred,' he pointed dramatically. Fred had left The Settlement before Derain had become part of their lives.

There was a decomposing and partly-eaten body lying beside the track, with what appeared to be a bullet wound in the back of the head. Tanya carefully turned it over and it was indeed Fred. She called the rest of the group.

'Obviously an execution,' said Roger. 'We'd better bury him properly.'

The group dismounted and, within half an hour, a grave had been dug and Fred's body was eased into it. Roger muttered a few words of prayer as the body was covered in earth and branches.

By mid-morning the next day, they arrived in a small village with less than a dozen houses. As they arrived, half a dozen dogs rushed out barking and several people dropped everything and ran into the bush in a blind panic.

Rachel chased after one woman and caught her, 'It's okay, we are here to help. There is no need to run,' she said to the frantically struggling woman.

After a few minutes, the woman started to cry and her struggles ceased. 'Do what you will, but please leave the others alone.'

Rachel brought her to rest of the group, already dismounted and unsaddling. The horses were released into a small paddock nearby. The woman looked around uncertainly.

'We are not here to harm you in any way,' Tanya said to her quietly, 'but to help if we can.' The woman looked distrustful. 'What happened to all your stock?' asked Tanya. 'There are plenty of hoof marks here, but no animals?'

'Men came and took all the animals, mainly cattle.'

'They did you no harm?' asked Tanya.

'A man came about an hour before the others and told us all to run into the bush or else we'd be killed. He was very convincing, so most of us did as we were told. We now think it was a trick. Other men came with a herd of cattle and just opened the gates and took everything. They seemed to be in a dreadful hurry.'

'Did the first man say who he was? Can you describe him?'

'He didn't give us a name,' she said, but described Fred in some detail.

'It wasn't a trick,' said Tanya. 'We know the man you describe. He was found dead, executed, about a day's ride from here. His name was Fred Costas.'

Gradually, when they realised the visiting party posed no threat, more people emerged from the bush. 'I overheard one man, maybe the leader, yelling at the men to get a move on and forget the people.'

'He said something about "getting Fred",' interjected another unkempt man.

'What did he look like?' asked Tanya.

'He was a big, well-built man with a Mediterranean complexion. He was quite harsh and the others seemed scared of him.'

'With good reason,' answered Tanya. 'The man was Demetriou Smith and he is dead now.'

'Dead? What do you mean?'

'I killed him.' She waved her automatic rifle about.

'We have a non-violent approach to the world here,' said the man quietly.

'Maybe I should tell you what Demetriou's group did to the people at The Bandstand, a settlement a few days' ride to the west of here.'

'We've heard of them and had contact in the past, but they cut us off when they felled all those trees.'

Tanya told them in graphic detail of what had happened at The Bandstand.

'God obviously protected us by sending Fred,' said the man.

'Fred died trying to warn you. He wasn't able to warn the people at The Bandstand.'

'God's will, he works in mysterious ways.'

Tanya looked exasperated and glanced around her group, all of whom imperceptibly shook their heads. 'We must get away soon,' said Tanya. 'If it's not against your non-violent principles, we potentially recovered your cattle. They are at our settlement.'

'We no longer have any horses.'

'Perhaps God will provide you with them then,' said Tanya acidly.

Tanya's group had a quick meal, watered the horses, and went on their way. One of the women from the village spoke to Tanya as they left. 'This group was founded on non-violent principles, but the new world seems to make that difficult to maintain.'

'Fred put himself at risk by coming here to warn you and your fatuous response was to say his death was God's will. If he hadn't come, all the men would be dead and you women would've been raped and enslaved. Now you are relying on others like us to return all your cattle, having risked our lives to do that. God or no God, you need to wake up.' She turned away furiously and the woman scuttled off.

Two days' ride away, Derain still managing to follow the faint trail, they found another little settlement, no more than a scattering of unprepossessing-looking huts. As they had now come to expect, a few dogs of uncertain ancestry rushed out barking, just keeping out of reach. A shot was fired over their heads as the group entered the small clearing.

Tanya and her group didn't react. Instead, she stood up in her saddle, with both hands held high. 'We come as friends, nothing else,' she shouted.

The response was another shot, hitting a branch not ten feet above the horsemen.

'If you want your cattle back, you'd better stop that. We come as friends,' Tanya repeated.

A man holding a battered, old Second World War mark IV .303 rifle, emerged from the scrub. 'There are ten guns all aimed at you,' he said aggressively. 'What do you want?'

'Some information,' said Tanya evenly. 'There was a raid here, we think, a few weeks back. They stole all your cattle and maybe some horses, but somehow you had a warning of the raid and ran off into the bush. Right so far?'

The man lowered his weapon. 'How d'ya know all that?'

Tanya ignored him and continued, 'The man's name was Fred.' She gave a clear description. 'He made off west to warn the next settlement along the way.'

'You mean the God Botherers,' said the man, now listening carefully. A few people came out from various hiding places and stood around.

'Yes, said Tanya, 'they lost all their cattle as well.'

'So you haven't come here to raid us again?'

'No, as I keep saying, we come as friends.'

Weapons were lowered by the bedraggled-looking settlers. By now, twenty adults and several children had emerged.

'If we may dismount,' said Tanya 'then we can explain ourselves.'

Nothing was said so the group dismounted and loosened horses' girths.

Tanya continued her dialogue, 'Fred warned the other settlement, but they lost all their cattle as well. Unfortunately, they found Fred out and executed him. He was by then on his way to The Bandstand. You may know them?'

'Yes, snooty bastards, we had some dealing with a man called Bill there a few years ago now.'

'He was one of the raiders, but that's not the point.' She described what had happened to the people there. 'That would've been your fate if Fred hadn't warned you.'

There was silence from the settlers; then one of the women said, 'We're sorry about Fred. He seemed a nice man.'

'We were warned by a survivor at our settlement and were able to surprise the raiders and recover all the cattle. All the raiders are dead now,' said Tanya.

The group shared their rations with the settlers, who seemed on the verge of starvation.

'Those cattle were our lifeblood,' said one of the women. 'Since they were taken we've been in a bad way.'

'Well, I see you have some horses,' said Rachel. 'Fetch your cattle any time.'

'The horses were taken by the raiders, but they reappeared one night.'

'When the cattle stampeded the horses just took off,' Tanya told them.

Later, Tanya asked, 'Are there any other settlements, to the east of here?'

'There were several,' said the woman, 'but they were overrun by people leaving Newcastle after the floods.'

'What are you going to do now, assuming you fetch your cattle and remain here?'

'Don't know. We've all been a bit shell shocked since the raid. Having our cattle back should put us back on our feet. But we'll need better security.'

'We may have something to suggest,' Tanya said, watching for a reaction.

'We don't really know who you are, but you look well set up.'

'We are from The Settlement, two days' ride west of The Bandstand. There are now more than four hundred people settled there.'

Eyebrows were raised, but the tall bearded man Tanya now identified as leader calmly responded, 'There were some rumours around about a very big settlement somewhere in the Blue Mountains, but since the flood we've heard nothing more.'

'How many head do you think you lost?' asked Tanya.

'About fifty.'

'Unbranded?'

'We don't brand our cattle.'

'There are something like one hundred unbranded animals among the group we rescued. I suppose the rest belong to the people you refer to as the God Botherers. If you wish, two of you can return home with us to collect your animals. You still have several horses, but the God Botherers weren't so lucky. So if you're happy to help them, I suggest you bring two spare horses and they can fetch their cattle at the same time.'

The bearded man pulled a face but said, 'Okay, I can see we all need to pull together.' He hesitated a fraction and continued, 'My name is Joseph by the way.'

A flurry of introductions followed.

'What do you call this place?' asked Rachel.

'"Banksia"; many of them grow in this area,' answered Joseph.

'It's unusual for a woman to be a leader of such a group,' observed Joseph in general conversation.

'There is no discrimination in our community; women and girls are encouraged to participate in all activities,' Tanya replied. 'We even have a military academy, where volunteers are trained as soldiers—women and men.'

There was an immediate spark of interest among the women in Joseph's group.

Tanya said, 'If it's alright we will spend the night here and leave with you early in the morning. It may take a week to get back home. And we have our own rations, so don't worry about that.'

There were looks of relief from the Banksia folk.

The group clattered off at first light. Tanya had persuaded Joseph and his wife Cath to accompany them. They had two spare horses for the God Botherers, who were initially suspicious, but soon persuaded it was in their best interests. Two men from the God Botherers accompanied the party, but they tried to keep to themselves during the journey.

Tanya had become aware that Tom, one of the young men in her group, had started to take more than a passing interest in her personally. *Stupid little shit. This is all I need.*

The night before the party was due to arrive at The Bandstand, camp was established in a place they had used on their outward journey. As was her now well-established habit, Tanya checked on the horses during the night and took the opportunity to relieve herself, hidden from the camp, behind some nearby bushes. As she returned, Tom unexpectedly appeared on the path. 'Hello Tom,' she said quietly as she tried to ease past him. He blocked the way. 'Tom, get out of the way, please, or you will get a lot more than you bargained for.'

Tom made a pass at her, and said, 'I love you, I want to make love to you.'

'Love, you stupid little bugger! Lust, more like. You are a good member of The Academy, but I have no other interest in you. I will count to three. If you don't let go of my arm you … '

When Tom tightened his grip, he found himself upended, his head smashed hard into the ground.

Momentarily stunned, Tom found Tanya's foot on his throat. 'Get up you silly little idiot and go back to bed. If I hear one more word of this nonsense you will be put on a formal charge.'

Tom stumbled off. Being tall and good looking, Tanya supposed he wasn't used to being turned down.

During the rest of the journey, Tanya gave Tom all the horrid little jobs that needed doing around the camp, such as collecting and burying rubbish and burying the fire. The women in the group somehow understood without a word being said and cooperated. Tom made no protest and tried to keep out of Tanya's way.

Rachel said to her quietly, when they were alone, 'It looks as if you sorted Tom out. He has been making all sorts of inappropriate comments about you for weeks now. Some of the other girls have had similar problems.'

The group arrived back at their home in the mountains a week after they had left Banksia, having spent a night at The Bandstand on the way through. Their guests were impressed by The Bandstand, even in its depleted state, but were completely overwhelmed by The Settlement. All were encouraged to stay a few days. The God Botherers soon found soul mates in Donald Weatherspoon and his church group, now an enthusiastic exponent of multi-faith activities, almost as if he had thought it up himself. Joseph and Cath spent their time at one of the dairies and with Graham and his furniture manufacture.

When Tanya had recovered and caught up with Mark and the family, she met with David and gave him a detailed update.

'Well, Caroline and I have now come to an agreement. The proposal is to formally merge The Settlement and The Bandstand. Caroline will have a seven and a half percent share of the merged company. The arrangement needs ratification by both our board and their management committee, but she doesn't see a problem as she is the owner there anyway. I will be moving to The Bandstand with hopefully fifty volunteers from here.'

'Okay, that is reasonable. But we also need to think about these two new groups. They are both extremely vulnerable, making us vulnerable too. Banksia is only a week's ride from here. At least another fifty people from here need somewhere to go, plus the fifty we hope will move to The Bandstand. Maybe the arrangement with Caroline will give us a basis for coming to some sort of agreement with both the other groups.' She hesitated before adding, 'If possible, only the strongest people should move, otherwise they will fail and we'll be in a worse position.'

'No need to rush. Absorbing The Bandstand is a big deal. Let's see how it goes and understand all the pitfalls first. If we encourage these other groups to visit, maybe they will come up with something we can work with, even if it's security related first.'

'When are you actually moving?'

'Soon, but I will be back at least monthly and I hope you will reciprocate. But, you wanted time to think … Are you comfortable with everything?'

'I'm quite comfortable,' said Tanya, without expressing any of her doubts regarding Mark. 'Mark thinks his role should focus on the wider security issues, bearing in mind the absorption of The Bandstand and these other new groups. And Jonathan has told him we should try to secure the Port of Newcastle sooner rather than later.'

'Newcastle's years away,' said David, waving his hand dismissively.

'I think things will be much the same, with you and me providing the impetus like always,' Tanya continued, more calmly than she felt. 'We do need to think of the succession down the track. How long can you continue at your current energy levels?'

'Dunno, that's why it's really important who accompanies me to The Bandstand.'

David was focussed on moving to his new life and wasn't yet prepared to have a wider discussion about the future. So Tanya tried to engage Mark in a philosophical conversation about the geographic expansion of The Settlement, the capacity, and the reasons for actually doing it.

'In order to secure ourselves, we need to somehow control the area from here to the coast,' she told him. 'Absorbing The Bandstand is a first step, but it needs to go beyond that.'

While Mark could see the sense in it, he was still getting used to the idea that Tanya would now formally take over. He hadn't considered that initiative and wondered if she was merely trying to exert further control.

Mark said, 'We need to make sense of the changes with The Bandstand, and possibly future associations with Banksia and the God Botherers. I think any kind of discussion beyond that is getting way ahead of ourselves.'

'Doesn't it make sense to have some sort of plan?' she argued.

'Too early,' he said.

Tanya thought, I will find someone else to bounce ideas off.

David openly discussed his plans to move to The Bandstand. He had recruited most of the settlers and was liked and well respected. Tanya, on the other hand, while well respected was seen as quite ruthless. They respected the times she had saved the community, but people still wished she could have handled things more gently. Many were still horrified by the death of the raiders.

Tanya tried to avoid the talk, but if confronted she responded promptly. 'You weren't there. Would you have preferred to see our people hurt or killed? Join the rescue party next time. And I can assure you there'll be a next time.'

Normally people scuttled off at that point, but many in the village wondered what life would be like without David's moderating influence. He had no difficulty in persuading twenty families, including some of the medical staff, to accompany him and move to The Bandstand permanently.

CHAPTER THIRTY
Expansion, Continued

When Caroline recovered, she and David quietly moved to The Bandstand.

Tanya accepted David's advice to occupy his office.

'I think it's really important as people need to see you as the boss. When I visit, I will take a small corner of Joe's office.'

Mark unobtrusively moved into her old office.

~

David was well acquainted with Bandstand affairs and left much of the daily business to Caroline. Initially, he focussed on aligning the rules of governance between the villages, including right of occupation for individual properties and settlement laws. All the individual business operations were sold off to the occupants in The Bandstand and "New Settlement Pty Ltd" was formed. David discussed every new proposal with Caroline before it was put to the board.

While Caroline was strong and fair, and had nothing but the interests of New Settlement at heart, she did not have Tanya's legal background, her ruthlessness, and her ability to think ahead. David missed Tanya's input so he arranged for Joe to rig up a solar-powered phone line between the two communities.

'It's just a direct line between your office and Tanya's office,' Joe told David. 'I don't have the equipment to do anything more elaborate. We should have done this long ago.' Now there was ongoing daily contact as well as the monthly reciprocal visit.

~

As a consequence of the raid, Caroline persuaded Mark to establish a branch of The Academy at The Bandstand. Many Bandstand people were already involved in The Academy, so the training and ethics were easily transferred.

'I will take responsibility for the training,' Mark told Caroline. 'I need to get closer to Banksia and the God Botherers anyway, to see how we can help them and incorporate them into New Settlement somehow.'

Mark and five Academy-trained people had helped return the stolen cattle to Banksia and the God Botherers. Joseph had seen the benefit of an association with New Settlement and had come to trust them, Mark in particular.

During the ten day cattle drive back to Banksia, Joseph confided, 'Tanya asked me about nearby settlements and I told her most had been destroyed. However, there's a large establishment I didn't mention, another four or five days' ride from Banksia. They've made their base in Brisbane Waters National park, near Woy-Woy. I've been there once at their invitation. Their leader calls himself Thor and they run the place differently. Thor is an absolute dictator and his word is law. Any dissent is quickly quashed, either by execution or expulsion. If you're looking for stability in this area, you'll need to meet with him.'

'What did he want from you?' asked Mark.

'I don't know. Maybe to frighten me. He knew we were too small to threaten his place. Perhaps he wants to expand his influence and was testing the water. I don't think he has any idea how to achieve his ambitions, other than by brute force.'

'Would we be safe and welcome if we tried to visit?'

'Maybe. I'll get word to him and see what gives.'

Mark spent the journey getting to know Joseph, trying to work out whether he could be trusted. He concluded Joseph was his own man and looked after his own interests. Neither Mark nor anyone else could rely on his cooperation unless loyalty was earned.

When he discussed it with Tanya later, she added thoughtfully, 'How do we cement our relationship with him?'

'If Joseph turns to Thor instead of us for support, it will diminish our standing. So the first priority is making sure Joseph sees us as his ally. And we'll need Thor's friendship too, or at least his neutrality. Any kind of conflict with him will undoubtedly harm us.'

'Okay, what do you suggest? You spent quite a long time over there.'

'We can offer immediate help with Banksia's security,' said Mark. 'Firstly, reducing access to their site from the East. It would make an attack from Thor more difficult. We might send Jason, and maybe Susan, to install solar on their houses too.'

'Once all that is done what sort of hold will we have on them?'

'Knowledge sharing—access to our stock breeding programs and Academy participation. We could encourage Thor's young people to join The Academy as well.'

'Okay, we'll have to discuss costs and the payback with David.'

CHAPTER THIRTY-ONE
Thor

After several months, word came from Joseph that a small party from The Settlement would be welcome to visit Thor's place, renamed by Mark as, "The Vikings".

Joseph also wrote, "Thor has asked to give him two weeks' notice of the visit."

'We need to be really well-prepared,' she told the board, and with a straight face, 'otherwise, it'll be like standing bare arsed to the northern wind … '

'Tanya!' said David, as they all laughed. 'Any suggestions?'

'Mark and I are concerned that if we take the invitation at face value, we might be vulnerable, from what we've learned of Thor.'

'What do you mean by that?' asked David.

'Well, if a small group of five went to The Vikings, with no back up, we really would be putting ourselves at Thor's mercy. He could imprison or kill us.'

'Why would he do that?'

'He may see us a threat. We know he tolerates no opposition at all within his own organisation. People have been killed or expelled for displeasing him.'

'Why communicate with him at all?' asked Patricia.

'If we just ignore him, Banksia will form an alliance with The Vikings,' answered Mark. 'That could be very dangerous for us. Banksia is less than seven days' ride away. Sooner or later, we will have to deal with The Vikings.'

'Okay, Tanya, please go on,' said David.

'Five of us will go to Banksia and continue on … '

~

She and Mark then spelt out in detail what they had in mind.

'Is all this necessary?' asked David.

'Yes,' interjected Mark. 'We cannot risk arriving there unprotected.'

'Goodwill!' said an incredulous Chloe, having considered the proposal. 'It sounds more like an invasion.'

'We will call it goodwill,' said Tanya smiling. 'By that time, Thor won't be able to do anything about it anyway.'

⌁

The room was uncomfortably silent; unsure about the plan.

'Do you think we should go at all?' asked Caroline.

Not answering directly, Tanya said, 'The raid on The Bandstand tells us we must protect ourselves. The best way of doing that is expansion. As Mark has said, Banksia is really waiting for us to show our credentials. If we don't go to The Vikings, Banksia will be lost to us and absorbed into Thor's group. That is dangerous. At the moment, The Vikings are quite a long way from here, but Banksia is much closer.'

'Why don't we use the helicopter?' asked Patricia.

'Once we land we are dead meat,' answered Tanya. 'We may never be allowed to take off again if there's bad will on Thor's side.'

The group gradually tried to absorb what they were being told by Tanya and Mark. Most wished they had never heard of Thor.

'If we sit here and do nothing, we will end up defending ourselves in difficult circumstances,' said Mark. 'Thor may be full of goodwill, and then the plan is unnecessary, but we should be prepared. We'll never be in a position to absorb their establishment, but if we are strong, we will be able to maintain a cooperative relationship based on respect. Thor will value that over time. We will benefit in keeping The Vikings confined to their own patch for the time being at least.'

'Who goes to The Vikings in the first instance?' asked David.

Many suggestions were put forward and for one reason or another rejected.

'We need to take some of our younger people,' insisted Tanya, once it had been agreed she and Mark would lead the group, 'to showcase our talent, so to speak.'

'Who do you have in mind?'

'Kim, Jason, and Rachel are the obvious ones,' answered Mark.

'Both our children,' said a nervous Patricia.

⌁

Tanya and Mark led a rapid ride to Banksia, taking just five days and bypassing the God Botherers' village. They had already sent a messenger to Joseph giving Thor the requested two weeks' notice.

'Keep your eyes skinned,' Mark instructed on arrival. 'My guess is that within half an hour of our arrival, a messenger will be sent to Thor advising there are only five of us. Don't do anything, we just need to know.'

The party was greeted warmly by Joseph and the Banksia residents. While Tanya and Mark were feted, the three younger members of the party tended the horses and set up camp, knowing there was no spare accommodation. All three had extensive experience in the bush and took it in turns to walk off unobtrusively into the surrounding areas to observe.

As they were about to return to the main festivities, Rachel said to the other two, 'The horse tethered fifty metres down the track over there has now gone. I did a quick count of the greeting party, but I'm guessing there will be one less now.'

Minutes after they had joined the main group, Rachel whispered to Kim, 'One missing, a young teenage boy. They must think we're really stupid.'

'We'd better tell Tanya.'

'No hurry. She probably knows anyway; she will have kept her eyes open.'

Later that night, Rachel quietly told Tanya what they'd observed. 'Teenage boy,' said Tanya contemptuously. 'I saw him creeping off. Totally predictable.'

'Joseph has agreed to accompany us to The Vikings. He seems very nervous,' Mark told Tanya as they retired to their two man tent.

'He may be playing a double game, or maybe Thor has found a way to force him into it. We are well enough prepared, I think.'

Two days later, they set off for The Vikings, with Jason leading a packhorse with a solar power unit, sent to Banksia in advance. He would be able to install it in a day or so. It was intended as a gift of goodwill for Thor.

Hours after Mark and Tanya and the group had left for The Vikings, much to the amazement of the remaining residents at Banksia, seventy-two, well-disciplined, well-armed Settlement troops clattered into the untidy village. As arranged, Roger, in charge of the whole operation, had instructed eight members of the group to bypass Banksia and cover all known exits.

'There may be more than one messenger,' advised Roger.

The group proceeded as planned, completely ignoring the local residents. Within half a day there was a loud explosion a short distance away.

The second group returned a few hours later. 'The trees are all down so that access route is totally blocked now.' Roger had checked and was satisfied that two access routes had been blocked, just leaving the gorge route open.

The group had a meal and it appeared to the bemused residents they were about to make camp and stay the night. However, Roger had separately instructed each ten person troop, 'Lead the horses on foot down the gorge route, be very careful in the dark and be quiet.'

In the morning Cath, Joseph's wife, stood with the remaining members of the village in the area where she had expected to find Roger's troop and tried to understand what was going on.

'There is only one way out now towards the East,' said one of the men. 'The two other routes are blocked, I just checked.'

'This has obviously been well-planned,' observed Cath. 'We'll just have to see what happens.' Secretly she thought they were in a good situation. *Tanya is too smart to put herself in a vulnerable position,* she thought. However, if Thor comes off best in this skirmish we'll be protected as we've done everything asked of us. If Tanya prevails, we'll deny any complicity with Thor.'

The eight who had bypassed Banksia altogether, in two groups of four, had set two ambushes. As expected the first messenger, a teenage boy, came galloping around a bend after negotiating the rough track. He was halted by a pile of bushes. Trying to pick his way around the unexpected blockage he was confronted by four Settlement troops, cocked rifles pointing at him from ten feet.

'Off!' said the leader. The messenger had no option but to comply. 'Right, tell us what you're doing.'

'Looking for some cattle that have stray—' he didn't finish the sentence, receiving a hard slap across the face. 'Strip him, there's probably a note.'

He was roughly and rapidly searched.

'Here, I'll read it. It's a bit of a scrawl but it says, "Another large contingent of Settlement people have arrived here at Banksia. All well-armed."'

'Tie him onto his horse,' said the leader. 'Look sonny, if there is any bullshit at all we will shoot you and the horse and leave you to the dingoes, understood?'

The boy whimpered, 'I just did what I was told.'

Suddenly, a burst of gunfire was heard from a few hundred metres away, followed a few minutes later by a single shot. 'It seems Susan has stopped another messenger.'

The boy looked terrified, but nobody said anything. In an hour they met up with the other four led by Susan. They said nothing until the boy was out of earshot.

'Stupid sod,' she said. 'Bloke in his thirties, tried to ride over us. We took the horse into the bush and shot it and we buried the man. We found a note. I doubt if anyone will ever find anything. Roger said, "no bullshit", so we stood no bullshit.'

The next morning the main group joined them. They camped in a suitable spot Susan had found.

'We will leave in the morning,' Roger instructed.

~⁀

Mark, Tanya, Joseph, and the three younger members of the entourage arrived as they had planned, mid-morning, at the main gate of The Vikings. There was a perfunctory but polite greeting from the two gate guards and they were allowed through, to be escorted to an encampment which Joseph had told them was about a kilometre from the gate.

Tanya looked about sharply, but apart from a few scrawny cows quietly grazing on the side of the track, she noticed nothing untoward. As they approached through the trees, they saw their first awe-inspiring view of the village, consisting of thatched huts set on a hillside, appearing to flow down like a stream to the main hut, dominating the centre. It was all neat and tidy.

A few dogs rushed out barking, but were silenced by a sharp word from an enormous man with shoulder length hair. He was dressed in animal skins, as were all the visible Viking people. The man stood up as they arrived and dismounted. Even Tanya was impressed and somewhat intimidated.

'Thor,' he said, extending his huge hand. He was expecting to shake Mark's hand, automatically assuming he was the leader. So he was surprised when it was first grasped by Tanya, followed by Mark, and Joseph. He ignored the others. 'Come,' said Thor. 'First I will show you around and then we can talk. Your people can unsaddle and put the horses in that small paddock over there.'

Carefully watched by Thor and some followers, Tanya pointedly strapped her short-barrelled rifle around her back, having ensured there was no round in the breech and the safety was engaged. The magazine was, of course, full. The others followed her example. Kim, Rachel, and Jason did as they were told and unsaddled and tended the horses.'

Tanya was impressed by the orderly village. The main hut was about ten times the size of the sixty-odd other huts, but they were all neatly thatched, with small single entrances, requiring people to bend double to enter. They were all facing downhill towards the big hut, as if they were paying homage.

'Maybe two hundred people,' Tanya whispered to Mark.

They were royally entertained for four days, with Thor introducing them to his children. Hercules sported the same physical characteristics as his father, Tanya guessing he was in his mid-twenties, and Venus, a beautiful, slim girl in her early twenties. Tanya was never certain who Thor's wife was as there were several women hovering around in a servile manner, never introduced.

Thor showed them his cattle, some for beef, others for milk, and his rather primitive milking parlour where the animals were milked by hand. There were extensive vegetable gardens and orchards. Many young men, armed with an array of guns from modern hunting rifles to old Second World War infantry rifles, wandered around in a disorganised fashion. One young man carried a Bren gun. But there was no evidence of any kind of discipline. The young men herded the cattle and moved them to where Thor directed. During their visit, various young men brought in native game obviously intended for the pot. The women milked the cows, tended the crops, and prepared all the food. Tanya could see the young men were itching for something to do, peaceful or otherwise.

She expressed her opinions to Mark.

'I agree. I bet Thor understands that perfectly and it fits in with his philosophy. It could cause us some problems.'

Tanya said to Thor during the second morning, 'We've brought you a complete solar power installation, as a gift. We've been wondering where it would be of most use to you. I think it would be dangerous to have it on a thatched structure, because of the fire risk.'

'Solar power! We've no electricity here, but we have wooden storage sheds. It would be useful there,' answered Thor.

A day and a half later, Jason was able to switch on the system, illuminating the extensive vegetable storage sheds, some of which were underground, to maintain a constant temperature. Thor was very impressed and was seen switching the lights on and off from time to time.

Hercules, completely smitten by Kim, took trouble to show her around and tried to engage her in conversation.

She told Tanya later, 'He may be quite smart, but he seems to have little or no education and is only interested in his horse and fancy hunting rifle. Hercules, what a fucking name! It gives him all the wrong ideas about himself. And I've noticed everyone is terrified of Thor, Hercules too. But Venus is very interested in everything we've told her. She said she would like to visit us, but she seems to have no concept of how we run our affairs. She is very sweet, but is afraid she'll be told to marry one of her father's lieutenants. I was introduced to two of them—large, smelly, overweight, middle-aged men; a ghastly fate.'

Tanya laughed at the description. 'They seem to be quite friendly ...' She stopped when she saw Kim's expression.

'Without doubt, there's something in the wind. I've seen the lieutenants trying to organise something. It's possible they're still trying to decide what to do with us. I also caught a glimpse of a face I recognise, but can't place,' Kim continued. 'He ducked out of sight when I looked his way.'

'Describe him,' instructed Tanya.

'Harold,' announced Mark, when Kim had described him. 'I wondered when we would bump into him again.'

He recounted, for Kim's benefit, the conflict with Harold and how it had been resolved .

'They certainly see us as a potential threat and they have Joseph's eldest son locked up here, by the way. Venus let that slip this morning. I pretended not to hear. Apparently, he proposed to Venus without Thor's permission, almost certainly an excuse. I suppose Thor can blackmail Joseph at will while his son in custody,' said Kim thoughtfully.

'No wonder Joseph, the stupid bugger, is behaving so strangely. Do you know where the boy is being held?' asked Mark.

They were able to talk quite freely since all The Settlement people were housed in one hut. Joseph had insisted on being housed elsewhere.

'There is a dungeon underneath the food store,' answered Jason. 'I stumbled across it when I was fixing something on the solar system this afternoon. There are about six people there in chains at present, but there is space for at least a dozen more.'

'This is all a bit of a wakeup call for me, I'll think about it overnight,' said Tanya.

The Settlement people found the huts warm and comfortable and the mattresses soft. Tanya and Mark quickly fell asleep.

When the older generation had gone to sleep, Jason asked quietly, 'When are the others due?'

'Tomorrow afternoon sometime. They won't be far away,' answered Rachel.

Jason sat up quietly. 'I have no intention of being locked up in that bloody dungeon, and tomorrow afternoon may just be too late. Rachel, come with me now, I have a plan. Kim, could you continue to distract lover boy in the morning. Bet you fancy a shag with him, anyway,' he said teasingly, ducking as his sister tried to cuff him.

'I'll look after him, don't worry,' said Kim. 'Are you going to find the main group?'

Jason nodded, 'Smart girl,' he whispered as he and Rachel crept out into the night.

Everything was quiet. They ran to the horse paddock and tacked up their two horses, hoping the other horses wouldn't make too much fuss about being left behind. They walked the horses until they were out of sight of the village and then cantered most of the way to the gate.

'Hang on for a moment,' Jason told Rachel, handing her the reins of his horse. 'There is bound to be a hole in the fence somewhere. I'll be back shortly. We don't want to alert the gate keepers, so be quiet.'

'Yup, Tanya could drive her helicopter through it,' he said on his return. 'Let's find Roger and the mob. Come.'

Riding slowly after clearing the immediate vicinity of the gate they made enough noise to attract the attention of their colleagues. They were challenged almost two kilometres from the gate.

'Halt, who goes there?'

'This is Jason. I need Roger, quickly.'

'Jason, what the fuck are you doing here?'

'Rachel's here too. We need to see Roger.'

Jason explained his plan to Roger. 'Nothing has happened so far, but something is planned for the morning, I'm sure. So we need to move fast. There are two goons on the gate. We've found a hole in the fence, so some of us should return that way, bang the goons on the head, and then let you lot in. If your troop gets to the main camp before eight in the morning I'm pretty sure we'll pre-empt a lot of nastiness.'

As the dawn broke, Jason, Rachel, and four others crept through the hole. They cautiously approached the two, sleepy guards, banged them on the head, trussed them up, and gagged them.

Rachel then opened the gate, allowing the troop to enter the base unhindered.

'Wait here for an hour and then march up the road. Rachel can show you where to go. I'm going back to the village now,' announced Jason.

Tanya woke up early, 'Christ, I have a headache,' she confided in Mark. 'Do you think they put something in the food last night?'

'Maybe. I slept well and feel fine. Where are the kids?' he said looking around. 'The beds are all cold. They must have gone off somewhere early.'

Kim appeared, followed by Jason. 'Breakfast,' Jason said.

'Where's Rachel?'

Jason shrugged and said jokingly, 'Maybe she fancied a roll in the hay with one of the Neanderthals. She'll be around.'

They all got up and walked over to the main hut. They were greeted warmly by Thor, but there was something different in the atmosphere. A number of ragged-looking armed men were standing around trying to look unobtrusive. Tanya helped herself to some fruit and sat down, as did Mark.

'Joseph told me you helped to recover all his cattle,' offered Thor conversationally, looking at Mark. He had not become used to the idea that Tanya was the boss.

'I had nothing to do with it,' said Mark. 'Tanya led the group and recovered all the cattle; all Joseph had to do was come and drive his cattle home.'

Thor looked nonplussed. 'What happened to the rustlers?'

Tanya drew her forefinger across her throat.

'What, all of …?' then Thor went pale and his eyes almost popped out of his head. 'What the fuck?' he exclaimed. He was looking down the main track leading from the gate.

Tanya turned around and saw Roger, with Rachel by his side, calmly leading the troop five abreast, all with their rifles held at the ready in their right hands, with the butts resting on thighs.

Some of the attendant Vikings started to fiddle with their weapons.

'Don't be fucking stupid,' muttered Thor. 'Can't you see you would be cut to pieces before you could say asshole. Put those things away.'

He watched as Tanya marched down to greet the troop, standing to attention on the front step of Thor's magnificent hut. She waved Thor over to stand by her side and held up his hand as if in partnership. The troop each fired three shots into the air in complete unison without a word being said.

Roger marched up the steps, saluted and said, 'At your command, madam.'

Joseph's eyes were focussed on the forlorn figure of the messenger boy bringing up the rear, tied to his horse. He worried about how he was going to explain the situation to Tanya. The whole situation had now dramatically fallen in favour of The Settlement.

Tanya saluted and responded, 'Dismiss and unsaddle. I expect you can camp under the trees over there.' She glanced up at the bamboozled giant towering over her.

Thor nodded.

With the faintest smile, she turned and walked back to her breakfast. It was all she could do not to burst into laughter. She refused to catch either Jason's or Mark's eye. She and Roger and the troop had practised that little charade for weeks before they ventured on this expedition.

They all watched as Roger, with Rachel assisting, put the troop through its final inspection. 'Two horses with loose shoes, one trooper on a charge with a dirty rifle,' announced Rachel so everyone looking on could hear.

'What does that mean?' asked Thor, watching in fascination. The idea that anyone apart from himself could exercise discipline and impose sanctions was beyond his imagination.

'Just watch,' answered Mark.

Once the camp was prepared, Rachel marched the hapless trooper to a flat stretch of track still clearly visible to the spectators. 'Attention!' she barked, and the girl came briskly to attention. 'Hold your rifle above your head. Now run, knees up, knees up, run run run.'

'But it's a woman,' spluttered Thor.

'There is no distinction in our Academy. All participants are volunteers, but we have more people wanting to become part of The Academy than we have room for,' Mark told him. 'The discipline is well accepted.'

'All this just for a dirty rifle?' Thor shook his head.

'Standards are important. This is an elite group, let one thing slip and you're on a slippery slope to nowhere.'

To his credit, Thor made no reference to the arrival of the troops, treating them as if they'd been expected. Tanya and Mark were secretly relieved they'd put plans in place to counter any of Thor's.

An hour later, the exhausted trooper was half carried by colleagues to her tent, then given water and a massage. Another hour passed and she was back on her feet as if nothing had happened.

Thor was astounded, but determined not to be outdone. He could see the fitness and discipline of The Settlement was beyond anything his ragtag operation could offer, but he had confidence in his own and his people's marksmanship. 'We challenge you to a shooting competition,' he said to Tanya. 'Three of yours against three of ours.'

'Okay,' answered Tanya, somewhat reluctantly. 'As you can see, we have only brought our short-barrelled rifles with us for use on horseback. Lend us some of your beautiful hunting rifles and we'll take you on. We'd each need a couple of sighters, of course.'

'Fine,' agreed Thor. He could see the proposed arrangement would give him and his people a distinct advantage. Thor selected himself, Hercules, and another young man Tanya had seen wandering about the base.

Mark was asked to select the three from The Settlement. 'Tanya, Roger, and Stephanie,' he said.

'Stephanie, d'you think she'll be okay after all that running?' asked Tanya.

'It's what we train for,' Stephanie answered, when asked.

They were all taken to an informal rifle range in the bush. The group of six, plus two assessors, and a half dozen boys for setting up and managing the targets, walked the few hundred metres. Thor led in his proprietorial way. Stephanie and

Roger had selected 30.06 Savage rifles from Thor's extensive gun collection, as they were much the same as the rifles they had used at home. Tanya had found a .300 Holland, which to her seemed perfectly balanced. All were fitted with scopes.

'Guests to fire first,' announced Thor. 'One of you, then one of us. Two sets of five shots each.' He felt very confident, and whispered to Hercules, 'Fancy choosing women on their team, we will knock spots off them easily.'

Targets were set up three hundred metres away. The Settlement people were allowed five sighters each. Thor's eyes widened when he saw the close groupings of the sighters fired by each of The Settlement contestants. All the shots were to be fired from a prone position on the ground.

Stephanie went first. 'Five in the bull,' said the adjudicators, one each from each side. Thor looked surprised, but said nothing.

The young Viking man produced the same result.

Roger had five bullseyes.

Hercules had five bullseyes.

Tanya had five bullseyes.

Thor had five bullseyes.

'Dead even at half time,' announced an apprehensive Thor. Tension was mounting.

Stephanie and the young Viking had no trouble in repeating the results of the first round.

Roger had four bullseyes and an inner. He winked at Tanya when nobody was looking.

A very nervous Hercules stepped up and produced four bullseyes and an outer.

Thor looked at him furiously.

Tanya produced four bullseyes and an inner. She tried to look despondent, slapping her thigh dramatically as she rose from her position on the ground.

'Five bullseyes will win it then,' said Thor.

Thor confidently stepped up, adopted his prone position on the ground, and produced the required five bullseyes. He whooped delightedly when the result was announced.

'Congratulations,' said Tanya. Thor was surprised when she kissed him chastely on his bearded cheek.

'You did very well,' he said to Stephanie, 'especially after all that capering about earlier.'

Stephanie glanced at Tanya and just answered, 'Thank you.' She was going to say, 'Well, that is what we train for,' but decided that would detract from Thor's triumph.

~

'I'd like to show you something else,' Mark confided in Thor, 'something that could be of value to you.'

After a sumptuous lunch for the leaders, on the verandah of Thor's enormous main hut, Mark and Roger set up ten makeshift targets along a bush track leading away from the village for a kilometre. They lined up fifteen of the troop, eight men and seven women, all on horseback, looking immaculate in their uniforms.

'These people were selected at random,' Mark told Thor. 'Every one of the people in the troop is trained to do the same thing.'

Starting about five hundred metres from the first target and galloping flat out, but carefully maintaining a twenty metre gap between each horse, they charged along the track firing three rounds at every other target. Within five minutes all the targets had been demolished and the troop had gathered and returned, two by two, in order. The leader approached the main hut and saluted Mark.

He, returning the salute, said, 'Thank you. Dismiss the troop.'

There were a few minutes silence before Thor asked, 'Can you help us train our people?'

'Yes, of course. Send them to us and we'll train them.'

'What about sending the trainers here?'

'In time that might work, but only when there is a core of trained people here.'

~

'Venus has asked if she could return to The Settlement with you?' Thor asked Tanya.

'Of course, Kim will look after her and assist her learning.'

During a lull in the conversation, Tanya ventured, 'There is a man called Harold here. He once caused us a great deal of trouble for no reason.'

'There is no Harold in this community,' answered Thor.

'Maybe he has changed his name,' said Tanya. She described him.

'There is a man who fits that age and description,' said Thor thoughtfully, 'but he calls himself Godwinson.'

Tanya laughed, 'Harold Godwinson, of course, the last English King who lost his country to the Normans. Your Mr Godwinson seems to have a sense of history. I don't suppose he mentioned us. He was known as Harold Monckton once.'

'No, he has never referred to you.'

'Maybe the arrangements here suit him better.' She explained the trouble Harold had caused The Settlement, his apparent connections with ASIO, and the now non-existent Australian Government. 'Could have sent us to the wall,' she told Thor as he watched her closely. 'Be careful of him.'

The Settlement people left the following morning and were given a big send-off by Thor, mounted on his large, white stallion and surrounded by his Vikings. Tanya carefully surveyed the crowd, but there was no sign of Harold. With Tanya and Mark leading, the troop cantered down the track in formation and out of the now open gate. A quiet word from Mark had ensured Joseph's son and the two messenger boys accompanied them.

During the journey back to Banksia, Kim had maintained a rear guard watch by doubling back along the track. 'There are two lots of three horsemen following us,' she told Tanya.

'Go with Venus and get her to tell them to go into the sex and travel business, otherwise they will get a backside full of lead.'

Kim smiled at her boss's humour and passed the message on verbatim to Venus. She looked uncomprehendingly at Kim for a moment and then laughed. 'I will come with you,' Kim told her.

'How did you know they were following us?' asked Venus.

'One just has to double back through the bush and wait, I will show you when you start with The Academy. Patience is critical.'

Returning to Banksia, they found David and Caroline had arrived and were anxiously waiting to hear about their visit to The Vikings. Cath had given them the sole use of a recently-constructed spare hut in the village, in recognition of their status.

Most of the troop returned home immediately, but Mark had agreed, at Joseph's request, to leave three behind at Banksia for security and training purposes.

Kim was given a special assignment. 'We've been told there is a group of women established in one of the forest areas, on your way home, some way south of the main track. See what you can find there. They've survived, so they must be pretty tough. Take ten of the troop, mostly men I suggest,' Tanya smiled. 'Maybe we can bring them under our wing as well.'

After two days with the main group, Kim and her troop broke off and turned south. Kim was proud and happy to be given the responsibility. She had asked Rachel to look after Venus until she returned.

Tanya and Mark gave David and Caroline a full briefing on the developments with Thor and The Vikings, talking privately in their hut at Banksia.

'I think Thor is onside,' Tanya reported, 'although it was marginal for a while. We really have to thank Jason for acting when he did. Thor was at least contemplating locking us up.'

David was horrified at the turn of events, but said nothing.

'Thor's daughter, Venus, has accompanied the troop back home, so Thor will be onside for a while. We really need to make sure she gets more than she expects from her sojourn with us. A husband would be good,' Mark added, attracting an approving glance from Tanya. 'We will have to keep building our relationship with him by providing other services he might need.'

'Like what?' asked David sharply.

'He would like military training for his people … '

'Giving him the capacity to attack us, and others,' said David more calmly. 'We will have to think about how we do that.'

'Maybe train just a few. Give them a taste for what is possible, without the capacity to harm us in any way,' replied Mark.

After some thought, David said, 'Intermarriage is more secure, and has a longer term impact. Finding Venus a suitable husband within the wider Bower family would be best.'

There were some uneasy glances around the group. 'Sounds a bit medieval,' said Tanya. 'I was just assuming Venus would fall in love with one of our wonderful young men.'

'If Thor behaves like a medieval potentate, family ties would make him into a powerful and committed ally,' David was warming to his theme. 'We could also find a wife for Hercules among the Bower family?'

'Hercules is like an untrained billy goat, needing a thorough wash,' said Tanya, a look of distaste on her face. 'Also he's totally under his father's thumb. Although, he did fall for Kim in a big way,' she added mischievously.

David looked at her enquiringly, 'Sounds ideal,' he said with a laugh.

'She kept him at arm's length. Mind you, the smell would have reinforced that.'

After a short silence, Caroline said in a firm but conciliatory way, 'I'm rather glad Kim left and didn't hear any of that. From her stay at The Bandstand after the raid, she gave us the impression of great inner strength. You won't be able to force her to marry anyone against her will.'

'Nobody will be asked to do anything against their will,' said David firmly, closing the conversation down.

~∂

Joseph and Cath were shuffling about, keeping their heads down, nervously waiting for a reaction from Tanya and Mark to the week's events. They were aware they might have overplayed their hand, but were thankful The Settlement people had come out on top.

Tanya was determined for Joseph to recognise that his duplicitous behaviour would not be tolerated in future.

'I will deal with Joseph,' Mark said, 'Now that we have him by the short and curlies, we can screw him for any kind of deal we want.'

'Is that the smartest thing we can do,' said Tanya quietly.

David listened intently. He could see Tanya was about to come up with one of her gems. 'We need to find a way of making him feel important to us, plus giving him and the people at Banksia a real stake in the operation. But it will include control by us, now and into the future. I will come up with a deal before we leave.'

David and Caroline stayed on, with David acting as the conciliatory elder statesman. Joseph, and particularly Cath, saw Caroline as an ally, more on their level. They were quite terrified of the sophistication of the Bowers, and Tanya's ruthlessness.

Mark deliberately waited until the main troop had left under the able leadership of Roger and Rachel before he tackled the increasingly nervous Joseph.

'Thank you for helping to rescue my son,' Joseph started. 'Him being in that dungeon put us in a very difficult position.'

'Yes,' Mark said gruffly, 'you could have told us about it though. We happened to be well-prepared, but … '

'Thor forced us into acting like spies,' Joseph said hurriedly.

'Mostly unsuccessfully,' Mark observed.

'How did you know … ' asked Joseph, hesitatingly.

'Tanya thought you would try to have a foot in both camps,' answered Mark. 'I presume that is no longer necessary?'

'No, of course not. Thor was very surprised by the arrival of Roger and his men, as was I. You didn't mention you'd planned to arrive in such strength.'

'No,' said Mark abruptly. 'We thought Thor might try something on. Jason took the initiative and fetched Roger a bit earlier than was planned. I think he arrived just in time to prevent Thor shoving us into that dungeon. You were a party to all that of course. It was part of the deal to have your son released.'

Joseph's mouth opened and shut without any sound emerging. He looked terrified.

'Denying it would do you no good, so don't try,' said Mark firmly. 'It would have gone badly for Banksia and The Vikings if we'd been incarcerated. Roger was always coming. But, it was only due to Jason's quick thinking that he arrived when he did, preventing a lot of nastiness.'

Joseph shook his head.

'There would have been a bloodbath in both villages. We instructed Roger to be completely ruthless; the training they undergo reinforces that approach. The Settlement has no capacity to house prisoners.'

Joseph looked blankly at Mark, completely intimidated.

'One other thing. What's Thor's background? Those people didn't grow up there.'

'Thor was originally part of a bikie gang on the central coast, drug running and so on. When things became too hot for them, they found a base in the forest. They had plenty of money and were able to set themselves up well. They may have paid off critical people so they were left alone. When the flood came, there they were, but without bush or farming skills.'

'How do you know all that?'

'I just do.' Mark could see he would get no more out of him.

Mark left Joseph with his thoughts for a few minutes. When he returned, Joseph had regained some composure.

'What are you going to do?' asked Joseph. 'You have already agreed to help us with security.' He hesitated. 'There was another messenger sent to The Vikings, who seems to have disappeared. Can you tell me what happened to him?'

'He was shot,' said Mark matter-of-factly. 'He tried to ride over Susan when she asked him to stop. He was shot in self-defence.'

'Susan! She seems a gentle sort of girl.'

'Joseph, don't underestimate anyone in our organisation. She was told not to tolerate any bullshit, so she acted accordingly.'

'What am I going to tell the people here?'

'Your problem,' Mark answered, indicating the subject was closed. 'And, I expect Tanya will come up with an arrangement welcome to you. I expect you will have to agree to some of our people settling here.'

'You're in a position now to take advantage of us,' said Joseph defensively.

'Yes, but I think Tanya's proposal will surprise you, it's likely to be generous.'

⌁

Tanya walked around Banksia with Joseph, familiarising herself with the property. The area was well-watered and fertile, but the residents had made little of their natural advantages; only running the small herd of cattle and growing vegetables.

'What land rights do you own here?' she asked Joseph.

'Nothing formal. We just came here, built a house, and occupied the place. Then others joined us.'

'How well defined is the area you use?'

'There is no fence.'

'Nobody has objected to you being here?' asked Tanya.

'The occasional person from the forestry department came and saw us before the flood. We've seen nobody for a while now.'

'What did the forestry people tell you?'

'They told us we'd have to move. But nothing happened, so we stayed.'

'So legally you own nothing.'

Joseph shook his head uncomfortably.

'This is what we can do,' she suggested. 'We need to place markers around the area you see as Banksia land. In twelve years, if there are no objections, the area will then belong to the person or organisation that enclosed the property.

We'll give you a small percentage of a company called New Settlement Pty Ltd, currently owning The Settlement as well as The Bandstand, in return for recognising that New Settlement has enclosed the land known as Banksia. Everyone who occupies a house here will have the right of occupation for one hundred years. We'd have to agree on some small annual levies, all of which can be paid through work in Banksia that benefits the community. You'll have to accept at least ten families from The Settlement each year for the next three years. They'll build houses here and have the same rights of occupation as you. If there's no objection to the land enclosure, the company will eventually own Banksia.'

'What percentage are you thinking of?' asked Joseph.

'One percent,' answered Tanya. 'At present you own nothing. This gives you a stake and ensures your security.'

'Can you write all that down? I need to discuss it with Cath and the others.'

Tanya handed him three typewritten sheets.

Two days later Joseph came to see Tanya with Cath in tow.

'We agree with everything,' said Joseph, 'but the percentage is too low. Caroline says she has seven and a half.'

'You can't really compare the two,' argued Tanya. 'We own The Bandstand property; here, we'll own land after twelve years if we're lucky. Their place is much more developed; she has three hundred head of cattle as an example. What percentage did you want?'

'Two and a half,' said Cath, not looking at Joseph.

'I could probably get the board to agree to one and a half.'

'We'll have to consult the others,' said Cath.

'We're leaving in two days,' said Tanya. 'We need resolution before then.'

David, Caroline, Tanya, and Mark were on their way two days later with a signed agreement in their possession, allowing the people at Banksia a two percent share of New Settlement Pty Ltd.

Dropping in on the group known as the God Botherers, they were surprised to see Donald Weatherspoon, his wife, and three others from The Settlement. Donald was embarrassed and tried to explain, 'We were just talking to the people here about helping them build a church.'

'Fine,' said Tanya. 'Obviously the same rules apply here as applied in our own community if you are proposing to use any of our resources.'

'I just thought we could help out here by bringing some people and some materials to assist them,' said Donald.

'Maybe I should try to deal with this one,' David suggested. 'We are close by and I know Donald quite well. He has his heart in the right place, so I will try to keep him involved without him compromising our position.'

Mark and Tanya returned home post-haste.

CHAPTER THIRTY-TWO
The Amazons

Intrigued by what they might find in a women-only settlement, Kim and her group, following poorly-defined paths, eventually found themselves in a pretty glade with a number of small cottages, well-built and in sympathy with the locality. It had taken longer than expected. The place was well hidden and they'd made wrong turns more than once.

They'd come across an old farmhouse on their way, approaching with caution. There were dozens of rusting abandoned cars in the yard. The place was silent. Kim dismounted, having handed the reins of her horse over to Stephanie. With one of the young men in the group, she banged the wooden steps with a large stick.

'Snakes,' she explained to her companion.

She opened the front door and was almost sick on the spot. The entrance hall and surrounding rooms were strewn with what appeared to be human bones, some still covered with remnants of clothing. Several of the corpses had firearms attached or nearby. The evidence suggested the people had been sheltering from an attacker.

Kim went outside to share the discovery. 'Stephanie, could two or three of you have a look around the yard. I need three more in the house.'

After an hour, the horrified group gathered and Kim asked Stephanie for a report.

Pale and shaken, Stephanie said in a near whisper, 'Maybe the remains of twenty human bodies … ' she shuddered involuntarily. 'Some bones of slaughtered cattle and sheep. Fodder, now completely spoilt, some sprouting in the bags. There are two cow carcasses in a pen. They would've died of starvation. The vegetable garden and orchard may have been stripped, but it's too overgrown to say for sure. Scattered human remains in the orchard, maybe dogs had eaten what they could and left the rest. That's about it.' She retched, before adding, 'Dear God, to think that might have happened to us, the way those people must have died … '

'Same for us,' said Kim, struggling to keep her composure. 'There are bones of something like a hundred bodies, in there, scattered all over the bloody place. The doors were all smashed to pieces. I can't believe what we saw in there.' This time she wept uncontrollably, taking a few minutes. 'It seemed people had tried to hide away, maybe with food they were hoarding, then they were attacked. This is why David and Tanya insisted on isolation at The Settlement. There isn't a scrap of food left and the electricity must have failed soon after the flood. I've now switched off the mains. I suppose when it comes to survival, we all revert to instinct and behave like animals.' She sat down on the front step and wept again.

'This was once a well set-up place,' observed Stephanie, still shaken, 'although they were obviously quite unprepared for the flood. If we're looking for places to expand towards, this is a good example.'

Kim nodded, 'We'll discuss it with Tanya and David, when we return. But let's go and see what this women-only place has to offer, hopefully that'll be a lot more cheerful.'

'Aren't we going to do something about all these bones here?' asked a young man.

'No point,' said Stephanie sharply. 'Let's get the hell out of here.'

Kim looked up, surprised, but said, 'Yes, we'll lock up and try to leave it as we found it.'

As the troop approached the village, two or three dogs barked furiously and then scampered after the few drably-dressed women as they dashed into a main building. Kim halted the group and they all dismounted and loosened the horses' girths.

Five minutes later, a severe, middle-aged woman with greying hair emerged. She was quite tall and exuded an air of authority. Like the others, she was dressed in hard-wearing workmen's clothes. After a brief glance over the intruders she said, 'We have very few visitors here. Who are you and what do you want?'

Kim answering said, 'We're from a group based in the Blue Mountains and are trying to establish contact with other groups in the region.'

'Is that The Settlement? We've heard of them.'

'Yes. We've already managed to make contact with a few groups between our base and the coast,' replied Kim.

'What is your purpose?' asked the woman suspiciously.

'Recently there was a raid on a place called The Bandstand, a two day ride north of here. Many of their people were killed and all their cattle stolen. So security is one concern.'

'Really, how awful!' said the woman anxiously.

'We recovered all their cattle and killed all the raiders,' said Kim quietly. 'We now cooperate more fully with two other groups and have taken responsibility for their security.'

They eyed each other for a few moments.

'Maybe we could discuss this over a meal,' said the woman. 'We've been very happy left alone. We'd like that to continue.'

'Can we camp here?' asked Kim. 'We have our own supplies.'

'Oh yes, forgive me. We've so few visitors I've forgotten my manners. No, food is not a problem. Please share our meal with us. You can camp over there under the trees and your horses can be put in the nearby paddock. Dinner will be at seven.'

By now about fifty women, from late teens to late forties, as well as about twenty female children, aged from about four to sixteen, had shyly gathered to listen to the conversation. There was no evidence of any male presence at all. As the conversation continued there was growing chatter, especially among some of the younger women.

At the appointed hour, Kim led her group into the main building, consisting of a large room and its utilitarian furniture, made up mainly of several large tables together with appropriate chairs. The kitchen and some smaller rooms led off the main room. There were places laid for all the adult members of the community as well as Kim and her ten strong troop. There was no electricity. Instead, the room was lit with smoky paraffin lamps. Kim guessed the community had run out of paraffin and the fuel used in the lamps was animal fat.

To Kim's amazement, most of the women had transformed their appearance, having changed into cheerful summer dresses, tidied up their hair, and applied makeup. The transformation couldn't have been more profound. Some of the outfits exposed attractive legs and some women sported low cut dresses, revealing maximum cleavage. Kim's group were directed to places scattered around so that each table hosted one or two of the visitors.

Kim was placed on a table with the leader, and other older women. The meal was plain but delicious; roast lamb and copious quantities of vegetables.

'My name is Irene, we didn't introduce ourselves earlier,' said the leader. Kim had noticed her looking around with satisfaction at the arrangements.

'Kim.' She shook hands rather formally with the women at her table. There was a gradual increase in the noise of conversation around the room.

'You're very young to be leading such a group,' observed Irene.

'I'm twenty-six,' answered Kim. 'I'd almost completed my medical studies in Sydney at the time of the flood, but have now had considerable experience at our hospital in The Settlement. So to all intents and purposes I'm a qualified doctor. I'm also part of an elite military training academy within our community. We're now increasingly glad we have this capacity. So I'm more than qualified to lead this group. I would be very happy to tell you all about The Settlement, and I would like to understand your situation.'

'Sorry! I wasn't trying to question your leadership qualities,' said an apparently contrite Irene. 'Please tell us more about The Settlement and then I will tell you about us and why we're here.'

Kim spent thirty minutes spelling out in some detail how the group started and what had been developed in the past eighteen years. 'So we have now combined our activities with The Bandstand, due to the misfortune they suffered, and have made contact with other groups between the Blue Mountains and the coast.'

There were many questions which Kim answered straightforwardly.

'A hospital,' observed one woman. 'We've lost one or two members, who with better treatment might have survived. Since the flood, transport has been a problem.'

'None of the major hospitals are functional anymore. But, we do have a helicopter, for use in emergencies.'

'Thank you for that information, maybe I can reciprocate,' said Irene.

Kim nodded.

Irene looked around the room, nodding in satisfaction. 'This place was created as a haven for women. Women have many reasons for joining us, but I suppose that mainly it's wanting more control over their lives, and for other reasons such as abuse. Some just want to live in a natural environment. My father left me a large acreage, including this wooded area, but we have significant areas under cultivation, a decent flock of sheep, and a well-managed herd plus poultry and horses. We comfortably feed ourselves as you can see. All the labour, the building, and the heavy lifting is done by the people you see around you.'

'I see there are a number of children here,' said Kim. 'If there are no men around, how do you have children?'

There were a few nervous glances around the table. 'Well, this is perhaps where we are a little less conventional than you might expect,' said Irene, without a hint of a smile. 'Periodically we invite individual men here who impregnate say two or three of the younger women. The men are allowed to stay a week or two and then they leave.' She made it sound like a stock breeding program.

'But there are no males here at all, not even children,' said Kim, looking expectantly at Irene.

'Any male children are put up for adoption at birth. We have, or rather had, a wholly legitimate relationship with an adoption agency.'

'I notice the youngest of the girls present appears to be about four. It must be more difficult to make contact with appropriate males since the flood.'

'We've had no male visitors since the flood and no female additions either.'

'Don't the male visitors have any rights regarding the children?'

'No, they sign away their rights on arrival.'

'Is that legal?'

'We've had no problems at all up to now,' was the evasive answer, 'Since the flood it seems irrelevant.'

Kim glanced around the room where there were some animated conversations in progress. The male members of her troop were very much the centre of attention, which was no surprise since there'd been no male contact for this group of women in at least four years. She smiled inwardly. *I imagine there'll be a few women impregnated, to use Irene's ghastly expression, within the next day or so.* 'How do you select the potential mothers?' asked Kim.

'Volunteers. We have no shortage of women wanting a child.'

'And the girls that produce a male child? What's their reaction?'

Irene shrugged. 'They all know the rules. Of course there is some emotional reaction, but we are well able to cope with that.'

'How have you managed to dress up tonight? Where did you get the makeup from?'

'Most of the women brought it with them. They don't have much opportunity to use it, so I suppose they've kept it safe somehow.'

'We've recently resupplied ourselves from Sydney for that sort of stuff, using our helicopter.' She laughed. 'There was a scramble for makeup and clothes when we returned.'

'Are there no objections to you doing that?' asked Irene.

'There's nobody to object as the place is deserted. Everything will go to waste unless we use it.'

'Deserted?' said Irene quietly. 'I hadn't realised it was quite that bad.'

Three of the younger Amazons, as Kim was now thinking of them, formed a small band in one corner of the room and were enthusiastically playing a mixture of Irish jigs and popular dance music. The younger people in the room were up and dancing, having pushed tables and chairs out of the way to make space. Already there were two notable faces missing from her own group. An enormous air of anticipation had crept into the atmosphere.

Kim watched as Irene glanced around the room. There was a quiet air of triumph on her face. Feeling that she had somehow fallen into a trap not of her making, she considered her options, wondering what Tanya would do in the circumstances. Should she just pack up and go? Persuading the males in her group to leave at this juncture would be nigh on impossible, bearing in mind what seemed to be on offer. Also it seemed important to continue to build a relationship with The Amazons. She wondered how she could turn the tables on Irene. How difficult would it be to persuade some of The Amazon residents to rejoin a mainstream community like The Settlement?

After her meal, Kim attracted the attention of her two female colleagues and said quietly, 'I think, unwittingly, we have fallen into a bit of a trap. Presumably, you've learnt about the purpose of this outfit, not that there is anything particularly wrong with it.'

There were nods from her colleagues.

'There has been a bit of a gap in their arrangements for procreation here because of the flood. Our arrival is, therefore, like manna from heaven from the point of view of our hosts.' Kim glanced knowingly at her colleagues. 'Earlier in the evening, I thought it would be a bit of a free for all, but it seems Irene has organised things in such a way as to maximise the probability of pregnancy. So one of their girls has been assigned to each one of our boys and that will last until we leave, making it less of a shagfest than I first thought.'

They all laughed.

'Anyway it seems our visit will solve some of their problems with the hope of multiple pregnancies, and I'm sure Irene assumes we'll adopt any unwanted male children.' Kim pulled a face. 'The leader, Irene, also showed considerable interest in the security that we could provide and our medical facilities. I hate being used in this way, but I suppose the boys will enjoy the ultimate male fantasy.' Kim thanked her lucky stars she'd taken Tanya's advice, meaning none of the troop members had any romantic attachments with each other. 'Let's make the most of this evening and find out as much as we can about this place. Question the women. Four years of complete isolation may have changed ideas about their lifestyle here. Some may wish to move to The Settlement … '

'Why don't we just let them be?' interrupted Stephanie. 'If that abandoned farmhouse is an example of what is available, we could just go and occupy that place and a few others without worrying about Amazons or any other fringe groups.'

'That is an option, but we are trying to establish an area at least sympathetic to our values, from the base in the Blue Mountains to the coast. In time we may try to reopen the port at Newcastle,' answered Kim.

'Thor and his gang have the same values as we do?' responded an incredulous Stephanie. Her companion laughed uneasily.

'Thor needs work, but at least he's now quite friendly and won't work against us, especially since his daughter is at The Settlement.'

'Two nights here?' questioned Stephanie. 'I hope that is all,' responded Kim. 'We should be able to leave early the day after tomorrow.'

'Not soon enough for me,' said Stephanie sharply. Kim looked at her; Stephanie was very gifted intellectually and could match anyone in The Settlement in terms of physical stamina, as she had amply demonstrated at The Vikings. But now she seemed to be deliberately making things awkward and flouting authority.

Kim thought, I'd better find out the reason.

The next day The Amazon women, despite what appeared to be demanding duties, generously showed Kim and her group around their establishment. Irene escorted Kim on horseback to the far reaches of her domains. There was no mechanisation—the cows were milked by hand and, when they visited the cultivated area, Kim was surprised to see one of the more robust Amazons laboriously handling a plough pulled by two oxen.

'We ran out of fuel for our tractors within weeks of the flood,' explained Irene. 'I presume you have the same problem.'

'No, we don't,' answered Kim to a surprised Irene. 'Our tractors are solar powered, as are our houses. No fires are allowed, for ecological and safety reasons. We do have a very large quantity of conventional fuel stored though, enough to last at least another ten years with careful use.'

'Solar! We had started to explore the possibilities of installing solar power when the flood occurred. We do have quantities of panels and some hot water tanks, which I purchased cheaply some time ago. Do you have a woman who could help us install it?'

'Yes, Susan.'

'You have to understand, we are anxious to maintain the integrity of this place as a refuge for women,' explained Irene, defensively.

Kim nodded, but thought Irene would probably have to compromise on that ethic. However, she decided not to challenge her at this stage in the relationship.

During their leisurely return to the village, Kim gradually established that an association between The Settlement and The Amazon community would be welcome. This included help with security, solar power, general technical assistance, and medical facilities, as well as with ongoing reciprocal visits.

'We must ask that all the assistance you provide will be female; it is important to maintain our fundamental purpose,' Irene firmly repeated her mantra.

'You have failed to mention the vital question of procreation,' Kim said quietly.

'Can't we just assume that from time to time some of your unattached males would come over here and impregnate suitable women. We can then continue as we have in the past?'

Kim was stunned by the total lack of any kind of emotion in the proposal. 'Irene, do you really think it will be that simple, like breeding bulls just appearing at your convenience? Previous visiting males presumably have just disappeared back into the major cities. But, we are only about four days' ride away, possibly less if we manage to open roads up again. Some of the "unattached males" will probably want to be a part of the lives of children they have helped to bring into the world.'

Irene looked irritated at the obvious point. 'Maybe we can explore that down the track. I would like to prioritise some of the services you have to offer.'

'There will be some cost, of course. A reciprocal arrangement for our efforts,' said Kim firmly.

Irene was unable to hide the disappointment on her face. 'Yes, of course,' she said.

Kim asked, 'How have you escaped trouble from raiders or any outside sources since the flood?'

'At first all our stock were kept in the wooded area, so the place looked uninhabited unless a traveller came right into the village. Anyway, we are well off the beaten track.'

'What, none at all?'

Irene looked at Kim speculatively, and then said, 'Three men arrived on foot about two months after the flood hit Sydney, having left their car on the side of a road. They died.'

'How?'

'Poison,' announced Irene promptly. 'They were up to no good and I could see they might encourage some of their friends to come here, so I dealt with them.'

Kim was amazed. 'Does everyone know what happened?'

'No, only one other. I told the others I'd persuaded the men to leave since this was a women-only refuge.'

'And they all believed that?'

'They had no choice.'

'How did you get the men to take poison?'

'I poisoned their water. They were out on the property doing a job I'd arranged and I took them some water and their lunch. A grave had already been dug nearby in the forest.'

'And your accomplice?'

'Oh she's still here. You met her at dinner last night.'

Kim was genuinely shocked at Irene's ruthlessness. She supposed she'd been told the story to indicate she was not to be trifled with.

'No trouble since?

'No, we kept an eye on the situation, or rather I did, and no more than three months after the flood hit Sydney, we were able to expand back into the wider acreage as we had before. You are the only visitors we've seen for four years now. I wasn't even worried about our security until you told us about that raid. Clearly, we need to do something about that and cooperation with you should help.' Irene hesitated. 'Please keep the information about the demise of the visiting men to yourself, there is no need for anyone else to know.'

Kim nodded thoughtfully, thinking there was more to Irene than was evident on first acquaintance.

Riding back into The Amazon village, they saw nothing except three lovesick couples. 'Where is everybody?' asked Kim.

'Still out on the property or in bed,' she was told by one of her smiling male colleagues.

We've assumed you'll join us for dinner again this evening at seven?' Irene asked.

'Yes, thank you,' answered Kim graciously.

There had been no mention of any kind of ablutions, so Kim, taking a towel and soap and a change of undergarments, wandered down to a shallow pool in a fast-flowing watercourse downstream of the village. She was surprised to find Stephanie in the same spot. Without saying much, they both washed sitting in the pool.

Kim glanced at Stephanie and tentatively ventured, 'I've noticed recently that you seem unhappy with your position in the organisation. Is there anything I can help you with?'

Stephanie looked at Kim for a long moment. Like most people in The Settlement, she trusted Kim and admired the way she had singlehandedly rescued Susan and her grandmother at the time of the flood.

'I will be frank with you,' she said eventually. 'I feel undervalued, probably because I'm not a Bower.'

Kim bit her tongue.

'I know I'm as bright as anyone in the village and I have been very diligent with The Academy. I'm the best shot we have, including Tanya. I'll have completed my vet training within months and I need more responsibility.' She stopped, perhaps wondering if she had said too much to one of the powerful Bower family.

'Tanya and David are well aware of your talents,' answered Kim. 'They hold you in very high regard; I think that was demonstrated by your inclusion in the shooting competition. You've just turned twenty-one?'

Stephanie nodded.

'I agree there's a need to expand the control beyond the Bower family and that's been discussed from time to time. Our current expansion program will create the need to maximise our collective talents. As I see it, the Bower family will have no choice but to widen the management group considerably, very soon. Please remember though, David and Tanya are the reason we are alive at all.' She stopped to collect her thoughts. 'I'm happy we've had this conversation and I'll respect the confidential nature of it. But I'll do everything possible to put you in a position of responsibility where you will need every ounce of the gifts you have.'

They looked at each other and embraced, just as Irene walked through the trees shielding the pool from the village.

'Oh, sorry,' she said as she stood her ground, 'I didn't mean to interrupt anything.'

'You didn't,' answered Stephanie as the pair slowly disengaged.

'I was going to suggest you could use the bathroom facilities in the main building, but I see you've already done the natural thing and washed in our beautiful stream,' said Irene as both Kim and Stephanie unselfconsciously stood up in the pool and carefully dried and dressed.

'Thank you,' answered Kim. 'This was very refreshing, but I'll mention your offer to some of the others.'

Irene looked curiously at both of the bathers as they walked back to their separate tents, trying to understand the relationship between the pair.

When Irene was out of earshot, Stephanie grinned at Kim. 'Best keep her guessing.'

Kim nodded and laughed.

～୬

The evening meal was just as delicious, but finished early in view of their planned departure the next morning. There were a few lovelorn couples, and the atmosphere was subdued, in contrast to the joyful tone of the previous evening.

Kim idly wondered how Irene could so easily dismiss centuries-old human feelings. Humans are not cattle and sheep. As sure as I'm sitting here, some of the couples Irene so carefully manipulated into each other's arms will have genuine feelings for each other.

Kim spent ten minutes after dinner ensuring everyone in the troop knew what the program was for the next morning. 'I would like to be back home in four days, so we can't tolerate any delays.'

She returned to the main building to confirm arrangements for the group's departure and to thank Irene personally for her hospitality. As she approached, she could hear the sounds of a furious argument. She stopped in the shadow of a nearby tree and listened.

'There's no reason to change anything,' shouted Irene. 'They'll leave, the babies will be born, and we'll live our lives as before. There may be some female visitors coming here from time to time, but that's all.'

'I want to visit The Settlement and leave with them tomorrow,' said a tearful voice.

'You understood the arrangements when you asked for refuge and came to join us. You don't have permission to leave. I can see you're temporarily infatuated with the boy I arranged for you. In days you will have forgotten him.'

There was silence and more crying.

'There'll be a visit to their place in the future,' she heard Irene say. 'But we need to leave our silly emotions behind, so I'll decide who goes.'

Kim was shocked at the exchange. She had no idea Irene had quite such a grip on her fellow Amazons. In a few minutes, a weeping girl ran from the building and disappeared into one of the nearby cottages. Kim waited five minutes, knocked on the open door, and politely entered the room where a group of older women were conversing quietly. The conversation abruptly ceased. Irene looked up anxiously, glancing at the open door regretfully.

'I just wanted to thank you personally Irene, for the hospitality we enjoyed here.'

Irene nodded, but Kim was made to feel she was intruding.

'We'll be leaving at dawn and I will follow up on the things we discussed.'

'Thank you,' Irene answered dismissively. 'Only female visitors please. We'll see you in the morning.' Irene waited pointedly until Kim left.

Kim decided she'd heard enough as the building's door was firmly closed behind her.

Pleased to see that Academy discipline had held up, as the first light appeared in the East, Kim proudly inspected the mounted troop. She rode around the camp area to see that there was no rubbish and that nothing had been left behind. Irene and a small group of Amazons stood by the door of the main building.

'Thank you and goodbye,' said Kim as she leant down in the saddle and formally shook Irene's hand. 'You can expect to hear from us shortly, within a month I would say.' They cantered out of the yard.

Half an hour along the rough path, they were surprised to see three Amazon women, on horseback, in the middle of the track ahead of them. Two were part of the "procreation" team.

One equally young woman, obviously taking the lead, approached Kim as the troop halted. 'I'm Felicity. We'd like to join you and visit The Settlement,' she said breathlessly.

'I know you need permission to leave as part of an agreement you signed when you were granted a place in the village. Do you have that permission?'

Felicity shook her head uncertainly.

'I assume that if you break the agreement, you stand to lose any rights you might have here?'

There was a sense of hesitation from the group. 'How did you find all that out?'

'It's true, isn't it?'

Felicity nodded.

'In time, you will be very welcome to visit us,' Kim continued. 'But we want to establish a long term relationship with your group. If you came along with us now it would upset that, possibly destroy any hope there may be of cooperation. Others in your group may miss out on their opportunity to interact with us.'

Felicity nodded.

'Visitors will be coming to your village, quite soon I expect. I'm sure this will break down barriers and get Irene to relax some of the conditions she's imposed on you. So, please reconsider your request and return to your colleagues. I'm quite certain that, within months, people from The Settlement will come to live here and that will be reciprocated on your part. This way no animosities will develop.'

'Irene is an impossible dictator,' said another one of the escapees.

'Yes, if our cooperation is to thrive that will have to change. I'm quite certain if you still want to live with us in around six months' time, you will be able to do that with Irene's full cooperation. Please don't rush things.'

The three went into a huddle. There were some tears from all three as Felicity returned and said, 'We are very grateful for what you've just said. You're right. We didn't consider the consequences. We'll go back now.'

'Go back by a different route,' offered Stephanie. 'You don't want to bump into anyone else on this track on your return, and you probably need to be sure your absence hasn't been noticed.'

'You really do understand how things work around here,' answered Felicity, with a frown.

The two girls kissed their lovers farewell and the troop watched as Felicity waved and then guided her companions onto another ill-defined path. They heard them galloping off.

'Good advice,' Kim whispered to Stephanie. 'Quietly see if you can find out whether the boys knew anything about the girls' plan.'

'My advice is not to pursue that. They'll have listened to what you just said and realised the plan was stupid. There's no purpose rubbing salt into the wound. I will do as you ask, though, if you disagree.'

'You're right, thanks, leave it,' she said as they cantered off.

Some hours later as the troop made good progress on their homeward journey they became aware of the sound of galloping horses. Shortly afterwards, Irene and a group of five Amazons came into sight. All the Amazons were armed, much to Kim's dismay. 'We are looking for some of our women who, without permission, were going to try and come with you,' announced Irene breathlessly and without ceremony.

'Really!' said Kim, feigning surprise and pointedly looking around. 'None of your people are here. We've not seen anyone else today. What makes you think anything else?'

'We heard rumours several of the women were planning on joining you down the track,' Irene had the grace to look sheepish.

Kim looked at her sternly, 'Irene, any relationship with us has to be based on trust. We haven't seen any of your people.' All the pursuers looked ashamed as Kim continued, 'If you are unable to trust us, then say so and we'll leave it at that. We do have other fish to fry.' Kim tried to look angry.

'No, no,' said the women in chorus, with panicked looks.

'We apologise,' said Irene. 'We've been isolated for so long we've forgotten how to trust people.'

Kim continued contemptuously, 'What on earth would you have done with that rusty array of weaponry. Chuck all that rubbish away is my advice. It's completely useless and doesn't look like it's been cleaned for years.'

The women looked around uncertainly.

'Let me see that thing.' Stephanie pointed at a revolver. The owner reluctantly handed it over. Stephanie gingerly opened the weapon. 'It's rusty,' she said. 'When was this last used? Look, the shells are more or less rusted in.' With some effort she prised all six shells from the weapon. 'I wouldn't trust any of those,' she said as she tossed them all into the bush. 'They would probably do you more harm than anyone you were aiming at. Properly cleaned up, this revolver should be serviceable though.' She handed it back to the embarrassed woman.

One of the other women handed over her weapon to the nearest member of Kim's troop. 'Perhaps you'd better look at this one too,' she said as Kim moved a few metres away with Irene.

'I'm serious. Do you still want to pursue the things we discussed yesterday,' Kim asked. She was certain she knew the answer, but wanted to further intimidate Irene.

A pale-looking Irene answered, 'Yes, certainly. We obviously overreacted. I unreservedly apologise for my suspicions. I would be grateful if you would continue as we agreed.'

'Okay,' said Kim, closing the discussion, as they rejoined the others.

Within a short time all the weapons had been examined. 'Of the six we have inspected, five are currently unserviceable,' announced Stephanie. 'A couple may, with a bit of attention, be useable again. Hang the rest on the wall as museum pieces.'

Irene and the very contrite group of women turned for home and cantered away.

~

Four days later Kim, asking Stephanie to accompany her, walked into Tanya's office to make a verbal report. Tanya had only been back from her own journey for a few days. She listened without saying much for the hour that it took Kim, with Stephanie making useful additions.

'What do you think we should do?' she asked, when Kim had finished.

Kim nodded at Stephanie.

'We should strike while the iron's hot,' answered Stephanie, confidently. 'Susan and two assistants should go and see what's possible to improve their technology, and a few more to start security training. We need to encourage attendance for some at our Academy as well. I think they're fortunate they've been left alone. If they'd been attacked they would have been destroyed.'

'I brought a few of the solar panels with me,' added Kim. 'I'll give them to Susan.'

'We'll have to think about how we can provide medical assistance in the longer term. Evacuating emergency cases back here by helicopter would be a start. I'm sure other issues will emerge, although their food supply is good.'

'What about the abandoned farmyard?' asked Tanya.

'And presumably many others,' said Kim. 'I suggest we treat that separately. After we get things going with The Amazons.'

'Okay, we need to get Mark and Joe into all this. Let's reconvene in the morning. Thank you both for a job well done.'

~

As they were about to leave Tanya's office, Stephanie talked about the changes they had observed in the countryside. Everything was much wilder than they were used to, although it was only a few years since the flood, the consequent de-population, and the increased rainfall. 'Perhaps the country will become forested again like it was before European settlement.'

'I suppose we must try to keep paths open,' said Tanya.

'Yes, if we're going to re-settle these areas. The longer we leave it the harder it'll be. Although, with the smaller population, the demand for land is much lower for now,' Stephanie continued.

Tanya thought, For someone so young, she really does have an extraordinarily wide perspective, I must see if I can tap into that somehow.

CHAPTER THIRTY-THREE

The Amazons, Continued

Within a few days, Tanya walked out into the village, found Stephanie and said, 'Can we just go for a wander. I've something I'd like to talk to you about.'

Looking surprised, Stephanie answered, 'Of course.'

She wasn't afraid of Tanya, rather in awe of her competence and necessary aggression. Stephanie hadn't been part of the posse that had destroyed the raiders, but had heard the stories, greatly admiring Tanya's audacity.

'I'd like to visit The Amazons and I want you to come with me,' suggested Tanya.

Stephanie was not going to be railroaded into some inconsequential situation, so she asked politely, 'What are your expectations of me?'

Tanya laughed. 'Smart question! You and I will try to come to an agreement with Irene and then I thought you could remain there and run the relationship.'

'Thank you. What do you think that will consist of, at least to start with?'

'Pretty well what you suggested a day or so ago when we met with Kim.

They agreed to take Susan and two assistants. Susan had told them she'd be able to use the panels Kim had brought back with her, probably just on the housing. They decided to take four women with a good Academy record to start a training program.

'While there, it'll really be up to you to bring ideas to the table and decide how seriously to pursue them,' said Tanya.

'I'm very flattered and would love to be a part of the plans for The Amazon establishment, but I have a few questions.'

'Go on.'

'I need to complete my vet degree and where does Kim stand with this idea? She broke the ice there after all. Also, where do you stand with this women-only business, which in my view will cause problems and is a brake on future development?'

Tanya looked at her shrewdly. 'Don't worry about Kim. She reacted enthusiastically when I broached the subject of you running the show over there. I've other plans for Kim, but just need to get my thoughts together on that one, so keep it under your hat. With the women-only issue, I understand from Kim that while some of the women may be gay, most seem to be hetero and might welcome a change in the environment.'

'Yes, many loved having the boys over there even though Irene had manipulated the situation to suit her. I've no doubt the "haven for women" theme has come to the end of its usefulness and many of the residents there would now welcome having a few men around.'

'You'll be the only vet in the establishment over there, so your practical experience will increase by leaps and bounds from day one. Take all of the books you need to complete the theoretical study and then return here for the final exam. What do you make of Irene?'

'As an individual, she is as tough as old boots, very strong and forceful. She has kept that group together through some difficult times, especially the recent isolation. She seems to be lacking in any understanding of people's emotions and feelings though; her philosophy regarding reproduction is wholly agricultural. And we know she reacts strongly when her authority is threatened.'

'You both handled the escapee situation well,' observed Tanya. Kim had told Tanya about Irene poisoning the men, but Stephanie still had no knowledge of the incident.

'Mostly Kim's doing,' said Stephanie. 'But Irene needs careful handling and is going to struggle to compete with the new authority represented by The Settlement, especially when The Amazons realise it's benign. I think, in a short time, most of The Amazons will come to see us as the authority and not Irene.'

Susan loved seeing young Barry, now four and a half years old, grow up; during her now quite frequent absences, she knew Chloe doted on the little boy and look after him like her own. Chloe had taught her almost everything she knew about rearing a child and she knew The Settlement was safe, children ran about everywhere in the village, free of wheeled vehicles.

Although she had accompanied the group on the trip to The Vikings, she was pleased to be asked to go with Tanya and Stephanie to The Amazons, despite having to again leave Barry behind. She had spent time with Joe and Jason making absolutely certain she was able to successfully install the solar panels and enjoyed the responsibility of helping to select two girls to assist her.

Two weeks after Kim's return from The Amazon village, Tanya, Stephanie, and Susan, together with four female troopers and Susan's two female assistants, set off for the village. Each member of the party led a heavily-laden packhorse carrying wiring and tools suitable for solar installations, and as many spare rifles and ammunition as they were able to accommodate, Stephanie's books, and the normal supplies for a four day trek through the bush. All were excited by the new venture, particularly the few who had never been on a mission before.

A small, fascinated group saw the caravan arrive in The Amazons' village at midday on the fifth day of their journey. 'We brought a lot of equipment and stuff with us,' explained Stephanie, having made all the introductions, 'delaying us by almost a day.'

'We weren't sure when you were coming back,' said a girl called Lola. Stephanie recognised her as one of the potential escapees from the previous visit. 'Irene is out on the property at the moment, so you'll have to camp under the trees as before. You can see that we've started to build another house in anticipation of you coming back to help us. We didn't expect nine of you though,' she said breathlessly.

'I will only be here for a few days,' answered Tanya. 'But camping is fine, we're quite used to it.'

Once the horses had been seen to and the camp established, the girls carefully stored all the equipment in a nearby shed with the help of a few Amazons.

'If most people are out on the property,' said Tanya, 'we'll just look around.'

'We can't offer you much for lunch,' Lola explained. 'You caught us on the hop a bit. But I'm sure Irene would want you to have dinner with us every night.'

'Don't worry. We've got food with us, but dinner would be great,' said Stephanie. While the others were busy, she took Lola aside and asked quietly, 'Did you get back here without being missed?'

'Yes, we've been thanking our lucky stars for your advice. Someone had overheard something about a plan and Irene and others had raced off after you, so there was almost no one about.'

'They caught up with us and Kim gave them a flea in their ears. They would've been a very subdued crew when they returned.'

'They were late, so we didn't see them. The next day there was some discussion about unserviceable weapons, although no mention was made of bumping into you.'

Stephanie nodded, thinking she would talk to Tanya about the sensitivity of the confrontation on their way home three weeks earlier. 'We've brought you some better weapons, which we'll teach you to use and look after properly.'

Lola changed the subject, pointing happily to her stomach. 'Pregnant, I think. Me and one or two of the others are often sick now, particularly in the morning.'

'Don't count your chickens just yet. If you can hang on to it for three months you should be safe,' replied Stephanie to a now concerned Lola.

Stephanie spent time getting to know The Amazons and within a few days had a dozen volunteers for the security training detail. Irene insisted that none of the potential new mothers were included. 'It looks as if most of them are carrying,' she said to Tanya confidentially.

'Irene really does just view the new mothers like heifers producing new calves for this place,' Tanya said to Stephanie later.

Within two days, Susan had successfully installed a solar-powered unit in Irene's cottage, providing light and hot water, much to Irene's delight. She found plenty of usable panels suitable for installing lights in all the buildings. 'But there are only enough hot water tanks for the main building,' she told Tanya. 'I need another two dozen tanks to have solar hot water in all the cottages.' She'd also had a look at all the vehicles and tractors. 'Most of them are in good condition, but we need all sorts of equipment to convert any of them to solar.'

'Maybe you could make a list and we'll see what we can do,' responded Tanya.

Susan handed her a list with a smile. 'I thought you might ask that.' She looked at Tanya wondering what her reaction would be to her next request. 'The girls should be able to finish the job of installing lighting in all the houses within about three months, and they don't really need me. So I'd like to come home with you. I've been away from Barry too much recently and I'd like to make it up to him. I can come back any time if I'm needed.'

Tanya looked slightly surprised. 'That's fine with me, but I'd like to talk to the girls to make sure they're happy about that. It's good to know we have such competent people.'

'I'm sure they'll be fine with it,' said Susan. 'I've already mentioned it to them.'

While Stephanie and her group were focussed on instilling some discipline into new recruits with early morning runs, basic drills, and weapons training, Tanya met with Irene to discuss formal arrangements surrounding the relationship between The Settlement and The Amazons.

'I was relieved to see you respected our philosophy that this is a haven for women, by only including women in your contingent,' said Irene, opening what she intended to be a very serious discussion.

Tanya was not surprised, but could see a very shrewd brain working overtime, trying to maintain her control. Not responding directly, Tanya said, 'I think it would be useful if some of your people were sent over to The Settlement for a period, for training. For example, Susan said it would take six months to train two of your people on many of the aspects of installing and maintaining solar power in your vehicles and water pumps, providing hot water and lighting, rather than people coming over from our place.'

'Six months? That seems like a long time,' responded Irene. 'Everyone here has a role. We would miss them.'

'Yes, I've thought of that,' said Tanya. 'It would be much more productive and efficient if some of your people were included in our military academy rather than trying to do it all here.'

'The same issue applies,' said Irene. 'We can hardly spare anyone at the moment. How long would that be for?'

'Twelve months probably,' said Tanya. 'It could be less or more; each trainee is regularly assessed and then completes a graduation process. When they have done that they'd return here.'

'Twelve months!' Irene was genuinely taken aback.

'Stephanie is an almost qualified vet,' Tanya continued. 'She can stay here for as long as you need her. Two of Susan's people will need about three months to complete the solar lighting installation, they could help out whenever needed, and our four Academy people will be available for general duties. They'll still have security responsibilities, and will continue with some training, but at a lower intensity. Your trained people will be able to take over when they return. The arrangements I've suggested will, in time, increase skill levels and productivity here immeasurably. Part of Stephanie's brief is to assess how else we can help, so if you agree this will add to the level of cooperation.'

'What happens if women training at your place are brainwashed into wanting to remain there?' asked Irene anxiously.

Tanya laughed in a relaxed manner. 'You must pay us a visit; brainwashing is not part of the curriculum. The women came here voluntarily and must value your *raison d'être* and so I presume they'd want to return,' said Tanya encouragingly.

Irene looked at her suspiciously.

'I think a more formal agreement between New Settlement and this place would be appropriate. What do you want to be called?'

'Well your people are referring to us as The Amazons,' Irene smiled at Tanya's mildly embarrassed expression, 'and we are quite happy with that, so you can call us "Amazonia".'

~

Over several days, Tanya found she was faced with a shrewd, tough negotiator in Irene, but was able to negotiate an arrangement where New Settlement Pty Ltd acquired all of Amazonia and its assets from the owner, Irene, in return for a five percent stake in New Settlement Pty Ltd and a seat on the board. Irene had to agree that all the residents, current and future, had a one hundred year right of occupation. She also agreed to eliminate some of the more onerous clauses in the present agreement with residents, such as having to get permission to leave Amazonia even for a day. The final agreement was much the same as the one that Tanya had made with Banksia.

Irene was eventually persuaded to agree to the new laws The Settlement had implemented. 'We've only had to impose corporal punishment once and nobody has been expelled since the flood. I hope that we'll never have to use the death penalty,' Tanya had said during the discussions.

'There is no chance of any of our women murdering children and such like,' Irene had observed as she tried to convince herself and others in Amazonia to accept the draconian laws.

~

During her downtime from the negotiations, Tanya chatted with Stephanie. She quickly began to appreciate how bright Stephanie was. At almost six foot, and slim with brown hair, she was pretty if not beautiful.

'What are you trying to do with all these new relationships with Banksia and now Amazonia, and then possibly the religious people? Won't they just become parasites; a drag on our own community?' Stephanie asked during one of their little chats.

'I hope not. If we just ignore them, especially a place like Banksia, they'll probably fall under the influence of groups like The Vikings and that'll spell trouble for them and us in the longer term.' This was just the sort of discussion she had wanted with Mark. She was very surprised that Stephanie had such strategic understanding.

'If we wanted to expand, we could just go to some of the areas that were abandoned after the flood and not worry about the philosophical differences that exist with people that have already settled in certain areas,' Stephanie countered.

'Those people are already there and we'll have to deal with them sooner or later. The smaller ones we can absorb. The Vikings are another matter. We need to understand them better and somehow create alliances with them so they don't actively oppose us. The objective is to unite as an Australian nation again. What we are doing is to secure a patch of the country which will eventually form one of the groups that hopefully come together. We also need places where some of our people can move to. The Settlement needs to maintain a population of less than three hundred and fifty. It is better that our people move into those other societies, firstly to help with their security, but to also help development. Our technology will transform smaller places, like here in Amazonia, very quickly. I'm hoping, in time, the places we absorb will have the same outlook and values we do.'

'The religious people may need a little convincing.'

'What about this place?' asked Tanya.

'Given a bit of time, they'll become more and more comfortable with our values. They may want to hang onto the women-only thing for a while, but I don't doubt they will become a very strong part of our wider organisation in time. I can already see non-threatening things I can do to move that along.'

'How do you think we should deal with The Vikings?' asked Tanya.

'Thor is likely to be a problem. Whatever you do, he will try to undermine you. And if you show any signs of weakness, he will take immediate advantage of that. Even if you form some sort of alliance with him, if he sees that he can diminish your power he will do just that, with no regard for the consequences. Thor seems to have no capacity to think very far ahead. Maybe a marriage alliance would help. I could see Hercules had his tongue hanging out over Kim, not that I think she would want anything to do with him. While he is alive he will be a problem, mark my words.'

Tanya was amazed at Stephanie's insights and wondered how she could further engage her in this type of conversation with Stephanie now living at Amazonia.

Ten days after their arrival, Tanya, Susan, Irene, plus four women destined for The Academy for twelve months and two women undergoing training with Joe and his technical team for six months, left Amazonia. Irene was scheduled to visit for a week. There was a great send off from the people remaining, and a great sense of anticipation.

'This changes everything,' Lola observed during the first evening meal after the group had left. 'Some of us could probably move to The Settlement if we wanted.'

'Maybe, but you should consider the women-only arrangements here. That situation doesn't apply outside Amazonia,' was Stephanie's diplomatic reply.

'Many of us feel that restriction has served its purpose,' said one of the other women.

A furious argument then erupted, with some women defending the current arrangements and others saying it was now redundant. Stephanie said nothing, but tried to assess who was on which side. She had attended many of the discussions between Tanya and Irene, saying little but learning all she could. Tanya had consistently consulted her and took her advice where it was appropriate. Irene consulted few others, relying almost solely on her own judgement.

⁓

'I thought it would take months if not years to achieve all that,' observed Stephanie to Tanya when the ink was dry on all the agreements. 'Irene has effectively agreed to water down the women-only mantra in Amazonia.'

'Maybe,' said Tanya. 'We'll see.'

⁓

Tanya's expedition spent a day on the way home with David and Caroline at The Bandstand.

'I have come to an agreement with the God Botherers,' David mentioned to Tanya, over a private dinner which included Caroline.

'You can't keep calling them that,' laughed Tanya.

'No, they want to be called "St. Andrews", which is fine by me,' was David's answer. 'Donald has been quite helpful and I think that he'll be part of a contingent of Christian settlers moving there from The Settlement. They have a one percent share of New Settlement Pty Ltd.'

'I'm not really comfortable having a wholly Christian enclave in our midst. We have integrated a multitude of different beliefs into our community. If we can, we should extend that to all the satellites.'

'That will take time,' said David. 'You seem to have made progress with breaking down the women-only restriction with Amazonia, with Irene agreeing to allow all those people to spend time with you in the Blue Mountains.'

'I expect that restriction to break down within twelve months,' said Tanya, 'as long as we can find a way of making Irene feel she's still in control.'

'Donald seems to have come around from his original bigoted stance. I'm getting on better with him now,' offered David.

'He gives me the fucking creeps,' answered Tanya.

'Tanya!' remonstrated David, amid laughter from both himself and Caroline.

'With him out of the way, their joint worship facility will function more smoothly. The Imam has a much better attitude than Donald and I expect it'll go from strength to strength,' Tanya added.

After her return to The Settlement, Tanya spent a few weeks making sure everything in the community was functioning well and that visitors from Amazonia and Banksia were fully integrated. Venus had settled down under Kim's tutelage and showed no sign of wanting to return to her father's domains.

Irene spent two full weeks at The Settlement absorbing all that she was able. She had frequent contact with the people involved in the various operations and kept her suspicious eyes and ears open for any signs of "brainwashing" as she thought of it. Irene, Isaac from St. Andrews, as well as Joseph from Banksia were formally inducted to the board during Irene's visit.

A motley crew, thought Tanya, after their first meeting.

Isaac tried to insist that Christian prayer was instituted into the proceedings.

'No,' said Tanya firmly. 'This is a secular organisation representing a multitude of beliefs. There is no reason you can't pray on your own before any meeting.'

CHAPTER THIRTY-FOUR

Newcastle

2032 AND BEYOND

Tanya was consolidating lists of things needed from various sources, including most of the satellite settlements. 'All this valuable equipment is sitting rotting in various warehouses in and around Sydney and will never be used,' she said to Roger, 'unless we use it. Find out from everybody where we might find some of it and bring anything light enough back in the helicopter. Jonathan seems to be working on finding us a much larger machine, which would make it all so much easier.'

Roger looked at her curiously. 'What are you going to use a larger machine for?'

'I'll tell you when I've thought it all through, but we are certainly going to need some heavy lifting ability.'

Roger, now aged thirty-four, had spent most of his life at The Settlement. At five foot ten, and slightly built with brown hair, he was quiet and thoughtful. He rarely pushed himself forward, but had shown leadership ability when it was needed, acting as Mark's second in command at The Academy and within the security operation generally. He had recently married an Amazon who'd been training with The Academy and they were expecting a child.

He knew Tanya would tell him what she had in mind when she was ready. With help from Graham, Joe, Susan, and many others, Roger made trips once or twice a week to various parts of Sydney looking for useful items. He collected solar panels and hot water tanks which he dropped off at Amazonia; spare solar tractor engines, one at a time due to the weight; and a plough and a harrow. Over several trips he replaced two complete milking machines as well as all the computers at The Settlement, and he provided Amazonia and Banksia with two laptops each. St. Andrews wouldn't participate because they regarded the computers as ungodly, and argued that just taking things without the owners' permission was theft.

Roger told Tanya later, 'All the main roads out of Sydney are still blocked with cars from all those years ago. We managed to land in an area next to the M4 at Penrith and had a look. Most vehicles had several bodies in or around them and we found notes in some of them. Here.' He handed over some scrappy pieces of paper. 'We are still seeing no signs of human life at all.'

When David mentioned the people of St. Andrews' concerns regarding the re-supply operations, Tanya said unsympathetically, 'Common sense is as rare as rocking horse shit in that community. Send some of them to us and I'm sure we'll change their minds. We're now breaking down the women-only ethic within Amazonia. Irene went ballistic when Roger told her he was to marry one of her people, but I persuaded her that if she were to accept some families, we would be able to send her at least a dozen hard-working people. She has now found that nobody is questioning her control, even with a few married men around, so her resistance is crumbling I'm happy to say.'

~⁹

'We still have quite a lot of fuel, but it's not being replenished so we urgently need another source,' Roger said to Tanya one day.

'I think I've found a place on the outskirts of Newcastle that ran a few helicopters for the coal mining industry. We need to check it out.'

'Well away from the flood-ravaged areas presumably,' answered Roger.

'I'm hoping to find fuel as well as a spare helicopter,' said Tanya.

~⁹

Days later, Tanya and Kim, with Roger piloting, flew the machine to the designated place. They hovered overhead and carefully flew around the area for fifteen minutes.

'I can't see anything living,' Tanya announced. 'We should go in. Roger, be ready to take off in a hurry and, Kim, please follow me and watch my back.'

Roger carefully landed the machine two hundred metres from a large, unmarked building. Tanya raced off, carrying her rifle, with Kim following, keeping a careful watch for any trouble. Tanya fiddled with the lock for a few seconds and it opened easily. With help from Kim she managed to prise open a small gap in the wide, heavy warehouse door, squeezing through. Pulling a torch from her backpack, she was delighted to see three large helicopters squatting in the gloom.

'Kim,' she shouted, 'everything okay? If it is, why don't you come in here? Look, this is unbelievable, they won't have been touched for years and will need a lot of attention, but that's okay. I want to get an idea whether they have any fuel here. Let's open the door for more light.'

They managed between them to open it about a metre, allowing a thorough search of the premises.

'Look over here!' said Kim excitedly, from the far side of the warehouse. 'Someone's living here,' she said to Tanya when she had found her way through the still-gloomy cavern.

Tanya shone the torch around. 'A bed, recently slept in, some food, wallaby skins, pots and pans. Here, this looks like a dog dish. This place is certainly occupied.'

'There is a door to the outside, here,' said Kim as a shaft of light from the now open door lit up the little space.

Tanya ran out of the building making for a small weed-infested copse at the rear of the property. She returned a minute later. 'There is most definitely someone here,' she told Kim, 'but he doesn't seem to want to be found. I caught a glimpse of a dog obviously following someone into the bush. There's no value in trying to find him. I'm assuming it's a him. I will leave a note for when we return.'

They spent another twenty minutes looking around, 'Here, Kim, look. There's a sodding great fuel tank. Must be for the choppers. No idea how full it is.'

They closed the warehouse up and locked it, leaving it much as they had found it.

'When we get back, I want you, Kim, to select fifty of our best people. You are to occupy that warehouse and the surrounds. The fifty will have to include Joe and some of his technical people. We must find a way of getting at least one of those machines operational. Roger and I will fly over and coordinate activities about two weeks after you have set off. We'll bring tools for Joe as well,' Tanya continued excitedly.

On the flight home, they silently observed the cluttered main roads filled with rusting old cars.

CHAPTER THIRTY-FIVE
Murder

'Look! What's going on?' said Kim, pointing as they circled to land, 'People all over the place; they seem to be looking for something.'

As the rotors came to a final halt, Mark came dashing out to greet them with a grim expression on his face. 'It's little Barry. He's been missing since early this morning as far as we can tell. I'm organising search parties. Some have already gone out and there are more to go. The best thing you can do is refuel and take the helicopter out for the hour or so while it's still light.'

'Where would you like us to concentrate?' asked Tanya, as Kim and Roger refuelled the machine.

'North, the bush up there. Some people have already gone there, but you could give it a good going over before dark.'

'What are we really looking for?' asked Kim.

'Primarily a child, but also if we see any suspicious movements, especially from an isolated individual,' was Mark's answer.

With Tanya at the controls they raced up to the northern end of the property and systematically, at a low level, skimmed the treetops, surveying the dense bush which had altogether recovered from the planned burn now many years back.

Tanya was using all her considerable skills as a pilot to keep the machine as low as possible. On their second slow traverse, just as Roger was saying, 'It's too dark to see, we should go back … '

Kim yelled, 'Look, over there, there's a figure running … just dived into the bush.' Tanya turned the machine around as quickly as she was able. 'If you can hover just above the ground in the vegetable patch, I can jump out. It's only a few hundred metres from where I saw the person,' said Kim. Tanya did as she was asked and both Roger and Kim clambered onto the runners and dropped onto soft ground.

Tanya landed the machine back at base, just as it was almost too dark to see. She refuelled again ready for first light. Finding Mark, she told him what they'd seen and that Roger and Kim were out in the bush looking.

'It will be easy to hide up there now in the dark,' he said, 'if indeed someone was trying to hide. But now we have a focus. There's no sign of the boy and search parties are returning because of the fading light. We'll start again before dawn.'

Tanya quickly dashed to Chloe's house where she found her very distraught mother-in-law. 'We were both here and Barry was playing outside,' she said tearfully, 'as he has done forever now. He's never wandered off before.' She wept. 'I just couldn't bear it if something has happened to him.' Tanya hugged her and tried unsuccessfully to give comfort.

Susan came in and clung to Chloe. 'Nothing, there is no sign of him and it's dark. He'll be scared. I don't know what to do.'

Tanya glanced at them. She'd known of their close relationship, but she could see Susan was like an only child for Chloe, making up for her loneliness since isolation. Tanya said, 'Susan, come with me in the helicopter in the morning. We can cover more ground that way.'

As she went home Mark found her. 'There's a rumour flying around that one of the Muslim men was seen hovering near Chloe's place earlier today. I personally don't believe that for a minute, maybe it's someone trying to misdirect the search. But with all the heightened emotions, there's a danger someone might try to take the law into their own hands. I've called a meeting at the hall right now. We need to nip this thing in the bud.'

Fifteen minutes later Tanya and Mark stood up on the stage in a packed community hall.

'You speak,' Mark said to Tanya.

She stood up, asking for silence. Right now, she really missed David's calm demeanour. 'We all know little Barry is missing. We don't know yet what has happened to him, but as sure as I'm standing here we'll find out. There are some ugly unfounded rumours circulating. Those rumours do this community no credit at all and whoever started them should be ashamed of themselves. If, as we suspect, those rumours were started maliciously, when we have found Barry, and that is a priority, we will also be looking for the people who started this nonsense and will take action against them. In the past, we have dealt successfully with crises when we have concentrated on the facts and that is what we need now. The search parties will start again at first light, so please be ready. Mark will direct the search, but we now have a focus northward, in the bushland. Thank you.'

Mark spoke individually to the leaders of the search parties and gave them clear directions. 'Please be on the parade ground at five am. We need to be in place at first light.'

At the conclusion of the meeting Kim and Roger appeared, looking tired and bedraggled. 'We've identified the area where we should concentrate the search, but it became too dark to see much beyond that. I'm quite sure I saw a man, but that is all we have to go on,' said Kim.

Tanya returned to Chloe's. She and Susan were still sitting there holding hands and looking helpless. She cooked them a meal and then encouraged them to go to bed. 'I will pick you up at five am,' she told Susan.

'I will be on horseback,' said Chloe, 'with a few others.'

'Take dogs,' said Tanya, 'one never knows what they might turn up.'

Groups started to gather before five am and were directed by Mark to various parts of the property. He was able to provide transport for a few people. Two groups of twenty cantered off north, one under Chloe and one led by Roger.

As soon as it was light enough to see, Tanya, with Susan and Kim aboard, flew the helicopter to the area where Kim and Roger were dropped off the previous evening. With hand signals Kim was able to direct two groups of twenty to the area where she had seen the apparent fugitive.

'There are enough people involved in that,' said Tanya. 'We should continue to do as we did yesterday and fly backwards and forwards over the area at low altitude to see if we are able to flush anyone out.'

'If there was someone here, maybe they managed to get back to the village under cover of darkness,' said Susan.

'Mark and some of his Academy people visited every house in the village to check. If anyone was missing, we'll soon know.'

By midday there was no progress. On one of her refuelling stops, Tanya asked Mark, 'Did you manage to account for all the residents last night?'

'More or less. However, there were a couple of people we didn't actually see as we were told they were in the bath or something. I'm trying to follow up.'

As people were becoming despondent, Roger, searching near the site where they saw the fleeing man, came across a dog barking frantically at a pile of recently-disturbed leaves. 'Keep right away,' he told his group. He took a spade and carefully scraped the leaves aside, soon uncovering a small leg and then the rest of a small boy; it was Barry. He appeared to be asleep despite the leaves, but his little body was cold. 'Get Tanya, quickly please, and all of you stay away, we don't want to contaminate the area.'

Within thirty minutes, Tanya had landed the helicopter, with difficulty, in the nearby vegetable patch and, holding Susan by the hand, she walked through the bush to where Roger was standing, 'I don't know what they've found,' Tanya said to Susan gently, 'but you may need to prepare yourself for the worst.'

Susan just held Tanya's hand tightly.

As they came into the clearing, Susan ran over to where Roger was standing and with an animal-like wail of anguish fell on top of her little boy. It took Tanya five minutes to prise Susan away from the body, which was placed on a stretcher and taken to the machine. Roger almost carried Susan to the helicopter and she clung to him as they took off and then landed minutes later on the parade ground.

The body was rushed to the hospital.

'We have DNA samples from every member of the community here, including all our visitors. If there is any evidence of abuse it will only take a day or two to find a match. It is not possible that anyone outside the community could be responsible for this,' said the doctor on duty.

'DNA?' questioned Tanya. 'I thought that was high tech science. Do we really have the capacity to analyse and match everyone's DNA?'

'Oh yes, we were originally given some testing kits from one of the Sydney hospitals and Roger has been able to provide more of them in his re-supply expeditions. The original science was a real breakthrough, but now the analytical process is quite simple.'

'You have done these tests here?'

'Yes, a few people were concerned about the paternity of a baby. We just dealt with it here in confidence.'

The search parties returned over the next two hours and, as with the previous night, everyone was asked to attend a meeting in the community centre.

There was an immediate hush as Tanya walked onto the stage. 'I'm sure you've all heard the news that we found Barry's body in a shallow grave earlier this afternoon. There's nothing I can say that sufficiently expresses all our feelings, but I'm sure I can pass on the deepest condolences from all of us to Susan and Chloe. As you all know, we have DNA samples from everyone in the community resident here today, so we will find the person who did this and whoever it is will face justice here in this very place. Again I urge you not to listen to rumours and let the justice system we've set up take its course.'

'How long will this process take?'

'Full analysis and matching will take about a week, I'm told. Then it will depend on what we find as to how long the rest of the process takes.'

'So you mean there is a child molester and murderer among us, without anything being done,' said an anxious voice.

Tanya looked grim, 'We're working as fast as we possibly can to identify the perpetrator. But we do need to clearly identify the person concerned, I'm sure you understand that. If you're concerned about safety, lock your doors. It won't be for long.'

Kim ran up on stage and whispered to Tanya, 'Donald Weatherspoon has left the village and, according to his wife, had plans to visit St. Andrews. She also said she hadn't seen him for several days. She's very upset.'

'Oh, shit,' mouthed Tanya. Quietly she said, 'I'll call David, but we need to try to intercept him as soon as possible in the morning. Does she think he was responsible?'

'I didn't ask.'

The crowd in the hall watched with interest.

'Any developments?' asked a voice.

'We asked everyone in the village to remain here until our investigations were complete,' she said reluctantly. 'I've now been told one person left on horseback this afternoon. As soon as I have confirmed the person's identity, I'll let you all know. Now please try to get on with your own responsibilities, we'll inform you of any developments. I realise this is important to the community as a whole, but I don't want to go off half cock on this issue.'

As the hall emptied, one person sidled up to Tanya and asked, 'Was it one of our Muslim brethren who left this afternoon?'

'No, it wasn't,' she said evenly. 'I will let you know who it is as soon as I'm certain.' *Stupid fucker*, she thought angrily. *Stupid blind prejudice.*

She walked over to see Chloe and Susan, and found Patricia there. 'The doctor gave them both a sedative and they're now asleep. I'll stay here the night and look after them for as long as needs be. I hear that someone left the property today.'

Anticipating the question, Tanya shook her head saying, 'I can't tell you who yet. I'm sure you understand the reason.'

Tanya phoned David to keep him up-to-date with developments.

'Donald?' said David. 'He's pretty harmless. Maybe I should try to find him and talk to him.'

'David,' Tanya almost shouted down the phone, 'don't go anywhere near him. He may be unbalanced and very dangerous. Please just leave it to us.'

Tanya then visited the team working on the DNA identification.

'The child will have Susan and Chloe's DNA all over him, so I must eliminate that,' said the doctor in charge. 'I can tell you he was strangled, so we have some fingerprints, and also sexually abused, poor little mite.'

Tanya took a deep breath before she said, 'Donald Weatherspoon was the person who left this afternoon. Maybe you should focus on him to start with, even if it's only to eliminate him as a suspect. Please don't reveal that information. One way or another we're going to have to make an announcement tomorrow or, at the very latest, the next day. I don't want people coming to their own conclusions and then acting on them.'

'We'll do our best. What you've told us is helpful.' Tanya didn't notice the sharp look the doctor gave her as she left.

At first light, Tanya, Kim, Jason, and Roger set out in the helicopter to find Donald. Jason and Roger had been equipped with harnesses so they were able to abseil down to the ground if needed. They traversed the known route from the eastern gate, but there was no visible sign of Donald or anyone else. Tanya flew north and then south of the regulation path to The Bandstand. They saw nothing in the acres of bushland and were just wondering what they should try next, when Roger pointed.

'There, under that tree, a man and a horse standing perfectly still, in the shade.' It took the others a few minutes to see what Roger was looking at.

'I'm going in,' said Tanya. 'You will have to be ready to abseil and quickly. Kim, be ready with that 30.06, I want the bastard alive, but not at the expense of one of ours.'

As Tanya hovered fifty feet above the tree, Roger and Jason abseiled down to the ground in a flash. Donald was quite unprepared, having thought he was safe with the helicopter hovering above. He didn't realise the crew had a method of reaching him in dense bushland. He made a grab for a pistol in his waistband, but too late, as he was suddenly dragged off the horse, his arms pinned behind him.

'Hey!' he yelled.

Jason ignored him, tying his hands and feet together and strapping him into a harness. Within twenty minutes of sighting him he was being trussed like a chicken into one of the seats in the helicopter.

'See that he has no other weapons,' Tanya yelled at Kim over the noise of the engine and the rattle of the rotors.

'I'm innocent, I didn't kill him,' yelled Donald.

'How did you know he was dead?' yelled Tanya. 'Gag him. I've heard about as much as I can stomach.'

Roger was then winched into the machine. 'Jason drew the short straw. He'll ride home.'

'I'm not sure who got the best bargain,' said Kim, hopping into the seat next to Tanya. 'Sitting next to that piece of dingo turd, even for only twenty minutes, doesn't sound like much fun to me.'

Tanya rapidly gained height and they landed just before noon.

'Remember this man is innocent until proven guilty,' said Tanya as they untied Donald and placed him in Mark's custody. 'He will obviously remain locked up until we have a case and then a trial. Nothing is to be said until this evening,' she added to anyone within earshot.

Another meeting was called for that evening. There was an air of anticipation in the audience and Tanya had to hold up a hand for silence. 'I promised I would tell you of any developments relating to the murder of Susan's child, Barry. Today, we apprehended Donald Weatherspoon and he is in custody.' There was an immediate hum of chatter, which subsided as Tanya held up her hand again. 'He left here yesterday afternoon and was found on a path south of the regular path to The Bandstand. When we have proper evidence, he will be brought to trial. We must all remember that he is innocent until proven guilty. So again I entreat you, do not take the law into your own hands as it will greatly damage this community should you do so.'

'If he'd been at The Vikings he would have been dead by now,' yelled a voice from the back.

'I don't think that has any relevance here,' said Tanya acidly. 'As I've said, do not take the law into your own hands; if you do, it will be you in the dock here facing the music.'

Earlier Tanya had spent time with Susan and Chloe, but both were still under sedation. 'We will have a proper funeral when all the DNA tests have been completed and the doctor is satisfied he can be released,' she told them. 'There will then be time for proper grieving and we'll do all we can to help you both face the future again.'

She had also phoned David, who said, 'Jason will tell you when he arrives that I found him half an hour or so after you had taken Donald into custody. But, I'm surprised. I always thought of Donald as a benign sort of person. Despite your advice, I was going to ask him to return voluntarily.'

Tanya bit her tongue and then replied quietly, 'He almost certainly would have shot you. But, we are still waiting on DNA evidence, so he's still technically innocent.'

'You think that he would have shot me?' asked David in surprise. 'We had developed a good working relationship.'

'He would have shot you!' said an exasperated Tanya. 'I'll phone when we have the DNA tests.' She cut the contact, something she'd never done before to David.

Three days later, a distressed hospital doctor came to see Tanya. Before she could utter a word he said, almost in a whisper, 'It's a perfect match; the semen on Barry's body matches Donald's DNA exactly. I have had the results checked independently, twice. That is why we've taken so long.' He looked down. 'I was part of his church group and would've done anything for another result. I thought he was a good man. He has let many people in this community down.'

David too, thought Tanya, looking at the doctor. 'Are you prepared to testify and confirm your findings in court?' she asked.

'Yes.'

'Mark, as head of security, will collect all the evidence we have and hand it over to the prosecutor. There is now enough evidence to charge him formally.'

The trial process within the community was well established, if used infrequently. The judge had retired from the New South Wales bench prior to becoming a resident and there were a number of experienced lawyers, also resident, prepared to act as prosecutor. Tanya had managed to persuade a woman from Amazonia, who had some experience, to act as defence counsel. Tanya had decided that, due to the personal connections, none of the Bower fraternity should be involved in any way with the trial, except as possible witnesses.

Roger, as second in command of security, formally charged Donald.

Lasting only two days, Donald's trial was unusually short and swift. He pleaded not guilty to abduction, sexual abuse of a child, and murder.

The prosecution presented evidence of Donald's flight; the DNA evidence; and two witnesses who had seen Donald hovering near Chloe's cottage.

Donald had insisted, against counsel advice, to take the stand.

'This whole exercise is a Bower family conspiracy against me personally. I'm going to expose them totally in that court,' protested Donald to his lawyer.

'You need to think about the evidence against you and deal with it. If you claim not to have been anywhere near the scene of the crime, you need to be able to put doubt in the mind of the jury that you are telling the truth. If you take the stand, in my opinion, you will almost certainly not be able to do that,' said Maureen, his defence counsel.

Donald shrugged.

'Donald, please tell the court where you were on the afternoon of the day in question, the day of the little boy's murder,' asked the defence counsel.

'In church. The church that I built, despite all the roadblocks put in my way by David Bower and his family.'

'Do you have any evidence of that?'

'Yes, there are several witnesses who will testify they saw me there.'

'Step down please.'

Three people were individually called to the stand.

The judge reminded each of them that they'd taken an oath to, 'Tell the truth, the whole truth, and nothing but the truth'. They were also reminded that perjury was an offence and could result in prosecution.

Two of the three withdrew their testimony.

The third man took the stand and testified he'd been in the church with Donald all day.

'It's the same man that has kept trying to direct the blame towards the Muslim community,' Tanya whispered to Mark. 'I don't like this, not at all.'

They need not have worried.

A triumphant Donald was asked to take the stand again. Maureen felt she had a least put doubt in the mind of the jury regarding Donald's whereabouts on the day of the murder. 'No more questions,' she said.

The prosecution then asked, 'How do you account for your semen being found on the boy's body?'

'It's just a Bower conspiracy.'

'All three of the medical staff here have testified there's a million to one chance that the samples they found are not yours, none of them are members of the Bower family and two are members of your church,' thundered the prosecution counsel.

'It's a Bower conspiracy,' Donald repeated mechanically.

'Why did you leave here in such a hurry?'

'I had many things to do at St. Andrews. The search had been completed and the boy's body found. I could make no further contribution, so I left.'

'You had supplies for two weeks. Why would you need so much for a four or five day ride to St. Andrews? You also had maps relating to territories far beyond St Andrews.'

'All that was planted on me. All of this,' Donald waved his arms about the court, 'is a Bower conspiracy to get rid of me.'

He was asked to step down and Roger was called to the stand.

'Roger, you were one of three people who apprehended the defendant.'

'Yes,'

'Are you a member of the Bower family?'

'No.'

'Please describe how the defendant was apprehended.'

'With Tanya flying the helicopter, Jason and I abseiled down to where the defendant was trying to conceal himself under a tree. We then apprehended him.'

'Was that difficult?'

'Not particularly, although he tried to pull a loaded pistol on us. We surprised him.'

'Did you have any supplies with you in the helicopter that could've been added to his load as he claims?'

'No, with the three of us, plus Tanya, and the abseiling equipment, there wasn't much room for anything else.' Roger was genuinely upset that he could be considered part of such an underhand arrangement.

'Did you place some maps in the defendant's luggage?'

'No,' Roger almost shouted.

Isaac from St. Andrews was called to the stand.

'Were you aware that the defendant was on his way to St. Andrews?' asked the prosecution counsel.

'No, we had agreed he would come and try to finalise arrangements for him to move to St. Andrews, but we weren't expecting him for at least another month.'

'No more questions.'

During a break, there was a flurry of activity and some whispered conversations.

'I call Mrs Weatherspoon to the stand.'

There was a look of fury and consternation on Donald's face.

'Mrs Weatherspoon, can you tell the jury where you were on the day of the murder?'

'I spent all day in the church, cleaning it and arranging flowers as I do on a regular basis.'

'Who was with you?'

'I was on my own.'

'Was the defendant with you?'

'No, I didn't see him all day. In fact I haven't seen him for several days now.'

'So he wasn't with you in the church?'

'No.'

'Could you confirm who else you saw in the church on the day in question?'

'I saw no one else. I told you I was on my own. That is quite normal I usually do everything on my own.'

Three others were then called to the stand. All testified that the man who'd said he was in church with Donald was actually with them, all day, dosing cattle.

The prosecution summarised. 'The DNA evidence is unequivocal. Three separate analyses were conducted and all came up with the same result, that the semen found on the body belonged to the defendant. When the defendant heard the boy's body had been found, he tried to escape. This was a well-planned exercise; he had supplies and maps that would have taken him beyond the jurisdiction of this community. The contention that he had some urgent business at St Andrews is pure fiction. The defendant claims he was in church at the time of the murder, but all the evidence relating to this claim has either been withdrawn or discredited. The defendant keeps stating that prosecuting him for this dastardly act has something to do with a Bower family conspiracy to get rid of him. Again, this is pure fiction. Members of the jury, I submit that it's your duty to find the defendant guilty on all counts and that the maximum penalty should be applied.'

The defence claimed that the defendant had been in church at the time of the murder and that somehow the DNA analyses were flawed. 'The defendant has done much good here. He is innocent and should be released immediately back into the community.'

The jury spent a day considering the evidence. To a packed courtroom the judge asked the jury foreman, 'Have you come to a unanimous conclusion on all counts?'
'We have m'lud'
'On the charge of unlawful abduction of a child?'
'Guilty.'
'Unlawful sexual abuse?'
'Guilty.'
'Murder?'
'Guilty.'
The judge waited for the gallery to subside.
'Mr Donald Paul Weatherspoon, stand up please.'
A shaken Donald stood.

'You have been found guilty on all counts. Sentence will be passed when the court convenes at ten am tomorrow.'

Every possible seat had been taken when the court convened the next day.

'Before I pass sentence, I ask if either the prosecution or defence counsel has anything to say. Prosecution?'

'The defendant has been found guilty on all counts by a jury of his peers and in a legitimately constituted court. I ask that the maximum penalty of death by firing squad be applied on all counts. There is no room for mitigation, the defendant is evil and the community needs protection from such a person.'

'Defence?'

'I question the validity of this court, the proposed sentence does not comply with Australian Law, and the proposed sentence will constitute murder.'

'Will the defendant please stand?'

Unsteadily Donald rose to his feet.

'Donald Paul Weatherspoon, you have been found guilty of the foulest deeds by this legally constituted court. Your behaviour during these proceedings has been nothing short of disgraceful. Do you have anything to say before I pass sentence?'

Donald shook his head.

'On the count of abduction, you will be expelled from the community and all your assets held in the community will be forfeited. On the count of sexual abuse of a child you will be expelled from the community and all your assets held in the community will be forfeited. You will also be executed by firing squad and your body will lie in an unmarked grave outside the boundaries of this community. On the count of murder, you will be expelled from the community and all your assets held in the community will be forfeited. You will also be executed by firing squad and your body will lie in an unmarked grave outside the boundaries of this community. There will be no right of appeal and sentences will be imposed within one week.'

He banged his gavel. The courtroom cleared almost silently, Donald was returned to the lock up.

People were genuinely shocked. All were aware of the law, but had never really envisaged it would ever have to be imposed.

Tanya said to Mark, 'You will have to organise the firing squad, but no Bower family member is to be present in any way. Roger or Rachel will have to be in charge. Also, I'm not going to repossess Donald's house as the court directed.

Mrs Weatherspoon has not been tried for anything. I am going to ask the hospital doctor, who knew the Weatherspoons well, to inform her she can stay in the house and continue to be a part of the community if she wishes. We will have the right to review the situation every five years.'

'I think that is fair and prevents the Bower family from gaining anything. Frankly, I don't have the stomach for imposing death sentences. I hope Roger and Rachel will be able to deal with it,' replied Mark. 'I have charged that bastard with perjury, by the way.' Referring to the man who said he was in the church all day with Donald. 'I'm going to throw the book at him.'

Tanya nodded.

Tanya told Kim she could now get on with planning the takeover of the warehouse in Newcastle. 'Take fifty of our best people, including as many of our technical people as can be afforded, including Joe, and plenty of supplies. Secure the area. I will be over there within two weeks. I have spoken to Joe and he thinks Susan can be left in charge of the technical stuff here at The Settlement. It might help to get her mind off the ghastly experience she has gone through.'

'How do you deal with all this?' asked Kim, 'I'm like a wobbly jelly, I don't know what to do with myself. I almost feel sorry for Donald.'

'It's the same for me,' answered Tanya. 'The only way I've coped is to try to get on with our plans and think ahead. In time, the scars in the community will heal. We also need to think of a little boy whose life was cut short. And Susan and Chloe's lives will never be the same without Barry, whatever they do. '

Mark gathered all the members of The Academy together, with the exception of those absent and the fifty who were now planning for a sojourn in Newcastle.

'There will be a ballot for eight people who will make up the firing squad. If your name comes up in the ballot you will have no choice but to participate. Roger will be in charge. The board has decreed that, as with the trial, no Bower family member will be part of the execution party. There is to be no possible thought that any of this is linked to personal issues such as revenge. Any questions?'

Most people felt the arrangements for Mrs Weatherspoon were fair, but there were one or two voices who said, 'It's a payoff for her testimony.'

'You can't win,' said Tanya angrily, when Mark mentioned the conversation he'd overheard.

An hour before dawn, on the appointed day of the execution, the party consisting of Donald, manacled and mounted on a horse led by Roger, the eight people who made up the firing party, three witnesses, the judge, and a doctor from the hospital, left The Settlement on foot by the occasionally-used western gate.

Two hours later, deep in the forest, Roger halted the party. 'There is a newly-dug grave just over there,' he pointed.

'Judge, will you read out the sentence.'

The judge asked Donald, who was still mounted, 'Do you understand the sentence, Mr Weatherspoon?'

Donald nodded.

'Do you have anything to say, perhaps to the victim's family?'

Donald shook his head.

The detail then made Donald dismount and escorted him through the trees and tied him to a stout post situated next to the grave. He was blindfolded. The rest of the party followed silently.

Roger had already briefed the firing party. 'Each rifle has one round in the breech, some of the rounds are blanks and some are solid. Under no circumstances are you to open the breech of your rifle either before or after the shot has been fired. This is to protect you, so at no stage will you as individuals be identified as having fired the fatal shot. I will personally collect all the weapons afterwards and clean them. I have already given you your instructions. Aim for the heart. You will only be ten metres away.'

The party came to a halt and stood still for a minute, with the firing squad ten metres in front of Donald. Roger, standing to the side, lifted his right hand and said, leaving a second between each order, 'Safety off. Aim. Steady. Fire.'

All eight shots were fired simultaneously and Donald slumped against his bonds.

'Safety on. Doctor will you please certify that Mr Weatherspoon is dead.'

The doctor spent a minute in front of the bloody corpse, checking for any sign of a pulse, 'I can certify that Mr Weatherspoon is dead.'

Without further word, the detail untied Donald's bonds and lowered the body into the grave, which was rapidly filled in and covered in branches. When the grave was dug, Mark had instructed Roger to plant ten saplings around the grave site. 'I don't think anyone will ever find this place, but when these trees grow it will be impossible to walk through here anyway.'

Not one word was spoken on the return. A notice of execution was pinned on the outside of the community hall, signed by the judge, the doctor, and the three witnesses.

A very upset Roger reported to Mark, and then Tanya, 'I have done many things for this community,' he said quietly. 'Don't ever ask me to do anything like that again.'

David had kept away during the whole process, but Tanya had kept him informed of progress. Once the execution had been completed and formalised, Tanya phoned him again and asked for his advice. 'Do you think there should be another community meeting, just to put all this to bed?'

David thought for a moment. 'Probably not. Some people will see it as an attempt at self-justification or even gloating over the outcome. Make certain there is a full factual account of the whole process, right from the murder to a mention of the execution, in the paper. People will make what they will of it all for themselves. I'm sure that for parents of young children especially, there'll be a sense of relief.'

'Okay, that makes sense.'

'I do have an apology to make to you though,' said David.

'Oh, what?'

'You warned me many times about Donald, but I thought I knew better. I'm sorry.'

'Not necessary, but thank you. If you hadn't been on such a slow horse the day we apprehended him, you wouldn't be around to make this apology. Frankly, I would miss you. I'm getting all bloody sentimental now.' She put the phone down and wiped away a tear.

Days after the execution, Susan and Chloe arranged a funeral service and burial for Barry. The service was held on the parade ground and everyone in the community who was able attended the emotion-charged event. David was persuaded by Tanya to attend and was asked to say a few words.

'This is the celebration of a life cut short before its prime. Barry will never go to school; he will not have the opportunity to attend The Academy; he will never marry. We will all remember him as a sweet, cheerful little boy. Most importantly, we need to understand the loss that Susan and Chloe have suffered. We must also remember that justice has been done and the scourge that we found in the midst of our society has been removed.'

The whole community accompanied the little coffin to the top end of the property, where it joined the few other graves already there.

CHAPTER THIRTY-SIX
Newcastle Again

Kim led her troop of fifty out of The Settlement a few days prior to the execution of Donald Weatherspoon. They were mostly under thirty, except Joe, and split evenly between the sexes. Some had wished to wait until after the execution, 'To create finality,' as they described it, but most were relieved to be away from The Settlement's now oppressive and stifling atmosphere.

Riding northeast, within a few days the troop emerged from the wooded areas to join the Putty Road towards what was once the small, attractive village of Wollombi. As with all the roads, there were now rusting cars jamming it up, many with the remains of occupants still inside. The village was a morass of all sorts of vehicles scattered in every spare corner, most with bones and remnants of clothing partly covering them. There appeared to be no sign of life.

Kim said to the horrified troop, 'We'll camp here for the night.' She directed people to organise the camp. 'We need to conduct a proper search,' she said to the rest of the party. 'Go into every building. It may be that there were absolutely no survivors at all, but I'd like to be certain of that.'

They searched high and low through the museum, the looted grocery store, the pub, all the houses, and the two cafés. Most people returned after an hour or more with the same story—human remains. Some had died peacefully in bed, but others had evidently been the subject of violent and horrific deaths. There was not a scrap of food to be had anywhere, other than the occasional tomato on an overgrown plant in the chaotic gardens.

As they were all gathering in the camp, one of the troop rushed up to Kim to breathlessly announce, 'I think I've found something, please come and have a look?'

Being directed to the very outskirts of the village, Kim saw a decrepit little cottage hidden away, almost overwhelmed by creepers. With difficulty, they forced the unlocked door open. It was clear the place was occupied, although there was nobody visible. Out the back of the cottage, there was an extensive, well-maintained vegetable garden and an orchard. Beyond that there were three or four contented looking cows, a bull, and a small flock of sheep.

'Hello,' Kim yelled, 'is there anyone here?' There was a deafening silence. She tried once more, with no effect. 'They may show themselves later. I will leave them a note. If they don't want to be found that's too bad. I wonder how they survived though.'

They looked around the establishment.

'There are definitely two people living here,' said Kim, 'and a child. I wish we could find them. If they need help we can provide it.' She tried calling again, but there was no response.

Kim briefed all the guards on returning to the campsite, 'There is undoubtedly someone living here. You need to keep your eyes skinned. It's possible they might try to creep into camp out of curiosity as much as anything. If they come innocently, we need to persuade them that we mean them no harm and may even be able to help them. So, double up on the number of guards.'

In the dead of the very dark night, one of the guards, Jim, saw a faint movement on the opposite side of the camp. He quietly crept around keeping to the shadows, hoping that the other guard on duty had seen him move and would come to help if needed. Something attracted his eye among the horses and he quickly moved in that direction. There was a man trying to loosen the tethers on several horses. Jim, unseen, raced around and using his strength and considerable bulk, took the man down with a ferocious rugby tackle. The other guard was on hand, helping to subdue the large, whiskery man who silently fought both guards as if his life depended on it. Some of the untethered horses started to move away.

'Tie him up firmly,' Jim muttered, 'and I'll take him to Kim. You'd better try to catch the loose horses.'

By this time, the rest of the sleeping troop had been alerted to the fracas. The horses were all recaptured, some with difficulty, then the fire was built up and the prisoner was dragged reluctantly into the firelight.

Kim said to him kindly, 'We are on our way to Newcastle and just happened to pass this little village. We mean you no harm, and if you wish to be left alone then so be it. We could be in a position to help you though if that is what you want. We would like to understand your story. How have you survived here when most didn't?'

There was no response from the man, who continued to struggle fruitlessly against his bonds. A minute later, an unkempt woman and a pretty child of about six were brought into the gathering. Kim could see that the woman, slim, with short brown hair, would have been pretty once, but she now looked tired and careworn. The man emitted a low moan and looked about wildly.

Kim repeated to the terrified woman what she had just said to the man. 'Please, just tell us your names and what must be a remarkable story of survival.

We are here to help if we can. We mean you no harm.' The child had accepted a warm drink from one of the troopers.

'I'm Mary and Joshua is my husband ... ' she waved a hand vaguely in his direction. 'Amy is our child ... We came to live here a few years before the flood ... We were strangers in the village and mostly kept to ourselves ... When all the people started to come into the village, after the flood, we managed to lock ourselves away. As you can see, the cottage is tucked out of sight. One or two people tried to ... '

'Shut up Mary,' said Joshua firmly. 'These people look like the police.'

'We aren't the police,' answered Kim. 'We'll tell you who we are. Anyway there are no police anymore. And, your child, Amy would have been born after the flood. How did you cope with her birth with absolutely nobody to help you?'

'We just did. We have cattle and sheep on the property, so we have a reasonable idea of what happens when a mammal gives birth.' She smiled wanly.

'What about medical attention?'

'We just do what we can. Amy had a younger sister who died a few months ago.' A tear slipped out, which was quietly wiped away.

'Have you seen anyone around here in the last couple of years?'

'You are the first people we have seen since those ghastly weeks after the flood. We didn't move from our cottage for more than two months and then we found that all the people in the village had died. There wasn't much we could do so, as you see, we left them alone.'

'Maybe you'd like us to tell you something about ourselves,' suggested Kim.

Mary shrugged. 'If you like.'

Kim then gave a brief account of The Settlement, 'We have a hospital and a school, for example, if that is of interest.'

'We want to be left here, alone,' said Joshua gruffly.

'If that is your choice then we'll respect it,' Kim answered. 'You should understand, though, that the comparatively few people who have survived have started to move about. It may not be very safe here in future and there are no police. You may be better off joining one or other of the nearby settlements, or encouraging others to join you here.'

There was silence while breakfast was cooked and served; even Joshua participated.

'Why did you try to release our horses, by the way?' asked Kim.

Mary looked uncertainly at her husband.

'We just wanted you out of here,' muttered Joshua unconvincingly.

Kim shook her head and didn't pursue the matter.

As daylight emerged, the troop efficiently packed up the camp and was ready to move by seven thirty. Joshua had been released from his bonds.

Kim said to Mary, just prior to departure, 'We are on our way to Newcastle on another mission. I will arrange for another visit from our people within a month or so, who can help you if you need any. You need to make up your minds, but the chances of remaining here in complete isolation for much longer are remote. It may become unsafe.'

The troop made their way through Pokolbin and the famous wine-growing area of the Hunter Valley. The roads as they had now come to expect were scattered with cars going nowhere. The once pristine vines were now wildly overgrown. One winery had been burnt to the ground and others, looking forlorn and deserted, were covered in creepers. The troop noticed, as Stephanie had mentioned, that the countryside was becoming overgrown.

'There may be the occasional pocket of survivors,' Kim said to the group. 'If they show any signs of wanting to be found, for want of a better word, then we can make contact and tell them who we are. If they want to be left alone, then so be it. We can't lose sight of our mission.'

The small, rather ugly town of Cessnock was utterly deserted. In days gone by it had been a fuel stop on the northern road from Sydney to Brisbane. One of the leading members of the troop sighted what appeared to be a ten year old boy as they left the small, nearby settlement of Kurri-Kurri.

'Some of us should follow the boy at a safe distance, so as not to frighten anybody. The rest should stay here for the moment,' said Kim.

They were nervously greeted by a group of adults and a gaggle of unkempt, dirty children. The four Settlement people dismounted and gave the children gifts of food.

'We are from a place in the Blue Mountains which we call The Settlement,' offered Kim. 'We're here to help, if you need anything. Somehow you survived and continue to do so.'

'Are you from the Australian Government?' asked one of the men.

'No, we have nothing to do with Government; it doesn't exist anymore anyway.'

'How can you help then?'

'We are well established and have such things as a hospital and school. We are looking to re-open the Port of Newcastle and perhaps re-settle some of the area between the Blue Mountains and the sea.'

'What do you want from us?' asked the man suspiciously.

'Nothing specific, although if you knew a short route to Newcastle that would be helpful. Also if you know the area it might help us decide on possible settlement opportunities nearby.'

'Such as?'

'Firstly, we need a source of food if people are to settle here, then we can re-establish schools and so on.'

'There is no fuel anywhere around here.'

'We have solar-powered tractors, which partly gets around that problem. We want to know if there are any other survivors in the area and if there are any other major settlements around.'

'We've seen no other people since the flood, but … ' he hesitated and looked for support from his companions, 'there is a group of quite wild people who come down here occasionally from the North. They raided us once recently and took away one of our young girls and some cattle. We have replaced the cattle, there are plenty of them running wild around here, but we are worried about what happened to the girl. They have not been back for a while … '

'They will be back,' said one of the women firmly.

'Okay, so security is a big issue. We could leave one or two of our people here if that would be of any help. Later we might be able to do something more permanent here for you, or when we have established our base in Newcastle you could move there.'

'We are quite well-established here, so we want to stay,' the man responded. 'There are plenty of places that were abandoned during the floods, so if people wanted to move here we could show you where to go. These people came in force last time. There were about fifty of them on horseback, so leaving just a couple of people here wouldn't be much help.'

'What do you really want?'

'Central services like education and hospitals would be good. And security, of course.'

'What do these wild men call themselves?'

'Barrington. I think they are based at Barrington Tops. They had horses and guns, but aren't as well set up as you. We had no real conversation with them, they just came in, took the cattle and the girl, and left.'

'What happens, in the short term, if these people from Barrington return?'

'We have a plan, but there are only a few of us. We're hoping we'll just be left alone.'

'If six of us stayed here until something more permanent was developed, would that help?'

'Yes, six would help.' He looked around for nods of agreement from his colleagues. 'Food is not a problem, we can feed them.'

'How many of you are there?'

'Ten adults and now fifteen children.'

Kim called the rest of the troop to join them.

'We need six volunteers to stay here until something more permanent can be arranged. None of the technical people please as they're needed in Newcastle.'

Within a minute, six hands had been raised, including Jim.

'Good, we'll stay here the night and make a plan. Security is paramount.' She told them about the raid and the abduction. 'Jim will be in charge, but this will only be a temporary arrangement. I'll talk to Tanya about something more permanent.'

During the rest of the day, with the help of the leader of the group, Richard, they surveyed the area on horseback. Over the evening meal they developed a security plan.

'Jim, have you looked at all the weapons here?'

'They are mostly okay. Some of them could do with a bit of upgrading. We'll look around the houses here and see what we can find over the next few days.'

Richard smiled, 'We have always been a bit reluctant to go and raid other people's houses, for all sorts of reasons, but you people don't seem to worry.'

'No, the owners are past caring, so anything you need will just go to waste if you don't use it. That applies to everything—tractors, cars, computers, and so on.'

'We have no fuel or electricity,' said Richard.

'Solar is what we rely on. We can probably fix you up with a solar-powered tractor.'

~

The Kurri-Kurri group were in a very good frame of mind when Kim's troop left at dawn. They were accompanied by an eighteen year old boy as a guide, who left them to return home once they reached the outskirts of the city of Newcastle. The boy led them down a little used, overgrown path and the city gradually came into view. It looked asleep, there was no movement, nothing, as they descended carefully into the built-up area. The troop stopped now and then to take in what they were seeing and to get used to the idea that this once thriving city was indeed a ghost town.

~

Two weeks after their departure from The Settlement, the now forty-four strong, well-mounted, disciplined troop, riding two by two, entered the eerily deserted streets of Newcastle. Much of the city centre was under water as were all the low-lying districts north of the Hunter River. There was no visible sign of any human habitation at all. The once pristine gardens were all overwhelmingly overgrown with a mixture of once-cultivated plants and rampant weeds. Everything gave off a seedy, decayed look.

Kim stopped her troop outside a large mansion at the top of a hill, 'I would like to have a quick look in here.'

Handing over the reins of her horse, she had to break a window to unlock the front door. Everything was very tidy and orderly, although smothered in dust. There was not a scrap of food in the kitchen, the garbage had been taken out, and the electricity switched off. Upstairs she found ten clusters of bones in a series of bedrooms—six adults and four children. There was no sign of any violence. There was a note on the bedside table in the main bedroom dated six weeks after the flood had hit the Eastern Seaboard of Australia.

It read, "Should anyone find this note, we completely ran out of food, the electricity failed within hours of the city being flooded, and there is no water in the taps. We took the only option open to us."

A list of names, with their respective ages, was added at the end of the note. Kim stood for a minute with her head bowed. *How many million times will this scene have been repeated in Australia and around the world,* she thought. *We must never let it happen again.*

Looking through the house, she found several laptops and, in the garage, three luxury cars, now rusted through and sitting on flat, decayed tyres.

Having relocked the door she returned to the troop and told them what she had seen. 'We'd better find this helicopter place,' she said thoughtfully, as they rode off.

After some searching they found the warehouse Kim had visited with Tanya a few weeks earlier. She knew it was close to the northern freeway. The troop was halted within sight of the warehouse.

'When we were last here there were signs of a person living inside. We must capture him without hurting him in any way. Maybe he knows something about this place.' She briefly explained the geography of the premises. 'There is a door at the back. When I open the main warehouse door, he'll probably try to escape through the back door, so if six of you,' she pointed, 'quietly go around the back while the rest of you surround this place. We ought to be able to apprehend him without too much trouble.'

Some members of the troop were detailed to hold the horses and the rest deployed as Kim had directed. Joe then picked the lock on the warehouse door, a skill that many from The Settlement had learnt from Tanya, and, with difficulty, pushed it open sufficiently to allow entry. There was the noise of someone or something scrambling away in the far reaches of the huge building. Then a flash of light as a door opened, faint signs of a struggle, and a lot of swearing.

Joe had been warned about the door and was busy oiling the runners when the detail from the rear of the warehouse brought a large, bearded, struggling man to the front.

'What the fuck do you want, just leave me alone,' yelled the man in a strong American accent. When Kim, the rest of the troop, and the horses became visible, he calmed down and said, 'Oh, I see.'

'We will explain ourselves,' said Kim, 'and then maybe you could do us a similar courtesy.'

The man looked warily about him and then said, 'There are chairs in the office upstairs.' He pointed.

Several troop members gingerly climbed the unlit stairway while Kim explained where the troop came from and what they were doing. 'Firstly we would like to be able to re-commission these machines.' She waved in the direction of the three helicopters. 'But our ultimate objective is to create a small settlement here and re-open the port.'

'And you think you can do that?' asked the man sceptically. 'What do you know about helicopters?'

'Three of us came here a few weeks ago by helicopter.'

'Small machine. These babies are a very different kettle of fish,' said the man defensively.

'Tell us about yourself. The rest of the city is deserted so we were surprised to find anyone at all living here. All we have found, apart from you, is piles of human bones. You seem familiar with this outfit?'

A few chairs were brought and dusted off. Now seated the man started to tell his story. 'My name is Eustace Thornbury,' he smiled at the expressions of amusement on the troop's faces. 'I work here.'

Kim was about to interrupt, but Eustace held up his hand. 'When the floods destroyed the city, all the people here disappeared and have not been seen since. A few days later, a group of Aboriginal people came here with their own food and persuaded me to go with them into the mountains, where I have been until about two months ago when they returned me to this place. They talked about a White Goddess and that I was to help her and her people.'

There were glances of understanding between Kim and members of the troop.

'I had no idea what they were referring to until you and another woman appeared something like a month ago. The other woman followed me, but gave up quickly, and then you came today.' He paused. 'Can I just call my dog? He will be terrified with all these people around.' He whistled and a brown Kelpie arrived, cringing, and went to sit next to Eustace. One of the group went out and produced some stale bread and gave it to the dog, who perked up and wagged his tail.

'You say that you work here,' said Kim. 'What is your job?'

Eustace smiled. 'I'm from the helicopter company in California and my job is to maintain these babies, and a few more in other places in New South Wales, but I'm based here.'

'Good heavens,' said Kim. 'Would you be able to get these birds flying again? That's what we're here to do, initially.'

'Well, I could of course, but you can't just come in and take over. What happens when the owners return and find that I've allowed you to steal everything here?'

'If the owners haven't been here since the flood, now more than seven years ago, they are certainly dead. Have you any idea what has happened to the world since you went to live with the Aborigines?' answered Kim. 'I don't suppose you've been paid for any of the intervening years either?'

Eustace looked uncomfortable and shook his head.

'Well, you can see what's happened to Newcastle,' said Kim. 'Every coastal city in the world has suffered a similar fate. Much of the world's population died in the floods or shortly afterwards. We've made contact with a few surviving groups, but they're few and far between. We're on a mission to try and widen our contact base and, in time, to re-establish some sort of government in Australia. It'll take us a while to create a viable operation here in Newcastle, which is why we need the helicopters, to bring supplies in from our base in the Blue Mountains. Also to possibly airlift some of our vehicles out of our place.'

Eustace looked sceptical, 'How can I believe you? All that sounds pretty farfetched to me.'

'The person your Aboriginal hosts referred to as the White Goddess will be here in a few days in the helicopter you saw. At our base, we have a library of recordings from around the world and our own videos of the local environment showing many details of the catastrophe. If you wish you will be able to return with her and view these things. I hope that will be enough to convince you. Anyway, it's no more farfetched than you telling us that you have spent the last seven years in the mountains with a group of Aborigines.'

'Okay, what are you proposing to do here?' asked Eustace.

Kim explained that the group would be camped somewhere nearby in order to start the Newcastle settlement.

'There are a number of things that need attention. I think we should be able to find cattle, even if they're a bit wild to start with. We need to plant vegetables and fruit and we will then start the unpleasant job of clearing a few houses for settlement. If we have the use of helicopters with a large lifting capacity, it'll make things easier.'

'Joe is here to install solar on this building and on some of the houses,' Kim continued. 'He and his team will be able to make this place operational and then get the helicopters airborne again, under your direction, assuming you're convinced of our bonafides by then.'

'There is a generator here. I haven't looked at it since my return, but it'll light up the whole place,' said Eustace. 'No need for solar.'

'Depends how much fuel is available,' said Kim.

''Bout a year's worth, when I last looked. Same for helicopter fuel. Maybe Joe and his people could get the generator going to start with. Then I can start to clean up some of these babies before the White Witch arrives.'

'Goddess,' said Kim to an uncomprehending Eustace. 'White Goddess. I'm sure she would prefer to be called Tanya though.'

Tanya and Roger arrived in the helicopter a week later. 'The aftermath of the whole messy business took a bit longer than I expected,' she told Kim, referring to the execution. 'Hopefully, it'll have returned to normal by the time you get back home.'

Tanya found Joe and two of his assistants on their hands and knees surrounded by a jigsaw of metal pieces all covered in oil, placed on some clean sacking.

'We have stripped and reassembled the generator,' said Joe, standing up and wiping his hands on some cotton waste, 'I'm sure it'll work fine. We're just putting the engine together, so we should have light in here sometime tomorrow.'

Tanya looked around. 'Did you find that person who was living here?'

'Oh yes, Eustace, I'll introduce you,' said Kim. 'But he's gone off to see one of the houses we're cleaning up.'

'Eustace!'

Kim explained how they'd established contact with him. 'Somehow the Aboriginal group who took him in know about the White Goddess. They told him when they returned him here that he was to look after "people who will arrive on horses". However, he's still concerned his bosses will arrive at any minute and, if we have commandeered these helicopters in here, they'll think we've stolen them and that he has helped us. You'll probably have to take him back home and show him some of the recordings we have. Anyway, he still thinks of himself as the maintenance engineer on these machines, or rather his "babies". If anyone can get them airborne he can.'

With Kim, Tanya reviewed progress on all the activities towards the development of a Newcastle settlement. Kim told her what they'd found in Wollombi and Kurri-Kurri. 'I told Jim and the people I left in Kurri-Kurri that we'd relieve them in a month, but it would be ideal if you could drop in on your way back to see how they're coping.'

'Okay, we'll see if that can be fitted in,' responded Tanya.

Kim's group had also found some cattle, still very wild not having had any human contact since the flood. 'We have them corralled in a nearby paddock,' said Kim. 'Hopefully, in time, they will become quieter.' They had found a source of cattle fodder, in a nearby wholesale business. 'It seems unspoilt,' said Kim.

Other members of the group had started to clean up nearby houses. One was quite empty. They were refurbishing it with quantities of paint and disinfectant found in a large DIY warehouse.

'Because of the smell we've had to remove all the furniture, bedding, and clothing, and burn it. 'Most houses will need the same treatment, as well as a thorough airing, before we can use them.' Kim reported.

Kim told Tanya where they were recording lists of names of previous, deceased, occupants. 'We have also dug a large grave so that any bones we find can be buried there.' They were able to furnish reconditioned houses from a nearby furniture store.

Tanya admired the large area cleared for growing vegetables. 'It'll be months before we'll be able to harvest anything from here. We also need to build a fence to keep the roos out.'

'They need a solar-powered tractor,' Roger offered, 'but it will take a few trips to bring all the bits here. With one of those new choppers, we could do it in one hit.'

'What are the priorities?' asked Tanya, when she'd seen everything.

'Transport,' answered Kim. 'I think if we could find a light diesel truck somewhere nearby and try to recondition it, it'd do the trick for the time being. We have a large quantity of diesel here. Then, if we had at least one of the helicopters going it would be easy to re-supply us from The Settlement so people here could focus on development.'

'I can see Joe is going to be pulled in all sorts of directions at once if we're not careful, said Tanya. 'Where is this Eustace? If needs be I will take him back to the Blue Mountains and show him some of the videos we have.'

They found Eustace buried in the engine of The Settlement helicopter. 'Ah, the White Witch,' he said, wiping his hands on his overalls.

'Just call me Tanya,' she said laughing.

'I was having a look at this baby here,' said Eustace. 'It's been well maintained, but will need major attention in the not too distant future; the machine is old now.'

'If you could get one of those other machines going, it would be easy to let you loose on this one for a while,' said Tanya, trying to size Eustace up.

'Yeah, but do you really think you can just come in here and take these machines and use the fuel that was left here? What happens when my bosses come back from San Diego? I'll be locked up.'

'The likelihood of your bosses still being alive is remote,' said Tanya. 'And there are two chances of them ever appearing here again, Buckleys and none.'

'Buckleys?' Eustace looked at Tanya. 'I suppose that's another peculiar Australian expression.'

'Yes, it means fuck all, in your language.'

Eustace laughed uneasily.

'Look, I'll happily take you back to the mountains and show you recordings of the effects of the flood all over the world, if that is what is needed to convince you? I'm fairly sure we have a clip on what happened in San Diego and other parts of California. Eustace, we really need your help. Come hell or high water, we're going to create a settlement here in Newcastle; it would be much easier with your cooperation.'

Eustace looked at her for a moment. 'Okay, I need another couple of hours to complete what I started doing to your machine and then we can go to your precious settlement.'

'It's an hour's flight. Unexpectedly, we'll have to drop off at a place a few minutes from here and I like to land in daylight, otherwise we'll have to wait until the morning.'

~♪

Taking off mid-afternoon, Tanya flew the short distance to Kurri-Kurri. After circling twice, they landed under Jim's direction in a grassy area near where Richard and crew had made their home.

'Just popped in to see how you're getting on and to introduce ourselves to our new friends,' said Tanya as they disembarked.

'There's been no movement from the North,' reported Jim, after introducing Tanya to Richard and his crew.

'Is there anything you need?' asked Tanya.

Jim laughed, 'Everything and nothing. In terms of the immediate security situation, we're now well set up. If the people from Barrington come here they will get a very unpleasant surprise. We do need to try to rescue the girl though, and then in the long term a solar-powered tractor would be good and we could install some solar electricity here which will help the group. There's a child needing hospitalisation, if you've room for her. We have looked at most of the houses in the vicinity, so our immediate needs in terms of tools and so on are well met. Your visit alone will make a difference; the people here now have hope.'

~♪

They loaded a very sick girl and her mother into the helicopter. 'Roger will just have to sit at the very back and keep still,' said Tanya to a nervous Eustace. On the return, they had to skirt one of the local thunderstorms. Eustace's eyes nearly popped out of his head as Tanya circled The Settlement, landing a few minutes before dark. Tanya left Roger to complete all the post-flight checks while she ran to the hospital, emerging a minute later with a doctor, nurse, and gurney. When she could see that the girl was looked after she took Eustace into the village.

He was introduced to Mark, who was asked to set up a selection of videos detailing what had happened to various communities at the time of the flood, including San Diego.

'I had no idea the place was so extensive,' observed Eustace, looking around.

'It's now more than twenty years since we started developing it. David and I have driven this development. We both came to the same conclusions in 2010 about climate change and acted on them accordingly.'

'Who is David?'

'My father-in-law, Mark's father. Joe is married to Mark's sister. Kim is Joe's daughter'

'Very much a family affair,' observed Eustace.

'I've put you in a spare cottage, belonging to one of Mark's brothers. You can have dinner with us and spend as much time as you wish watching the videos in the community centre.'

'I see most of the men are clean shaven,' said Eustace during dinner, 'I ran out of blades years ago.'

'We go on raids … 'said Mark.

'Re-supply expeditions,' Tanya interrupted.

'Re-supply expeditions,' Mark continued, 'into Sydney and its surrounds. All the supermarkets and food warehouses were looted within days of the flood, but most other shops and warehouses were untouched, so we develop lists and then take the helicopter and get whatever we need. I can give you razor blades, and any amount of clothing. If we had one of those big choppers that Tanya described we could haul in more substantial items such as washing machines and dishwashers; all the ones here in the village are aging. Vehicles too. There is nobody about, so if we don't use what's available it will go to waste.'

'Why don't you take vehicles into the city? It would be much easier than using a chopper.'

'At the time of the flood we deliberately isolated the place, so people are unable to get in here. Now of course we can't get out. Also most roads are still blocked with cars where people just stopped and were unable to go any further.'

'What happened to the people?' asked a troubled Eustace.

'They died,' answered Mark. 'Tanya and others went on a few exploratory expeditions within weeks of the flood hitting Sydney and found bodies in cars and near roads. There was no food and nowhere for them to go.'

'Is this what I am going to see on those videos?'

'No, most of the pictures we have are from official sources, which we recorded as the floods hit. They all went off the air within about two weeks of the flood arriving in their locality. We do have some recordings of the aftermath of the flood in Sydney. I can show you some of those if you wish.'

After dinner, Mark escorted a silent Eustace to the community centre. 'Each video is clearly marked with the subject and date when it was recorded. We felt we needed a record of what had happened in the hope that future generations will not make the same mistakes we have,' Mark explained.

There was no sign of their visitor, so after ten o'clock Tanya announced to her children, 'I'm just popping out to see what Eustace is up to.' Mark had disappeared.

In the community hall the videos were all neatly stacked and Eustace was sitting there crying his eyes out.

'What's wrong?' asked a concerned Tanya.

Eustace looked up at her. 'I had no idea; I thought they might all still be alive.'

'Who?'

'Wife and three little kiddies. I saw the recordings of the San Diego and Los Angeles areas. I just had no idea. For years I've tried to imagine what they were all like and what they'd grown into. I imagined my homecoming. None of that can ever happen now.' Another tear escaped down his cheek.

'Here, you need a stiff drink,' said Tanya. She switched off the video player, collected all the clips and escorted Eustace back to their cottage.

Mark was strangely absent, so Tanya spent until early morning listening to all Eustace's reminiscences. When Mark crept in, Tanya looked at him curiously.

Unasked he said, 'Just checking on a few things.'

Eustace eventually went to sleep on the couch in the lounge with a blanket over him. He was woken abruptly by Tanya's two teenage sons tearing through the house at six am yelling at each other about which horse they were to ride that morning before school.

'Oh,' said Chas when he realised there was someone on the couch, 'who are you?'

'I'm Eustace; I'm here to help the White Witch steal some helicopters.'

'White Witch? You mean Mum! That's a good name, we'll call her that when she gets too uppity.' The boys tore off.

A clean shaven and neatly dressed Eustace appeared at the breakfast table just as Tanya and Mark sat down, 'Thank you for the clothes,' he said, 'I feel much better now.'

There was silence for a few minutes while they all helped themselves to quantities of scrambled egg and toast. 'Being isolated, we made ourselves self-sufficient some time before the flood. Obviously that is still the case and it's what enables us to expand our influence,' explained Tanya.

A dry-eyed Eustace said, 'Thank you for your sympathy last night. It's going to take a while for me to come to terms with what has happened. Anyway, I now understand what you're about and I'll certainly help you all I can, including making those choppers airworthy again.'

'You need to tell us what support you need,' said Tanya.

'How many pilots do you have?'

'Two, that is me and Roger and two in training. I presume you're a trained pilot and can help.'

'Yup, bit rusty of course. Showing no disrespect, but those babies in Newcastle are a bit more of a handful than your own machine. We'll need to make absolutely certain that anyone who flies them is one hundred percent competent. Anyway, for the moment I need Joe and one other to help me. It may take a month to get one of the machines refurbished and ready to take to the air.'

Roger took the passenger seats out of the helicopter and flew to Newcastle with Eustace and a large quantity of supplies. They were relieved to see the lights in the warehouse blazing as they landed. Roger continued the supply process on his own, over the next few days, while Eustace and Joe planned the refurbishment of the choppers in the warehouse. Within two weeks, the girl from Kurri-Kurri was up and about and, within another week, she and her mother were on their way back to Kurri-Kurri, with Tanya piloting the helicopter.

CHAPTER THIRTY-SEVEN
Jason and Venus

Tanya spent time with Susan and Chloe trying to help them overcome their loss. Often when she arrived, Susan made some excuse about her responsibilities now that Joe was in Newcastle and left her with Chloe. *The stupid, stupid bugger*, Tanya thought, referring to Mark.

Tanya had realised that Jason and Venus were an item when Jason came to see her to announce that he and Venus had decided to get married, 'I have just told Mum. She's thrilled. She knows and likes Venus.'

'Congratulations,' said Tanya, kissing her nephew on the cheek. 'But be careful. We must be sure Thor is comfortable with everything. We don't want to upset him in any way. I expect he will want one of us, either David or me, to formally ask for his approval and he'll certainly ask for a bride price.'

'What?'

'In some primitive societies, like The Vikings are mimicking, it is customary for the groom's family to provide gifts to the bride's family on the occasion of the marriage of a daughter. I am slightly surprised Venus hasn't mentioned the subject.'

'You mean Venus has to be paid for,' said Jason aggressively. 'Why can't we just get married like everyone else round here?' He started to leave.

'Jason, sit down and listen to me.' He had too much respect for Tanya to ignore her, so he sat glaring at her. 'I'm thrilled you and Venus are in love and are to marry. You have been to The Vikings and your actions saved us a lot of unpleasantness, so you realise things operate very differently over there than they do here. Thor will see a marriage between you, a Bower, and Venus, as an important political alliance, so we just need to be aware of that.'

'What sort of bride price are we talking about, some more solar installations or something?' asked Jason, now more calmly.

'Thor will want a bargaining process, which could take a few months. I expect that when he sees this place he'll ask for something like one hundred head of cattle.'

Jason sat there with his mouth open for a few seconds. 'Where the hell am I to get a hundred head of cattle?'

'You won't be involved in the bargaining process. The matter will probably be settled between Thor and David. Thor may not want to deal with me because I'm a woman,' Tanya replied.

'You will pay Thor one hundred head so I can marry Venus?'

'I don't expect to have to pay quite that much, but yes, in principle.' Tanya laughed at Jason's discomfort. 'You have to understand this alliance is very important to us as well as Thor, so it must all be done properly. Don't under any circumstances go running around telling people, it will just wreck everything. Then you won't be marrying Venus anyway. '

'You've certainly knocked the shit out of the romance of it all,' said a very subdued Jason. 'I feel like a pawn in some political game.'

'Only temporarily,' said Tanya. 'Once this is all sorted, and the ceremony is over, life will go back to normal.'

'Ceremony?'

'You don't think that Thor is going to let his precious only daughter go without a big hoo-ha, surely,' said Tanya laughing, putting her arms around Jason. 'Come on, this is going to be fun! We've got to play it right and this sort of stuff is just up my street. Just one other thing,' she said to an apprehensive Jason, 'please do not get Venus pregnant.'

Jason left muttering and shaking his head, 'One hundred fucking head of cattle.'

~♪

Having spoken to David on the phone, Tanya decided that just she and David would pay a visit to Thor, and arranged to do so two weeks after the marriage discussion with Jason. They had been to The Vikings twice since the first encounter, once with Venus.

'What the hell have you got in the back there?' asked David, laughing as Tanya picked him up at The Bandstand.

'A present for Thor. It's a pure bred bull calf. I'm sure he'll like it. I had a discussion with him on the subject on our last visit, so I have taken the opportunity to surprise him since the seats are out for the supply trips to Newcastle.'

'But the bloody thing will crap all over the back of the machine.'

'It's firmly tied into a sack. It can't really move and will crap, or should I say has crapped, in the sack,' she laughed. 'We're just getting ourselves into Thor mode.'

Within forty minutes, they were unloading an unstable calf in front of a pleased Thor.

'No Venus this time?' he asked.

'Mark had some training exercise planned, so she had to stay,' explained David.

After making sure the calf would be properly looked after, and offering his guests a refreshing drink of fruit juice, Thor looked at David and said, 'You didn't come here just to deliver a calf.'

'We've been wondering how we might further cement the relationship with you and your outfit here,' answered David.

'What do you have in mind?'

'You already have some of our people here helping you with military training exercises. We could help you install more solar, where it is appropriate. We could certainly help to improve the quality of your herd,' Tanya interrupted.

Thor looked at them both quizzically. 'One certain way would be to arrange a marriage between my family and yours, the Bowers I mean.'

Tanya looked at him, saying nothing, hoping he would expand on the intermarriage theme.

Thor continued, 'Hercules would like to get to know your Kim better, but she does not seem interested. She is very strong, maybe too strong for Hercules.'

'Would you have any objection if Jason were to court Venus?' asked David.

Thor's eyes widened as the real purpose of the visit was now unveiled.

'Jason? Oh yes, the smart one. I actually had one of my senior lieutenants in mind for Venus. She can marry him when she comes back from your place.'

'And if she doesn't like him?' asked Tanya.

Thor laughed. 'She'll do what she's told.' He frowned. 'It makes no difference whether she likes anyone or not, she'll get to like the person I choose or get beaten.' David winced, but Tanya didn't bat an eyelid.

Thor looked at them shrewdly and then said, 'I don't know Jason very well, so send him here for two weeks. He can come in the helicopter, maybe with some more solar installations and that military rifle your people seem to carry. He can ride well?'

'Yes, very,' said David hurriedly.

They spent an hour walking around the area immediately surrounding Thor's palace, admiring some of Thor's new initiatives.

Then Tanya said quietly, 'We are in the process of creating a settlement on the outskirts of Newcastle and expect to be able to open the port within a year or two.'

Thor looked at her sharply.

'You don't go anywhere near Newcastle, do you? I could take you over there in the helicopter one day if you were interested,' Tanya continued.

On the way home David said, 'He seems to be set on marrying Venus off to one of his cronies.'

'I don't think so,' answered Tanya. 'He understands perfectly all the implications of a deal with us. Having Jason there for two weeks is just the start of a lengthy bargaining process. I can tell you that although he will play hard, this deal will go through.'

'Deal, you just see it as a deal?' David said in a horrified voice.

'Sorry, I didn't mean to de-romanticise everything, but in the end this d … er, arrangement will be bigger than either Jason or Venus, as far as the uninterrupted growth of The Settlement is concerned. In the end it will be a deal, but I will confine my conversation and thoughts in that direction to you.'

'In all the years I've known you, you never fail to surprise me,' said David. 'One step ahead of the sheriff, as always.'

'Only one? Just watch me. I'm going to have a ball with this one.' Tanya smiled.

CHAPTER THIRTY-EIGHT

Barrington Bandits

Tanya went looking for Derain on their return home. Once she'd found him, or he'd chosen to be found, she told him about the Newcastle initiative and asked whether he knew Eustace. 'He knows about the White Goddess.'

Derain shook his head. 'Ancestor very powerful, he might tell other group to find and look after this man you are tell me about. Maybe ancestor think that Derain have already too much to look after.'

Tanya decided Derain would probably never divulge whether he knew Eustace or not. 'I want you to come with me to Newcastle in the helicopter.'

'Helicopter, no, this will crash and then I'll not be able to look after White Goddess.'

Tanya laughed. 'I've been flying the machine for many years now, it won't crash. I need your help with something, with two things actually.'

After much careful persuasion, Tanya managed to get Derain into the machine. During the flight, he changed from holding his head saying, 'This very big noise machine crash,' to excitedly pointing out well-known landmarks.

On the way, Tanya told him they'd found some isolated people in Kurri-Kurri and that one of their people had been abducted, 'We will go there first. I want you to find out all you can about the gang in Barrington Tops, we need to try and rescue the girl.'

They landed and introductions were made. At the end of the visit Derain said, 'No need for big, bang-bang rescue. I bring girl back here. I need one person to go with me who the girl recognise. Maybe I need two week.'

⁓

On the short flight to Newcastle, Tanya explained the newly-established relationship with Thor and his people. 'That Thor, very bad man, do not like Aboriginal people.'

'You know him?'

There was a mumble from Derain which Tanya took to mean "yes".

'Derain think that he, Thor, might try something silly with our people in Newcastle. Then you go shoot them. That is best thing for that man, anyway.'

'No, we can't do that, Jason will marry Venus and we need Thor and his people to accept us. We don't want to fight with them. If they come to Newcastle, I want you to give them a very big fright, like ghosts or something. Something that will scare the shit out of them, and keep them away for a very long time. It'll become part of their storytelling through the ages.'

Derain grinned from ear to ear, 'I see White Goddess still very smart,' he tapped his head.

After landing, Tanya took Derain to meet Eustace, but there was no flicker of recognition between the two. 'Either they really don't know each other or they are both very good actors,' she told Joe later.

'Eustace has described his Aboriginal home, where he stayed all those years after the flood, in some detail,' said Joe. 'It bears no resemblance to Derain's place.'

'I have some concerns about what The Vikings may try to get up to here in Newcastle,' Tanya told Kim. 'He is worried we may become too powerful. Have you seen any sign of them?'

'Strangely enough, yes. We've caught glimpses of some people dressed like them in skins.'

'Brief Derain and leave it all to him. I don't want any violence though. It's important The Vikings stay onside.' Tanya smiled and then said mischievously, 'Hercules still fancies you, you know. A marriage between us and The Vikings would secure our relationship.'

Kim was about to respond angrily and then saw the amused expression on Tanya's face. 'Marriage with Billy Goat Gruff you mean?' She laughed. 'Two chances—Buckleys and none.'

Derain made his own way back to the settlers at Kurri-Kurri. 'One person come with me, a person girl recognise. We go through Barrington village, pick up girl, and go north before come back here. People there will think you people here have rescue girl and will jump on horse and try to kill you all. Maybe you can lay ambush for them.' He shrugged. 'I bring girl back here, we need two horse.' He left with the girl's mother Josie, who could ride and shoot as well as any of the men. She was armed with her own rifle and a handgun. Derain was unarmed. Jim handed Josie twenty handwritten notes which said -

We have taken back what belongs to us.

If you attempt anything against us in future

You will regret it bitterly.

We want peace, nothing more.

'Drop them all over the camp,' Jim continued. 'It may stop them taking action, but if not, and they come here, we'll destroy them. Derain and I have selected a place for an ambush.'

Josie looked at him uncomprehendingly for a moment and then nodded. 'Peace is better,' she mumbled.

It took three days for Derain and Josie to find the Barrington village in the very rugged and steep slopes of Barrington Tops. The camp was well hidden and far into the area. Increased rainfall had made the undergrowth thick and impenetrable at times.

'Wait here, I be back.' Derain told Josie.

Two hours later he returned. 'There is girl with rope tied round neck. Must be daughter Emilie. You must see.'

They tethered the horses firmly to a tree well out of sight of the camp and Josie accompanied Derain to the outskirts of the large, untidy bush camp. There were several scruffy huts, one log cabin, and a central building, perhaps their community centre. There were many tents which had seen better times. Ragged-looking people were wandering around in a disorganised fashion; some were engaged in cooking a meal. A paddock held more than fifty horses as far as Josie could make out. They could hear noises from cattle, but they were held some way from the camp.

'There,' said Derain, 'that is Emilie?'

Josie drew a sharp breath as a girl of about fifteen was dragged about, with a rope around her neck, by an older woman. The girl was absolutely filthy.

'Yes,' she said shakily.

Derain held her by the arm. 'Don't worry, I bring her back after dark.'

They had a small meal, without lighting a fire, and rolled up in the sleeping bags for a few hours. Just after midnight, Derain woke Josie and they packed up the camp.

'You lead horse quietly to other side of camp, just past horse paddock. I bring Emilie to you.'

Josie handed Derain the handwritten notes. 'Jim says we must drop these all over the camp, could you do that please.'

Derain shrugged, 'Jim told me, I think it will do no good.' He took the notes and crept off into the bush.

It took Josie an hour to lead the horses around the camp. She found a spot beyond the horse paddock as she had been directed. She waited for a few minutes when Derain suddenly appeared carrying what appeared to be a large bundle. Josie looked at the bundle. It was indeed the terrified Emilie.

Josie hugged her. 'Shh,' she whispered. 'You're safe now, but we must make no noise.'

'Go that way, I come soon,' Derain pointed, as he helped the pair onto Josie's horse.

'Where ... ' but Derain had disappeared.

Josie moved as quickly as she was able in the dark, down the path indicated, leading both horses. She heard more horses neighing nervously and then the noise of cattle lowing and shouts from the camp. Derain silently appeared. His white teeth flashed a grin in the dark. 'I make all horse and cow run into camp, maybe keep all people busy for few hours. They never find us anyway.'

It took the Barringtons several hours to regain control and to gather the various animals into their respective paddocks.

'The girl has gone, she is nowhere to be seen,' shouted one of the women. A frantic search ensued during which several of the notes Derain had scattered were produced.

The leader went white with anger, 'Okay, saddle up, we're going to teach those bastards at Kurri-Kurri a lesson they'll never forget.'

'Be careful,' warned one of the women. 'This rescue took a lot of organisation and planning ... '

All she got was a very hard slap in the face. 'Be quiet woman, those people are weak and disorganised. Anyway, they'll cease to exist when I've finished with them.'

'But they offered peace.'

She was ignored as forty-five men clattered off on horseback down the path towards Kurri-Kurri.

Jim had prepared his ground well. The children and some of the older women were hidden in a basement they had found in one of the nearby houses, already refurbished by the Kurri-Kurri settlers. Altogether, for the ambush, he had the six people including himself from The Settlement, seven of the adults from the Kurri-Kurri settlers, and five of the older children. He had made sure they could all shoot and that the weapons they had were serviceable with sufficient ammunition.

'They'll be able to see the cattle in the paddock over there,' Jim pointed to the uneasy group. 'That will guide them down this narrow roadway, which they will only be able to negotiate in single file. We need to be spread out for say one hundred metres along the west side of the roadway, which is raised above the level of the road. You must all be well hidden. One Settlement person will be accompanied by two Kurri-Kurri people. I will be in front and will take down the leading two or three horses, probably including the leader.'

'And then?' asked a voice.

'I'll make them all dismount and drop their weapons.'

'And if they don't?' insisted the voice.

'If there is any resistance, I will shoot the leader, just to wound him if possible.'

'I think we should just blast them off the planet.'

'That is the fall back position. If they continue to resist I will give the order to fire, and you should all be prepared to kill.'

'Are you sure they will come at all?' asked one of the women.

'No, but it's better to be prepared. They probably assume you are weak and unable to defend yourselves. We now know differently.'

'I'm uncomfortable about shooting at and killing another human being,' said another.

'They've already taken one of yours, heaven knows with what intent. Have no doubt they will have no compunction in raping the women here and then killing the men. If necessary, we should all shoot to kill. Have no hesitation. At that point it will be either you or them, 'Jim replied firmly, but quietly.

They were all in place a full day before a small cloud of dust was seen in the distance. Jim had made certain the defenders had food and water and were able to sleep comfortably in position. He had moved between them regularly during the wait.

'Here they come,' he told everyone. 'They'll be here within an hour or so. Remember, don't fire until I tell you.'

They could see the cloud of dust rapidly approaching and, within the hour, the group with horses all of a lather came galloping down the lane in single file as Jim had predicted. Jim took down in rapid succession the first three horses, their riders crashing down to earth. One of them lay there moaning. Some of the other riders were unable to avoid the mayhem and there was a tangle of men and horses all trying to avoid each other.

Jim fired a burst over the heads of the raiders. 'Drop your weapons and put your hands in the air.'

Some members of the group reluctantly obeyed, but the leader who'd recovered from a heavy fall from his horse, yelled, 'Take no notice. It's just a couple of farmers.'

Jim aimed his rifle and shot him in the leg and the man fell down screaming. 'Drop your weapons. Now!' Jim yelled. 'All of you! I will count to three—one, two, three … '

Most complied. Two started to wave their weapons about, supposedly looking for their assailants. Jim shot them both, one in the leg and one in the arm.

After a few minutes, a very subdued group were standing in the laneway with their hands above their heads, having dropped their weapons.

'All of you, move twenty metres down the road in the direction of Kurri-Kurri. Move!' He fired a shot over their heads and the now thoroughly intimidated group shuffled along the road. 'Now lie face down. Quickly.' He fired another shot.

He and the five other Settlement people emerged from hiding places. Two herded the now very nervous horses into a nearby paddock. Three searched the raiders lying on the ground. 'Look for hidden weapons. Woe betide any of them that have kept a weapon of any sort.'

One man leapt up brandishing a revolver. There was a shot from one of the still hidden Kurri-Kurri settlers. The man dropped down dead.

'Any more of you lot with bright ideas?' asked Jim in a loud voice.

There was silence.

'Okay, tie them up,' Jim instructed. The Kurri-Kurri adults emerged and within thirty minutes all the raiders had their hands tied behind their backs, still lying in the road.

The Settlement people gave first aid to the three wounded raiders, but the dead man was left where he was.

'Why did you do this to us,' asked a plaintive voice. 'We come in peace.'

'We will have little Emilie back here shortly,' Jim replied. 'Perhaps she will have something to say about what happened to her. I know what you intended here—murder, rape, enslavement, and theft.'

Derain, Josie, and a still very dirty Emilie arrived on horseback shortly after the raiders had all been pacified. Emilie, still perched on her mother's horse, shrieked and hid her face in her mother's dress when she saw the men.

'Do you know what happened to her during the months she was away?' asked Jim.

'She was treated like a slave, a rope tied around her neck. She was raped, almost daily,' answered Josie. 'Do what you will with these men. I must get Emilie cleaned up and start helping her get through all this.' She rode off with Derain accompanying her.

'You heard all that,' said Jim. 'So much for coming in peace.'

He asked for one of the horses to be brought. The dead man was loaded onto the animal and firmly tied on. Two Barrington men, under guard, were detailed to gather all the water and food the raiders had brought with them.

The raiders all looked anxiously at Jim, 'You are to walk back to your village. When you get there you will make plans to leave the district altogether,' Jim said harshly to the group. 'If any of you are seen again, you will be shot out of hand.'

'What about our horses and guns?' asked one of the men.

'Your actions have forfeited them altogether. I will allow you to take two rifles for hunting and a few rounds of ammunition. Now get going before I change my mind.'

Three Settlement people, on horseback, escorted them for two days and then, as Jim had instructed, rode on to the Barrington village ahead of the raiders.

Several women scattered when shots were fired into the air on arrival. They told the one or two that had remained visible, 'We have come to take back what belongs to those people in Kurri-Kurri, no more, no less. We have the girl back, badly damaged, and we are going to take back the cattle you stole. If you resist in any way you will be shot.'

The women looked blankly at them and one of them then asked anxiously, 'Where are all the men that left here? What has happened to them?'

'Most of them will be back here in a day or two, very much the worse for wear,' was the unkind answer.

'Most of them?' one woman shrieked.

'You will find out. In the meantime, you'd better start packing this place up. If we return and find any of you here, we'll burn the place down and you'll be shot.'

They drove the selected cattle off, amid shrieks of anguish.

In Kurri-Kurri, the wounded were moved to one of the houses while their injuries were attended to. A week later, Tanya passed by in the helicopter. With a frown on her face, she listened to Jim's report. 'As a priority, I think Emilie and her mother should be transferred to our hospital. The girl was raped and seems to be pregnant. She also yells blue murder at the sight of one of our captives in particular. As for the wounded, you can do with them what you like. I wish we had shot them all dead, to be honest.'

'You have done well,' Tanya responded. 'The sooner we can get some of our people here permanently, the better.'

During Tanya's visit, the stolen cattle were returned. The one wounded Barrington man, who was mobile, looked on forlornly.

Once Emilie and her mother had been properly accommodated, the wounded raiders were transferred to The Settlement hospital for treatment. Mark agreed with Tanya that the prisoners were to be kept completely isolated. The staff tending them were changed at regular intervals, so there was no chance of any sort of personal relationship developing.

'When these people have recovered from their wounds, we must decide what to do with them,' observed Mark. 'It would've been much easier if they'd died.'

Tanya looked at him, Somehow we have risen above our animal instincts.

When Emilie's condition was confirmed, she and Josie asked if the pregnancy could be terminated. She was also able to confirm that one of the wounded men had raped her on many occasions.

'I'm not going to run an elaborate court case for any of this,' Mark announced, after a discussion with Tanya. 'When these bastards have recovered, we'll have a very short court session during which I will make my recommendation regarding their punishment. We'll then dump them back in the bush and they can rejoin their ghastly compatriots.'

A few weeks later, when the three had sufficiently recovered, a notice was published in the newspaper detailing the incident at Kurri-Kurri and the fact that, undeservedly, three of the wounded raiders had been treated at the hospital. It finished by stating one of the men had been found guilty of rape and had been sentenced to forty lashes with a cane and that the other two had been given sentences of twenty lashes each for their part in the raids on the Kurri-Kurri settlement. All the sentences had been administered and the three had been expelled.

Mark, with Roger piloting the helicopter, dropped the three men off halfway between Kurri-Kurri and Barrington Tops. They were given three days' food.

Mark told them, 'The fact that we treated you and saved your lives is more than you deserve. If any of you ever appear in this vicinity again, you will be shot.'

CHAPTER THIRTY-NINE
Jason's Appraisal

When Jason was dropped off at The Vikings, with another bull calf, after the usual friendly greetings, Tanya suggested to Thor, 'Perhaps you would like to visit Newcastle with me today. It might be interesting for you to see what we're doing.'

Thor shook his head. 'I hear bad things of that place, ghosts and terrible whooshing noises in the night, fire in the trees, then with no sign of any burning the next day. No thanks, you are welcome to it. I will stay here among things I know.'

After take off, Tanya thought to herself smiling, 'Thank God for Derain. We're getting Thor into a place where he will no longer be any kind of threat.'

Tanya had told Jason on the journey to The Vikings, 'They will challenge you to all sorts of competitions such as riding, shooting, and hunting; if there is anything left to hunt in that place. Whatever happens, firstly understand what the competition is all about and then totally thrash them, which you will be able to do. There is one exception to that.'

'Hercules?'

'Smart boy! Yes, let him win, but only occasionally. And one other thing ...'

'Decline all the fanny offerings that will come my way?' answered Jason.

'You took the words out of my mouth,' Tanya smiled. 'Remember the prize.'

'Venus,' said Jason firmly.

'For you, yes. For another thousand or more people, peace. Just keep a small part of your mind on that.'

Jason started to install solar power in Thor's palace. Using the well-established discipline taught by Joe, he always checked his earlier work at the start of each day. On the second day he took one look at the uncompleted installation and immediately tracked Thor down.

'I installed this yesterday and some ungifted nincompoop has messed with it in the night. If I hadn't seen what had been done, when the sun comes up in an hour or so it would have set fire to your palace. It would only have taken a few minutes for it all to go up in smoke, including you probably. I don't really care whether or not you want solar power, but if you do please have all this nonsense stopped. If you don't want it, tell me and I will pack everything up and take it to Banksia.'

'Banksia has solar?'

'Yes, they are paying for it. Maybe I should suggest to Tanya that you might appreciate it a bit more if you were asked to pay as well.'

He re-examined all his work each day after that, but had no more trouble.

Most evenings he was obliged to join in heavy drinking sessions with many of the young men. Jason was quite unused to alcohol, especially the home-distilled variety on offer. He managed to pour away most of what he'd been given, but he often still felt somewhat unsteady when he was allowed to leave. On the fourth night, just as he entered his hut, he noticed a fresh, feminine smell. Remembering his discussion with Tanya, he turned on his heel and quickly left, spending the rest of the night sleeping on a couch in the semi-public area in Thor's palace.

Thor found him at dawn the next morning. 'Don't you like your own place,' he asked acidly.

'It's very nice,' answered Jason. 'I was late after all the drinking, and there was another person in the hut I thought was mine, so instead of disturbing anyone I came here. I've slept very well.'

Thor looked furious, but said nothing.

Jason had no difficulty in beating the dozen or so opponents who challenged him in various contests. Although, on one occasion, he allowed Hercules to win a riding competition by a short head.

Earlier he had talked with his two colleagues that had been assigned to train The Vikings.

'The problem is lack of discipline,' he was told. 'None of them attend all the training sessions. They only attend when they feel like it, so sometimes we have a fairly full group, but for tougher things like long runs or cross country riding, only one or two turn up and often none at all. There are no sanctions, nothing like being put on a charge like we have at home and Thor takes very little interest.'

A week into what Jason considered his two-week penance, he was walking briskly to complete one of his solar installation projects. To his horror, he saw a small girl of two or three on the path walking unsteadily, as children of that age do, with hands outstretched, towards an enormous black snake which appeared to be dancing on its tail threatening her. A woman emerged from a nearby hut, took in the scene, and immediately started shrieking, attracting many bystanders.

Jason knew he had to act quickly, and, without a thought for his own safety, he dropped his workbag, picked up a nearby fallen tree branch, broke it in two, and rapidly approached the child and the snake who were now less than a metre apart. The snake sensing the new threat focussed on Jason, rather than the girl.

Derain's first lesson, the thought flashed through Jason's mind. Keeping the stick in his left hand to attract the snake's attention he slowly moved around, snatching the snake up by the tail and in a whip-cracking movement he broke the snake's back. He then stood on its head, killing it.

Jason gently picked up the crying girl, and walked the fifty metres to return her to her hysterical mother.

'It's alright, she wasn't bitten,' said Jason gently. 'No harm was done. Easy.' He put his arm round her shoulder until the sobs had ceased.

'Oh, thank you, thank you!'

A small crowd gathered to comfort the woman. When Jason could extricate himself from the melee, he collected his discarded work bag and picked up the dead snake.

Later, having skinned it and removed its head, he took it to Thor's kitchen and suggested to the woman in charge that it could be eaten for the next meal.

'Thor won't eat snake,' said the woman.

'Tell him its chicken, he won't know the difference'

The woman laughed

~っ

'Enjoy the meal?' she asked Thor and several of his lieutenants when the plates had been cleared. The only subject of discussion at the meal was Jason's apparent heroism.

'Yes, it was delicious,' most of them chorused.

'Jason's snake,' she told them, to many disbelieving looks. One of them clutched his throat as if to be sick.

Although horrified to start with, Thor recovered his composure quickly and said, 'Snake? Delicious, seems a bit like chicken. Maybe we could include it as a regular in our diet.' He winked at Jason. All his lieutenants quickly followed suit and made positive remarks.

~っ

For the last ten days of his stay, Jason was treated as an honoured guest. He had several long discussions with Thor, especially about the military training. Resulting from that a "volunteer" group of twenty trainees was formed with

Thor personally administering the discipline. Dawn runs and uniforms were introduced, and any transgressors were severely punished.

'If they really fuck-up, I have the dungeon,' he said to Jason conversationally, as if it was the most commonplace punishment in the world.

The Settlement trainers suddenly had a real job on their hands and said laughingly to Jason, 'Pity we didn't have the snake incident earlier in the piece. Seriously, within a few months, this squad will be up to the standard of The Academy.'

Jason was ready to greet Tanya and gave her a full briefing when she arrived to pick him up. Leaving nothing out he said, 'I really don't think there'll be any problem getting Thor's permission to marry Venus. I thought she might come with you; I'm looking forward to seeing her. And no mention has been made of the bride price issue, by the way.'

'It wouldn't enter Thor's head to discuss that with you. He may mention it to me later. I suggested to Venus that she should come today, but she seemed focussed on making sure you had a warm welcome when you returned.'

Thor was very polite and said to Tanya, 'Exceptional young man, your Jason. He has been very helpful here in the last two weeks. He will have told you about saving that child from the snake? We now have a very good military training program and he has installed solar in many places. He has my permission to court Venus as you describe it.'

'Thank you,' said Tanya quietly, 'as you say he is an exceptional young man.'

'If she agrees, we'll have to discuss the question of a bride price, it is … '

'I understand the concept,' Tanya interrupted. 'Normally, his father would be involved in this discussion, but in this case the possible marriage represents an alliance between your family and the Bower family.'

'Yes,' said Thor excitedly.

'So either David or I will be having those discussions with you.'

Thor nodded. 'If you can finally agree terms, then I am happy to deal with you.'

'I can agree to terms, the matter doesn't have to be signed off by anyone else.'

Thor looked surprised.

On the way home, Tanya said to Jason with a half-smile on her face, 'You have permission to court Venus now, you obviously did well.'

Not taking the bait, Jason responded, 'The snake incident made the difference; before that I had to put up with all sorts of crap.'

'Being a woman, Thor thinks I'm likely to be a soft touch when it comes to negotiating a dowry, so he's agreed to deal with me on the issue.' She paused and smiled. 'Don't worry, I'll have him tied up in a cock lock and ball press like he has never dreamt of, and he'll think it was all his own idea,' she said aggressively.

Jason laughed. He then added, 'There are a couple of other things you should be aware of.' Tanya looked at him curiously. 'There was a man called Harold who gave you a lot of grief in the early days of The Settlement.'

'Yes, I was sure I saw him during our first visit to The Vikings.'

'You did. I found him shackled in the dungeon when I went in there to fix something related to the solar system. He pleaded with me to get him released. Apparently you said something to Thor about him, so one of Thor's lieutenants searched his hut and found all sorts of compromising documents related to his connections with ASIO and so on. Thor apparently was part of a bikie gang in the past and Harold was sent there as a spy.'

'I knew about the bikie gang,' said Tanya. 'What are they going to do with him?'

'They've done it,' answered Jason.

'What?'

'They apparently executed him two days ago; almost nobody knows. He's been in the dungeon since our original visit. Thor just told everyone he'd left one night. I doubt anyone believes him, but if you want to survive in that place you ask no questions. Hercules let it slip one day when I mentioned there was one person less in the dungeon. According to Hercules, two of the lieutenants took him off into the bush one night, shot him, and buried him where he won't be found.'

'Jesus, he was a nasty piece of work, but he didn't deserve that,' said a shaken Tanya.

'I just thought you should know.'

Tanya nodded, 'Perhaps you should keep that story to yourself, don't even tell Venus. Are you quite sure he was actually executed? What you were told might just be a smokescreen. Harold, or whatever his name is now, might easily have been sent off on some secret mission by Thor, as an option down the track to undermine us somehow.'

Jason looked at her and said, 'I certainly believed Hercules at the time, but you may be right. As I understand it, Harold has a grudge against us and may have been willing to undertake an underhand scheme, especially if his life depended on it.' He had no intention of telling anyone else.

'Also, they treat their women like slaves.'

'That's quite obvious from the behaviour we've witnessed.'

'It's worse than you think. While we are there they tend to behave, but the trainers have been there for a while now and periodically the men go on a drinking binge, after which any woman is fair game. Any of them,' repeated Jason. 'And there are no sanctions, but there has always been one exception.'

'Venus.'

'Yes. Maybe that was one reason she was keen to come and stay with us,' said Jason. 'Don't completely trust Thor. My guess is he'll try to do us some damage if he possibly can. He felt he was made a fool of during our first visit and he'll try to get his own back at some stage regardless of any marriage treaties. He wants power, nothing else.'

They landed back at The Settlement a few minutes later. Tanya phoned David to give him a brief report on her visit to The Vikings.

She also told him about Harold, 'I think Thor could be playing a double game here. Either Harold was done away with or, far more likely, Harold has been sent off somewhere to a place that doesn't share our values and will be hostile to us. This is just for your information,' said Tanya, 'nobody else knows, save Jason of course.'

David reflected for a moment and said, 'When we started The Settlement I had no idea of the sort of compromises we would have to make and the sort of company we would eventually be keeping. Oh well, it's done now. The stupid bastard Harold had something coming to him; but as you say, it's all too convenient. Maybe Thor has something more up his sleeve after all.'

CHAPTER FORTY
Jason's Wedding

Within the promised month, Eustace, with Joe's help, had moved one of the big choppers out from the hangar and started the engine. 'I've been reminding myself of all the little tricks to flying this thing,' he said to Joe, 'but I think it's better that I take her up on my own first, just to make sure all is well. No need for two of us to go down if I've made any mistakes putting it all together.'

Returning an hour later he said, 'She's a real beauty, like she always was.' Then he added, 'Probably scared the shit out of all the people in that funny place with all the grass huts. They were running about all over the place.'

'Sounds like The Vikings. I haven't been there yet, but I think our son Jason is going to marry Thor's daughter, so there could be a bit of a party.'

'Thor! That's almost as bad as Eustace.'

'Yes but he chose the name. I'm guessing you still have the name your parents saddled you with,' said Joe, laughing.

'What kind of an asshole would call himself Thor?'

~

Tanya flew backwards and forwards to Newcastle, taking the opportunity to have a few lessons from Eustace in flying the new machine. 'We'll only have to supply the base here once or twice a week with this machine,' she said to Eustace. 'We must train Roger and the other two to fly it as well, and I would like your help in moving a couple of our solar-powered vehicles out from The Settlement so we can use them on the roads. We also need another source of fuel.'

~

A month after Jason's visit, Tanya took Venus and Jason back to Thor's in the old helicopter, now with its full array of seats and having been fully reconditioned by Eustace.

Shortly after arrival, Venus had a private word with her father. 'Jason has asked to marry me,' she said. 'I would like your blessing.'

'He will need to come and ask directly and I still have to finalise a few details with Tanya. But yes, in principle, you have my blessing,' he said gently, looking fondly at his only daughter.

Jason was waiting and received much the same answer to the question. 'I'm sure you will look after her very well,' he said. 'All the things you set up here have worked.'

Tanya later told David on the phone, 'As predicted, he asked for one hundred head as a bride price. I told him they would all die since he doesn't have enough grazing for his own cattle, let alone another hundred head. I also told him that his beasts were not much bigger than goats anyway and why would anyone want animals like that.'

David laughed. 'He would not have taken that nonsense from anyone but you. What happened after that?'

'We agreed he would have to expand the area he occupies into the more open areas north of where he is now so he can run a decent herd of cattle. We will help him identify those areas and secure them, and then stock the new areas with a base of forty heifers and a bull from The Settlement. The area will be jointly owned. I have it all down in writing, signed sealed, and delivered.'

David started to laugh. 'But that was what we had planned anyway.'

'Yup, also those idle bastards sitting on their fat backsides over there at The Vikings, doing nothing, will now have to do some work. Some of the women will move as well. Once they are no longer under the immediate thumb of Thor, they will blossom.'

Tanya had asked Stephanie to help out with the establishment of the areas to be settled jointly with The Vikings, since all her responsibilities in Amazonia were under control. Two of the solar vehicles in The Settlement had been lifted out with the new helicopter, creating easy and quicker access than having to travel by horse everywhere. Mark continued to have overall responsibility for security, including the whole Viking establishment.

David sighed and paid her the ultimate compliment, 'What would we do without you?'

'You'd find someone else. Nobody is irreplaceable.'

'What about plans for the wedding?' asked David.

'Probably late September, as the weather is warming up. I'm sure Thor is planning a huge splash.'

Tanya popped in to Amazonia from time to time on her way to and from Newcastle, mainly to check on progress with both Irene and Stephanie. But she also took the opportunity to talk to Stephanie, privately, about the wider issues. When Stephanie had been briefed and accepted the responsibility of helping The Vikings extend their area, Tanya told her about Harold and her suspicions regarding the double game.

'Do you think Harold represented any kind of threat to Thor?' asked Stephanie.

'Before the flood, maybe he did, but now I'm sure he doesn't.'

'I don't think Thor would kill people just for the sake of it. If he did execute Harold, it would be because he represented a threat or he wanted revenge for some transgression. If he merely wanted revenge, why stick him in the dungeon at all. You may be right, it's certainly possible Harold has been sent off somewhere and will re-emerge to create some sort of mischief, if that suits Thor, down the track. I'll discreetly keep my ear to the ground and see if any of The Vikings sent to the new areas know anything.'

Tanya patted her on the shoulder in acknowledgement.

As promised, the wedding was truly spectacular. A day before the scheduled date, Roger and Rachel arrived with eighty of the best from The Academy. They camped as they had on the first visit. Venus had been staying with her father for two weeks before the nuptials. A woman Tanya had now identified as Venus's mother flitted around excitedly in the background.

An hour before the appointed time, Tanya arrived in the new helicopter with Chloe, Susan, Mark, David, Caroline, Irene, Stephanie, Isaac, Joseph, Cath, and Uncle Jonathan, who'd been persuaded to join the celebrations from his army base near the deserted city of Canberra. Ten minutes later Kim, piloting the old helicopter, arrived with Joe, Patricia, and the groom.

There had been some discussion about what to wear for the occasion.

'Thor and his associates will be wearing new animal skins,' Tanya told them. 'Venus has the most beautiful traditional wedding dress imaginable, which her mother has dredged up from some secret hiding place. I think, where possible, we should all be in pristine academy uniforms. I did consider wearing what I wore to Evan's wedding all those years ago, but the moths have put paid to that idea.'

Chloe, Patricia, Caroline, and Cath found pretty dresses, Susan wore academy dress, Joseph an old suit, and Isaac wore his clerical dress. Jonathan wore his Australian Army dress uniform with General's insignia, a feature that was not lost on Thor. Eustace surprised everybody by arriving at the last minute in the second of the choppers from the Newcastle warehouse. With him were two of the mechanics who'd worked on the machine, plus Derain, and six of the Aboriginal group. They were joined by a party of one hundred from Derain's village and the village that had rescued Eustace. It had taken them two weeks to walk through the bush to attend the wedding.

The day was, as hoped for, beautifully warm and sunny with a light breeze, perfect for such an occasion. Thor, sitting on his white stallion and accompanied by a now considerably more disciplined armed troop, was completely outshone by The Settlement contingent, but he greeted everyone with a calm smile. He had been warned by Tanya that the Aborigines would arrive in numbers. Although he was not entirely comfortable with what he saw as an incursion, he made an effort to welcome them as well. The women of The Vikings were all busy preparing the wedding feast, and were allowed to attend the ceremony held in front of Thor's palace.

A very manly and military-styled Jason and a stunning Venus in a pristine white wedding gown were alone at the front of the throng, some seated, many sitting on the grass. To everyone's surprise, a well-rehearsed ceremony was conducted by Thor personally. The format was similar to the Anglican wedding service, but with no reference to the deity. Thor gave the blessing and pronounced them man and wife. He even produced an official Australian marriage register for all parties to sign.

At the conclusion of the service, The Settlement troops, mounted and accompanied by The Vikings' militia, fired the now usual three shots into the air. Thor was thrilled at this unexpected addition to what he had planned, especially as his people were able to participate and had not spoiled the spectacle, all shots being fired in complete unison.

Guests were invited to help themselves to the sumptuous feast that had been provided. Key visitors were invited to be seated at a large table on the verandah of The Vikings' palace, together with Thor, Hercules, and his lieutenants, but including no Viking women. The other people seated themselves on the surrounding lawns.

Thor's speech, congratulating Venus and Jason on their marriage, was long and rambling, and detailed the history of his establishment. In conclusion, he said, 'We stand for being independent of central authority and being able to live our lives as we see fit.' He continued rather clumsily, 'The formal association with The Settlement, now cemented by the marriage of my daughter Venus to Jason Bower is important in this regard. It means we can continue to live side by side in peace and harmony, while we respect each other's way of life and values.' He sat down to continued applause.

David reciprocated, by congratulating Jason and Venus on their marriage, giving a brief history of The Settlement and the science behind its establishment. 'We welcome all races, creeds, and cultures to the re-establishment of our civilisation after the devastation of the flood.' Then he said firmly, 'We need to be mindful of the mistakes the human race made that resulted in the devastation we experienced so we don't repeat them. We also need to keep a watchful eye on the unsustainable practices the white settlers made here in Australia during the past two hundred years. We now have a chance to repair some of those mistakes. Sustainability, not greed, should be our watchword, as well as the self-reliance that isolation has forced on us. We should listen more often to our Aboriginal friends, who we found shared our vision that the world as we understood it would cease to exist. They will have something of their own to say later. Over the next several decades, long after my demise, we will rebuild Australia, hopefully for the better. As Thor said, we ought to be able to develop together, but be able to respect each other's values and way of life.' He sat down to rapturous applause.

Then the whole Aboriginal group, led by Derain, including a half dozen from The Academy, still in their uniforms, started a traditional dance lasting about twenty minutes. Derain, traditionally clothed, in an outfit noticeably similar to Thor's, through an interpreter, made a speech, welcoming and congratulating Jason and Venus on their marriage and wishing them well. He concluded by saying, 'White people's houses and food make us ill. We do not need white people's guns and cars. You all talk about welcoming all races and creeds to this society, yes, but that has all been said before. This time, it should include the Aboriginal people as well. We can help you better understand and look after the land, but we need free access to that land. We can share this land with you, but you must not take it away again. We share the view of David and Thor that we should be able to live together and respect each other's values and way of life.' Led by Tanya, there was a slow but sustained applause as Derain stepped down.

Joe and Patricia had long since realised the wedding was a catalyst for a much wider understanding and association between the two groups. Joe was not good at making speeches and he and Patricia had said all they needed to say to the couple in the months before the wedding. For her part, Patricia was looking forward to having her attractive daughter-in-law living nearby and was expecting to be helping to nurture a grandchild in the not too distant future.

While not overawed by the situation, Jason had understood after his discussions with Tanya that this was a marriage of two very distinct parties, not just himself and Venus, so he confined his words to, 'Venus, a very warm welcome to the Bower family. You have to know that this is the happiest day of my life and I will dedicate my life to making you as happy as I can.' He had realised that anything else he might say under the circumstances would not be particularly relevant.

Thor had no knowledge of Jonathan's existence until he arrived, but said to David in a private moment, 'Maybe it would be useful if your son from the

Australian Army could say a few words. He represents a new dimension as far as we are concerned.'

David gave a brief introduction to his youngest son, now aged forty-three and the most senior person in the Australian military to have survived.

'My name is Jonathan Bower. Before I say anything else, congratulations to my nephew Jason and the spectacularly beautiful Venus. Your life is sure to be adventurous and I hope that it will be happy as well.' He paused for a few moments, not wishing to spoil the occasion with a lengthy speech.

He explained that the military had ten thousand troops scattered around the country and in ships and submarines on the coast, supported by strong family networks, food supplies, hospitals, schools, and so on. 'The focus up to now has been maintaining the geographic integrity of what was Australia. This has involved dealing with a few incursions, mainly from the North. These incursions are at a low level, but we don't want anyone getting the idea that this continent is unoccupied territory. The area is vast, so it's an enormous job. Our objective, in the longer term, is to re-establish some sort of Government over the whole continent. Having heard what has been said here today, all of us need to bear in mind that people wish to be more in control of their own lives. That philosophy should form the basis of any central authority. There are possibly as many as one hundred groups around Australia that survived the floods and all of them need to play a role in deciding what sort of Government should exist.' Muted applause greeted him as he sat down.

For most attendees, the earlier speeches reflected their present aspirations, after all this was a wedding, not a political occasion. Festivities continued for most of the night and gradually guests and residents stumbled off to bed, followed by the bride and groom.

In the morning, as they were helping themselves to breakfast in the entrance to Thor's palace, Tanya and the guests became aware of an excited group of women shrieking their heads off as they emerged from the now empty bridal suite. They were waving a sheet around streaked with blood.

Tanya took one look at the group and said to Mark quietly, 'It's supposed to be virginal blood, proving that Venus was a virgin before her marriage, and that the marriage has now been properly consummated. Who the hell do they think they're kidding?' She shook her head just as a beaming Thor appeared. 'Probably chicken blood,' whispered Tanya. 'They'll have the chicken for lunch, but we'll have left by then.'

CHAPTER FORTY-ONE
Susan and Hercules

On their return to The Settlement, and after a few attempts, Tanya managed to corner Susan alone when Chloe was out on an errand. 'Come here,' she said and hugged a somewhat resistant Susan to her. 'You're pregnant aren't you?'

Susan started to cry and nodded.

'I know who the father is, but I would like you to tell me please.'

'Mark,' was the tearful response.

'I should be angry, but I'm not. Just tell me why.'

'When Barry was killed, Mark was so sweet to me and his mother. He came here a lot and it helped. One day, Chloe was out, and it just happened. It's all stopped now. Before Jason's wedding, Chloe confronted me. We had a discussion and then I put a stop to it. I'm so sorry.'

'About two months?' asked Tanya.

Susan nodded.

Tanya held her for a minute and then said, 'How well do you know Hercules? I saw you talking to him a bit at the wedding.'

Susan smiled through her tears. 'He's okay actually, once one gets over all the bluster and he's away from his father.' She looked at Tanya suspiciously. 'Why do you ask?'

'He has asked permission to marry you.'

'Marry?' said Susan uncomprehendingly.

'Yes. You'll have to agree of course, and maybe you should talk it over with Chloe, who, I might add, is aware that I'm here talking to you about this.'

Susan burst into tears again.

Ten minutes later, Chloe appeared. Susan, still red eyed but quite calm, was sitting holding hands with Tanya.

Tanya nodded at Chloe. 'I'll see you later.'

Susan started crying again and clung to Chloe for a few minutes.

'What happened?' asked Chloe.

Susan told her and said, 'She was quite sweet actually, not angry. She wants me to marry Hercules.'

'Tanya has been aware of your relationship with Mark almost from the beginning. She came to talk to me about it months ago. The marriage proposal is all Hercules' idea though. Nobody is going to force you into anything you don't want to do, least of all Tanya. You have to want to do it for yourself. The arrangements can be put into place very quickly, if you agree.'

'I see,' said Susan. 'It solves a lot of problems like the paternity of the child and my presence here. I can also be very useful at The Vikings. Maybe it's not such a bad idea.' She shed a few more tears as Chloe held her tight.

'Are you in love with Hercules?'

'Love! Don't be daft. He's not as bad as everyone makes out though, but I hardly know him.'

'Did you sleep with him at Jason's wedding?'

Susan smiled through her tears. 'No, but he wanted to.'

Chloe found Tanya in her office, busy tidying up.

'She'll certainly agree,' Chloe announced. 'She just needs a few days to get used to the idea. We should put everything in place now—a wedding here and some dowry discussions. I will be going with her, but you probably guessed that.'

'Going with her? That is a surprise.'

'She's like a daughter to me. Moving over there will make a clean break from the memories here. I might even be able to help civilise Thor and his mob a bit.'

'It's a surprise, but the whole project would welcome your presence over there. It'll make a big difference.'

'I'm not going there for "the project" as you call it. I've never really felt part of it and won't be sorry to leave here. Susan and Barry gave me something to live for and I hope to recreate that at The Vikings.'

Tanya walked around the desk and put her arms around her mother-in-law. 'I know, I really do understand.'

'What are you going to do about Mark? I've told him what he did was the worst possible thing from all our points of view,' said Chloe. 'Stupid bugger.'

'I'm dealing with him, but I expect it will be alright in time. The project needs him badly and so I need him.'

'Do you still love him?'

'Probably.' She shrugged.

'There is one other personal thing,' said Chloe.

'Yes, anything.'

'When I die, I'm not to be buried here. I've told Susan that I want to be buried on the headland to the north of Manly Beach, looking out to sea.'

'Buried?' Tanya looked surprised, but seeing the faraway look on her mother-in-law's face, said quickly, 'I'm not expecting to have to bury you any time soon, but I'll certainly make sure that happens when the time comes.' She hugged Chloe.

'I'm seventy-five, it'll happen sooner or later,'

'Later; you're still very fit.'

The wedding was arranged with indecent haste and a very elaborate ceremony took place within a month at The Settlement.

Thor was pleased and said to David, 'We're now joined at the head and the hip, it's almost one family.'

Six months later Susan gave birth to a big bouncing boy, 'A few weeks premature,' Chloe told Thor. Thor was thrilled with his new grandchild and whatever thoughts people may have had on the subject, no questions were asked.

'He'll be called Mars,' announced Thor, consulting nobody, 'after the God of War.'

Round one to The Vikings, thought Chloe, or perhaps round two. I suppose marrying Susan off to Hercules was round one, with The Settlement edging out The Vikings.

During one of her trips to The Vikings, Tanya had asked Thor what surname Mars would have.

'Surname?' answered Thor. 'If your name is Mars, there is no need for a surname.'

Round three to The Vikings, thought Chloe.

CHAPTER FORTY-TWO

Vale David 2036

2036

Tanya now shared her time between the orderly, civilised place that The Settlement had become and the chaos of Newcastle, where Kim was happily in charge of the developments. Tanya tried to ensure people working there returned to The Settlement periodically, and were replaced if that was what was wanted. Within another year, the achievements were considerable and she was able to tick them off on her fingers Newcastle had become partially self-sufficient. Another year, and it would be almost totally so.

All three Newcastle helicopters were now functioning. Eustace had advised that one machine should always be on the ground being serviced while the other two were working. 'For all sorts of reasons,' he explained, 'not the least of which is if we have an accident there will be a rescue helicopter available.'

They had reconditioned twenty houses around the new Newcastle base. Tanya herself had the use of one small cottage.

A large mass grave had been dug where any bones were laid. Where possible, names of the deceased were entered in a register together with their addresses.

A dozen, conventionally-fuelled, four wheel drive trucks and six larger trucks had been made serviceable.

Many roads in the area had been cleared. Again trouble was taken trying to identify the remains of people found in vehicles on the roads.

Jonathan had confidentially told her of a fuel dump in the Newcastle area. It had not been touched since the time of the flood. The site was unmarked and all the storage tanks were underground. Joe had reconditioned pumps on the site.

All their vehicles used on the ever-expanding farms were, as a policy, powered by solar.

A plan had been devised to build a port in Newcastle. Some equipment was needed to start the project.

Most of the land between the Blue Mountain stronghold and Newcastle was now occupied by New Settlement. Settlement people had moved to Wollombi and Kurri-Kurri.

Derain and his people were happy. They had free access to all the lands that New Settlement occupied as well as the Blue Mountain range. They were always welcome and they continued to conduct bush craft lessons for all the settlers as well as advising at times of crisis.

Tanya consulted David constantly, but at eighty-one he travelled little and was content to remain at The Bandstand, now comfortably prosperous. Jonathan, now he had the time, also made contact once every two or three months. Sometimes he visited, but often Mark or Tanya flew to the military base near Canberra.

'Most of the settlements you've uncovered,' Jonathan said, 'except The Bandstand, seem either to be very small or their survival is based on what I think of as fringe beliefs. I have now unearthed another place that have kept themselves well hidden all these years in the Kanangra-Boyd National Park, in the southern Blue Mountains, west of the Warragamba Dam. They are smaller than The Settlement, but have similar beliefs to you. Access is very difficult, either on foot or horseback, although we've visited there a couple of times with a helicopter. An association between them and you would create a reasonable base for a renewal of a democratic government in New South Wales at least. I will try to arrange a visit.'

Mark and Tanya nodded, but said nothing.

'Also I have, now, after four or five years of silence, had word of Evan,' he said, 'from Jakarta. I wasn't able to speak to him, but I understand that he and Beryl are both still alive. I'm not sure how well they are. It's almost ten years since the flood. If he ever gets back here, he will certainly have a story to tell. They were trying to find some sort of fishing boat off the coast of Java, to bring them back here.'

Tanya was, unusually for her, sitting in her office savouring the stability she and David had created and wondering where it could now take them, when the phone rang.

'Hello David,' she said cheerfully into the mouthpiece, 'everything okay?'

'It's Caroline,' said an unhappy voice at the other end. Tanya immediately knew the worst had happened. While she had a good relationship with Caroline, they rarely spoke to each other on the phone.

'Tell me' said Tanya quietly. 'It's about David isn't it?'

'He died of a heart attack about an hour ago,' was the answer. 'We tried to bring him around, but he must have been dead before he hit the floor.'

Tanya tried hard not to, but she just wept. 'I will have to call you back,' she said amidst the tears. 'Give me ten minutes.'

Thirty minutes later, Tanya tried to be her normal, businesslike self and managed to have a sensible conversation with Caroline on the phone. 'He will have to be buried here,' she said. 'You know the little hillock he used to go and stand on, making plans and building dreams. He has to be laid to rest up there. I think that is what he would want. How are you holding up?'

'David had slowed down a lot over the past few months, and we had conversations about his death, so it's not a complete surprise. I'm actually holding up well. I would like to come over to you for a period anyway to get away from all this. There are people here that can keep things going,' answered Caroline.

'Okay, I'll pick you up in the chopper and bring David back here. The funeral is going to take some organising.'

~

The same evening Tanya asked everyone to the community centre for an important announcement. When people saw Caroline on the platform with Tanya, and no David, they had an inkling of what was to come. Tanya managed to compose herself and said without any ceremony, 'I have to tell you all that today is one of the saddest days in the life of The Settlement. David, our founder and mentor, died this morning of a heart attack.'

There was shock around the room, although many had guessed.

Managing to keep her composure, she continued, 'He did not suffer. His death was sudden and painless. Deepest condolences to Caroline and the immediate Bower family. All of us will miss him deeply for his humour, his humility and counsel, and most of all his calmness.'

There were many sniffles throughout the room, and then Tanya said in a more businesslike way, 'The funeral will take a few weeks to organise. People will want to come from all over the place, and many will have to come on horseback or on foot. All I ask is for all of us to accommodate as many as possible in our homes. Mark, do you or Patricia want to say anything?'

Neither was able to speak and merely shook their heads.

~

It took almost a month for everyone to gather for David Bower's funeral. Almost two thousand people attended. They were all assembled around the base of what became known as David's Hill. Caroline had consulted with Chloe about the arrangements and they both felt comfortable with Isaac from St. Andrews conducting the service.

Chloe advised him, 'You have to take account of the fact that many of the people attending not only have no Christian background, but also may have altogether different beliefs.'

'Of course,' said Isaac. 'If he taught us nothing else, David taught us tolerance, something our own religious beliefs preach, but don't always do very well.'

Jonathan arrived in an army helicopter as everyone gathered. 'Who the hell is that man with long hair and that wild-looking woman with him?' asked Tanya as she was about to start the proceedings.

Mark rushed off. 'I think it's Evan and Beryl!' he yelled. And it was.

There had been much argument about who would perform the eulogy. Tanya said that one of David's children was the most appropriate, probably Mark.

'You, Tanya, have worked closely with him for more than twenty-five years,' argued Patricia. 'This whole project is about him, David, and you as much as anyone else here. He regarded you as a friend, and if he needed advice on anything you were the first port of call.'

'Any dissent?' asked Tanya. 'Mark?' He shook his head. 'Patricia, Joe?' Both shook their heads. 'Okay, I will prepare something and ask Chloe and Jonathan when they arrive if they think it's appropriate. I'm really not sure that it's absolutely the right thing, but if anyone else wants to say something they should feel free to do so.'

Chloe, and all those who'd known Evan, rushed over to see him and Beryl. The funeral proceedings were delayed by an hour.

Jonathan explained, 'We picked them up in a helicopter a few days ago at a remote community west of Darwin. Army people up there eventually believed Evan's story and alerted me.'

'Indonesian fishing boat,' said Evan shakily, once he had tearfully greeted everybody. 'We spent three weeks on a fishing boat and they dumped us at that community, but that is another story.'

The family all stood on David's Hill and, once Isaac had conducted a very sensitive service, Tanya rose to her feet. 'Almost against my better judgement, I have been asked by the Bower family to talk about David. Before I do, most of you don't know Evan, here.' She hugged Evan. 'He is the third child of David and Chloe. He was in England at the time of the flood and he and Beryl, his wife, have somehow found their way back here after more than ten years.'

There was growing and sustained applause from everyone as they tried to understand the implications of what the pair had done and must have endured.

Once the applause had died down, Tanya continued, 'As you all know, David and I have worked together on this project since its inception, so I got to know him very well indeed.'

She went on to describe his early life in detail. 'He was fifty-five, probably looking forward to a gentle retirement during the following ten years, when he concluded that the Ross Ice Shelf would collapse with disastrous consequences for the world at large. He found this place and we all know what happened after that. The reason that the few of us here managed to survive the flood was because of his foresight and willingness to risk everything to create this haven, despite scepticism and opposition from many people.'

Tanya spoke for an hour, detailing the trials, achievements, and setbacks of creating The Settlement. She made no reference, at all, to her part in its creation.

'For my part, David was a friend and mentor, and on the few occasions we disagreed on things he always came up with a creative solution to the problem. He was always the voice of calm reason and that was the atmosphere he created here in The Settlement, allowing us to develop as we have done. He listened to anyone who had anything to say.' She hesitated as a tear escaped down her cheek, 'I for one will miss him deeply and I'm certain that I speak for all of you here today.'

Several more people stood up to speak, including Derain, and even Thor. Then, the coffin was lowered into the ground and covered up, once Caroline and Chloe had each sprinkled a handful of earth on top.

~∾

A modest, rough stone plaque had been erected next to the grave site with its inscription.

David Bower

Visionary

1955-2036

~∾

The visitors drifted off over the next week. Evan and Beryl were installed in the cottage that had been built for him twenty years earlier.

During the funeral, Tanya had noticed Chloe, although she had been totally involved in the ceremony, often stood next to Thor. When she thought nobody was looking, she'd had a half smile on her face and looked very happy.

It can't be, thought Tanya, I'll have to follow that up.

Thor had already told Tanya that Susan, Hercules, and Mars would be moving over to the new areas agreed upon at the time of Venus and Jason's wedding. 'You will be going with Susan, presumably,' Tanya innocently asked Chloe later.

'Maybe, maybe not. I've found a bit of a niche at The Vikings and am helping the women there make more of themselves. I can always pop over and see the family now that the roads are being opened up.' She flushed slightly and avoided Tanya's gaze, but gave nothing further away.

Jonathan stayed on for a few days after the funeral, partly to see Evan. The only occasion he'd seen his brother in the past twenty-five years was at Evan's wedding in England. Tanya had also asked if he'd stay on. She often bounced ideas off him when she was able and used him to discuss strategy. They had a fruitful discussion for a couple of hours which helped them both forget David's passing for a little while.

'There is one thing I need to tell you,' Jonathan said. 'I've thought long and hard about this, but I think I have to tell you.'

Tanya raised her eyebrows without saying anything.

'You remember the settlement I mentioned at Kanangra-Boyd, in the southern Blue Mountains?'

'Yes, we haven't had a chance to do anything about that yet, but we'll get to it. Don't worry.'

'Well, I think you need to know,' he said reluctantly. 'I've just discovered that Virginia Andrews is one of the leading lights over there. I haven't told Mark.'

She looked at him and said, 'Thank you. I'll tell Mark myself when the time is right.' An involuntary shiver went through her as she said to herself, *I thought I'd left that pile of shit behind years ago.*

Tanya suddenly felt very lonely.

Guy Hallowes has lived an international lifestyle; born in Kenya, and qualified as a Chartered Accountant in the UK, he has also lived in South Africa, Botswana, and Canada whilst settling with wife Diana and their four children on Sydney's leafy north shore.

A senior executive in a major international publishing company for twenty years, Guy always harboured a wish to write—a wish that has now been more than fulfilled with four novels dealing with the "transition" in Africa from Colonial to Majority rule.

Icefall is Guy's fifth novel and the first of a series of thrillers based on the aftermath of cataclysmic events brought on by global warming.

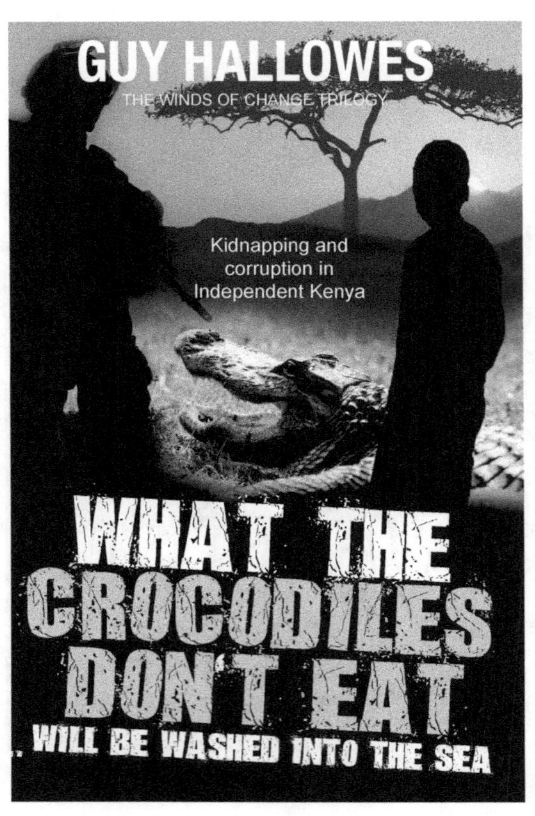

What The Crocodiles Dont Eat Will Be Washed Into The Sea

Book Two of 'Winds of Change' Trilogy

No Peace for the Wicked
Book Three of 'Winds of Change' Trilogy

Rough Diamonds